"I WILL NEVER MARRY!" YSABEAU DECLARED.

He caught her wrist easily, before she could strike him. He looked down at her flushed face, with her veil now lying askew, and her breasts heaving, and studied her for a moment.

They were quite alone. Ysabeau was suddenly aware of his size, and her own defenselessness. He could do anything to her—anything!

"I won't hit you," he growled. "I'm just going to prove how foolhardy your last statement was." And before she knew what he was about, he had gathered her into his arms and with one hand holding her head still, he was kissing her—thoroughly and expertly, his lips so warm and persuasive against hers that his tongue met with no resistance. . . .

Also by Laurie Grant:

DEFIANT HEART

LEISURE BOOKS NEW YORK CITY

A LEISURE BOOK

Published by

Dorchester Publishing Co., Inc.
6 East 39th Street
New York, NY 10016

Printed in the United States of America

To
my parents
and
my daughters,
Dani and Steffie.
Thank you for being you.

FOREVER
LOVE

Part I

Chapter One

"When the soft breeze turns harsh and drear,
And leaves fall from the boughs above,
When birds' songs less sweetly strike my ear,
I sigh, and sing the pains of love,
Love holds me captive in his lake,
And never have I made him mine."

"*Ma Duchesse,* a thousand pardons for this interruption," the courtier murmured apologetically as the last sweet notes of the *viole* died away. He stood blinking in the bright sunlight that bathed the Duchess' pleasure garden, though the lady he addressed sat in the shade of one of the many lime trees, surrounded by half a dozen of her ladies-in-waiting and as many knights. The air was redolent with the herbs that grew in nearby beds—sage, mint, coriander and fennel—as well as with the perfume of roses and lilies.

"Yes, Arnulf, what is it?" Eleanor, Duchess of Aquitaine and Normandy, Countess of Anjou, sighed, regretting the need to shift her attention from the troubadour's mellow tenor. His voice had been echoing her sweet melancholy at being parted from Henry Plantagenet, her bridegroom of only three weeks. The Duke was in Barfleur, punishing the French, and Eleanor, truly in love for the first time in her thirty years, was bored and fidgety without him.

"*Le Sieur de Ré*, your grace. He has with him his daughter, and is in hopes that you will take her into your household."

Eleanor arose gracefully and greeted the spare, lean nobleman who stood at the courtier's side.

"My lord, I bid you welcome to the Palace of Poitiers," she said graciously in the sensual, husky voice that had mesmerized so many troubadours and nobles alike. Her words gave no hint that she was wondering how to tactfully refuse the Lord of Ré's request.

Now that Eleanor had returned from the colorless, dreary court of Paris, Aquitaine was once again the center of sophitication and culture, and many wished to be at her side. But each rustic nobleman's daughter seemed more lumpish than the last. The Duchess of Aquitaine would have only those about her whose beauty and charm mirrored her own.

"Your grace is kind to receive us," the old man said, bowing low. "May I present my daughter, Ysabeau?"

Eleanor's clear, gray-green eyes betrayed none of the surprise she felt as the old nobleman moved aside, revealing the young female who had stood, huddled in his shadow.

The girl curtseyed diffidently, clumsily, then stood still. Her brown eyes grew enormous in a small oval face as the Duchess inspected her. Her flush accentuated a sprinkling of freckles over high cheekbones and a pert little nose that fell far short of patrician elegance. She reached a hand up self-consciously to replace an errant strand of brown hair that had strayed from its thick braid beneath her veil.

"Your grace," she murmured. Though only two words, quietly said, they gave promise of a pleasing, mellifluous voice.

Here was no beauty as defined by current fashion. She was neither blond, nor tall, nor pale-eyed. Her complexion, possessing none of the translucent pallor praised by troubadours, spoke of a life outdoors. Her bearing was that of a wild thing that suddenly finds itself caged. The court ladies would find no reason to be jealous of her garments, either. Beneath the girl's worn, serviceable brown mantle, Eleanor glimpsed a faded blue gown of no particular style. She sensed a challenge here, and began to be intrigued with its possibilities.

"Your grace, your seneschal informs me you already have many young ladies to serve your needs, but I beg you to consider my daughter," the old man said. "She is much in need of polish, for I have been a widower since Ysabeau was three, and she has lacked the tempering influence of a lady. I have been much away from my island castle since her mother's death, having joined your grace and King Louis on crusade. I was captured there by the Saracen and held to ransom, and my health has suffered ever since." He hesitated, studying the Duchess for traces of impatience.

Eleanor shifted her gaze from the girl and said encouragingly, "Continue, *mon seigneur.*"

"I came home to find that, in my absence, Ysabeau had become accustomed to running half-wild. Perhaps it is my fault—I had allowed her to spend part of the time in the home of my mistress, a widow in La Rochelle. Her son is of an age with my Ysabeau and became her constant companion. Jean and she would go on expeditions into the *marais*, the marshes near there. He's a good lad, and certainly would not harm a hair on Ysabeau's head, but it's no life for a gently born *damoiselle*. My sister, who is a *religieuse* in Bordeaux, saw to her education and now offers her a place among the nuns, but she is my only heir and somehow I feel that is not right for her either. . . ."

"Ah, *non*, I quite agree," Eleanor interrupted decisively. "I will take her." And I will transform her into the jewel of my court, she added to herself.

She was touched to see tears of gratitude in the clouded dark eyes of the *Sieur de Ré*. There was, however, a curious mixture of grief and rebellion on the face of her newest lady-in-waiting, whose gaze was now directed at her aged father.

"You will want to make your farewells privately, no doubt. When you have finished, Ysabeau, come inside and someone will direct you to your quarters," Eleanor said. Then she gestured for her entourage to follow her, leaving the elderly noble alone with his daughter in the garden.

Simon de Winslade had just arrived in Poitiers and was brushing the dust of travel from his tall, lean form near the side entrance of the Maubergeone Tower. He had been told the Duchess was in the pleasance and intended waiting upon her there shortly.

He found the garden empty, however, except for an old man who stood listening to the impassioned entreaties of a chestnut-haired, slender young girl. Unseen by them, he drew near, under the shade of a quince tree, intending to merely ask if they had seen the Duchess; but he became curious as he saw tears begin to flood the poorly dressed young woman's cheeks.

"Please, *mon père*, don't separate Jean and me. I love him! I wish to be his wife, even if it means living in a cottage. What is a title to me?" She flung her arms widely and dramatically, then caught at the old man's sleeve as he turned away from her.

"Ysabeau, my dear and only child, we have been through all this before. You cannot marry a peasant. It would never do. No one understands this better than Jean himself, though he knows he is wrong to have gone off with you as if you were—the butcher's daughter! You have a responsibility as an heiress, my dear, to marry a lord who can protect you and your lands when I die. You are a different breed from Jean, as surely as a palfrey is different from a horse that pulls a baggage wain."

"But I love him! I will marry no one else! And why bring me here, Papa? I know nothing of the ways of court, of fancy gowns and mincing lords. I would rather be riding up the canals in the *marais* in Jean's boat, listening for the curlew's cry."

Behind the tree, Simon smiled wryly.

The old count said with light-lipped firmness, "You argue foolishly. That will be enough! You are a lucky girl to have a place with the most renowned noblewoman in Europe, and can learn much here if you apply yourself. Make your sainted mother proud of you, if you do not care for my feelings!"

His words seemed to touch her heart at last, for the girl, head bent, said in a small voice, choked with tears, "As you wish, my lord."

"*Au revoir*, Ysabeau. God be with you."

"Goodbye, Papa."

The old man, face impassive though his hands were clenched so tight the knuckles were white, walked slowly toward the gate without a backward glance.

Simon stood rooted to the spot, unsure for a moment whether to steal away without being seen and spare this Ysabeau further humiliation, or ask about Eleanor. Before he could do either, however, the *damoiselle* began to speak out loud, obviously thinking she was alone.

"I'll not do it! I will run away and marry Jean. He can't keep us apart—we are meant to be together."

He laughed spontaneously then, before he could stop himself, and she whirled, scarlet with embarrassment and indignation.

"Just what is so funny?" Her eyes took in the tall form, as it stepped out of the shadows, richly dressed in a short tunic and cloak to which the dust of the road still clung. Thick, tawny-gold hair fell low on his brow and brushed his collar in the back. His arrogant face was lit by a pair of startling azure eyes and he had a thin patrician nose. A mustache of the same burnished gold as his hair called attention to a pair of sensual lips and gleaming, even white teeth.

"It is amusing to think of you enjoying life as the wife of a pleasant, *ma damoiselle*. Why would you want to be a haggard old woman when you're thirty, with a hutful of ragged brats, married to a toothless, smelly old man who probably beats you—*if* he has not perished fighting for his lord during the days he is obligated to serve him."

She launched herself at him then, her hand raised to slap his face. "How dare you?" she screeched. "You don't know him. Jean is everything good and kind to me, and he'll never be smelly and toothless. I'll never love anyone else, ever! If I cannot be Jean's, I will never marry!"

He caught her wrist easily, before she could strike him. He looked down at her flushed face, with her veil now lying askew, and her breasts heaving, and studied her for a moment.

They were quite alone. Ysabeau was suddenly aware of his size, and her own defenselessness. He could do anything to her—anything!

"I won't hit you," he growled. "I'm just going to prove how foolhardy your last statement was." And before she knew what he was about, he had gathered her into his arms and with one hand holding her head still, he was kissing her—thoroughly and expertly, his lips so warm and persuasive against hers that his tongue met with no resistance as it brushed against her teeth and entered her mouth. She felt that she had been swept off the earth into a hot whirlwind of feeling where no one else existed but herself and this man. She felt as if she had known him always, that the hand that was roaming at will now over her neck and shoulders—and, dear God, cupping her breast—had been there before. She melted into him, a moan forming in her throat, realizing that Jean had never kissed her like this, nor, she knew intuitively, did he know how to do it so well. She was experiencing so much more now than she had ever imagined existed on those few occasions when Jean had dared to kiss her timidly. She wanted this raging fire to rise even higher . . . she was willing to let it consume them both. . . .

Suddenly she realized that his lips had left hers and he was no longer stroking her skin, which felt on fire even under the rough wool of her dress. He was just holding her, but, in truth, she would have fallen if he had not. Dazed, she opened her eyes, focusing with difficulty on his blue eyes, which glinted with amusement.

" 'I'll never love anyone else, ever! If I cannot have Jean, I'll never marry!' " he quoted in a mocking falsetto. "*Eh bien, mademoiselle*, whether you marry or not remains to be seen, but I think I have proved you were made for loving."

She felt like the Apostle Peter after the cock crowed thrice. He had made her respond in a few heartbeats' time, made her cling and moan and open her mouth—indeed, herself—to him. She had allowed him such liberties as only a wanton would permit.

Fury followed shame so closely as to be almost indistinguishable from it. How dare he make fun of her! She was Lady Ysabeau de Ré, daughter and heiress of a count. She slapped him then, the blow landing with stinging force, leaving a livid mark on his left cheek. Then she stood there, paralyzed, knowing she should run now that his arms no longer held her, but somehow unable to do anything more than gaze in fascinated terror as his eyes turned into blue shards of ice.

"I suppose you expect me to beg your pardon for my boldness," he said, "when, in truth, all you deserve is a sound spanking." For a moment he looked as if he were about to do it, but to her credit, she did not shrink from him. "You're quite lucky your father did not beat you, you know. He would have been within his rights. He's correct, you are lucky to be here, but I wonder how fortunate Eleanor is to have you? It will be quite a while before you are worthy to be called a lady, from what I have seen."

He dropped her hands then, and stalked off, giving her a contemptuous parting glance. She watched him go, her mouth forming a soundless *O* as inwardly she writhed in shame.

Who was he? He had not even given his name. He had spoken in the *langue d'oïl*, the tongue spoken by the northern French, rather than the more fluid *langue d'oc* spoken here in the south. She fervently hoped the marks of travel indicated he was someone who would not be long at court. Perhaps he was merely a messenger whom she need never see again. Perhaps he was not even noble, and had no more right than Jean to be so high-handed with her. But his aristocratic bearing indicated otherwise, and his clothes, though dusty, were of too good a quality to belong to a mere peasant.

Well, whoever he was, he would never have cause to criticize her again. From now on, she would be as elegant as the Duchess herself.

Once inside, she motioned to a page lounging at a window embrasure, and the young boy guided her up a twisting, steep staircase to a room with a heavy door of dark wood.

Ysabeau knocked shyly, then pushed at the door and let herself in.

"So you're the new one," a sulky blond said, uncurling herself from a window seat. "I am Blanche de Limousin. Her grace told me to await you here and see what you needed to prepare yourself for the evening meal." She eyed Ysabeau from head to toe, her hands at her hips, wide mouth compressed into a thin critical line.

"Well, it's obvious that a bath is the first priority," she said severely, "and then, surely, you have something more suitable to wear in those chests." She gestured disdainfully at the two leatherbound coffers that held all of Ysabeau's clothes.

For a moment Ysabeau could only stare, dismay forming a cold lump at the pit of her stomach.

"My clothes are all clean . . . but they were my mother's. I know they are out of style, but I needed no fine gowns on the *Île de Ré*. . . ."

Blanche had thrown open one of the chests and was rifling through the contents with obvious aversion. "Well, you are not on the island now. These gowns will never do at the most sophisticated court in Christendom. And look at you! You won't be able to borrow my things until you grow some curves, my girl, even were you tall enough. We'd almost be able to outfit you as one of his grace's pages and none would be the wiser." She gestured at Ysabeau's petite form, then at her own lush curves and height.

"And that hair—it hasn't got the slightest trace of a curl, has it?" She continued her careless assessment, unknowingly targeting one of the things Ysabeau most hated about her looks, though none who saw it later, dark and shining, would have disparaged its thick beauty.

Blanche did not wait for an answer, but strolled languidly out to summon the bath water, leaving Ysabeau stinging with resentment at her first two encounters at the court of Poitiers.

She stared, wide-eyed, at the rich, vivid tapestries that graced the stone walls of the room while she waited for the lady-in-waiting to reappear. There was a large comfortable-looking bed with wine-colored velvet hangings to one side of the room; Ysabeau wondered how many ladies she would have to share it with. Nearby stood a tall wooden wardrobe, which she was just about to explore when a sloshing noise outside the door heralded the arrival of the tub and buckets of steaming water carried by several menservants.

"Ah, good afternoon, my lady," said an amazingly fat, short woman with a beaming smile. "I regret that I was not here to give you greeting. I am Marie, tiring-woman to you and the others who share this room. Lady Blanche said to tell you she would see you later."

Ysabeau smiled uncertainly in return, and both women waited while the men set up the large oaken tub and poured in the water.

"Go ahead, undress, and I'll help you wash," Marie instructed briskly after the last man had gone out the door. She pulled over a large wooden screen decorated with mythical beasts.

"I'm sorry you had to meet Blanche de Limousin first. She can be as spiteful as a cat," the little woman said a few minutes later, as she expertly massaged Ysabeau's scalp and worked the sweet-smelling soap into her thick brown tresses. Marie had added a handful of dried herbs and flower petals to the water, and the delicious scent rose around her nose in the steam. Ysabeau leaned back gratefully, feeling the hot water soothe the ache of saddle-weary muscles.

"You will also be sharing the room with another lady, Matilde de St. Gilles, who is by far pleasanter company. She's a bit older, a widow, but you'll probably never have to share the bed with more than one of them at a time, because one of you will always be on duty with the Duchess at night, in her anteroom. And when she's not on duty, Matilde is frequently with her lover, which may explain her sweeter temper." Marie gave a deep chuckle. "*Eh bien*, I mustn't be shocking you."

"You haven't," Ysabeau protested faintly, but she sensed Marie was not convinced, and was surprised to feel that the tiring-woman seemed to approve of her innocence. Ysabeau was not ignorant of what men and women did together. Anyone growing up around the many serving wenches and lackeys in a castle would have observed interrupted caresses and subsequent swollen bellies on the women, followed by hasty weddings. Such sights had aroused odd feelings in her that became more disturbing as she got older; lately these had become hard to ignore when she had gone anywhere alone with Jean. He could never be persuaded to do more than hold her hand or give her a quick kiss, however, which left her puzzled and frustrated.

Chapter Two

Ysabeau, seated at a trencher with the haughty Blanche, looked about her as the great hall filled with lords, ladies, pages, and servants. They were sitting at one of the many lower trestle tables that radiated out from the table on the dais at which only the highest nobles and churchmen were privileged to dine with the Duchess and Duke; yet they were still above the massive silver saltcellar that was the social boundary between the gentlefolk and the commoners.

The buzz of conversation rose to a din as everyone found their places and servants began to bring in great platters of food. There were eels in a spicy purée, roasts of venison, pork, and veal, as well as a magnificent roasted peacock on which the feathers had been replaced before serving, fresh fish, plentiful loaves of soft white bread, and a multitude of fruits and cheeses, accompanied by goblets of hippocras to wash it all down.

Ysabeau, however, had eaten little and what she had consumed tasted like bitter gall.

La Fille du Marais, they were calling her, or simply, *La Maraise*—the marsh girl. Those sitting around her had witnessed her introduction to Eleanor and taken note of her outdated clothes and unsophisticated mien, and now seemed to revel in tormenting her. One mischievous young lord had even gone so far as to stand, flap his arms, and give a screeching cry as if to imitate a marsh bird, though Ysabeau thought caustically that he had only succeeded in playing the fool.

Matilde de St. Gilles, her other roommate, had been introduced to her and was sitting nearby. She was a comely woman with auburn hair who appeared about five years older than Ysabeau's 16 years—certainly not as much older as Ysabeau had imagined when Marie had told her Matilde was a widow. She had smiled in friendly fashion and Ysabeau had sensed that she was, as the tiring-woman had promised, kinder than Blanche. But Ysabeau had been distracted by the dark handsome noble on her other side, and had had little chance to talk to Lady Matilde.

Blanche made no attempt to integrate her into the conversation that flowed all around them, so at last Ysabeau gave up and tried to eat, eyes downcast.

"Ah, what a beautiful animal," Blanche murmured aloud, as if to herself, and Ysabeau looked up, following her trenchermate's gaze to the high table. Expecting to see a prized lap dog, Ysabeau was surprised to realize that Blanche had referred to the man seated to the left of the Duchess. It was the tawny-haired Norman, her tormentor in the garden! Eleanor seemed to have been highly amused at something he had just said, for she was laughing gaily and touching his wrist in a flirtatious manner.

"Who *is* that?" Ysabeau dared ask at last.

"Simon de Winslade, a baron from England," sighed Blanche rapturously, preening and trying subtly to catch the nobleman's eye.

"Oh, then he is not of this court, he is English," responded Ysabeau with a heartfelt sense of relief.

"Of course he's not English—they're a conquered race of serfs, mostly," pronounced Blanche superiorly. "He's Norman-French, with English lands. But I imagine he got that golden hair and those blue eyes from some Saxon ancestor." Blanche gave a delicious shiver, as if suggesting that that added an element of fascinating savagery to his character. "But he's certainly not a Poitevin. His manner is all Norman—cold, hard—and he gets what he wants. I hear he's at court to deliver a message to Duchess Eleanor from her *belle-mère*, the Empress Matilda, in Rouen."

"You know him, then?"

"No, but given the chance, I will," answered Blanche with lazy certainty. "I believe I have just picked my new partner for the game of *l'amour courtois*."

"Courtly love?" repeated Ysabeau in confusion.

"I forget, you are *une rustique*," Blanche purred condescendingly. "Yes, the *gai savoir*, the game in which a lady becomes the object of selfless worship, the man, usually of lower degree, her adoring slave. He serves for the joy and honor of her merest smile, not because he dares hope she will give anything more. He grows pale in her presence, and sleepless if she but frowns at him." She smiled as she continued to gaze with narrowed, hungry eyes at the Norman lord.

"And you think this baron would be content with that?" Ysabeau questioned dubiously. Somehow she could not visualize the cynical Norman participating in such an artificial ritual with so little reward. "Would he not eventually expect to wed you?"

Blanche broke into peals of laughter which their tablemates noted. "*La Maraise* thinks the goal of courtly love is marriage!" the young lord who had mocked Ysabeau earlier hooted derisively. "Love and marriage? They are mutually exclusive, *ma chère*. One marries for land, for position, to ensure an heir. That tedium done with, the lord and lady are free to go their own ways and amuse themselves—discreetly, of course."

Ysabeau, her cheeks flushed with shame, nevertheless persisted. "But what if the lord finds out?"

"On my faith, you *have* been immured on that sandy island, haven't you? The husband is not likely to object, since he will probably be pursuing some lady himself. That is the game, my innocent!"

"But how is a man ever sure his heirs are his own, if this is so widespread a pastime?" Ysabeau continued seriously.

There was an uncomfortable cough from the young lord, whom Ysabeau later learned was Joscelin, bastard brother of the Duchess. But Blanche broke the brief silence by saying archly, "There are lapses, of course, but the goal of courtly love is for the woman to be adored only. For her to allow liberties . . . she might just as well be a scullery maid!" She shuddered as if the idea was unthinkably distasteful.

Ysabeau glanced at Matilde de St. Gilles, who was gazing adoringly at her swarthy partner. "Is that what you are, my love, a lapse?" She did not trouble to lower her amused voice. The handsome lord at her side merely smiled and gallantly kissed her hand.

Blanche de Limousin pouted until Lord Joscelin came to her rescue. "It would add luster to the honor of any man's name to merely carry Lady Blanche's handkerchief. Simon de Winslade would be a fortunate man, indeed."

"I am sure he has noticed me," Blanche remarked confidently. "I shall have to arrange a meeting—accidentally, *bien sûr*."

Ysabeau gazed back up the dais, surprised, for she had not noted that the baron's attention had ever wandered from his hostess, Duchess Eleanor. His hair gleamed in the light shed by the flickering oil lamps hung at intervals between the tapestries on the wall. As she watched, the startling blue eyes narrowed, and he glanced down the high table at the assembled lords and ladies of this scintillating court. He appeared impatient with the interminable, elaborate meal. The fingers of one hand drummed restlessly on the snow-white linen beside his trencher.

Why, he feels as caged as I do, thought Ysabeau as she studied the powerfully masculine, virile figure at the high table.

The Duchess, perhaps sensing his impatience, smilingly addressed a remark to Simon de Winslade, and his harsh, high-cheekboned features relaxed into an easy grin, transforming his air of discontent into heart-stopping charm. He threw back his head in amusement at whatever Eleanor had said; the mellow sound of his wholehearted laugh reached Ysabeau even over the buzz of the dinner conversation and the musical accompaniment coming from the gallery.

She watched as he ran a hand through the dark gold mass of his hair and pushed it away from his forehead. Then, with regret, Ysabeau saw him bow elegantly to her mistress and excuse himself. The eyes of all the women in the hall followed the compelling, tall figure as he strode out without a backward glance.

"Ah, too bad," sighed Blanche. "I was just beginning to have hopes of meeting him during the dancing after dinner. I'm certain he would make an entrancing partner. Don't you agree, little Ysabeau?"

The patronizing tone irritated her. "Not to me. We have . . . ah, met . . . already, and the Norman lord has all the *politesse* of a Saracen."

"Oh ho!" crowed Joscelin. "*La Maraise* has decided she is too good for him. Your quarry is safe, Blanche."

"Oh, I never considered Ysabeau competition," replied the blonde sweetly, but her eyes flashed fire, for Ysabeau had disparaged her prize, and Joscelin, the strength of her appeal. "She had better cut her teeth on smaller fare, since she is so new in court. Some lonely squire, perhaps."

Ysabeau would have been amazed, indeed, to know that Simon de Winslade had, in fact, been staring in their direction, but at her, not her overconfident trenchermate.

He had seen the shy figure, dressed in an outmoded gray bliaut which did not suit her, enter the crowded great hall at the side of the haughty blond lady in waiting now sitting next to her. He had watched as the court sophisticates had alternately ignored and mocked her, and Simon was offended for her. He was the only one to see that tears threatened to spill over those fine, doelike eyes.

His irritation from their meeting in the garden was forgotten as he mused over how different she was from this painted, perfumed crowd of raucous peacocks who were treating her so cruelly, despite all their fine manners.

He had been wishing himself home again at Winslade, even with all its problems, or at least that Henry of Anjou was here. His suzerain was much too restless a fellow to sit patiently through endless banquets, and would have been off a long time ago, charging into some new activity, with Simon at his side.

Duchess Eleanor had interrupted his reverie

then by asking about affairs in England, and he had no more time for thoughts of the odd little damsel at the lower table. After an amusing exchange of words with his hostess, he had bid her adieu, remembering that he was to depart for Rouen at dawn.

Chapter Three

Ysabeau had cried herself to sleep that night. She had hated the knowing, triumphant look on the face of Blanche when she asked to be excused just as the dancing started in the great hall after dinner, but she could not take any more tonight. Pleading fatigue, she had fled to the sanctuary of her room, correctly guessing she would find it empty. Marie would not have expected any of her charges to be back so soon, so Ysabeau undid the lacing of her gown awkwardly and took it off, lying down on the bed.

She was grateful to be alone, for the tears came then, building to great, racking sobs. Desperately, she wished herself back on Ré, where the soothing swish of the water in the bay would have lulled her. At last, exhausted, she slept.

Though they continued to call her *La Maraise*, the girl of the marshes disappeared over the next few weeks spent in the Maubergeone Tower.

The transformation began the very morning after her arrival with a fitting for new garments. She had barely broken her fast when she was summoned from the great hall by Marie.

"We'll soon have you as gorgeously arrayed as any of her grace's ladies," the heavyset woman promised cheerfully as they climbed the steep stairs winding up into the cool gray heights of the tower. "Lady Blanche had no right to mock your clothes, you being new to Poitiers and all. Why, you have no need of such garb at home, though I do hear you lived in a castle there too."

"It wasn't much of a castle, really," panted Ysabeau, keeping up with the serving woman with difficulty on the dimly-lit steps. She thought of the ramshackle little keep with its tumbledown walls on the narrow, sandy Île de Ré, and a wave of homesickness washed over her again. She missed every one of its few inhabitants, from the score of peasants and men-at-arms to her absent-minded, dear old father, the Count.

"How . . . do you . . . manage these stairs so easily, Marie?" she asked.

"You mean, as fat as I am?" She gave a chuckle at Ysabeau's embarrassed face. "They're nothing, my lady, after years of rushing to and fro to serve the nobility, who are usually in a hurry, wanting everything yesterday." She paused to let Ysabeau catch up.

"Well, you'll soon look as fine as anyone after Yvette has tended to you, so no one need know how small your keep is at home."

The woman in the little room at the top of the stairs was as bony and spare as Marie was well-rounded; she wasted little time in chatter as she measured Ysabeau's petite form and held various colors and fabrics against her sun-kissed complexion and rich brown hair.

Ysabeau's eyes fed hungrily on the lengths of luxurious velvets, lustrous silks, and diaphanous sarcenets piled high on tables nearby.

"Her Grace said you were to pick enough for several gowns, as befits a lady of her court. Well, my lady, what hues do you fancy?" Yvette questioned.

"I don't know . . . there's so much to choose from," Ysabeau replied.

"No pale, sweet blues and pinks for you, I think," pronounced Yvette decisively. "You are not one of those pallid lilies from the ladies' bower, so let us use your fresh color to advantage."

In a trice she had selected jewel-bright colors that complemented the natural rose blush of Ysabeau's cheeks for her outer gowns: emerald green, peacock blue, scarlet, and magenta.

"I'll make three up into lovely bliauts, Lady Ysabeau, just as soon as I can. Marie has told me how you are being treated by that nasty Blanche. Soon, *voilà*, there will be no one but the Duchess herself more splendid! Of course, I will also make up some undergowns of the finest linen, and chemises of Egyptian cotton, and later, when summer has left Aquitaine, a warm mantle. But for now," the seamtress dismissed her briskly, "let me get to work."

Ysabeau made .her way back down the winding stairs with Marie, who had waited for her, knowing she would need guidance to Duchess Eleanor's bower. As they went, the tiring-woman described a typical day in the life of the Duchess of Aquitaine and the ladies who attended her.

"The Duchess is a very active woman. By this hour she will have attended Mass, broken her fast, pursued her correspondence, and will be attending to the business of the duchy in her lord's absence, while her ladies stitch on altar cloths and such. A *jongleur* usually plays softly in the *viole* or psaltery and sings sweet songs. If she is not very busy, her grace and the ladies will discuss romance and sometimes invite young nobles in for a court of love."

But Ysabeau was not to have any further preview, for they had reached their destination, and with an encouraging smile, Marie left her to enter alone. Ysabeau remembered the scornful Blanche and took a deep breath before going in.

Within Eleanor's large apartments, however, nothing resembled the serene picture of court life just painted by Marie. Confusion reigned as ladies rushed about the room laden with stacks of clothing, dashing from wardrobes and large chests to smaller traveling coffers.

The tall woman in the center of the room was sorting through a small jewel-encrusted casket, her palm crowded with rings, brooches, a sparkling necklace, and colorful, gleaming enamels.

"Ah, there you are, Ysabeau." The Duchess straightened, handing the selected jewelry to one of her ladies. "Pack these carefully, Giselle, as well as the pearl coronet." Her lovely face was lit with excitement as she turned back to her newest lady. "You are just in time to help my ladies pack. My lord has come home, you see, but he tells me we are going on progress—tomorrow! Only a man, and especially an Angevin, could think a departure on such short notice possible." But the Duchess looked as if she would fly to the moon in a moment if her young, impetuous bridegroom asked her to.

"We will go *en chevauchée,* so that my Lord Henry can see his new duchy—the vineyards, the olive groves, the salt marshes, Landes and Saintonge, where the finest horses are raised, Talmont, where we'll hunt and hawk—ah, he will love Aquitaine, this jewel of a duchy I have given him. And they will love him, my Poitevins and Gascons; they will adore Henry of Anjou just as I do!" She whirled and clapped her hands delightedly, and her joy was so infectious that Ysabeau smiled back.

"And I, your grace? Do I attend you on your journey? I have only just come from the seamstress. I fear—"

"No, of course, your new raiment will not be ready in time, I am quite aware," Eleanor said, then noticed Ysabeau's crestfallen look. "Do not be sad, Ysabeau de Ré. I have room only for a few ladies to accompany me—my sister, Petronilla, Mabelle de Bordeaux, Blanche de Limousin—" Ysabeau did not miss the arch, triumphant look shot at her by her spiteful roommate. "And besides, you are probably fortunate not to go. My Lord Henry travels as he does all else—like a demon!" She gave a rueful laugh.

"Ysabeau," she went on, "I would like you to use this time while I am away wisely, in learning the ways of court life. I will leave you in the good hands of Matilde de St. Gilles, with whom I am informed you share a room, and that rascal over there, Philippe de Melle, my sweet-singing troubadour."

The wiry young man sat curled on the window seat, idly plucking his lute with a quill, but at Eleanor's introduction he arose and bowed, grinning at her. The smile, set against tanned aquiline features, was so engaging that Ysabeau could feel her disappointment and uncertainty dissolving as she returned his greeting.

"Philippe will teach you the *chansons* of romance, of lovers such as Tristan and Iseult, and Lancelot and Guinevere," Eleanor went on, delighted at the instant liking she sensed between these two. "Between Philippe and Matilde, I am confident you will soon be a credit to the court. Meanwhile, *vite*, run to the chapel, *ma petite* Ysabeau, and fetch my chaplain to me. Tell him to bring the jeweled reliquary—he will know the one."

Ysabeau was by no means sure she could find her way to the chapel, but with Blanche still smirking at her, she could do no less than nod competently and reply, "Yes, Your Grace, I will be back in a few moments."

"But a few moments" threatened to become hours as Ysabeau found her way down the stairs and threaded the maze of corridors that made up the second floor of the Mauber-geon Tower, which Eleanor's grandfather, the scandalous Guilhelm IX, had built for his paramour.

Serving maids and men-at-arms walked by, all seemingly intent on their errands, surely too busy to note that the newcomer was lost. Ahead, a pair of ladies sat on a bench, chattering animatedly with a courtier whose back was to Ysabeau. Surely they would direct her—but then she recognized Joscelin, the derisive joker who had mocked her the night before. She would not play the country fool for that one! Ysabeau merely nodded civilly to the trio and passed on.

The minutes ticked by and she imagined her mistress beginning to grow impatient. The very first task entrusted to her and she could not handle it! Perhaps Eleanor would even re-consider her kindness in allowing Ysabeau a position in her household. Now that she resolved to ask the next person she found, no matter who it was, the passageways were deserted.

She began to quicken her steps. Rounding the corner at a near-run, her breath coming in gasps she collided with great force against a solid object, and fell to the cool stone floor.

"Oh, Saints, I *do* apologize, *ma chère damoiselle*! It seems we both were in too much haste," chuckled a rich voice, whose Provençal French had a distinctly Angevin accent.

She had managed to appear the gawky, inept fool again. Completely mortified, she dared not look into the eyes of the man who was now proffering his big hand to help her up, but instead stared at his sturdy arm, gleaming with reddish-gold hairs.

"How are you, then? No bones broken, I hope?" he laughed, and Ysabeau at last assessed the stocky figure before her. He was powerfully built, though of no more than average height, and had fiery red hair over a ruddy, wind-roughened face, lit by merry blue eyes. His cheeks had not felt a razor for days. He smelled strongly of horse. He wore a much-traveled russet cloak over a shirt and chausses, with a dagger tucked in at the belted waist.

Who was this, Ysabeau wondered. The master of the stable, perhaps? He offered no introduction, but continued to smile in a friendly fashion as he returned her gaze curiously.

"Well, don't you have a tongue, beauty? Who are you? You were not here before I left, that I would swear!" He reached out a hand; his large rough fingers felt strangely gentle as he touched her flaming cheek.

But how dare he handle her so familiarly? Shame at her clumsiness, mixed with rage and frustration, made her voice icy.

"I am Lady Ysabeau de Ré," she answered, trying to imitate Blanche's unapproachable hauteur, "new lady-in-waiting to Her Grace, the Duchess of Aquitaine. I have been sent on an errand of great importance, fellow, so kindly direct me to the chapel and I will not trouble you further."

"Ah! I beg your pardon, *ma damoiselle*!"

The stocky figure was now the picture of abject humility. "I meant no harm in my friendliness—it is just my way. I would be delighted if you would allow your humble servant to show you the way. I fear you have gone in quite the opposite direction. But never fear, I will guide you there myself!"

Mollified somewhat, she accepted his arm, but firmly ignored his grin. As they made their way back through the passageway, Ysabeau could see she had indeed gone the wrong way, and said so.

"Oh, you will catch on soon. Only months ago, I was new here myself, and yet here we are at the chapel, safe and sound." He nodded at the entrance with its pointed, Romanesque arches, and bade her enter.

As her eyes adjusted to the cool, dark interior, lit only by tapers on the crimson velvet-covered altar and by votive candles flickering to one side, she sought and found a dark-robed figure who was poring over a large illuminated book on a carved wooden podium.

"Father?" She realized her mistress had not furnished her the chaplain's name as the gray-tonsured man looked up from his task and smiled. Then, seeing the man behind her, he bowed respectfully, leaving Ysabeau mystified and uncertain once again.

"Your grace," the priest murmured, "how may I assist you?" His eyes were focused on Ysabeau's companion, not on herself.

"This is one of my dear wife's new attendants, Ysabeau de Ré. I have merely guided her steps to you, my good Father André," the man said in that deep, rumbling voice.

Ysabeau suddenly realized whom she had addressed so harshly. Forcing herself to remain calm, she briefly explained her errand and watched as the cleric strode in back of the rood screen to fetch the reliquiary before she whirled around, curtseying deeply. "Oh your Grace," she gasped, "I apologize for my rudeness. I did not know who you were."

"Of course you did not, my dear." Henry Plantagenet was mightily amused. "I am usually mistaken for the keeper of the hounds, the falconmaster, or suchlike. I don't exactly dress the part of Duke of Normandy and Aquitaine, and Count of Anjou, do I? No matter. I am all those things, and married to a beautiful wife who brings me rich possessions and a court peopled by lovely ladies, such as yourself."

He bent to assist her up again, sliding both forearms under hers and allowing his hands to remain for a long moment at her waist as he continued to gaze warmly down at her flushed, pretty oval face. "Of course, you did quite right to put such a forward lout in his place, my dear. You have absorbed the manner of the court lady quite quickly."

"My lord . . . but I did not know . . ." she continued to stammer.

"Hush, it is naught." He smiled, showing white, even teeth, and let go of her as the chaplain's quiet footsteps returned. "And now that I have placed you in Father André's care, I trust he will help you back to my wife."

Ysabeau felt overwhelmed by his potent Angevin charm, and suddenly knew why

Eleanor of Aquitaine had braved the Church and King Louis to throw herself and her duchy at the feet of this man, ten years her junior.

Chapter Four

Simon de Winslade reined in his black destrier by the ravine in which the River Clain ran as it curved around Poitiers. That city, set on the slope of a hill, was his destination.

He pulled his cloak more closely about him, thinking that even the ever-present sunlight of Aquitaine could not warm this November afternoon. He hoped the great hall at the palace would have a cheerful fire awaiting him and a good joint of roast meat turning on the kitchen spit, for he was weary from his journey.

He was not seriously concerned about the comforts awaiting him in Poitiers, however. Like most Normans, he was of the opinion that the southern French were a bit too addicted to the pleasures of life. "The Normans to battle, the Provençals to table," went he saying

No, his chief cause for concern was that he

might find Henry Plantagenet still on his honeymoon trip around his new duchy. The Duke had left Poitiers himself, on progress in August, not long after Simon had last visited and the last news that had reached him in England was that Henry was still touring Poitou and Gascony and being royally entertained.

Damn Eleanor, if she's changed him into a fat, soft troubadour like the rest of these southern fools, thought Simon disgustedly, though knowing the energetic Duke as well as he did,he doubted that such a transformation was possible, even by a woman with the potent charm of Eleanor of Aquitaine. Simon had genuinely liked the slim elegant Duchess when he had visited the court in the summer, but England was being torn apart by civil war. It needed the strong rulership Henry represented too much now for Simon to be patient while the Plantagenet Duke enjoyed an extended wedding trip.

Perhaps I'm envious of my liege's happiness, Simon mused, blue eyes staring at the sluggish river water, his lips compressed beneath his golden mustache. Certainly Winslade keep is provides me no peace and pleasure these days, for when I think of home the sound of my heir's squalling fills my ears, th son whose coming meant the loss of Rohese.

Rohese, the flaxen-haired, comely daughter of a neighboring baron, had always seemed full of boundless energy and health. She and Simon had been promised since they were children, and once wed, had looked forward eagerly to the first of many children.

Yet for all her robust health, three days

after the long and difficult birth she lay dead of a fever, and the babe had been given into the care of a wet nurse from the village. It was not an unusual thing for a woman to die of childbed fever, but why should that comfort him? For days after Rochese's death, he had been like a crazed animal before deciding that he could, perhaps, assuage his grief by working in a larger cause.

England had suffered ever since Henry I had died without a male heir, leaving its people caught between the rival claims of his daughter, Matilda, and nephew, Stephen of Blois. The latter, whose claim was much less justified, had finally succeeded in driving Matilda from England, but Stephen had proven such a weak, ineffectual monarch that evil flourished, unchecked. Many said that Christ and his angels must be sleeping.

Though Simon recognized the legitimacy of the Empress Matilda's claim, he had found her arrogant and selfish, as had many of the English. But Stephen was no great improvement. Simon had tried not to take sides, but it was becoming increasingly difficult, especially when his elder brother and twin, Gervase, had given his allegiance to Stephen. Gervase had always been for the winner in any situation, and Simon hadn't trusted him since they were boys. His lands lay to the south, and had been the principal manor of that first Norman, Guy de Bayeux, who had crossed the Channel with William the Conqueror. Gervase might well have been Simon's overlord, except for their divided loyalties. Their father had been a vassal of Matilda and her father, Henry I, and had arranged for Simon to pay homage for his lands directly to the Empress, rather than to Gervase, whose loyalty went to Stephen of Blois—at least, as long as he was winning.

Strife and divisions of this kind were now rampant all over England. No longer could one merely rule one's fief in peace and ignore what went on elsewhere in the land.

Henry, we need you! Pray God you are there, and will heed me, thought Simon, turning his horse towards the palace.

But Simon was fated to be disappointed, for upon arrival at the Palace of Poitiers, he was informed by their graces' seneschal that Henry and Eleanor were still on progress and had sent no word of their date of return. Nor did the seneschal know their precise whereabouts; the last message from the Duchess had been sent from Saintonge. Baron de Winslade would be best advised to wait here, he was told. Surely, with all those lands to govern, they must be home any day now, and meanwhile, there was no more comfortable, pleasurable court in Christendom.

God's Blood, swore Simon to himself as he strode disgustedly from the great hall to see to the quartering of his retinue and stabling of their mounts. Across the Channel, my fief may be overrun by Stephen's brigands and I have no redress. I am advised to beguile myself by listening to *jongleur's* music!

He had just time enough before the evening meal to order a bath and soak away the stench of travel.

As he was leaning forward in a soothing tubful of steaming, soapy water, having his back scrubbed energetically by a buxom serving wench with a lilting Provençal accent, the idea of whiling away the time in such an enjoyable fashion began to have a certain appeal.

Rohese had been dead for two months, and in that time he had not had a woman, not even one of the agreeable scullery wenches in the hall at Winslade. It was as if the shock of her sudden death had stilled the needs of his young, healthy body.

Why not, he suddenly asked himself. An amusing dalliance would pass the time quickly until he could speak with Henry Plantagenet and accomplish his mission. He leaned back in the large oaken tub, enjoying the ministrations of the fresh-cheeked blond. On an impulse, he reached a dripping arm behind him and pulled her into his embrace, kissing her full on the mouth.

The bath was over.

". . . and then he said, 'Give me but a ribbon from your hair, *midons*, lest I die from loving you.' So what else could I do? The dear man would have wasted away. His face was so pale, his hand trembled . . ." reminisced Matilde de St. Gilles with a smile, her eyes dreamy.

Matilde, Ysabeau's other roommate, was black-haired, and had been wed briefly to an aged count who had died, leaving her a handsome portion. His grown son, however, had not wanted his stepmother around, and so

Matilde had come to court.

The two sat in front of the pleasantly crackling fire in the ladies' solar, companionably embroidering to pass the dreary late fall afternoon. In the months that had passed since Ysabeau's arrival at court, she had become particularly close to Lady Matilde.

"Now, it's about time you picked a lover, Ysabeau," drawled Matilde, startling the brown-haired girl so that she pricked her finger with the needle. Ysabeau licked away the drop of blood that appeared on her fingertip, looking at her friend with a confused expression.

"I? A lover? Who would want me?"

"You're no longer a little marsh bird, you know. You've been at Eleanor's court long enough. It's you who should do the selecting, and there's any number of men who would be your devoted slaves, starting with Philippe de Melle. Ah, if he were only of noble birth . . ."

"Ha! He, like all the rest, is in love with Duchess Eleanor! And I am neither blond, nor blue-eyed, nor tall."

"It makes court life pleasurable," replied all that you differ from the clasic ideal," Matilde answered her warmly.

"*Grande merci*. But why would I want to play this game? It seems to me that lovers aren't happy unless they're suffering," observed Ysabeau, rethreading her needle.

"it makes court life pleasurable," replied Matilde practically. "Keeping up with her grace can be exhausting. I should know—I was with her on crusade with King Louis. And this Plantagenet she has wed is never still. A lady needs something of her own, the knowledge that she is desirable in a man's eyes, to hug to herself in this court. It takes the claws from spiteful cats like Blanche to have a gentle lover to serve one's every whim. All too soon you will be wed to some powerful lord who will be better informed about the amount of your dowry than the color of your eyes. Enjoy your youth and freedom while you can."

"But there are married ladies of the court who have . . . admirers."

"Ah, yes, it can be done, but one must be so much more careful. One never knows when some crusty old baron will take offense that his lady has a handsome young *chevalier* mooning over her, and haul her off to his dank dark castle in the middle of nowhere, and proceed to fill her belly with one brat after another, till she is such a hag no handsome man would look twice at her." Matilde rolled her eyes dramatically, and Ysabeau had to chuckle.

"But I have a lover, actually," Ysabeau reminded her. "You remember, I told you about Jean. . . ."

"A peasant boy from the marshes certainly does not count, nor should you even mention him if you want to be considered worthy by some gentleman," Matilde told her firmly. "Above all, don't let Blanche get wind of it! You are a lady of the nobility, my dear, and, as such, must not consider one such as your childhood friend, Jean, worthy of being your lover. Frankly, you're quite lucky he was too honorable to take advantage of you. Meaning no disrespect to the Count, your father, but I can't imagine what he was thinking of to let you run wild like a goosegirl! Believe me, Ysabeau, it's best you forget your past, and do as I've suggested, if you would survive in this court."

"I will think on it. Perhaps it would be amusing . . ."

"I wonder whom you will pick?" mused Matilde. "It's plain that no one at court now has caught your eye. *Eh bien*, there will be many new faces now that Eleanor has wed the Plantagenet." She glanced at the hour candle burning on a low stand nearby.

"Oh, my dear, where has the time gone?" Putting her work aside, she called over her shoulder as she flew from the room, "I won't even have time to change, Ysabeau. I have an assignation, so I'll see you later, perhaps. . . ."

Ysabeau likewise left her work and made her way back to her tower room, where Marie waited to assist her into an emerald green *bliaut* that laced tightly in the back, accentuating her slender waist, high, proud breasts, and gently rounded hips. The gown had deep sleeves whose lower edges dangled nearly to her knees. She wore a double girdle of gilded leather that passed around her waist and then low around her hips, ending in long, silken tassels. Marie had quickly rebraided her thick lustrous brown hair, deftly weaving gold thread in with the strands and binding the ends.

"I think the Duchess would be proud if she could see you now, my lady," praised the plump little tiring-woman, "and Lady Blanche so jealous . . ."

The compliment brought a smile to

Ysabeau's face as she scanned the great hall with its colorful banners hanging from the rafters. It was filled now with benches and trestle tables and crowded with lords and ladies beginning the evening meal while pages rushed to and fro, bringing in great platters of meat and flagons of wine.

Usually she sat with the other ladies-in-waiting who had not gone with Eleanor. Sometimes they were joined by Philippe de Melle, who was witty and amusing and much in demand as a trencher companion. It was plain that he had taken his charge from Eleanor seriously, for he had obviously adopted Ysabeau, always having a helpful tip for her, an encouraging, flirtatious remark, or a new *ballade* to play for her.

At the moment, however, Philippe was nowhere to be seen, and all the ladies she knew were already partnered at their trenchers. A basically shy person, Ysabeau still felt hesitant about seating herself with someone she did not know well. Sharing a trencher, a large flat piece of stale bread that served as a plate, involved a certain degree of intimacy, after all.

She saw Joscelin, the Duchess' bastard brother, leering at her from across the hall and pointing invitingly at the empty place beside him. Determinedly, she looked the other way as she walked down the aisle behind one of the long trestle tables.

It was then that she felt a hand at her wrist, stopping her.

"I would be honored if you shared my place, gracious lady," said the deep, resonant

Norman voice, as Simon de Winslade rose politely to gesture toward the empty seat beside him.

It was the Norman noble who had taken liberties with her on the day of her arrival, she realized with a start, gazing at the devastatingly handsome lord. She felt a *frisson* of excitement—or was it fear—at the base of her spine; now, as before, she found him distinctly predatory.

"I thank you for your courtesy, my lord, but I believe I am expected with her grace's ladies," she replied hesitantly, though a part of her wished to stay and be drawn further into those inviting azure pools of his eyes.

"Nonsense. By the time you find them the meal will be over, and you will have to go hungry," the baron chided. "Come, sit down. Your court is famed for the welcome it gives strangers. Do not disappoint me, gentle *damoiselle*."

There was no way she could gracefully refuse. Gingerly, she sat down at his side, watching him warily as he began to serve them the choicest bits of meat from nearby platters, while his tow-headed squire poured her a cup of wine.

"I am Simon, Baron de Winslade, from England, *damoiselle*," he said, drinking in her beauty, the power of which, he sensed, she was largely unaware. Those eyes, dark brown and expressive as a doe's, stared at him, as if she thought him a ravening lion. She caught her full pink underlip self-consciously between her teeth.

Finally he queried, "And you are—"

Her cheeks flooded scarlet. "Ysabeau de Ré, my lord, I am sorry."

"No need." His smile changed, became reassuring. "Perhaps my thick northern accent is hard to follow." He paused and then said, "We have spoken before, when you were newly come to court."

"*Oui*," she responded with a rueful smile, grateful that apparently he was willing to start afresh and not make reference to what had passed between them before.

But she was not going to escape entirely. "And are you still in love with the peasant, Jean? Does he send you passionate messages of undying love?"

She gave a little gasp, then lowered her eyes that he should not see the pain in them. It had been she who had sent missives to Jean in La Rochelle. She had had no reply, no word from her former companion to prove that he was thinking about her, that he longed for her at all—that he had ever loved her as he'd said.

"But perhaps I trespass," he said lightly, sensitive to her mood. "We will speak of other things. How is it you are not with Eleanor? Surely that would have been enjoyable?" he asked, raising an eyebrow at her as he took a small knife from the jewelled scabbard on his belt and cut their meat.

"Only a few could go, and they left two days after I came. But yes, I would have enjoyed it, to go on horseback through the countryside of Poitou and Gascony in summertime. . . ."

She found herself responding to his questions, despite her initial wariness. But she was careful not to reveal the unpolished girl from the island she felt she still was, deep inside, under the new gowns and thin veneer of sophistication. Perhaps it was the pain of Jean's rejection of which he'd reminded her, but suddenly she wanted to dazzle him.

"And you, Lord Simon? Do you bring a message from the Duke's mother again? Will you have to wait on the newyweds?" She gave him a flirtatious sidelong smile, but kept her tone casual, as if it were a matter of no great moment.

"This time the word I bring is from Henry's supporters in England, who cry out for his presence there. Perhaps you have heard, even in your comfortable keeps in Poitou, that England is a war-torn land in which no man or woman is safe." His mouth twisted wryly. "So I was cursing the time I must, perforce, spend away from my demesne, waiting on Henry, until you appeared before me. I think now, maybe, I will not mind passing the time away at this court, *ma petite* Ysabeau."

Ysabeau felt dazzled, transfixed by that sensual mouth so near hers, smiling as he offered her a morsel with his fingers. She understood enough of the *gai savoir* to know that she must regain the upper hand in this conversation. It would be all too easy to drift still further into the spell being cast by those compelling eyes. Who would have thought that eyes the color of a clear winter sky could be so warm?

"And how will you help me pass the time, Ysabeau?" he persisted, taking advantage of the noise provided by the entrance of some jugglers and tumblers to whisper intimately into her ear as his slim, elegant fingers cupped her chin. His breath, faintly wine-scented, was not unpleasant on her neck.

He had to be stopped—now. It was obvious that he was attractive enough to have any woman he liked, but if she played the game the way he obviously expected, she would be merely one more in a series of conquests. So the northern gallant thought to have her to warm his bed. . . . She would give him more of a challenge than he bargained for!

She straightened her back and turned to face him, all flirtation gone from her manner now. His hand fell away from her face as he brought the flagon to his lips, watching her speculatively.

"I think we had better start, *mon seigneur* de Winslade, with some lessons in manners as practiced by a civilized court, where gentlemen do not paw ladies whom they have just met." She had intended to go on and explain how one who would add honor to his name must serve his lady nobly, unselfishly, and chastely for weeks before she deigned to grant him so much as a smile.

But his spirits were not dampened by the quelling look she gave him, or by her words. He merely grinned, and shot back maddeningly, "How long must I know you before I may touch you again?"

The supper was not over, but she had to escape those knowing eyes, that sensual, cynical mouth, or she would slap his confident face before all the assembled nobility of the court of

Aquitaine.

"Excuse me, my lord, I feel a headache coming on." She arose, ignoring his murmured protestations of concern. They were false; he knew there was nothing wrong with her head. She declined his offer to escort her to her room. She dared not remain in his company a moment more.

"Sweet dreams, then, my dear—I am sure we will meet tomorrow. . . ." he called after her as she fled the great hall, trying to keep to a dignified pace. She nearly collided with two pages bringing in an enormous sculptured marzipan peacock, complete with feathers.

Yes, Simon thought, as around him the *jongleurs* broke into a merry tune, accompanied by tabors and pipe, this stay at court should prove *very* interesting. . . .

Unknown to either Simon or Ysabeau, however, their encounter had been witnessed from the gallery above by a very interested pair of eyes, and the owner of those eyes now moved quickly to intercept Ysabeau before she gained the sanctuary of her chamber.

Very good, my girl, the man thought, you are learning the game well. You didn't fall captive to the Norman scoundrel's blandishments. He was surprised at how much that pleased him. Could that mean she was worthy? But he forced himself not to complete that thought. It was too early to tell. He must be wary. . . .

Just then, he caught sight of the fleeing figure in the becoming green velvet gown. She was just rounding the corner ahead of him, and he called out, "Hold, Lady Ysabeau. Where are you going so fast? Did some poor gallant offend you?"

She turned and faced him, her cheeks still flushed, her dark eyes still flashing, her chest still heaving in indignation. "Oh, it's you, Philippe. No, of course not. Whatever would make you think such a thing?" she protested, essaying a laugh.

"Someone or something has upset you," he countered, his gaze penetrating.

"Nonsense. I merely have a headache, and I'm eager to retire for the night. And where were you this evening, my friend?" she asked too quickly, obviously eager to change the subject.

He looked away suddenly. "Oh, I visited a sick friend in Poitiers. I am honored that such a beauteous lady deigned to miss me," he concluded with a grin.

She didn't believe him, he could tell that. She probably assumed he was out wenching at a nearby tavern, he thought as he watched her disappear down the hall. If she only knew how far off the mark that was. But his flirtatious compliment was entirely what she would expect of a troubadour, and she would not press him further about his whereabouts. Perhaps someday she would understand . . .

Chapter Five

Matilde caught up with Ysabeau as the girl, accompanied by Philippe de Melle, was leaving Mass the next morning.

"My dear, it is all over the palace!" she giggled, laying a small beringed hand on her friend's wrist. "Philippe, have you heard what our pupil has been up to? I must say, Ysabeau, you've made a good choice. He's quite a catch."

"Matilde, what on earth have you heard?" Ysabeau asked, amazed at how her simple *tête-à-tête* had been distorted by the court gossips.

"They say the Norman lord paid marked attention to you at supper last eve, that he is obviously mad with love of you. *Mon dieu*," she sighed dramatically as the trio strolled through the corridor, "isn't it wonderful, Philippe?"

The troubadour remained silent and fell back a step or two.

"We merely shared a trencher," Ysabeau protested, but smiled at her friend's enthusiasm, nevertheless. They made their way to the great hall, where breakfast was laid out.

"They say the looks exchanged by *La Maraise* and that magnificent male creation were like lightning bolts. 'Merely shared a trencher,' eh? You sly thing! I applaud your choice, though. Were it not for my hot-blooded, jealous Rene, I would want him mad for me."

"The only thing he's maddened with is lust," Ysabeau returned tartly, as they broke their fast with white crusty bread and watered-down red wine. "But he will have to revise his expectations of me. I will not fall like a ripe apple into his bed!" She caught Philippe's approving eye, and felt vindicated.

"But it sounds as if you *have* decided on the Norman," Matilde pried.

"Perhaps . . . if he is not too uncivilized to play the game," Ysabeau allowed, gesturing with a remaining crust, her eyes thoughtful. Neither woman noticed Philippe crush a piece of soft white bread in his hand with surprising vehemence, or paid much attention when he excused himself and left the table.

"You might have more fun if you played it his way . . ." Matilde offered irrepressibly. "But won't it be fun to see Blanche's face when she returns! She'll be livid with jealousy. She thought to attract him herself, you remember, the last time he came to Poitiers, and he never even noticed her."

The thought did lend additional spice to the notion of making Simon de Winslade her adoring slave, she agreed to herself, picturing the spiteful Blanche de Limousin watching hungrily as she and Simon strolled by. Of course, the Norman would have eyes for only Ysabeau.

"Pardon, Lady Ysabeau," an adolescent voice said.

Looking up, Ysabeau was surprised to see the towheaded youth who served as squire to Baron de Winslade.

"My lord bid me request the pleasure of your company, if your duties do not press you this morning. He will meet you by the pear trees in the pleasance."

Ysabeau, eyesbrows raised, exchanged a look with Matilde, who murmured with a smile, "The game begins."

"Matilde!" Ysabeau protested. "He thinks he has but to snap his fingers, and I will jump as high as he commands."

The young lad had a ready reply to her objections, however. "If you seemed unwilling, I was to give you this."

He handed her a folded parchment sheet, on which were written the words:

"Beautiful lady whom I adore, permit me to atone for my disagreeable behavior which so displeased you yestereve. Come, show me the beauty of an autumn day in Poitiers, which will be but dull in contrast to your own dark loveliness. Do not disappoint me, or you will break my heart.

Simon"

Without a word she passed the missive to her friend, conscious of a growing excitement within her that made her stomach feel cold while everywhere else she felt hot and alive.

"Well, what are you waiting for, *ma chère*? You have no special duties that cannot wait, with Eleanor gone. Go get your cloak," Matilde ordered, giving the girl a gentle shove.

When she arrived at the pear trees, bare of leaves now in the late November sunlight, she found him waiting.

He was more handsome than any man had a right to be, dressed in a royal blue knee-length tunic that challenged the glory of his eyes, with a darker blue mantle of the same length edged in squirrel and fastened by a gold brooch in the center of his chest. On his legs he wore red knee-length stockings with cross-gartering over his linen chausses, and on his feet, shoes of soft leather. All this she noted in the blink of an eye; it was his engaging smile that transfixed her, as the sunbeams burnished the dark gold of his hair.

"Good day, my lady, I am honored you have come," he said, bowing. He had studied her also as she had approached, and was pleased by her slender figure in the gown of pleated scarlet wool which laced up at the sides, showing a snow-white *chainse* beneath the full, long sleeves and gold-bordered hem. Her hair was covered with a veil and barbette, also of pure white linen, which framed her face enchantingly and set off the deep brown pools of her eyes. She wore a cape of a deeper crimson hue, which matched the red leather slippers that peeked from under her hem.

"Last evening, I thought you should wear only green, Lady Ysabeau. I can see now I was wrong," he said in his caressing voice.

Was the high color that stained her cheeks a reflection of her gown's color, or due to his compliment? He could not be sure, but thought it had not been there until he spoke.

"You have Matilde de St. Gilles, another of Eleanor's ladies, to thank for my coming," answered Ysabeau, essaying a haughty tone and distant expression, determined to seize control of the situation from the beginning and hold it. "It was she who persuaded me to give you another chance."

If he noticed her coolness, he gave no evidence of it. "I am grateful. It promises to be a lovely day, surely one of the last of the year, and I thought we could walk in the city. Surely there are sights in Poitiers that even a crude Norman baron like myself would find diverting."

Was he mocking her? She met his dancing eyes, but could not tell.

"Just you and I, my lord?" she asked suspiciously.

"Naturally, I would not so compromise your honor. Geoffrey, my squire, waits at the main gatehouse, and will walk with us."

She gave him a skeptical look which clearly said that if he were up to any devilment, the presence of a callow youth would do nothing to hinder him; but she acquiesced with a graceful inclination of her head.

"I thought you might like to see the oldest Christian building in France first, my lord," she said as they passed through the gatehouse with Geoffrey in tow.

Simon gave his assent, then, without asking permission, put her arm through his, for the streets were narrow and steeply inclined.

Simon walked in silence, but frequently glanced over and studied her. The wealthy burghers' houses they were passing presently required no comment. The weather had already been remarked upon. The quiet made her uneasy. At last, she desperately sought conversation. "What part of England are you from, my lord?"

"Winslade lies in Hampshire, in the south central part of England."

"Is it a goodly fief?"

"Assuredly—or was before the unrest in England began. It lies on the North Downs, which are chalk hills, and is richly forested, full of game, has a prosperous village and reasonably industrious villeins. Of course, it could all be a smoking ruin by the time I return." His face was somber and troubled.

"Conditions are so dangerous, then?"

He nodded. "Stephen can't keep order. Those bent on evil do precisely as they please, waylaying travelers, torturing them for their valuables, killing—so much for knightly virtues."

"Do you not fear to leave a wife behind in such conditions?"

He looked at her sardonically. "Think you that I would be pursuing you, if I were wedded?" He guessed that her query had been a probe to find out his status, but was surprised at her reply.

She gave a very Gallic shrug. "What has one thing to do with the other, my lord? Do not men do as they wish, but expect their wives to remain virtuously at home, keeping the hall and hearth warm?"

"I have no wife," was all he said. He could not bear to speak of Rohese, whose golden fairness was so different from the dark French beauty who walked beside him now. He thought briefly of his son . . . but, no, he would not mention Aimery either, since he would not talk of the boy's mother.

They had arrived at a small rectangular building. "This is the Temple of St. Jean. It was originally merely a baptistry, and was built, it is said, some six hundred years ago. The narthex was added early in this century, though," Ysabeau informed him as they stepped down into the entrance, which was slightly lower than street level.

"There was once a piscina—a basin for draining the water used in baptisms—in the center of the temple, but," Ysabeau said, "it was filled up at some previous time."

He studied the few frescoes and sarcophagi whose faded color somewhat relieved the plainness of their surroundings. But there was not enough in this small building to absorb his attention for long. She could feel him watching her, and looked up to catch a speculative gleam in his eyes.

"Next, shall we go to the Church of St. Radegonde?" she said quickly. "It is also very old."

"As my lady decrees," he answered blandly.

A jowly monk, caretaker of the building, hastily appeared at the door, looking flustered at having almost missed a donation from a wealthy noble. Simon handed him a coin, brushing aside his obsequious offers to answer any questions they might have about the history of the Temple.

Radegonde's church was not far away. "St. Radegonde was a Thuringian princess, a Christian, forced to marry the pagan Frankish King Clotaire. She was not happy with this wicked man and his godless ways, so after a time she obtained leave from the Church to separate from him and found the Order of St. Croix here. She enjoyed a close relationship with the chaplain of the order, the poet, Fortunatus."

They had stopped in front of a niche to the right of the nave, which contained a footprint, supposedly that of Christ when he appeared to the saint.

"Close? How close?" he interrupted with a maddening grin.

"Theirs was a relationship of the spirit," she said, trying very hard not to smile. "His greatest hymns were inspired by their pure love."

"Indeed," he returned dryly, and read from an inscription in front of a poorly executed statue of the saint: " 'Human eloquence is struck dumb by the piety, self-denial, charity, sweetness, humility, uprightness, faith and fervor in which she lived.' Not too dumb, it would seem. Truly a model to whose virtues any woman should aspire!"

She had not missed the comical rolling of his merry blue eyes. "Why limit those virtues to women, my lord? There have been male saints, too. What I found admirable about Fortunatus was that he extolled her virtues without asking anything of her."

"At least, he doesn't *admit* asking anything base of her. How very selfless of him, if it is true."

She resented this cynical tone, but was more alarmed at how close to her he had inched in the dim light. "Is that too selfless an ideal for a Norman? The gentlemen of the *langue d'oc* dedicate themselves to serving their ladies, and pleasing them."

"They must be very patient men," he murmured as they moved out of the chapel back into the nave, his eyes glittering in the strange light cast by the stained-glass clerestory windows. An old palmer, with the cockleshell badge denoting a pilgrimage to St. James Compostela, strolled past them with a benign smile.

"And you are not?" she parried daringly.

"It depends on the goal," Simon answered. "For something truly significant, I can wait as long as needed." He gave her a wolfish smile.

And which of those goals am I, she wondered, as they went back into the bright sunlight and were rejoined by the squire.

"That is probably enough for one day," she said, as they trudged back uphill to the palace. "I have duties to attend to, even in her grace's absence. I have enjoyed showing these places to you, my lord."

"As I have enjoyed your company,"

admitted Simon. "My men-at-arms need drilling, else they'll grow fat on this rich Provençal diet and enforced idleness. But surely there is more to see of Poitiers than churches?"

"Ah, but we did not even see the richest of the churches, Notre Dame La Grande, St. Hilaire . . ." She chuckled to see the wry face he made. "You do not like churches, *mon sieur*? I am told the Normans are all very devout."

"Oh, we are, and I've admired what I've seen today for its antiquity and beauty. But there is that about being in the company of a beautiful maid which draws one's mind away from religion."

"I see." Her full ripe lips curved in a smile at the compliment. "But there is another sight you might find interesting. However it is across the Clain," she dismissed the idea regretfully, "and perhaps too far to walk in November. Perhaps, if you are still here in the spring—a picnic?" she suggested impishly.

"Even Eleanor cannot keep a man from duty that long!" he said, mock-severely. "If I am still in Aquitaine then, I may as well sign my fief over to King Stephen's brigands!"

She noted a shadow which crossed his face then, and wondered at it, for he seemed to have forgotten her utterly for a moment. She could not know he was thinking of little Aimery; he was worrying about his son's fate should might continue to triumph over right in England, should his brother, Gervase, attempt to add Winslade to his possessions.

Chapter Six

Ysabeau spent the afternoon with the other ladies, readying Eleanor's winter clothes for her use.

"They will return soon, they must," Matilde said. "I can almost feel it. Any day now an outrider will arrive to tell us their graces are but hours away."

The rich velvets, woolens and heavier silks that had been left behind were inspected for minute rips or stains and signs of wear. Embroidery was mended, and gowns that had been left in the back of the clothes press were taken out to be aired. Each garment was as elegant, stylish, and as unique as its owner. When Ysabeau realized that Eleanor had many more with her on her journey, the magnitude of the Duchess' wardrobe seemed staggering.

"Here, Ysabeau, take these to her grace's

almoner, who lodges in the gatehouse," Matilde said, handing Ysabeau a couple of Eleanor's older gowns and chemises. "He will distribute them to the poor, as her grace would wish."

Ysabeau smiled at the thought of a Poitevin peasant in one of the sheer linen chemises with its delicate lace trim, still luxurious though a trifle worn. She welcomed the chance to escape into the cool air outside. Here in the Duchess' bower, while her hands were busy, her thoughts turned all too often to the Norman baron.

She crossed the inner courtyard with her burden, her way familiar now, and delivered it efficiently to the old priest whose sole job it was to dispense charity in the name of the Duchess.

Leaving the small apartment with the blessing of the kindly almoner still echoing in her ears, she was startled to hear her name being called by a familiar voice from outside the portcullis.

"Jean!" she cried gladly, after she recognized the figure being questioned by the gate guards. "It is all right, let him in," she instructed the guards, who then raised the portcullis with much creaking of the winch from the chamber above.

She could hardly believe he had come, the person she had longed for, wept for in secret as the days stretched into weeks and months and still no answer to her letters came. She gazed fondly at his well-loved, somewhat stocky figure as he waited patiently for the barrier to be fully raised, and stared back at her with a shy smile.

As soon as the portcullis no longer separated them, she went flying toward him. He looked at her, grinned, then snapped his fingers over his shoulders at something beyond, hidden by the gatehouse tower. The next thing she knew, she was being bowled over by a flurry of brown and black fur.

"Ami!" she squealed joyously, dodging an enthusiastic wet tongue, as the huge mastiff gave her a slurpy greeting. "Oh, *mon chèr*, you have grown so big!"

She righted herself by pulling on the fur of the shaggy brindle shoulder of the dog, which the animal bore patiently, tongue lolling out as he gazed from his master to the fondly remembered girl who had inexplicably absented herself from their outings in the *marais* of late.

"You look wonderful, Ysabeau," Jean said, staring at her so that the wistful note in his voice escaped her for a moment.

"Ah, so do you." Her eyes took in the familiar russet jerkin, the rough serge trousers, cross-gartered woolen hose and coarse, short boots that were so typical of him. His curls were wind-tousled, his features, weathered and regular; but his smile, she saw at last, was somehow constrained.

"What do you here, Jean? Is aught wrong with *mon père*?" She felt dizzy with alarm suddenly; had he come all this way only to bring bad news?

"Nay, don't worry, Ysa. The Sieur de Ré is hale as ever, though his joints begin to ache as the cold draws near. The grape harvest was excellent—the cellars of the château are crammed full of this year's vintage."

"Then, what? Have you come at last to

take me away? Have you missed me as I have missed you? You didn't answer any of my letters . . . I didn't know what to think. . . ." Hope flared wildly, then died as he let go of her hands and looked down at his feet.

The silence punctuated only by the mastiff's happy panting as he sat on his haunches, lasted until she thought she would go mad.

"Ysabeau," he said, almost as an adult speaks to a child, "I can't write, and the priest had to read your letters to me. But you knew it was impossible. You knew it was over—it had to be—when you left to come to court, to finally be the lady you were born to be. I came to say goodbye, since I couldn't write you a fine farewell on parchment, like some fancy lord."

She stared at him, stunned. Her enjoyment in charming the Baron de Winslade was forgotten now. "No, no! I love you—and I don't want to be a lady!"

"Ysabeau," he began again patiently. "Perhaps Ami wants to be a heron, but he cannot be, for he is a dog. Don't you see what I'm saying? For all that my lord, your father, sometimes shares my mother's bed, we are still peasants, and there can be nothing between you and I. I knew that, always."

"But you kissed me . . . you said you loved me!" she cried brokenly.

"Yes, because in your company I forgot myself, and it was very wrong. Had your father let you remain at home, I might have done you a great disservice, for I felt for those few moments that we were the only two people in the world."

Ysabeau closed her eyes then, and as the

first tear escaped under her dark lashes, she remembered the lush green foliage that had hung all about them in the *marais* that day when he had beached the dinghy on a small islet with overhanging beech, willows, and elms. His declaration of love then was as fervent as her impassioned plea was now.

She flung herself into his arms, tilting her lips to his, clutching his broad shoulders against her.

"But if we truly love, then anything is possible, Jean! My father would see you were knighted, he'd have to if we were wed."

"You're dreaming, Ysa," he said, using the childhood nickname again to force her to listen. "If he knew I was here, he'd probably have me flogged, and perhaps he would be right. But I had to see you one more time, and tell you my news, and bring you Ami."

"But he's yours, Jean. I gave him to you." She remembered the black ball of fur that had been Ami only last year. The runt of the litter, the Count had said, and never noticed when the pup disappeared after weaning.

"There won't be room, where I am going to be living, Ysabeau," he said. "I am marrying the widow Aela."

Instantly a picture came to Ysabeau's shocked mind of the plump widow, who, with her brood of children, occupied a humble house next to the tavern she operated by the city gate.

"Aela?" she squeaked, her voice rising in disbelief. The thought of Jean, her Jean, wed to the widow of the tavernkeeper was staggering. "But, why?"

"I was lonely when you left," he admitted with a shrug, "and she was always there to listen, with a cup of wine she'd left on the hearth to warm for me. She's been alone a long time. She needs a man to help her run the tavern. It's full of coarse louts, day and night, trying to paw and pinch her. . . ."

Her fists tightened as she said spitefully, "And why not? She's one of them."

"So am I, Ysabeau, though you won't see it," he replied patiently. "Please don't make nasty remarks. They're not worthy of you. And she loves me, too. She's been very good to me."

"*She'll* never let you go punting in the marshes for the sheer joy of it," Ysabeau persisted, stung. "She'll have you fetching flagons of her cheap wine for the customers."

"Yes she will, for she recognizes the value of the fresh fish and fowl I can catch there. We plan to expand the Sign of the Heron to serve meals, too. But it will always be you I picture beside me in the boat.

"I've brought you Ami," he repeated. "Do you think the Duchess would allow him here?" His eyes pleaded with her to understand, and at last she could no longer ignore the obvious truth.

It was over. She was the *Damoiselle de Ré,* daughter of a count, and there was a great gulf between her and the peasant freeman who stood before her. She had been fooling herself to think that a life with him would ever have been possible.

She took hold of the dog's collar, and studied him through tear-filled eyes. "*Au revoir*, my Jean. God grant you a happy life."

"And you, my lady." He put a hand on her shoulder and lowered his lips to hers in a last, brief, bittersweet kiss.

The dog whined low in his throat, puzzled to see his master leaving so soon after being reunited with his mistress. But he made no move to follow Jean when he left, and instead transferred his gaze trustfully to Ysabeau.

In her heart she had known it was over, of course. But as long as she had not heard Jean say it, she had clung to her hopeless love. Still a part of her must have known it, else why would she have begun to play with the likes of Simon de Winslade? She did not think she was, by nature, a coquette, so some portion of her being had already accepted the end of one era in her life, and had begun another.

Nevertheless, she went about the rest of her duties that afternoon like a puppet, ignoring the curious glances of the others. When it came time for the evening meal, she did not feel equal to enduring the bustling great hall, or, more importantly, to the chance of encountering the probing azure gaze of Baron Simon. After picking at a selection of foods brought to her from the hall by Marie, she stroked Ami's head as he lay by the bed. Occasionally, a tear trickled down her cheek. Sometimes she smiled to remember a particularly happy time with Jean. At last she fell asleep, still in her scarlet gown, with her fingertips dangling onto the dog's large brindled head.

An hour later, after the fire in the brazier had died down to glowing embers, the mastiff raised his head in the dim light. He heard something above the soft sighing of his mistress' regular breathing . . . the sound of feet shod in soft leather boots in the corridor beyond the heavy wooden door.

Had there been any threat to his newfound mistress, a low growl would have begun to rumble in the massive animal's throat, and his hackles would have risen. But he sensed the person outside the door meant only well toward Ysabeau; he listened to the indecisive pacing, cocking his head in puzzlement as the footfalls became more distant, and at last died away.

Simon at last struck his fist into his open palm in frustration and made his way back down the tower stairs into the great hall, where Philippe played for the few still dancing. At a small table near the firelight, two courtiers were engaged in a long drawn out game of chess. Farther from the light, another young knight fondled the lady in his lap, his explorations punctuated by her soft giggles.

He had looked forward to her company ever since he had left her at noon. He had caught himself daydreaming while drilling his men at target practice with their crossbows. Her hair would feel like silk as he loosened it from its disciplined coils under the veil . . . her lips would be petal-smooth under his own. . . . His imagination had dared go even further while aloud he commended an especially skillful shot by Geoffrey. . . . Her breasts would be alabaster-smooth in his cupped hands, the hardening of a small nipple palpable beneath his thumb and finger . . .

And then she had not even appeared at the evening meal! He had scanned the hall many times, feeling like a foolish page in the first flush of an infatuation with a comely scullery wench, and resented her for returning him to such adolescent weakness. But there it was—he could neither stop looking for her nor pay proper attention to the somewhat overblown charms of the lady who'd sat beside him. It was a relief when the meal was over, and he could at last speak to Matilde, who had been sitting across the hall.

"Ysabeau retired early, my lord," she informed him when he inquired after her with studied casualness. "She complained of a headache." But then the handsome young woman had laid a hand on his velvet sleeve and confided, "She'd had a visitor from home, she said, and afterward she looked *si triste*. . . ."

It had to be that peasant, he guessed angrily, wishing he could run the lout through for the hold he apparently still had on the delectable Poitevin girl's heart. Before this evening she had begun to relax in his company, and flirt back at him, and his goal had appeared attainable after all. But then, the women of Aquitaine flirted as if there were no tomorrow, and strove to turn men into their tame birds. . . .

Simon knew not how long he would remain at the court of Poitiers. But he intended to continue on as the hunter, with Ysabeau the prey, no matter how much the courtly love fables indicated matters should go otherwise. He wanted her. He would have her, and both of them would enjoy it. Beyond that, he did not think.

But he could take no steps toward that end with her sequestered in her room. He had asked directions of Matilde, ignoring her knowing smile. He had not planned what he meant to do there. Perhaps he'd run into her casually on the stairway, or she'd just be happening to leave the chamber as he passed. He was anxious not to appear a lovesick fool. What else would more thoroughly convince her he was willing to submit to this ridiculous Provençal ritual of playing at love? Still, if it helped him find his way into her affections, perhaps it was worth assuming the guise. . . .

Indecision plagued him, and no petite dark-haired beauty appeared at the door, nor could he hear any sounds within that encouraged him to knock. At last, he strode away, wondering what the morrow would bring.

He smiled ruefully to himself as he turned on his heel and left the great hall, after surveying the tapestry-hung room for only a few moments.

He knew he should be hoping for the return of the Plantagenet and his bride, so that he could transact his business and be on his way back to England. He did not believe in love any more—you could give your whole heart to a woman, and it was still no guarantee she would not leave you, as Rohese had done in death. That was how he saw it. Love was too ethereal. But he did believe in earthly pleasure, and had been too long without it. He would hate to have to leave Poitiers without experiencing a few hours of delight with Ysabeau de Ré.

Chapter Seven

Ysabeau had not been overly worried about accepting Ami. Here, as in other palaces, dogs were ever-present, spending much of their time in the halls, especially during meals, when bones and choice morsels were thrown to favored ones, often resulting in a struggle for possession. Ami, however, was easily the largest dog, and his size made it easy for him to assume effortless mastery of the others, while his good nature allowed him to rule without bullying.

Ysabeau was amused, watching Ami explore the hall for the first time the next morning at breakfast. Several of his fellow canines greeted him, but he held himself stiffly, head erect, until the other, in each case, began to wag its tail in fawning submission. He then investigated the humans, aloofly ignoring the blandishments of some, and allowing others to pat him.

Ysabeau almost laughed aloud, for her pet's reactions to individuals of the court uncannily matched hers. When Lord Joscelin had called to him, holding out a tidbit, the huge mastiff had turned and trotted back to her.

"Who is your large companion?"

Simon de Winslade extended a long leg over the bench facing her, and straddled it, his gaze taking in the violet shadows under her somewhat reddened eyes. The *balourd* had made her unhappy, then, he thought.

"My lord, may I introduce you to Ami? He was brought to me by—someone from home. He was the runt of the litter, but you'd never guess it to look at him now, would you?" She smiled proudly at the dog, then watched how Ami behaved toward the Norman baron.

They got along immediately. The mastiff greeted Simon like an old friend, his tapering tail whipping around ecstatically, his big pink tongue lolling.

"Hello, big fellow. *Ça va*?"

Ami sat down and presented a massive paw, which was accepted gravely.

"I see you have passed inspection, Lord Simon."

"Dogs are good judges of character, you know," he said with a wink, leaning down to scratch the mastiff's ears.

"I have always heard it said," she answered, allowing a note of sardonicism in her voice.

"I'm sure you have his primary loyalty," he answered blandly, his blue eyes limpid pools of innocence. "Perhaps he could serve as our chaperone today."

She eyed him skeptically.

"The weather has continued benign, despite the time of year," he explained. "But it cannot be expected to go on, so let us seize the moment. You spoke of some further sight just outside of Poitiers yesterday, do you remember?"

"Oh, yes, but it is a little far to walk, even on a sunny day. . . ."

"*Bien sûr.* I have anticipated that problem." He spread his hands wide, grinning. "I have secured the loan of a sweet-tempered lady's palfrey for you, and I have my destrier. But we shall not, *hélas*, have the company of Geoffrey. My squire sampled too much Bordeaux last night and lies abed with a splitting head and queasy stomach this morning. So you see, we shall need your formidable companion there," he finished, indicating Ami.

His eyes were full of sparkling mischievousness, daring her to accept a second outing with him, this time without a human chaperone—not that Geoffrey had been much assistance yesterday, she remembered. He had waited outside of both churches and Ysabeau had no doubt he had been instructed by his master to do so.

"Ah, please, lovely one, come out with me in the crisp fresh air and banish the shadows from your eyes," the Norman coaxed.

Ysabeau was reminded of her restless night's sleep, haunted by dreams of Jean, who had consigned their affection for each other to the past. Why shouldn't she ride out with this charming, handsome noble with the dangerous smile?

Because he had a dangerous smile, and because her resentment of Jean's rejection was making her foolishly rebellious—these were reasons enough to be cautious. He was aware that she had grown up far from the sophistication of a ducal court, but did he really think she was as naive as all that? Ysabeau had gained quite an education in worldly matters in the few months she had been at court.

She thought of the lurid stories Matilde had told of young heiresses who had been kidnapped when they traveled outside castle walls without an adequate escort, and forced to marry some ugly, impoverished knight; others, she'd been told, were raped by brigands who left them to be found in their shame.

She certainly doubted de Winslade intended to abduct her, but she did sense he was seeking a little dalliance. He wanted her, his single-minded attentions since his return had proved that. She wanted him, too, but as a courtly lover, though she sensed he had little regard for the restrained conventions of *l'amour courtois*.

Suddenly, an answer to her dilemma occurred to her. She'd ask Matilde and Rene to accompany them. Their presence should be sufficient to keep Simon de Windslade's intentions honorable.

"It sounds like a lovely outing," she replied sweetly, and was pleased to see the grin her acquiescence brought to his lean features. "But I fear you will have to wait just awhile, my lord. I am obviously not dressed to ride, I have an errand to accomplish first. Shall I meet you at the stables in an hour? Meanwhile, if you will apply to the kitchens, I am sure they would be willing to supply us with a bit of refreshment to take with us."

He bowed low with his catlike grace, taking her hand in his and brushing it briefly with his lips. The warmth of his mouth, with the accompanying soft bristles of his moustache, sent a shocking wave of pleasure washing over her. She was sure he was aware of its effect on her as he straightened, watching her. One could practically see the plan for seduction forming in those eyes, she thought, though his actions and subsequent words were the perfect parody of the courtly lover:

"I will langish until then, *ma chérie*. But I am overjoyed you will honor me with your company."

A little over an hour later, Ysabeau and Simon rode over the Clain, heading northward out of the city, their horses' hooves echoing on the wooden planking of the bridge. Simon's mighty black destrier made a heavier sound than the dainty clip-clop of Ysabeau's petite chestnut mare, and she had to look up if she wished to speak to him, for the warhorse was several hands higher.

Ami led the way, alternately trotting merrily in front of the horses and dashing madly ahead, nose to the ground, on the scent of some small animal. He was clearly enjoying the brisk, windy morning.

Matilde and Rene rode just behind them, deep in conversation, using only their eyes.

Simon had betrayed no hint of dismay when

Matilde and Rene had arrived with Ysabeau at the stables, also dressed for riding, but had slanted an amused look at Ysabeau's innocent expression, as if he'd known exactly what she was about.

Greeting the Poitevin *chevalier* and Ysabeau's friend, the baron had exclaimed with pleasure that he was relieved to see them, for the scullery wenches had pressed more food on him than just he and Ysabeau could consume!

"You have shown no curiosity about what we ride to see, my lord," Ysabeau said, breaking the comfortable silence as they descended the slope past an olive grove. The dense, dark silvery-green leaves of the squat trees were in marked contrast to the stark, bare branches of other trees they had passed.

"I am merely content to bask in your beauty," he answered lightly, "and I know it can't be much further on."

"No, it is only a league or two beyond the bridge."

They covered the distance quickly, and soon turned off the road.

"Here we are, my lord," she said when they arrived in a little valley ringed by oak trees.

Within this circle leaned several massive granite stones, with a huge gray slab lying on top of them. Each stone was taller than a man, and together they looked like the forgotten playthings of a giant child, who had built a platform with his blocks and left them on a whim.

While the quartet rode into the grove, the sun disappeared behind a puffy gray cloud. The air seemed suddenly heavier. There was an eerie quiet about the place, as if even in warmer months, no birds dared chirp freely from the boughs.

Ysabeau had been shown the dolmen before, when a party from the palace had ridden out on a hot summer day, and had noted the same unnatural air about the area then also. "This is called the *Pierre Levée*, my lord," she said as all four dismounted and walked over to examine the stones more closely. "No one knows who put them here, though of course there are legends. There were pagan tribes here in Roman times, so those stones may have had something to do with their worship."

Simon nodded, looking at the stones thoughtfully and feeling the solemnity of the atmosphere, as Ysabeau had. "We have some of these in England, and I've heard they are plentiful in Brittany. I'm told the druids made sacrifices on them."

"Of young virgins," put in Rene sardonically.

"Thank goodness I am safe, being a widow," Matilde laughed. She and Rene turned away to see to the horses and unpack the food, having seen the dolmen before.

Joining in the playful spirit of the others, Ysabeau flung herself dramatically against the surface of a cold, upright stone.

"*Hé*, druid, do not harm me," she cried, bearing her white throat to the imaginary knife.

Before she knew it though, Simon advanced on her, falling into the role of druid. He unsheathed his dagger. The blade gleamed dully as he ran his long, tapering fingers over it to test its sharpness.

Ysabeau could not look away from his spellbinding blue eyes. Her heart began to thump wildly within her; a shiver traveled up the length of her spine. So too must the maidens of the dark times past have felt—paralyzed, unable to flee from the fate that awaited them.

He came closer. She could see the pulse beating rapidly in his throat, the individual tawny hairs of the mustache above the sensual mouth, the gleaming teeth. Then came his gravelly, caressing voice, murmuring, "Your *life* is not the sacrifice I would take from you, maiden," as he sheathed his blade, and took her into his arms.

He did not pull her away from the stone, but used the hard length of it to imprison her firmly against his body as his mouth descended hungrily on hers. His was initially gentle, slowly and thoughtfully exploring the boundaries of her luscious mouth, tasting the honey as his lips persuasively urged hers to part, and his tongue touched hers.

She was dismayed at the magnitude of her own desire as the heat spread and she became aware of his powerfully muscled chest pressing against her soft breasts. He lifted her off her feet, and she could feel his growing need for her as his arms locked her closer to him. Recklessly, she returned his kiss.

Behind them Rene cleared his throat, saying, "*Excusez-moi*, but our repast is ready. Perhaps you two could be persuaded to nibble on some chicken, instead?"

Ysabeau's face flamed scarlet as she edged away from the stone, every nerve screaming with the fleeting sensations he had aroused. What was this Norman lord, that he could cause her, for a long moment, to totally forget that two other people were there? It was a good thing she had persuaded Matilde and her lover to come, for Ysabeau felt certain she would not have done anything to stop Simon's sensual attack on her will. Even now a part of her resisted the interruption. . . .

She glanced at him again as they walked over to where the meal was spread out on a soft cloth, and was relieved to see there was no smirking triumph there, just a small half-smile that played about his lips as he ran his tongue over them, as if to catch the last sweet drop of her.

In her mind, she remained distressed, aware that if she did not guard the circumstances carefully, de Winslade would take from her anything he wanted, and she would give it freely. Here was no pliable courtier to be turned into a two-legged lapdog! Well, then, he would look in vain for such an opportunity.

Simon had not exaggerated the bounty of the meal sent by the palace kitchen. Perhaps, Ysabeau thought cynically, he had read her mind and had known she would have someone accompany them all along. There was cold capon, figs, apples, a bright golden cheese, flaky quince tarts, and a leather bag containing sweet hippocras.

Seated on their saddle blankets, the four devoured the feast. Ami was not forgotten, catching tidbits thrown to him. Nearby the horses grazed, oblivious of the dark deeds that had once taken place in this grove in centuries past.

Ysabeau felt the calm reassurance of Matilde's gaze, as if the other woman could see into her soul and read the agitation she still felt. She looked up to meet her friend's warm, sympathetic hazel eyes. Had Matilde ever felt like this before she was wed to the elderly noble? Did a woman feel this way again, this consuming fear of vulnerability, after she was no stranger to passion, as when Matilde and Rene had become lovers? She would have given much to know.

She watched as Simon and Rene debated the merits of various weights of broadswords. She was pleased to see how well he and Rene got along, for Rene had once said he disliked the Normans and was dismayed Eleanor had allied Poitou with them. But now, the swarthy Poitevin was chattering away with the Norman baron as if they were old friends. Simon was a man of considerable charm.

"We had better resaddle our mounts and return to Poitiers," Rene said practically, pointing a finger at the darkening sky. Ysabeau saw that while she had been eating, immersed in her doubts and fears, the autumn wind had capriciously blown quite a number of rain-heavy clouds overhead.

Simon, how had been lounging indolently on his side, agreed and arose with characteristic grace, beginning to gather up the utensils.

"Leave that, my lord. Matilde and I can pack up while you gather the horses." She laid a gentle hand on his wrist shyly, and was rewarded by his warm smile.

"We should arrive back well before the storm," Rene pronounced confidently, squinting as he scanned the ominous clouds.

It had seemed he was right, until they had gone half the distance back. Then a tremendous crack rent the sky apart, and a livid slash splintered an aged olive tree on the horizon. The rain began to fall in torrents.

Matilde's horse panicked, seizing the bit and plunging off madly toward the city. Rene was in immediate pursuit. In a moment they were gone, covered by sheets of rain which only increased in intensity with each passing second.

"We're already soaked," shouted Simon above the downpour, leaning to catch at her rein. "Isn't there somewhere we can take shelter?"

She thought quickly. "Yes, a hermit's cave I was going to show you on the return trip," she said, turning her horse's head with a beckoning wave.

Her palfrey was of steadier, more biddable temperment than the excitable mare Matilde had ridden, but lacked no speed as she responded to the girl's drumming heels. The black destrier followed, and in a few moments they had reached the shelter, which lay under the olive grove.

The cave had been chiseled out of a limestone hill. Simon speedily tied the horses to an oak sapling growing at a precarious slant outside, while Ysabeau watched from the mouth of the cave for her dog, but Ami was nowhere in sight.

"Your dog followed Matilde's runaway mount," Simon told her, sensing her concern as he sloshed inside, his cloak dripping rivulets over the hay-strewn stone floor. "I think he was trying to slow it for Rene."

"Mastiffs are always happier when they have something to do," she said lightly, but she realized her last protection from Simon was gone.

The hermit who had lived out his ascetic life here had long ago gone to his heavenly reward; but it was obvious from the firewood piled in a corner and the rushes on the floor that the cave was occasionally used, probably by the orchard keeper or a shepherd.

"The storm looks to go on awhile," stated Simon flatly, walking away from the cave's entrance. He began to pile the logs and dried brush together, and by dint of some tinder and flint and evident practice, managed to start a warming fire close enough to the entrance of the cave that the smoke drifted outward.

"You'd probably better get out of some of that wet clothing," Simon observed practically as he began to strip off his sodden cloak and tunic.

She stared at him as if he'd just suggested slitting her throat. "Undress? In front of you? *Non*, my lord, it's out of the question."

"I'm only suggesting down to your chemise," he said reasonably. "If we hang the garments over this boulder—like so—they will probably be dry by the time we are able to depart."

She could not, however, be persuaded to

part with more than her mantle, and sat, shivering, as he continued to shed layer after layer of clothing, until at last he was clad only in his shirt and *chausses*. The fine linen of the shirt clung wetly to his powerfully muscled arms, revealing the magnificent physique of one who wields a heavy broadsword.

"You're going to catch lung fever, I fear," he chided, watching her teeth chatter. "Why don't we at least share our body heat? Come," he invited, raising an arm to indicate a place for her against his side.

"I'm sure many maids have lost their virtue on flimsy pretexts such as that," she retorted archly. "Surely you do not think me gullible as that."

He raised a brow reprovingly. "*Chère damoiselle*, I have no motives but to warm you, and less importantly, myself. When I make love to you, I promise it will be in more romantic surroundings than these." He nodded at the bare stone walls and the brittle, musty hay on the floor.

When I make love to you. The arrogance, the conceit of this Norman *salaud*!

"You are very sure of yourself, my lord," she replied. "You have already taken more from me this morning than a lady grants even a favored lover in many months here in Aquitaine."

"I am sure we both wanted what happened this morning," he said evenly, his eyes locking in combat with hers across the fire. "Your lips welcomed mine."

"I am not an alabaster Madonna in some

dim chapel!" she cried. "Nevertheless, the kiss was imposed on me. I imagine you are used to treating the dairymaids in England so, my Lord de Winslade, and think the ladies-in-waiting here are of no more consequence. There are *filles de joie* in Poitou, if that is what you require." Her words were heated, but laced with a cold hauteur. She was aware that she took a risk if she made him angry. There was no one here to say him nay should he choose to force her. But her fear of the situation, and, perhaps, the wine she had so recently consumed, made her reckless.

She looked so young, so vulnerable in the dancing light of the little fire. Her dark brown hair hung in damp strands on her shoulders, giving her the look of a much younger girl. There was a bluish tinge of cold about her lips, and the flesh around her arms was dotted with gooseflesh as she pushed up her sleeves to warm herself by the flames. How could anyone think to seduce a waif such as this?

"I repeat," he insisted, "that I only wish to keep us both warm by holding you. On my oath as a knight."

She came close to refusing once again, indeed, and her mouth opened to utter the words, when a chill seized her. It was a full minute before she could keep her teeth from chattering enough to reply, "Very well, my lord, you are on your honor."

Ysabeau snuggled gratefully against his chest, the clean male scent of him mingling with that of wet horse, damp wool and the woodsmoke that hung around the mouth of the cave. His arm held her securely as she leaned back against the stacked wood. His skin warmed her, but she imagined her still-sodden clothing must not feel very pleasant to him. Yet he only sighed with pleasure at her nearness, and she relaxed by degrees in his embrace.

The lightning and thunder had subsided, giving way to a steady downpour that was hypnotic as it drummed on the ceiling of their cave. The wine and the secure feeling she had in being held in his strong arms worked its magic on her, and she dozed.

Moments after her regular, deep breathing told him she was asleep, Ami slunk in, abjectly apologizing in his demeanor for having so abandoned his mistress.

"Hello, old fellow, where have you been?" whispered Simon softly. "You have certainly failed in your task as chaperone—a good thing I am such a trustworthy fellow," he added, scratching the dog's ear with his free hand, "this time, at least."

Chapter Eight

True to Simon's dire prediction, Ysabeau fell ill the following morning, waking up with a congested head, a racking cough, shaking chills alternating with a fiery fever.

The evening before, it had been the hour of vespers before the rain had let up enough for them to journey back to Poitiers. Ysabeau, still blinking drowsily after awaking in the Norman's arms, had ridden the still-wet palfrey through the palace gate behind Simon's destrier, only to be met in the courtyard by a worried Marie.

"It's been at least three hours since Lady Matilde and Lord Rene returned, my lady," the tiring-woman scolded. "I was just about to have the captain of the guard send out a party to search for you." She'd rounded on Simon angrily. "Why, she's drenched through, my lord! She'll catch her death. Is that how you take care of ladies in England, *mon seigneur*?" She'd clucked angrily and shaken her head.

Simon had taken the reproof meekly. "I tried to get her to shed her wet garments, but she would not."

"I'll warrant that you did!" the servant had replied tartly, then led her weary charge off to her tower room for a hot bath.

Marie devoted herself to Ysabeau's care, bringing her hot soups and clean handkerchiefs and tea brewed of willow bark, which seemed to lessen the raging heat that flared within her.

Matilde made arrangements to share quarters with another maid-of-honor while Ysabeau was ill. But as she was gathering up her possessions, she saw that her friend was awake and regaled her with a tale of Ami's heroism. The mastiff had charged after the runaway mare, heedless of the danger from her hooves, forcing the horse to slow her mad flight until at last Rene was able to catch up and grab the palfrey's bridle. Then the dog had run back to Ysabeau and Simon.

"I was so terrified while my horse was running that I could think of nothing but my fear of falling off," Matilde confided, sitting on a stool near Ysabeau's bed. Then afterward, I felt like such a fool. Rene was all kindness, and said not a cross word, the dear. . . . But you two waited out the storm in a cave, I hear. How very romantic! What a charming companion to have in such a situation, Ysabeau. I'm sure the time passed quite . . . pleasurably." She grinned and added, "Already the court is buzzing with speculation."

Ysabeau sneezed several times in rapid, explosive succession, then glared at the older girl. "If I had been doing what you imagine, I doubt I would be suffering as I am now!" she said indignantly.

But Matilde only laughed. "As you say, little marsh bird. And be assured that it is not Rene or I spreading the tale."

"That Norman popinjay—" began Ysabeau angrily, but Matilde shook her head firmly. "Men like that do not brag of what they have done or would like to have done with a woman. No, I think you can lay this at Lord Joscelin's door. He was in the hall when just Rene and I returned, and knew that four of us had left together this morning."

Ysabeau could well imagine the Duchess' half brother gleefully embroidering the scandalous story, so that her honor was more shredded each time he told it. "Damn that *bâtard*!" she said, weakly sinking back on the plump goosedown pillows, pounding a fist on the mattress in frustration.

Ysabeau spent the next two endless days in bed. Her boredom was lessened only by visits from Matilde, who kept her informed of court gossip.

"There is no sign of the Duke and Duchess. Philippe has composed a new *sirventes* and can't wait to perform it for you . . . Lord Joscelin tried to needle Lord Simon about the afternoon he spent with you and found himself backed into the wall at sword point! The poor man's eyes bulged so in fear, I thought they would fall from their sockets."

"Ah . . ." Ysabeau kept her voice casual. "And how does our Norman emissary?"

"Very bored and restless, I think—drawing his sword on the Duchess' brother while he is a guest at court proves that. Fortunately there were enough witnesses that Joscelin was casting aspersions on your honor to justify his actions."

"How very gallant of him—*achoo*!"

"But don't you see? Fighting for a lady's honor is one of the marks of a true lover's worthiness," Matilde gushed with an ecstatic sigh. "Surely, now you could show him some little sign of favor . . . a smile in public, perhaps, nothing big, mind you, just a small reward."

"I'm surprised he hasn't found some lady with whom to while away the time," said Ysabeau, still feigning disinterest. "Or do Normans have ice water running in their veins, rather than blood?"

"As to the race in general, I could not say, Rene being a hot-blooded Poitevin. But that one—ah, *non*, there is nothing icy about him. The ladies swarm around him whenever he comes to the hall," Matilde said, watching the invalid under her lashes, and was rewarded by the reaction Ysabeau strove to hide.

"You make him sound like nothing but a big, stupid flower, and all the women bees," Ysabeau snapped pettishly.

"Hurry up and get well, Ysabeau, that you do not miss the honey. . . ."

"Bah! I hope he's not holding his breath waiting!"

* * *

Simon's attempts to visit Ysabeau on the first day of her illness had been firmly thwarted by Marie, who made it clear she held him responsible for her mistress' misery. The tiring-woman had set up her post in the corridor outside Ysabeau's room, and at each sally the Norman baron made up the tower stairs, he was repulsed by the formidable little figure.

Simon had missed the approving twinkle in the woman's eye as he had been turned away. Marie was playing a deeper game than the Norman realized, for the more she refused him entrance, the more he wanted to storm the door.

His obsession made him feel faintly ridiculous, but he could not alter it and he continued to watch for a chance to visit Ysabeau.

At noon on the second day it came.

He had already drilled his men that morning in sword practice, inspected their mail, and checked on Noir in his stall. The big horse had stamped a ponderous hoof as if to echo his master's mood. He had gone into Poitiers and purchased a gaudily painted toy rattle and a ball made of leather over a pig's bladder, which he packed away in his coffer for his son, Aimery. Now he was pacing the parapet restlessly, alternatively watching and bustling activity in the bailey and looking out over the tile and timber rooftops of Poitiers.

Aha, there was Ysabeau's tiring-woman below, carrying a covered basket and exchanging pleasantries with the sentry as he opened the portcullis for her. Simon watched as the rotund woman strode purposefully into the city on some errand.

In a few moments he had climbed down from his lofty viewpoint on the palace wall and was ascending the stairs of the tower, a delighted grin across his handsome features.

Ysabeau awoke in the big bed that she had occupied alone since she became ill, feeling another presence in the room. Was Marie perhaps back already from her errand into town? She had agreed to go in an effort to placate her mistress, who had insisted on getting up and walking to her room and sewing near the window.

"I'm feeling much better, Marie, honestly. And I cannot stand being confined to that bed anymore, or having the shutters closed so tightly—I feel I will suffocate. It's a mild day, it won't hurt to have them open so I can see to sew a bit. And I'm so tired of this broth you keep bringing me. I want some real food."

Marie had never seen Lady Ysabeau so resistant to common sense. She was rushing her convalescence, and would undo all the progress she had made, but she would not listen, stubbornly sitting near the drafty window at her stitchery for several hours. As a result, she had begun to look very pale and wan, and finally agreed to get back in bed if Marie would go to the place where she heard oranges were for sale, brought from far-off lands. Oranges in winter! Ah . . . she could taste the succulent sweetness now.

Her eyes fluttered open to see Simon de Winslade seated there on the stool by her, and she was instantly fully alert.

"You! How did you get in here?" she said, pulling the blanket up to her chin, aware that her nose and eyes were red and her hair was spread in wild abandon over the pillow. She hated to have him see her like this. Her first feeling on seeing him, however, had been a mad joy, and Ami, who had been lying watchfully in the corner arose and advanced to greet him, his tail whipping around happily.

"Hello, sleepyhead. It's about time you awakened. I have been sitting here for several moments just watching you sleep."

How dare he look so magnificent while she felt so drab and ugly?

She could not know how responsible he actually *did* feel that she had caught cold in the rain. He had sought an excuse to get her off by herself, away from the court, and she had paid for it. He was relieved now to see that she was awake and that her cheeks were flushed with color. Her eyes still held that velvety sparkle in their brown depths.

"You have not so much as a sniffle," she said resentfully, her words emerging as *you hab dot zo much as a snivvel.*

He smiled smugly. "I dried my clothes, *ma damoiselle*. I offered you the same opportunity. I truly regret to see you unwell, but . . ."

"You told me so."

"Exactly. However, I did not watch so anxiously for your dragon-guard to leave" —here he noted a smile break across those beautiful lips—"to tell you that. I came to assure myself I was not going to lose you. I would truly not have been able to go on, were that so." His manner was overdramatic, so that she could not see how sincere he really was. "I rejoice to see that although your illness is annoying, you will live yet to smile upon me." He blew a kiss to the air, in such skillful parody of the slavish lover that she was hard put to smother a giggle.

"Perhaps," she managed to say distantly.

Ah, very good, my lady, the all-knowing blue eyes said. You play *la belle dame sans merci* to perfection. Only we both know how your lips responded to mine. The words bored into her brain as if he had spoken them, but he only said, "My joy is in hope. Now, if I may be of service? Perhaps I could fetch you some cool wine, some delicious morsel . . ."

"Perhaps some fresh water from that jar over there would be best." She pointed to the bedside stand, and he obeyed her request.

The action of accepting the cup forced her to stretch one bare arm from beneath the concealing covers. His eyes feasted hungrily on its slender gracefulness.

Damn the man, she thought as she drank. I'm roasting with fever, yet I'm forced to stay covered up to my neck, and still his eyes devour me. But I can't . . . it's too hot, she decided. The room began to grow hazy as the fever rose within her again. Fretfully she pushed away the covers, careless that it bared her body, clad only in a thin linen bedgown, to his gaze. "So hot . . ." she murmured.

His face was suddenly creased in concern. Perhaps the fever would be mortal after all. He touched his hand to her cheek. "Ysabeau!

Surely you should not be uncovered! Where are more blankets?'' He was alarmed at the sudden dullness of her eyes.

''*Non, j'ai chaud*,'' she insisted, but he re-covered her, nonetheless, grimly watching as the excess internal heat turned to a bone-shaking chill just he located some extra blankets in a brass-bound chest near the shuttered window. He stirred up the smoldering coals in the brazier and placed it closer, then went to the door to bellow for a servant.

''I want a physician sent for immediately! The Duke and Duchess' own physician! What do you mean, he went on the progress? Send into town then. And summon my lady's tiring-woman back to the bedside. She should not be off on frivolous business while her lady lies ill!'' Raw worry vibrated in his voice, yet Ysabeau did not hear. The room seemed to recede as she fought to retain the very warmth she had been struggling against only moments before.

Chapter Nine

It was three more days before Ysabeau was pronounced sufficiently recovered to get out of bed, and another before she was allowed to dress and come down to the hall. The physician, a monk skilled in healing arts, summoned from the abbey, had pronounced her fit as long as she took up her duties gradually and ate nourishing foods.

Cheers rang out as she made her way into the hall at the midday meal, with Matilde hovering solicitously at her side. Her cheeks had lost much of their fresh color, but her step was graceful and sure as always, and her bearing confident as she smiled in pleasure at the courtiers' greetings.

"My lords, my ladies," she said, inclining her head, covered with a sheer linen veil. She did not fail to notice that a place was being held for her next to the man who had paced outside her room like a caged tiger and scolded Marie unmercifully when she had returned with the promised oranges.

Simon de Winslade was pleased to see she did not pick at her food as she had reportedly done for the last two days. The truth was that Ysabeau had been plied with broth, bland, unspiced food and well-watered wine until she was sure she would starve out of sheer boredom. However, she had been energized by the mere act of putting on something besides her bedgown and having her hair arranged rather than merely brushed free of its tangles. Leaving the stale air of her chamber had been the final enticement to her awakening hunger, and she attacked her food with gusto.

At one point he teased her: "Look at poor Ami. He is afraid you will leave him nothing." Indeed the big dog, lying behind her bench, watched each move her hand made from the trencher to her mouth with such seriousness that she had to chuckle.

"Has no one had a tidbit to spare him while I was ill? I suppose the pale women of the north pick at their food like this," she said, mimicking a lady of dainty appetite. She was slightly embarrassed to realize she had been eating like a starving peasant let into a feast by mistake. "I see you are a hearty trencherman yourself, my lord—not exactly the pale lover, too sick with emotion to eat."

"Ah, *non*, my lady, I merely want to keep up with any activity you undertake," he whispered brazenly.

She hoped he could not see the accelerated pulsebeat in her throat, hoped the warmth within would not spread to her face as a telltale blush. One was always struggling to retain the upper hand with this man. . . .

"I am not about to undertake any activity this afternoon, my lord," she said dismissively. "I am just recovering from a fever, you know. I planned to lie down and rest."

Simon de Winslade cocked a skeptical brow at her and said, "A very good idea. I would be delighted to accompany you and read to you from some improving work—perhaps Ovid's *De Amore*. I imagine it is in Eleanor's collection."

At the thought of that gravelly, masculine voice reading Ovid's frank treatise on love, she blushed, but nonetheless riposted, "A Norman noble who can read—how refreshing!"

"As is a woman who understands Latin."

"But of course. This is Aquitaine, the home of sophistication and culture."

"And I speak to one of the most sophisticated and cultured, I know," he said in a sincere voice, but his blue eyes mocked her, made her feel she was, indeed, no match for his will and wit. "I would be devastated to be deprived of your company this afternoon, when we both know that at any moment my mission will be completed, and I will have to return to England," he coaxed.

Matilde, seated across from Ysabeau, had heard Simon's last entreaty, though he had kept all his other remarks low. "There is to be a court of love after the meal, my lord. Ysabeau, surely he should not leave Aquitaine without being exposed to *le gai savoir.*" She winked broadly.

Ysabeau was gratified to find an excuse to stay in his company, yet make it appear she was merely condescending to help in his refinement. In truth, she longed to spend every possible moment with him, and dreaded his return to England.

She nodded her head graciously. "All right," she agreed. "I suppose I would not find that too taxing."

Philippe sat in a cleared corner of the room, strumming a psaltery while the lords and ladies found their places on benches, chairs and cushions in the herb-sprinkled rushes.

"Who calls me greedy does not lie;
I hunger after love remote
No joy within my grasp can vie
With that of winning love remote . . ."

After finishing, Philippe laid down the instrument and announced, "In the absence of Her Grace, the Duchess of Aquitaine, I am authorized to conduct this court of love. Has any of this assembly aught to bring to my attention?"

There was much whispered conversation and meaningful looks, but none volunteered. Philippe was not at a loss, however.

"It is frequently useful to speak of the question of love in the abstract before we address specific cases," he said easily. "*Eh bien,* let us consider the question, *mes dames*, 'Is it better to love a handsome man who is not forever faithful, or an ugly man who loves devotedly?' "

There was much discussion as to the importance of looks, a flippant remark or two about putting out the candle so that ugliness was of no importance, but most of the luxuriously gowned ladies were of the opinion that faithfulness was of more value than handsome features.

"I cannot, of course, speak for the ladies," interrupted one jovial fellow, "but I myself would prefer a homely lass who loved me madly and forgave my frequent indiscretions with the beautiful ladies whose affections were less constant."

General laughter greeted this sally.

"My lord, I have a case to bring before the court of love," said a lady toward the front of the group. She ignored the whispered protests of a sulky-faced lord who had risen as she did, in an obvious attempt to dissuade her from speaking.

There was an anticipatory murmuring from several in the crowd.

"Listen well, my lord," Ysabeau whispered, slanting her eyes at Simon.

"But, of course. I'm sure it will prove instructive," came his urbane answer.

"To the court of love I bring complaint against the Sieur de la Jarne," the woman said in an aggrieved tone, pointing to the lord beside her. "He pledged himself to love me faithfully, but I found him in carnal dalliance with a lady who shall remain nameless, though she knows who she is."

Ysabeau stole a look at Simon to gauge his reaction.

"That's the Comtesse de Rochefort, is it not?" he whispered to her. "The *Comte* himself is at court. How dares she mention her adultery so openly?"

"Wait and see, my lord," Ysabeau answered cryptically.

"Mon seigneur de la Jarne, have you any defense against this accusation? Had you, in truth, pledged yourself to her?"

"Yes, but my lady had not granted me any sign of her favor, though I had served her patiently for weeks, months. I had become a wan shadow, but does she show any pity? *Mais non*! A man has needs, you know," the noble finished emphatically, his lower lip jutting out.

"The true lover subjugates that baser part of himself to worship at the shrine of his love," Philippe said loftily. "*Ma dame, la Comtesse*, did you give your lover any sign that you encouraged his suit?"

"Indeed. He wore my ribbon on his lance at the tournament this last Easter," she said triumphantly.

Her words seemed to settle the matter, judging from the disapproving looks directed at the Lord de la Jarne. Simon glanced at Ysabeau, whose lovely eyes were sparkling with amusement.

"You think the old *comte* should haul his flirtatious wife off to his faraway keep and lock her in the highest tower room, never to see the light of a day again?" Ysabeau challenged in a whisper.

"But it's not fair—don't you see? The Countess has someone else—her husband. The *Sieur de la Jarne* is a bachelor, is he not?"

"Oh no, my lord." Her laughter tinkled melodiously. "He has a wife."

He shook his tawny head as if to clear it. "And all this adultery is openly discussed?"

"Adultery? There is no adultery being discussed, Lord Simon, unless it is that in which the lord was caught with the other woman. We are speaking of courtly love. And if aught else is done, then it must be discreet, according to *le gai savoir.*"

"You're a fool if you believe one can play at love, taste it in small sips. . . ."

"It is merely a higher form of love than you have experienced," she replied. She was surprised by the vehemence of his reaction. She thought he might be mildly amused, even skeptical, but he seemed genuinely irritated that she subscribed to this philosophy of love.

"This is merely playacting at the real thing, for those afraid of the risk," he retorted. "However, if that's the way you wish to play it, *ma chère* . . ."

Geoffrey, his squire, interrupted with a beckoning gesture from the outskirts of the throng. Simon stepped over to speak to him, leaving a curious Ysabeau who would have given much to know what he meant by his last remark. She caught the words, "At last," and then the Norman's face became thoughtful; he rubbed his chin, continuing to speak low to his squire, as if giving instructions.

In his absence, sentence had been passed, and the Sieur de la Jarne had been judged guilty of a serious crime against love, that of disloyalty. He was sentenced to carry the Countess' handkerchief on a silken pillow seven paces behind her for a full month, if he wished to be considered worthy of her at some future time.

The baron seemed content at his penance, and raised his fingers to his lips toward his lady. When Ysabeau told Simon of the outcome, however, his well-chiseled lips curled in derision, but he said nothing.

Ysabeau settled back to hear what else would come before the court, as eager to see Simon's reaction as anything else. To her surprise, though, he rose to his feet, drawing the attention of Philippe with a gesture.

"My Lord Judge, I am a newcomer to court, but I have the right to bring a case to the court of love, do I not?" Simon asked, to Ysabeau's astonishment.

"Of course, my lord. Humble supplicants at this court are always kindly received," Philippe answered gravely, but with a twinkle in his hazel eyes. No one could have been less humble in appearance than this powerfully built Norman lord in his dark gray velvet knee-length tunic and scarlet chausses, showing his sinewy calves. He paced before the court, an earnest expression settling over his compelling face.

"As I have said, I am a newcomer to the court, and one whose time is limited, uncertain. Nevertheless, I have come to deeply appreciate the tenets of courtly love, as I have heard them expressed by the loveliest maiden in Aquitaine."

Ysabeau nearly gasped aloud. How dare he lie so outrageously about his feelings toward courtly love, and pay her an enormous compliment all in one breath! The lie must necessarily cast suspicion on the sincerity of his praise. Flatterer! Deceiver! He had not named her, but already covert looks were being sent her way.

"I understand that the would-be lover must be willing to serve without counting the days before he is entitled to receive the smallest smile from the lady he adores," he said. "But I plead—nay, I beseech the court of love to consider mine a special case, since I may have to leave very soon. My soul thirsts for some sign, some faint indication that the object of my worship returns my affection in some small way, before I leave. I have done much to make myself deserving. During the time I have been here, I have had eyes only for this lovely lady, despite the charms of the many beauteous flowers of womanhood around me. And I have fought to preserve my lady's honor against the vile accusations of another—surely a worthy act for a lover."

"Oh, indeed, my lord Simon, indeed," agreed Philippe, as around them, each lady's eyes grew misty with wishing he'd defended her. Ysabeau fumed, her hands clenched in her lap. Dare she inform the court just how Simon really felt about this ritual of courtly love? The ladies might cease sighing so enviously if they had heard his remarks to her only moments ago.

But Simon had gambled successfully that she would not expose him, guessing she'd be afraid of being called ungrateful after the well-known incident in which he had drawn steel on Lord Joscelin.

"Does this lady favor you, my lord?" Philippe inquired, clearly enjoying this role which allowed him to pass judgment, despite his lack of noble status.

"I believe she does, though her maidenly fears cause her to doubt the strength of my adoration," Simon answered. All the while, his blue eyes dueled with Ysabeau's shocked brown ones over the heads of the gathering.

Damn him, Ysabeau cursed to herself. Adoration! All he wanted was for her to acquiesce to him!

"Well then," Philippe's voice broke into her furious thoughts. "I believe we are all in agreement that you deserve at least some slight reward for your devotion, my lord. I decree that you are entitled to two kisses from your lady fair, before the end of your stay. And—" he broke off as Lord Joscelin arose and whispered something into his ear which caused the troubadour to smile. "And at the suggestion of the Duchess' brother, I further decree that one of these should be given in front of this court, now, and the other should be in private, at the discretion of Baron de Winslade."

Ysabeau jumped up, indignant, not sure at whom she was the more angry—Simon, who was now grinning widely, or the smirking Joscelin, who had suggested the two-part penance which contained both public and private humiliation.

Before the right words could find their way to her trembling lips, Simon reached her side. "With all my heart, I thank the court," he said, pulling Ysabeau into his powerful arms, "and will carry out the first part of your judgment without further delay."

Swiftly he bent his head, and with one hand cupped her jaw, so that there was no escape. Before she could protest, his mouth met hers, inexorable; demanding; he pulled her tightly against him as if they were the only two people in the great hall. Cheers and catcalls rang out, but he ignored them as his lips punished hers sweetly, his tongue commanding her response, mandating the racing of her pulse, the weakness of her knees, the reaching of her arms around his neck to make the kiss go on forever. She was lost. The room spun around them, and she truly forgot the others present, for they had fallen silent, witnessing the passion raging between the two of them.

When at last he raised his tawny head, his eyes were shining. Softly, he said, "That is but one of two, *ma damoiselle*. I look forward to the second."

The remark brought her back to earth from the stars, made her conscious of all who had watched her clinging wantonly to him, for all the world like a complaisant serving wench. She felt naked before them, as if all could see her erect nipples and feel the tingling burning at the lower center of her. Her face flaming scarlet, she raised her hand and slapped him; the sound rang in her ears as she fled from the hall, tears streaming from her eyes.

Chapter Ten

The news came when Matilde began moving her possessions back into their room late that afternoon. The Duke and Duchess lay overnight at Sanxay, and would be home by midday.

So that was what Geoffrey had whispered to Simon, Ysabeau thought. The return of the woman she had come to serve seemed almost unreal to her, since four months had intervened since their brief meeting. The days had been drifting along without any great urgency or purpose. That was about to change, Matilde warned her as she put her gowns back in the clothes press.

"The Duchess is up with the birds and can dance until dawn," Matilde informed her, taking in her friend's swollen eyes and tear-stained face. "And Duke Henry is worse. Your time of leisure to learn court ways is over, *ma chère*. Though I know she'll be pleased to see how you've come along," she added, trying to cheer Ysabeau up, but failing to elicit a smile. "Back in the summer, you'd never have dared slap a baron's face, though why you did so is still a mystery to me. All he did was kiss you thoroughly, and magnificently. I vow, it made me go hot all over just to watch," she chuckled, ignoring Ysabeau's glare.

"He did it to humiliate me," Ysabeau exploded, punching the bolster with her fist.

"*He* didn't pass the sentence, the court did," pointed out Matilde logically. "He just carried it out, and rather well, too!"

"Matilde, how am I supposed to maintain control over this relationship if the court hands it over to that man?" Ysabeau gesticulated wildly, pacing about the room. "How can I remain the cool lady on the pedestal, if they've practically given him permission to seduce me?"

"Hardly that," her friend said calmly. "It was just a kiss, after all. But," she added on a rising note, "you do owe him another one, remember, and he doesn't seem the type to let such a delicious debt go unpaid."

And the next kiss was to be in private, Ysabeau recalled. "Just a kiss," Matilde had dismissed it, not knowing how the touch of his lips made her world revolve crazily, made her weak and dizzy, made her resolve to remain in control seem impossible, and not even desirable. When he kissed her, she only wanted the embrace to go on, to deepen, to become whatever he wanted it to be. She feared the whirling vortex of passion that swirled within her whenever he touched her. No, a kiss with Simon de Winslade could not be dismissed so lightly.

She had tried to calm herself with the reassuring thought that the ordeal could be postponed if she was clever and elusive; but now, with the advent of Eleanor and Henry, Simon's departure seemed imminent. She guessed that he would need very little time to impart his message to Henry, and might be ready to begin his journey back home as early as the day after tomorrow.

She tried to ignore the voice in her head that grieved at the thought of his leaving—of being bereft of his piercing azure gaze, the feel of his strong arms around her, the masterful touch of his lips. That voice within ignored the clamoring fears of becoming his wanton creature, and pleaded with her to be daring enough to explore the world of his passion and his love.

"Well, he'll not collect his debt tonight," she said decidedly, "for he'll not find me waiting around like the fly emmeshed in the spider's web."

"Ah, don't be so serious, *ma petite*," Matilde advised as she presented her back to Ysabeau for assistance in lacing up the *bliaut* she'd changed into. "*L'amour courtois* was meant to be fun. But if it's any consolation to you, if you evade him tonight, both of you will probably be kept much too busy by their graces to worry about it."

After Matilde left, Ysabeau spent the evening thoroughly bored in her room, feeling like a fugitive, almost ready to admit that it would have been better to have gone to the great hall and chance meeting Simon, rather than sneaking down the tower stair like a thief to exercise Ami in the outer courtyard and beg dinner at the kitchens, like a pauper. Once back in her room, she listened for Simon's footsteps in the corridor, until, at last, she fell into an uneasy sleep.

Those at court who wished to lie abed had forgotten the amazing energy of their new Duke. Just as the palace was breaking its fast following Mass, an outrider clattered into the courtyard with the news that Henry and Eleanor and their retinue were on the outskirts of Poitiers.

The whole palace turned out to watch the newyweds' triumphal return. Lining the parapets, the men cheered lustily while ladies fluttered bright scarves and delicate handkerchiefs from all the windows. Dried flower petals were brought out and rained upon the mounted couple—a miraculous floral snowstorm on this, the first day of December.

Henry and Eleanor, both clad in crimson velvet with capes of squirrel, were mounted on matching bay palfreys caparisoned with gold cloth trappings. They waved at their welcomers all around the inner bailey, dismounting with equal grace, bowing and curtseying, holding each other's hand. Then both entered the palace, and went to their own state apartments to reorganize their lives as Duke and Duchess of Aquitaine.

Eleanor's ladies-in-waiting who had not gone on progress were in her bower to meet her when she and her retinue arrived.

She swept grandly into the room, trailed by Petronilla, Blanche de Limousin, and Mabelle de Bordeaux. The ladies-in-waiting curtseyed as one, their dark skirts billowing around them.

"Arise, all of you. My, you are a treat to my eyes, ladies, as is this palace. I have certainly had my fill of bouncing along on horseback, and of tents, and of the hospitality of others. Would that I could stay here forever!" She then greeted each of the ladies individually, embracing and speaking a few words to each one.

She came last to Ysabeau, studying the emerald green silk *bliaut* that, of all her new gowns, Ysabeau felt most became her. She desired the Duchess' approval fervently and had instinctively chosen well, for Eleanor touched her cheek warmly, saying, "Ah, our little bird of the marshes has traded in her drab feathers for brighter plumage. *Comme tu es belle*! I trust you are now comfortable at court, *ma chère*?"

"Yes, your grace. I am glad you have come home."

"Thank you, my dear. And is she doing well under your tutelage, Matilde?"

"I believe she is fully prepared to serve you, your grace. I have trained her in the routine as well as possible without your presence."

"I have no doubt of that, Matilde," Eleanor said. "Yet I meant more than that. I left a scared little country girl here, and what I see now is a lovely young woman," she continued, keeping her eyes on Ysabeau's flushed face. "Has she come to feel at home in the *Palais de Poitiers*, eh? Does she feel at home in the courts of love?''

Ysabeau inwardly squirmed; she was being discussed as if she weren't there, but she felt no resentment, for she knew Eleanor's interest was kindly meant.

''Ah, your grace, you will be well pleased to know that *La Maraise* is already breaking hearts. She has the Norman Baron de Winslade twisted about her little finger,'' crowed Matilde, shooting the suddenly livid Blanche a triumphant look.

''Simon is here? Ah, wonderful! That rascal is quite a man, *ma petite* Ysabeau, and the woman who can keep him dangling quite skilled in Venus' arts! I'll be interested to hear more of this later. Meanwhile, ladies,'' she said, beckoning, ''we have much to do. Henry and I have enjoyed our travels, but they have taken their toll, so there will be clothes to mend, correspondence to attend to, unpacking. . . .''

Simon had been fortunate enough to catch Henry's eye as he strode to the ducal chamber, and since the duke knew his presence signaled important news, Simon found himself closeted with him within the hour.

''Come in, Simon, old friend. I am delighted to see you!'' Henry said from his seat in the window recess, where he was reading dispatches by the fitful late afternoon light that filtered in the panes. Already the stocky young Angevin had changed into the casual, rough clothing he loved, the tunic and trousers of coarse russet which had caused Ysabeau to mistake him for master of the horse.

In a corner of the room his falconer was coaxing the Duke's favorite falcon onto his perch with a bit of meat. The peregrine was sidling temperamentally onto the perch with much hissing and tinkling of the small gold bells, engraved with the Plantagenet broom emblem, that dangled by scarlet cords from its legs.

"A handsome bird, your grace," murmured Simon, going over to admire the large bird with its gray-barred feathers.

"Indeed so, old friend. She brought down a heron only this morning, which you shall see at supper. But I have a gryfalcon eyas being gentled in my mews even now, Simon, which I can't wait to loose in the air." Henry swiveled around in the window seat, setting his booted feet on the floor and leaning forward intently. "Does your visit concern my right to fly a gryfalcon?" His eyes, a paler blue than Simon's, bore intently into those of his vassal.

He was not speaking of falconry, both men knew. But the art of falconry was so entangled with the conventions of chivalry that one's rank carried with it the privilege of using certain types of hawks—and only a king was entitled to a gryfalcon.

"Yes, it does, your grace," Simon answered the duke solemnly. "England needs you. It needed you months ago when Reginald of Cornwall was sent to you, and groans even more for you now. We cannot take much more of Stephen. You are in full control of the duchy now, my lord, which can provide the cause with much-needed funds. These will be supplemented by lords at home who supported the Empress

Matilda, your mother—Chester, Hereford, Norfolk, Lincoln, and more every day."

"Succinctly put, my Lord de Winslade, though I know you could say more. I was on the point of coming this summer, you know, just a fortnight after I married Eleanor, when Louis' antics on the Normandy frontier forced me to go and teach him a lesson. I stopped back in Poitiers, intending to stay only long enough to try for an heir once or twice," he said, a twinkle in his eyes as he clasped his hands around his knees, "when it became apparent to me that not only did my lovely duchess deserve a more thorough honeymoon, but that I would benefit from knowing my Poitevins and Gascons better. I thought it was wise to know what kind of subjects I had at my back before I went charging off across the Channel."

"And what was your impression, your grace?"

"Fiery and opinionated, like my lady," responded Henry. "They seemed to think they only owed me the respect due the spouse of their Duchess, but we soon taught them otherwise, particularly the Abbey of St. Martial in Limoges. Don't look so disapproving, Simon—let me tell you what happened." He recounted the tale of how the abbey had failed to send the customary provisions to their tent, because it was pitched outside the city gates; the abbot contended that his feudal obligation existed only if Henry and his retinue lodged within the walls.

"I don't mind being just the spouse of the duchess most of the time," finished the Duke blandly, running his dagger under his fingernails, "but that was a bit too much quibbling to suit me. I razed their walls and their newly built bridge, so there need be no question of where their hospitality to their duke should begin and end."

Simon did not bother to tell him that he had already heard rumors about Henry's initial reaction to the disrespect of Limoges: a typical Angevin temper tantrum, witnessed by the whole retinue, with shrieking, writhing on the floor, and fists lashing out at anyone within range. Such a display of bile must have been rather frightening to Eleanor, Simon mused, but he merely said, "I'm sure they'll not fail you again, your grace."

Henry gestured dismissively. "So much for Limoges. What of yourself? You say you have been here nearly a month? We're sorry to have kept you so long from your fief. However did you occupy yourself, all this time?"

He beckoned to a servant, who served them cups of a rather indifferent wine. "We brought this from one of the vineyards that Eleanor boasted of near Bordeaux." He made a wry face. "I've tasted better."

Simon offered no opinion of the wine. "I have kept myself and my men fit, my liege, and . . . this and that." He was not one to boast of his conquests, particularly when there was nothing of which to boast, thanks to Ysabeau's elusiveness.

"Ah ha! The women of Aquitaine are justly famed, *hein*?" Henry was adept at reading between the lines.

Simon grinned. "I admit they are lovely," he answered noncommittally.

"No success, hey? You have to learn to play this courtly love nonsense, my tall Norman friend. It gets you in bed eventually, *mon ami*, but certainly by a longer route.

"By the way, Simon, I was awfully sorry to hear of your young wife's death," Henry said, suddenly changing the mood of their talk. Simon was astonished he even knew. "Truly a tragedy for you."

"Your grace is most kind."

"Yes—now back to the reason for your visit. I'm for Rouen tomorrow, to visit *ma mère* and ask her for further funds and advice."

Any other man would have rested at home for awhile after such a lengthy trip, but not the young Plantagenet. Simon knew him too well to be surprised.

"From there, I am for Barfleur, to embark as soon as possible for Bristol, something I should have done at least half a year ago. Will you come to Rouen with me? I know my mother'd love to set eyes on you, you rascal. She always did have a good eye for men—married Geoffrey le Beau and had me, isn't that proof?" he asked with a chuckle.

There it was, the promise of an invasion by the Plantagenet. The purpose of his journey was accomplished at last. Yet England would not be safe simply because Henry succeeded in landing, Simon knew, as well as the duke. There would still be King Stephen to contend with, an ineffectual monarch, but one nevertheless determined to pass his throne on to his son,

Eustace, as vain and contentious a creature as Christendom had ever known. There would be fighting and more wanton destruction before England could know peace again.

But, Simon thought, there would be time enough for warfare and battles, sieges and the clash of swords. Tonight was his last chance to collect a debt—the tenderest of debts—and he did not mean to ride out on the morrow until Ysabeau had, at the very least, paid at least what she owed him. And perhaps he could collect more, if he were skillful and lucky.

He would have to be singleminded once he left this seductive, soft life of the *langue d'oc*, and put off its lazy, pleasure-loving ways, or he would never survive the coming period of struggle. If he could just bed the wench, perhaps he could forget her. But right now he felt her captive, and all the more so because she maintained that haughty, controlled pose that was prized in the south of France as it was nowhere else. Though troubadours carried the songs and legends of Tristan and Iseult and King Arthur's court into the castle halls of Normandy and England, women there were basically of two sorts: the serfs, with whom a lord could do much as he wished, and the ladies, under the control of their fathers or guardians until control was handed to a husband. Rohese, of course, had been one of the latter and he had accepted her soft submissiveness as what was to be expected.

It hadn't occurred to him that he loved Ysabeau, as much for the fiery spirit she'd demonstrated by denying him, as for her beauty. And what use had he for love, even had he admitted it? He would have time after the war was over to find an heiress to mother his son, and whether she was lovable or not would hardly enter into it. He had had a lady with both looks and lands before, and he had loved her, and she had left him by dying. Since he had no use for love, he identified the pang he felt at the thought of leaving Ysabeau behind as just the normal ache a man would experience after a long period of abstinence.

Well, he had only himself to blame for not taking any of the many other women around to assuage that ache, he told himself. But now that he had succumbed to the charms of Ysabeau de Ré, neither scullery wenches nor free and easy court ladies seemed worthy quarry.

She had escaped him last night, he thought, remembering sourly how he had watched for her with delighted anticipation, only to see that no female face in the hall was hers. But she would not escape him tonight, for the dinner would be a state occasion, and all the court would be present to welcome Henry and Eleanor home.

Chapter Eleven

She had assisted the Duchess into a gown of gold samite figured in silver thread, a costly fabric from Champagne, and had been pleased to receive the Duchess' compliments at the deftness of her fingers as she laced up the back. She knew clumsiness was considered a deadly sin by Eleanor, and had feared her awe of her mistress might render her all thumbs. She was about to place Eleanor's coronet on top of her just-arranged golden tresses and sheer sendal veil, when the circlet was abruptly snatched from her by Blanche, who had coiffed her mistress and was jealous of what she considered were her prerogatives.

It was clear that Blanche's animosity had only flourished while she was gone, and Matilde's announcement of Winslade's supposed attachment to Ysabeau had fanned the flames.

Eleanor stared in the mirror held up for her and smiled. Blanche was then excused to go and change. Ysabeau hoped her sigh of relief was not audible as she winked at Matilde.

"Ysabeau, you're already dressed for dinner, aren't you? Assist me, then, with my train when we go down to the great hall," Eleanor commanded. That snuffed out Ysabeau's hope of slipping unobtrusively into the hall at the last moment so as to avoid Simon. She would be among the last to enter, and Simon, already at his place, would certainly spot her behind her mistress.

She had been fortunate in evading him all day, she thought later in the narrow passageway as they waited for Henry to join Eleanor and make a grand entrance. The air buzzed with conversation from the hall as the lords and ladies found their places and greeted their trenchermates. The smoky, hot smell of burning oil from a nearby cresset filled Ysabeau's nostrils as she watched the stocky figure of the duke stride toward them and take his wife's hand in his.

"Ah, there you are, my love," the duchess greeted her younger spouse in her husky, caressing tones. The magnetism between the two of them was almost palpable. "A busy afternoon catching up with state matters?"

"Of course. De Winslade's brought messages from England—I'll tell you all about it over supper."

Surprisingly, the ginger-haired young duke noted Ysabeau then as she stood behind Eleanor, holding her train.

"Why, hello, it's *Lady* Ysabeau de Ré," he said teasingly, the penetrating blue eyes lighting up, the smile clearly indicating he remembered their first violent meeting well. "I see court life agrees with you. You look charming," he continued, eyes boldly assessing the changes in her raiment and bearing.

". . . *Grande merci*, your grace," she said, blushing furiously, a little overwhelmed by the bold compliment in the presence of his wife. She darted a quick glance at Eleanor, but the Duchess evidently saw nothing objectionable in the courtly compliment, and they went on to speak of other things as they waited for the seneschal to announce their entrance.

Just then she heard a voice in her ear say in soft, low tones: "I will see you after the banquet, *ma chère*. There is a little matter of an unsettled debt."

"I'm sorry, my lord," she answered as the blood surged in her head and her heart took up a runaway rhythm. He was standing right behind her, so close in the press of attendants that they were almost touching. "But that will be quite impossible, as I am attending my lady tonight,"

"You won't be needed all night, by the saints," he snapped, his lips so close to her ear that she could feel his breath.

"Ah, Simon, you charming rascal," greeted Eleanor as she looked over her shoulder and saw him talking to her lady-in-waiting. "I've been waiting to greet you. You're to sit on the dais between Petronilla and myself. I hear you've news of England, and I vow, I cannot wait to hear it."

Ysabeau was surprised to feel a pang of regret that he would not be with her at her trencher. Did he feel it too? His glance raked over her briefly, opaquely, then he answered with a deep bow, "I would be honored, of course, your grace."

He was gone before she had a chance to reiterate her excuse. It was customary for at least one of her ladies to sleep in Eleanor's bed-chamber, to be available for anything the Duchess might need. Even if the duke joined her, the lady would only go as far away as the anteroom, to remain within the sound of a call.

Once seated at a place near the high table on the dais, Ysabeau was able to view the baron at close range. With Eleanor at his left and Duke Henry just beyond her, and Petronilla at his right chattering animatedly to him, his attention was claimed and she could study him undetected.

He was dressed in a black velvet dalmatic tonight, startling in its stark simplicity and richness of material, and devastating against the tawny gold of his mustache.

The banquet was interminable, the rich food carried out on platters in endless courses, the wines free-flowing, but it could have been peasant's pottage for all Ysabeau noticed its taste. Matilde, for once without Rene at her side, shared her trencher and tried to interest her in court gossip. Had Ysabeau heard the rumors that Eleanor's monthly courses were late, and that the Duchess believed herself *enceinte*?

Ysabeau was momentarily diverted. The Duchess pregnant? That would be a wonderful thing, to present the virile young Duke with an heir within the first year of their marriage. King Louis would probably gnash his teeth, up in the Île de France, since in all his years of marriage to Eleanor, he had only managed to sire two daughters on her. That Henry of Anjou might give Eleanor only daughters did not seem possible.

"He is quite a man," agreed Matilde, studying the duke on the dais, "but your baron quite outshines him."

"He's not my baron," growled Ysabeau, stubbornly looking down at her food rather than up at the high table, her lower lip jutting out pugnaciously.

"So you say," soothed Matilde, "but it would be interesting to know what just passed between the Norman and Eleanor. They were both gazing at you, and Eleanor looked as if she had just learned something very interesting. Petronilla, on the other hand, is pouting about something."

Ysabeau could not prevent her eyes from going instantly to the dais. Eleanor, by now, was deep in conversation with Henry, but Simon raised his golden cup in a mocking salute and then drained it slowly and deliberately as his eyes devoured her. When she at last looked away from him, she saw that Petronilla did, indeed, look petulant.

Gossip had it that Eleanor's younger sister had found very few men in her year of widowhood whom she could not captivate. But, Ysabeau noticed, while Simon was polite, charming and attentive, he remained outside her orbit.

After the banquet Ysabeau found the duchess in an expansive mood as she assisted her out of the heavy ceremonial robe and into a fur-trimmed woolen bedrobe.

"Henry tells me we will not be resting long in Poitiers, Ysabeau," Eleanor said, as she sat on a cushioned, backless bench while Ysabeau combed out the heavy golden mass of the duchess' hair.

"Indeed, my lady? But you have just come home," Ysabeau replied, letting her gaze wander about the luxurious bedchamber. The walls were whitewashed, and hung with tapestries of jewel-bright colors, depicting the Garden of Eden and subsequent temptation of Eve. The floor was of richly colored tile, covered in places with plush Oriental carpets rather than the usual rushes. There were opaque panes of glass in the narrow little windows. In one corner of the room lay Eleanor's massive bed, hung with crimson velvet, so high off the ground that a wooden stair stood ready to assist Eleanor into it. The air was pleasantly scented with the duchess' favorite sandalwood incense and the sweet-scented oil she preferred for use in the cresset lamps.

"Yes, but in the morning my lord will depart for Barfleur to board ship. The news from England is good, at least for the Plantagenets. They've had a bellyfull of Stephen across the Channel. While Henry is there, I will guard his interests here and in Anjou. Aquitaine is peaceful enough now, so as soon as possible we will move to Angers."

"God speed Duke Henry's cause," Ysabeau answered mechanically, for her thoughts were on another man who would cross to England even sooner. Eleanor, holding up the silvered glass mirror, saw the faraway look in her lady-in-waiting's eyes, and, putting that together with Simon's words at dinner, smiled secretly to herself.

Just then the door opened and Duke Henry appeared, grinning at the sight of his wife's sleek dishabille.

"By the eyes of God, you're a beautiful woman!" he breathed.

Ysabeau curtseyed and murmured, "I will be in the anteroom if your grace should require anything during the night."

She was heading for the door as the duchess spoke. "There's no need, Ysabeau. You are dismissed for the night. Blanche will be with me in the morning. Thank you—you have done well." Then she turned into her husband's eager embrace, her lady-in-waiting already forgotten, and Ysabeau's protest died on her lips.

If she wasn't to be in attendance on the duchess, then how would she avoid Simon, she thought in panic. Could she make it to her bedchamber without him knowing?

Her hope died as she saw Simon de Winslade lounging on a bench outside the Duchess' bower, long legs propped comfortably out in front of him.

"Good evening, my Lady Ysabeau. I am delighted to see that you are done with your service for the night."

"You might have waited here all night for

nothing," she taunted. "Normally the lady on duty stays."

"Ah, but the loving couple within won't need you." He jerked his tawny head toward the silent room beyond the door. And I do, his eyes said in the flickering torchlight.

"It appears they won't," she admitted, "but I am tired. It's been a long day." She walked on past him.

"There's a debt to be paid first," he said huskily, as his arm shot out to stop her. His grip on her forearm was steely, but it softened as he saw her flinch.

"Go ahead, then, kiss me," she said submissively, and turned her face up and closed her eyes. Get it over with, her mind screamed, so I can begin the sooner to forget how very nearly you've made me abandon all that I've worked so hard to achieve at court.

A moment later she opened her eyes, to find him still studying her with an amused quirk to his lips. "But my lady, the court of love said this was to be private."

Just then a pair of lackeys passed them in the corridor as if to underscore his words. Firmly he placed her arm through his, and whispered, "Come with me."

He closed the heavy oak door to his room behind them, and gestured to two backless chairs, between which was a low table; on this table sat a flagon and two cups. A brazier with smoldering coals and a fat hour candle by the bed cast the only light in the room. The room was strewn with thick Oriental carpets, a singular luxury when normally only rushes were used.

He waved her toward the chairs.

"I see you haven't had to share a chamber with any of the Poitevin courtiers," Ysabeau said, chattering to fill up the enormous silence between them. "In the crowded Maubergeon Tower, that is a signal honor."

"I've always gotten along well with Henry," he answered casually. "I've known him since we were boys. I only met Duchess Eleanor recently, but she's been very gracious—although I wish she'd call off her sister, that Petronilla," he said with a rueful laugh. "Perhaps it is not very gallant of me to say that."

She had to smile. Since the death of her husband, the Count of Vermandois, the Duchess' sister had been very predatory around all the handsome men at court, so much so that ladies feared for their lords' fidelity.

He poured her a cup of hippocras, and said as she sipped the hot spiced wine, "No doubt you've heard the plans. I leave for England tomorrow, and Henry is to come soon."

"Yes."

"And your mistress will take up her regency at Angers. That's quite an honor Henry pays Eleanor," he remarked.

"She is certainly capable of handling it as well as any man," Ysabeau said a bit defensively, thinking he needled her.

"Ah yes, of a certainty. I didn't mean to imply otherwise. Will you miss Poitiers?"

"It is not home. My place is with the Duchess." She saw he was making conversation, trying to relax her with words and wine, but she was determined not to make it easy for him.

"I will miss you, you know."

The remark surprised her. For a moment, the only sound that could be heard was a hissing from the candle as the flame sputtered in a sudden draft.

"I can't imagine why. You have scarcely got what you wanted from me."

He reached out a hand to touch her wrist with strong, elegantly tapering fingers.

"Poor Ysabeau, trying so hard to be the cool, distant lady on a pedestal because that is what she's been taught to value here," he said. "You won't even allow yourself to admit that you'll miss me."

She didn't know what it was, perhaps the gentle tone of his suddenly husky voice, instead of the mocking quality she had expected; or maybe it was because when she opened her tightly shut eyelids, he was kneeling at her side, holding her hands; but for whatever reason, she found herself awash in tears, the tension bursting the dam of her pent-up emotions. And in the next moment she was in his strong arms, her tears being thoroughly kissed away before he turned his attention to her waiting lips.

Her lips met his with all the remembered sweetness of the afternoon at the dolmen, but also with a hunger she had only hinted at before as he claimed her face between his two large hands and his tongue persuaded her lips to part.

Instinctively, her body arched toward him and he pulled her gently off the chair, so that they were both kneeling on the carpet, his arms encircling her, one hand against the small of her back. There was a wild swirling in the pit of her stomach as the tip of his tongue traced the borders of her mouth. Her hands slid past the hardness of his beard-shadowed jaw to bury themselves in the tawny mane of his hair.

Then he was whispering into her hair, "I want you, Ysabeau," and the raw need was naked in his voice as she buried her face against the midnight velvet covering his chest. She could feel the accelerated thud of his heart. She was conscious of the orrisroot scent he wore, mingled with the crushed herb essence embedded in the carpet. His hands had stolen into the neckline of her emerald gown, pushing it down, as his lips descended once more on hers, his kisses slow, deliberate, and drugging as she was pressed even closer into the contours of his lean, hard body.

The magnitude of her desire did not dismay her now, for her will had suddenly become his through the alchemy of his touch. Suddenly she did not want him to leave the court of Poitiers without receiving the gift she now so freely offered him.

His mouth seared a path down her neck and shoulders, distracting her partially while his fingers unlaced her *bliaut* in the back, as deft as any tiring-woman. She gasped as the cool air touched her newly bared shoulders, but he went on pushing down the emerald folds of the gown and its creamy linen undergown. Then his hands were exploring the hollows of her back, warming that flesh beneath his hands. A moan escaped from her throat as his mouth lowered to a rose-tipped breast while he cupped the other one, his thumb encircling and teasing the nipple till it tingled as much as the first did, tantalized by the rough tickle of his mustache.

"Simon . . ." she breathed, and knew not whether her cry was a plea for mercy or a sigh of encouragement; but he knew, for his eyes kissed hers as he lifted his head and lowered her back gently onto the lush pile of the carpet.

She knew this was the last moment she could turn aside from this dangerous passion that had been building since the first moment he had returned to Poitiers, but all she could do—all she wanted in this world—was to caress him with her eyes as with sure, efficient movements he pulled off the black dalmatic and snowy linen shirt, and turned his attention to the belt that held his chausses taut on his finely muscled legs.

She had seen his powerful shoulders and chest nearly bare before, when he had stripped to shirt and chausses in the cave, but now she had the full magnificent effect as he stood still in the flickering light for a moment, watching her as she became aware of the sign of his need for her.

"Ysabeau . . ." he breathed, and knelt to pull the gown over her hips. Her name became an exclamation of delight as he bared still more of her slim perfection to his azure gaze. "You are beautiful."

In a moment she was as naked as he and he stretched out his long, hard frame next to her, pulling her close against the soft mat of hair on his chest. "Ysabeau?" he said again, his lips nuzzling her neck and tingling in the shell of her ear, shattering what little was left of her composure. To the question in his voice there could only be one answer: yes.

She surrendered completely to his masterful initiation into the art of love. His hands went on a roaming, ravaging quest, stroking her belly and down her hips, then started upward from her slender calves, worshipping her body as he touched, speading the fire. She could not get enough of him, and clutched at him, as one of his hands strayed upward to the joining of her thighs, where he stroked and fondled until she felt literally aflame with need. Her back arched and she moaned again, till at last he accepted the invitation and lowered himself fully onto her.

There was a moment of piercing agony-ecstasy as he breached her maidenhead, and he drew back for a moment, staring at her flushed face, as surprised by his discovery as she was by the momentary pain. Then he smiled encouragingly at her as he filled her completely with one powerful thrust, leaving hurt behind and bringing her only mindless, fiery pleasure. Each stroke hurtled her closer to the abyss, as his hands cupped her buttocks, joining her to the pace he set until at last her world shattered into a million sparkling shards, while he murmured, "Ysabeau, *ma chérie*, my perfect one, ah, yes, that's it!" A heartbeat later, as she caught her breath, he reached his peak, and he groaned as if in the grip of deep pain, convulsively shuddering against her.

They may have both slept for a few moments, numbed with contentment, for she was aware of the passage of an uncertain amount of time before he was lifting her against his chest and carrying her to the bed, outlined dimly by the dying embers in the brazier.

"Simon," she began sleepily, "I really must go. . . ."

"Hush, now, darling," he said firmly. "It's late. Sleep now, for awhile." He lowered her gently and settled her with exquisite care as the rope-frame mattress creaked softly, then pulled the coverlet of furs over them both and brought her into the warm haven of his arms.

Sleep now. Yes. She would waken early in the dawn, so there would be time to speak of their love and the changes it would bring about. She would persuade him to delay his journey but a day, so she could obtain release from Eleanor's service and ready her possessions to go with him. And later, before evening, there could be a wedding in the chapel, unless he preferred to marry her in England. Yes, they would speak of all that in the morning. . . .

Sometime in the night she awoke, lying on her side with her back to him, fitted perfectly against him, conscious that his questing touch was rekindling the flame as his lips sucked coaxingly at the nape of her neck. She sighed, pushing her small firm buttocks more impudently against him, chuckling softly as he groaned, the degree of his reawakened desire already apparent. He turned her to him, and before she was fully awake, he had powerfully roused her with honeyed kisses and passionate lovewords, so that she eagerly acquiesced as his knee parted her legs. There was no pain this time, just a tantalizingly slow buildup of sensation as he kissed and stroked and sucked, until she thought she would scream for release. "Please . . ." she moaned.

"Yes, my love!"

Then there was not one abrupt peak, but a series of shorter, increasingly delightful ones, until at last they exploded together and sank back, exhausted, into the soft mattress.

Chapter Twelve

The loving, dawnlit conversation never took place.

Ysabeau was first conscious of a diminishing of warmth, and pulled the furs higher over one shoulder while reaching out with her other arm. But her searching hand met only a vast expanse of empty, cool sheet.

She opened her eyes, peering drowsily around the room in the misty grayness of the morning light. He was not there.

Fully awake now, she jumped to the window embrasure, pulling open the window shutters and gasping as the chill December air hit her bare chest. She gazed past the outer bailey, horrified at the sight ofthe Baron de Winslade already cantering out of the barbican at the head of his retinue.

"Simon!" she screamed, but, of course, he

could not hear her from the distance, and over the squeak of harnesses and the clank of armor. In the courtyard beneath her a man-at-arms looked up, grinning at the sight of the beauty with her long brown tresses partially hiding two luscious breasts. As she realized this, she hurriedly withdrew, slamming the shutters closed, and hoping he had not identified her.

In a welter of confusion she looked wildly about her for some hastily scrawled love note, some word of farewell, some explanation. There was nothing, no sign that Simon de Winslade had ever inhabited this chamber, not an article of clothing left behind.

Her bare foot touched a stiff place in the carpet below where they had lain the night before. She stared at the spot—the bright red already turned a dark brown as blood will shortly after it is shed—the blood of her maidenhead, carelessly shed by a foreign lord who never even looked back as he rode away.

Fortunately, the palace's inhabitants were mostly in the chapel hearing morning Mass as she stole guiltily up the stairs in her rumpled green sendal *bliaut* laced up crookedly in the back due to her lack of assistance. She hoped she would not have to face Matilde or Marie, and certainly not Blanche, for they would know immediately that she had not spent the night in attendance on the Duchess. Only Ami was there, his dark eyes gazing thoughtfully at her as he sensed her mood and suppressed his eagerness for his morning walk around the bailey.

She gazed into the small square of silvered glass that served as a mirror, dismayed at the swollen redness of her lips, the violet circles under her bleak brown eyes, the tangled disarray of her hair. She put her hands up to her face, feeling the stinging of tiny abrasions around her chin and cheeks from his beard, aware, too, of the slight ache between her legs, so much subtler than the blinding pain of his betrayal. She removed her clothes, choosing a woollen gown of sombre hue. But before she put it on, she took a cloth dipped in the icy wash water left at least an hour ago, and sponged herself off all over, trying to remove every trace of his scent and the blood that still streaked her thighs.

It was well that the household was in an uproar over the impending move to Angers when she joined Eleanor's ladies in the bower a short time later, for no one had time to notice that *La Maraise* was quieter than they had seen her since her arrival; she smiled not at all, going about the tasks assigned her with a tightness about her lips and downcast, joyless eyes.

The chaos was even greater than when Eleanor had gone on progress, for this time all the ladies were going and there was so much more to pack: clothing, plate and cutlery, bedding—even the beds themselves were disassembled and the panes of glass removed from the narrow windows.

Only a few palace servants would be left behind, with orders to clean the Maubergeon Tower more thoroughly than it ever could be when the nobility were in residence. Moldy old rushes were thrown out, matted with forgotten bones of countless feasts and the soil left by the many hounds and lapdogs that had gone with their masters and mistresses. Walls were re-whitewashed and the garderobes were sweetened by treating them with quicklime. When the duke and duchess returned, all would be pristine and ready for them, but no one knew when that would be, for the duchess expected to leave Angers only for England, as its queen.

Simon, riding north as if the Devil himself were chasing him, was as confused by his desire to turn his destrier's head and return to Poitiers as Ysabeau had been by his leaving. He had what he wanted, didn't he—the promise that Henry of Anjou would take the crown at last from Stephen's bungling hands. And he had spent the last night of his stay in Poitiers in the arms of the girl he had wanted since he had first set eyes on her in the garden, months ago.

He had thought her a virgin then. But from the taunting way she had teased him and held him at arm's length during the month, only to surrender so willingly to his embrace when he finally got her alone, he assumed that she had been bedded by someone else—damn whoever it was! Then, when he had thrust into her, he found he had been correct after all, that she had merely adopted the guise of the bold lady of the court, teasing poor men into madness so they could grovel at her feet. Inside she was still the innocent, half-wild creature from the island, and while a part of him exulted in the knowledge that he was the first to possess her, another finer portion of his heart recognized that he wanted to be the only one, ever, that he wanted her for his lady, to grace his hall, to bear him more sons, and, especially, dark-haired, dark-eyed daughters to capture mens' hearts someday as she had his. He loved her completely, now and forever.

But there wasn't time now. Surely she must understand that. He had a fief to defend, and a kingdom to help the Plantagenet Duke win. After their victory there would be time to return to claim her—or, perhaps, by that time, she would be on English soil herself, for Henry would be joined by Eleanor as soon as it was safe, he knew.

It still bothered him that he hadn't awakened her to make his farewells, but he couldn't bear to disturb the perfect picture of her that he would carry with him: Ysabeau sprawled, prone on his bed, a faint flush to her cheek, her long chesnut hair partly covering her face and graceful, slender back.

By the time he reached Barfleur, however, the need to ensure that she would wait for him was so great that, before taking ship, he purchased a sheet of parchment and some ink and wrote her. He declared his love and passion for her and asked that she wed him as soon as he could claim her either side of the Channel.

He handed this missive to an earnest-looking youth he found lounging near the quay, who said he knew of a garron he could borrow. Simon gave him a *livre tournois* for delivering the letter, with another to be kept by the priest of a nearby church until the youth returned with Ysabeau's answer. Her message—or perhaps even her lovely self—was to be put aboard the next ship bound for England.

Part II

Chapter Thirteen

Simon arrived back in his demesne in time to celebrate Christmas in his keep at Winslade before traveling on to Bristol, where Henry was expected to land.

He went immediately to see his son, but Aimery and Hulda, the wet nurse, were nowhere within the hall or the rest of the keep. Thomas, his seneschal, informed him that Hulda was most likely in her cottage in the village, where she frequently took the boy.

"Stupid wench," he growled in annoyance, for now he must trudge back across the bailey in the biting sleet and out into the tangle of wattle and daub thatched hovels that huddled against the walls of Winslade Castle.

"Why not just send for her, my lord?" the seneschal, a practical Norman from Caen, inquired mildly, but Simon was already gone.

He found the buxom wench contentedly stirring a pot of stew over the fire while his son rolled about like a little puppy on a wolf fur a safe distance from the hearth.

She looked up as he entered the rude, low-roofed dwelling, a glad smile of welcome lighting her handsome features. She ran a hand distractedly through her disheveled straw-colored braids, and smoothed the grease-stained homespun kirtle over her well-rounded hips.

"My lord, I didn't know you'd be returnin' today, or I would've had yer wee lordling at the castle for ye! I just came to mix up a pottage for Mam here." She indicated an old woman dozing on a pallet in a corner of the small room, who had not been aroused by the cold draft his entrance had created.

"Hulda, I might just as easily have been one of Stephen's brigands come to rape you and steal my heir," he answered her angrily in her English tongue, gesturing at the babe, who had ceased crawling about on the fur and lay staring at the stranger with the loud voice. Then the child broke into a wail of fear. The cry did little to sweeten Simon's temper. "I provided you with a very adequate chamber in the keep. Why are you not using it?" He was aware that his wrath was only making matters worse, but he couldn't suppress it. This wasn't the way he'd pictured his reunion with his son. The child should have been awaiting him in the hall, smiling delightedly as he was handed to his sire to hold. Awkwardly, he dropped the rattle and ball he'd brought from Poitiers onto the fur, but the baby made no move toward him.

"My lord, ye're scaring the wee boy," admonished the peasant woman bravely. "I do spend most of the day at the hall, but who's to see to Mam? Besides, we've had no trouble here. I guess Sir Hugh's seen to that."

She referred to his father by marriage, whose lands adjoined his. The relationship between the two men had always been cordial, but he'd seen Rohese's father only once since her death.

"*Bien*. What of Gervase?" he inquired.

"He hasn't been here, though Alf Carpenter saw him passing through the wood not a league from your boundaries, with a dozen men-at-arms."

"And what was Alf doing in my wood, taking one of my deer?" Simon growled, but with no real anger, though poaching was a serious crime.

Hulda made no answer to his last remark, seeing his attention was now on his son, where it should be. She sat down near the fire and bared a large, blue-veined breast, which the baby began to suckle contentedly, ignoring the noisy intruder.

Simon stared at the babe, whose dark downy hair had been a complete surprise to him, since he and Rohese both had lighter hair. A throwback to old Guy de Bayeux, he mused as he watched the boy stroke the breast he was suckling.

Hulda studied the silent man who sat on the hovel's only other bench, and at last his eyes rose from the babe to hers.

"He grows well. . . ."

"Indeed he does. He's twice as big as when you left."

"More like thrice. He's healthy?"

"Never a sniffle. He's started rolling over, and he's cutting a tooth."

He tried not to stare as she pulled her bodice back over her rounded breast. It strained against the rough cloth, leaving a damp circle where her milk had leaked. He looked away from her bosom and into her eyes. His mouth was dry.

She knew what he was thinking, somehow. "My lord," she said softly, "Yer son will be asleep in a moment. If you needed anything else, Mam wouldn't waken, I'm sure." Her eyes strayed as if by accident to the other pallet in a dark corner of the dwelling.

It would be so easy. Just a few moments tumbling about on the straw-filled pallet and he would rest well tonight, free of the teasing images of the Poitevin girl, of her white thighs open to him, her dark hair tickling his nipples as she bent to kiss him, her lush lips moist with invitation. And Hulda made it clear since he'd placed Aimery in her care that she would be glad to console the grieving father, as well.

"What about Alf Carpenter?" he asked shrewdly in his Norman-accented English.

He could see that his blunt question surprised her. Why should the lord care what her sweetheart thought?

"He'll never know, nor would it matter greatly. That's just the way it is between folk like us and you. He was the father of my babe that died, you know."

Simon had suspected as much.

"We'd like to marry, my lord. In a few months, when Aimery's weaned."

He was touched by her thoughtfulness on his son's behalf. Another pregnancy would dry up her milk for Aimery.

"You have my permission, gladly. But I think I must decline your offer." He met her surprised gaze, thinking of a darker pair of eyes. You would be pleased to know I will sacrifice that much to the conventions of love, Ysabeau, he thought. I will not use another as a cheap substitute, when I cannot have you.

"It was good between us once, my lord. It could be again." Her eyes were puzzled; she clearly didn't understand why he hesitated to take her now, for he had done so on another occasion, several years ago, when he was a barely bearded young squire drunk on harvest ale.

"You made a man of me, Hulda. Never think I do not remember that." He offered her no further explanation, nor would she have understood the truth of why he didn't take her now. He rose to go, leaving Hulda sitting quietly by the fire.

It would have made no difference, had he eased himself on Hulda, he knew; his thoughts would still have been on Ysabeau as he stalked back up to the hall.

He imagined her receiving the letter in which he had poured out his heart. He could picture her so well, perched in a window embrasure to take advantage of the light, perhaps wearing the emerald green *bliaut* that complemented her dark beauty, her eyes widening as she intently scanned the missive, her slender fingertips touching the parchment, the same fingertips he had guided to touch him . . . God's blood! He was more aroused now than when he knew Hulda's body was his for the taking, moments ago.

Would she be surprised to hear that he was so smitten? Or had she known since their first meeting that there was no other woman in the world for him, that it had only been a matter of not giving herself too soon, until he was well and truly ensnared by those entrancing honey-brown eyes, her lyrical voice, the soft pink of her lush mouth, the sweet curves of her body?

He had no fear that she would show the letter to the other ladies, her laughter trilling at his foolishness. He had seen from the first that the role of the haughty lady was an assumed one, although unnatural to her. Certainly, he would worship her. But it would not be a worship of a distant, untouchable object. His would be a passion-filled, much more earthly love, and she would be content to return nothing less, he was sure. A virgin when he had pulled her into his arms, she had nevertheless responded like an experienced woman, with a trusting confidence that banished fear of the momentary pain and replaced it with joy and pleasure. The way she'd returned each kiss, each caress, made it clear that she expected they'd have a lifetime together.

Chapter Fourteen

Ysabeau remembered the trip into the Loire valley in terms of sensations and emotions rather than sights: the icy slash of winter rain, the sodden misery of riding to the next available shelter, leagues away, the bone-numbing chill of wet clothes, the boredom and impatience when baggage wains became mired in the mud and had to be dug out, the weariness of listening to Eleanor's bastard brothers and her sister jostle for pride of place at their overnight stops at keeps and abbeys along the way. Others, like Philippe de Melle and Matilde's lover, Rene, went out of their way to make life bearable, assisting the ladies at fords, going to work like servants when repairs were necessary, and maintaining good spirits with their entertaining songs and stories.

Their efforts had no effect on Ysabeau,

though, who, numbed by her misery, saw each day as a cold, damp ordeal to get through. She went about her duties to Eleanor competently, but quietly, assisting the Duchess at rest stops, seeing to it that Eleanor had all possible comforts, making suggestions in the kitchens as to her preferences, making sure that the litter was ready should Eleanor prefer not to ride on any given day—for it was known now that the Duchess was *enceinte*. The knowledge enabled Eleanor to endure the winter journey with a breezy serenity that Ysabeau envied.

Ysabeau was relieved when her monthly courses began while on the journey, despite the cramping and inconvenience. Certainly she could not have shared Eleanor's serene radiance if that night of passion had left her carrying Simon de Winslade's child.

On the latter half of the trip, Ysabeau began to notice that the troubadour, Philippe, had appointed himself her constant companion. It was as if he sensed her bitter sorrow, and after a few glances into his clear gray eyes, Ysabeau felt certain he knew what had happened to her. She accepted his undemanding presence gratefully, for he seemed to want nothing more than to be near her, while even Matilde seemed to avoid her quiet roommate when there was Rene to keep her in smiles.

Near the border of Anjou and the end of their journey, they stopped at the famed Abbey of Fontevrault, a convent of nuns and monks unique in that it was ruled by an abbess. This had always been Eleanor's preferred religious establishment, since its founder at the end of the last century had been convinced of the superiority of women. It had been for decades the chosen retreat of noblewomen, wearied by the cares of their world, eager to forget demanding lords, ungrateful sons, and court intrigues. Its abbesses were already noble widows. Here Eleanor stopped their northward progress for two days, waiting for the cessation of some frightening cramping.

On the final day of their journey, a bright January sun appeared, shining brightly as if to atone for the entire miserable, damp journey. Even Ysabeau summoned forth a smile when Philippe told her they would be behind the secure walls of Angers by evensong. The city, he assured her, was full of churches, schools, philosophy, and poetry, and, of course, he added with a twinkle of his gray eyes, the climate of the Loire valley produced a very admirable *vin rosé*.

Just before they reached the outer gates they were joined by a young man with curly red hair who had dancing leaf-green eyes and a handsome countenance. He asked the escort of men-at-arms to introduce him to the Duchess of Aquitaine, and his mien was so poised and charming that they did.

Due to the rest and improved weather, Eleanor was mounted on her white palfrey rather than riding in the litter. Ysabeau and Philippe, sitting on their mounts nearby, witnessed the meeting of the unknown man and their mistress.

"My Lady Eleanor," he began, bowing low before smiling winningly up at her, "I am

Bernard de Ventador, the best troubadour in Europe. I see that you are justly famed for your beauty and *politesse*. I bid you welcome to Anjou, and Angers, and humbly beg to serve you with music."

Ysabeau felt Philippe stiffen at her side. "That squawking, conceited magpie!" he hissed.

She laid a gloved hand warningly on his, for his whisper had been rather loud. But Eleanor made no sign that she had heard it, nor did Bernard seem disconcerted in the least.

Eleanor replied in a lazy, amused drawl. "The best, Master Bernard? Surely that was Marcabru. Besides, I already have some very able musicians in my train." She gestured elegantly toward Philippe, who smiled thinly at the upstart.

"Were they trained by my master, Eble de Ventador, the second of his noble lineage, who maintained a school for troubadours at his chateau? I never saw him there," Bernard continued arrogantly, staring back unblinkingly at Philippe. "I beg but a position in your court, gracious and lovely Duchess, the embodiment of charm. There is certainly room for all who would sing your praises," he concluded magnanimously.

The Duchess appeared thoroughly won. With an appreciative flush on her cheeks, she accepted his offer, while Philippe continued to mutter threats and imprecations heard only by Ysabeau as they crossed the bridge over the Maine and entered the principle city of Anjou.

* * *

The Duchess and her retinue had been gone from the Palace of Poitiers for several days, the youth was told at the city gate.

"*Merde*!" he snorted disgustedly, sitting back in his saddle on the swaybacked bay and wincing at the painful message of protest his saddlesore posterior was sending to his brain. "And where are they now?" Probably across the sea, he thought, where he'd never be able to deliver his message and earn the other *livre*.

"Angers Castle."

Angers wasn't so bad, he realized. It was, at least, on his way back home to Normandy. Still, this was not turning out to be such easy money after all. Curse the baron for not knowing where his ladylove was—he could have journeyed to Angers and back in half the time!

He deserved a stop at an inn to warm him, he reasoned later that day, having made good time northward. He'd just spend a few *sous* on a mug of mulled wine, then gallop onward to an abbey where he could lay his head down safely without fear of having his throat cut for the coins he carried.

A buxom, apple-cheeked serving wench showed him a goodly bit of cleavage as she leaned over to take his order. He had to impress her. Maybe he'd spend a few more *sous* on another bodily need before resuming his journey. He wasn't used to having money to spend on a woman; he usually had to rely on what he could charm the local sluts into doing for free. The thought of this willing maid excited him.

"D'ye know you serve the trusted

messenger of the Baron de Winslade?" he whispered as she brought his wine and brushed teasingly against his shoulder.

"No, really?" she said skeptically. "You look like just another Norman to me." His accent was grating to Poitevin ears.

"*Vraiment*, my good woman. You see, here is but a small portion of the reward he paid me for carrying this important message," the youth replied, stung by her disbelief into revealing the gold coin in the pouch with the parchment that hung from his neck.

"Oh, I see. Well, in that case, perhaps you would like to enjoy your drink privately?" She jerked her head toward the ladder leading into the few loft rooms rented out to travelers. She cuddled close, grabbing his arm and pressing it against the soft, plump flesh of her breasts as she sat next to him, giving off a cloud of musky scent that clouded his senses.

"Certainly, I could spare smaller coins for more comfortable surroundings," he said, arrogant again after her seeming deference. "You're surely not suggesting you're worth more than, say, the cost of another mug of this indifferent vintage?"

Her mouth tightened, but he wasn't watching, and he only heard her respond in dulcet, husky tones, "Ah, no, *mon seigneur*, I know my place, but for two *sous*, you'll never have better."

He never would have better, for in a grove of trees two leagues away from the inn and not far from the Cistercian abbey where he planned to spend the night, he was set upon by brigands who had been tipped off by the wench. Though they were on foot, they efficiently grabbed the garron's bridle, yanked the youth off his horse and cooly slit his throat, ending his scream in a gurgle of blood. The gold coin was found and the corpse stripped bare, for his leather jerkin, braies, and coarse leather shoes were sure to fit one of them. The parchment letter was dismissed as a thing of no importance. It fluttered against the body for a moment, then blew away in the wind.

"Look how her color heightens when she looks at him," observed Ysabeau to Matilde softly as they sat stitching with gold thread on an altar cloth that was to be given to Fontevrault Abbey. Several of Eleanor's ladies were bent over the same task, but Ysabeau's whisper was pitched to reach her friend's ears only.

Bernard de Ventador, the copper-haired troubadour who had given Eleanor such a dramatic welcome to Angers, had just entered the duchess' solar and was settling down with his lute at Eleanor's feet.

The elegant Duchess was dressed in a gown of delicate peach hue, trimmed in bands of peach and silver embroidery, and wore a veil of sheerest pale peach over her gleaming blond coronet of braids. As yet, her pregnancy was not apparent; what was obvious was that she was happier anytime her new favorite troubadour was in the room.

"Do you think she could be in love with him?" Ysabeau asked Matilde, shocked.

"No, not in the way you mean," Matilde

answered, amused. "Everything is black or white with you still, eh, *La Maraise*? No, not in a way that would dishonor Henry. Eleanor just enjoys being adored. She's finally left that monk Louis behind, even more completely than she had at Poitiers, because here she is the complete mistress, without even Henry to dictate to her."

"I should think she'd miss him terribly," sighed Ysabeau, "and be worried about the danger he could be in."

"Bah, not her—she's not the type to sit and pray and make baby clothes," answered Matilde practically, cutting her thread neatly with a small dagger kept in her girdle. "She'll light the proper candles, of course, and pay for Masses, but deep down she knows Henry Plantagenet's more than a match for that Stephen, and she won't spend her time worrying."

Ysabeau nodded as she reached down to pat Ami, who lay dozing at her side, his head resting heavily on her slippered foot. In the background, Bernard sang plaintively.

> "The course of this our love I vow
> Is like the hawthorn on the bough
> At night, on the tree's branches toss'd
> It shivers in the rain and frost
> But morning sunlight comes and then
> Shines on each leaf and branch again . . ."

His music did not quite drown out Ami's low growl as Philippe de Melle sat down next to Ysabeau on the low bench.

"I should've known Eleanor would need no psaltery music when she had him to play and make eyes at her."

"Sssshh—your jealousy is showing," cautioned Matilde, trying to tease him out of his black, glowering looks.

Ysabeau was still staring at her dog. He'd never given the slightest negative reaction to any one of her friends before. Some, like Marie, Matilde, and, inexplicably, Simon de Winslade—God rot him—he adored, and showed it by the still-puppyish gyrations of delight he went through when any of those people greeted him, presenting his head to be patted, his back to be scratched, or if one was greatly honored, gravely proferring a paw. He treated Duchess Eleanor with the greatest *politesse*, and was a welcome visitor to her bower. Ysabeau had been asked to allow him to sire a litter on one of Eleanor's prize mastiff bitches.

Ami had always been rather indifferent to others, like Blanche, or Petronilla, or Philippe, tolerating their attentions impassively.

Ysabeau looked again at the big dog at her feet. He had shifted position so that instead of lolling indigently at her feet, he had his ebony eyes trained on Philippe.

Perhaps the dog was reacting to the aura of bitterness that had hung about Philippe ever since the Poitevin household had come to Angers, Ysabeau mused, concerned for the man who had shown her a great deal of kindness. Envy of the rival troubadour who had so completely captured his patroness' attention was souring his once-sunny nature to a disturbing degree. He had become caustic and reserved with everyone save Ysabeau, in whom he confided.

"Such are the ways of the great," he'd said. "Watch that you don't come to depend on her fondness for you, either. She'd banish you from court in a moment if it suited her."

Ysabeau had come to be one of the attendants Eleanor most liked to have around her, often complimenting her for her natural manner and deft, competent fingers. So when Philippe spoke disparagingly of his mistress, she pointed out the duchess' great kindness to her, and that Philippe *had* been given a place in the household here at Angers, that he had every reason to expect it would continue.

"Why, just yesterday she asked you to play for all of us after the midday meal, and serve as judge of the *sirventes* presented by the others," she had reminded him.

"Ah, *oui*, a bone thrown to a starving mongrel, while the fat lapdog sat sated at her elbow," he'd retorted. "I tried to tell Eleanor the truth I learned about her green-eyed darling, but she paid me no heed."

"Oh, and what was that?" she asked, humoring him.

"He left the illustrious Eble's household not because the great count had taught him all he could, but because Eble took exception to Bernard's seducing the countess." He looked smug, then disgusted as he reported Eleanor's response: " 'It's a great wonder that more of these silly bored noblewomen left with little to do aren't thus led astray.' "

Philippe seemed increasingly to need the comfort of Ysabeau's company, and Ysabeau, still stinging from the callous way Simon had treated her—seducing her with his magic touch and mesmerizing voice, then abandoning her without a word—did nothing to forbid him. However, she sometimes felt inexplicably ill at ease in his presence. There was an unspoken hunger in those clear gray eyes, sometimes, a hunger that had naught to do with carnal matters. . . .

At least, when he was around, it discouraged somewhat the attentions of the ever-increasing number of courtiers who found *La Maraise* fascinating. Her bitter disillusionment over Simon had translated itself into a cool hauteur that was ironically the air she had been trying to cultivate all along, before the Norman baron had come into her life. Ysabeau found herself the subject of *cansos* of passionate, if badly written, love verses. There were certainly plenty of would-be poets to write them, for Eleanor's court had become famed for its generous patronage of the arts, and those who knew Henry Plantagenet cared little for such things, flocked to the Duchess' side in his absence.

But Ysabeau chose none of them, much to their satisfaction, it seemed, for it gave them an excuse to go about wan and listless, sighing, taking little food when they were at table with her. Since she made no indication that any met with favor in her sight, all felt encouraged to continue in their languishing and hint that they would die if the dark-eyed, chestnut-haired beauty never smiled on them. But since they were behaving in a fashion decreed honorable by the *gai savoir*, they begrudged her not a moment of her aloofness.

Eleanor was amused at their antics, and not the least jealous at the attention her youngest lady drew.

"I saw your potential from the moment you came to court," she had said only last evening as Ysabeau had helped her prepare for bed. "I saw you could be a jewel, and you are—though I cannot decide if you are more like the glowing green of the emerald or the crimson of the ruby. And lately you have the hardness of ice, though I am puzzled as to what has brought this about. . . . My dear, I hope you are happy at court?" She turned to face Ysabeau, her gray-green eyes probing, though kindly. "I hope you would feel free to confide in me, if anything, or anyone, grieved you? Joscelin has not been too free with his hands again, has he?"

That Eleanor even knew that her bastard brother had bothered her was astonishing to Ysabeau. Nothing in her domain escaped Eleanor's notice.

"Oh no, *ma dame,* he . . ." She had flushed in embarrassment.

"No matter. He bothers all my ladies at one time or another. He's like a honeybee, never knowing whether he'll get lucky and a flower will accept him. But feel free to send him on his way just like anyone else. Joscelin has a wife, as you'd know if he ever bothered to bring her to court, instead of immuring her at his chateau with a new brat issuing from her every year. But I sense Joscelin is not the cause of the new air you have about you," the duchess had continued shrewdly, coming back to her original point so suddenly that Ysabeau was caught off guard. "You have been, perhaps, disappointed in love?"

Ysabeau had no need to answer. To her horror, her eyes widened, then flooded with tears she was not able to control. She dropped the silver-backed, jeweled hairbrush in confusion and covered her face with her hands. "Your grace, I am so sorry. If you feel I have dishonored your trust I will return to Ré," she sobbed.

To her surprise, Eleanor had enfolded her in her arms, laughing gently at her. "My dear girl, I would be a sorry hypocrite, indeed, if I banished you for mistakes I made at an even earlier age! You cannot think that, being raised in the free and easy way I was, I came a virgin bride to Louis Capet!"

Her confession shocked Ysabeau, and the distraction succeeded in stopping her tears.

"*You,* Your Grace?"

"Don't tell me you haven't heard rumors. I've been accused of everything, including carnal knowledge of my uncle, Raymond of Poitiers, while on Crusade with that monk, Louis." Her elegant mouth had wrinkled in distaste. "I only wish I'd enjoyed half the things I'm supposed to have done in my thirty years!

"The point is, it's not the end of the world. Any man worth having doesn't set so much store by bloodied sheets the next morning. Is it not possible that things will work out with this man who has meant so much to you?"

"I have heard nothing from him, your grace," Ysabeau had murmured, eyes downcast.

"He is not at Angers."

Aha, mused Eleanor. I *thought* it was that rascal Norman. She had intercepted some looks so searing between Simon and the petite girl from the island, that they rivaled even those Henry had given her in the gloomy Cité Palace in Paris, only two years ago—and those had been enough to convince her to divorce Louis. But Simon had a good heart, of that she was convinced, and was not a callous lecher. Perhaps this story would have a happy ending yet. . . .

"*Soyez tranquille*, my girl. Things are very confused in England right now. It may not be possible for him to write love letters as he might wish." She had smiled as the girl turned startled eyes on her, realizing that she knew exactly who had stolen her heart.

The song was interrupted by the entrance of a page, accompanying a travel-stained messenger from England.

"Ah, news from Henry!" Eleanor jumped up and clapped her hands, not troubling to await the end of Bernard's song. Ysabeau could see a real contrast now between her reaction to the troubadour and the suffusion of radiance at news of her lord. Let the gossips take note, Ysabeau thought, of the difference between Eleanor's fondness for worshipful flattery and this passionate love she obviously felt for Henry! In a rush of love and loyalty for Eleanor, Ysabeau hoped that Henry Plantagenet would always return that feeling as he did now.

Eleanor read aloud: " 'To the Duchess of Aquitaine and Normandy, and Countess of Anjou, etc., my beloved wife and mother-to-be of my heir. I rejoice in your news of the coming babe, and urge you to behave with moderation, so that by August when you indicate my son is due, the matter will go well for you and him. I treasure you all the more that you have given me the promise of an heir so speedily.

" 'I hope soon to add Queen of the English to your title, though I realize nothing will be handed me easily. We made a good landing at Wareham with thirty-six ships, one hundred and forty knights, and three thousand footsoldiers on the sixth of January, and on the advice of Baron de Winslade, went immediately to Devizes where we were joined by Chester, Cornwall, Hereford and Salisbury. We then laid siege to Malmesbury, chiefly to divert Stephen from Wallingford, which de Winslade informed me was the expected target. It seems I was well advised, because Stephen came and camped on the Avon, but made the excuse that the river was impassable and did not attack. The real reason, I am proud to report, dear wife, is that King Stephen could not trust his barons to follow his lead, so many had made separate agreements with me. Stephen has been forced to make a truce, and we are to go our own ways for six months here in England.' " At that, Eleanor sighed deeply.

" 'I am for Bristol again, where I plan to hold Easter court. I will keep you informed, but it is wonderful to know that I have left our lands in such capable hands as yours, my dear duchess. I long to be with you, but wish more to give you a queen's crown.' It is signed," Eleanor went on, " 'Henry Plantagenet, Duke of

Normandy and Aquitaine, Count of Anjou, and if God wills it, King of England.' "

Eleanor was obviously moved by the letter and happily acknowledged the ladies' compliments on Henry's graceful turn of phrase and good news.

Ysabeau, however, was shaken by the two references to Simon de Winslade. She was surprised, for he was but one of many barons. Nonetheless, his counsel was apparently valued as much as that of older, more seasoned nobles of higher rank. Now she felt Matilde's eyes on her, for Matilde had guessed weeks ago what had happened the night before Simon left.

"It seems I cannot avoid reminders of the fellow, even though he has put the Channel between us," Ysabeau said with a shaky attempt at laughter. Her face suddenly looked bleached of color against the rich blue of her gown.

"He certainly seems high in Henry's estimation," Matilde observed. "He is a man to watch, a man who will go far in the duke's service, mark me."

"Hush, Matilde," Philippe scolded, much to both women's surprise. "Can't you see that poor Ysabeau is in agony at the very mention of his name?"

Chapter Fifteen

Spring held the Loire valley in joyous captivity. In the oak forests the red deer led their fawns into glades spread with dog violets, lily of the valley, sweet woodruff, and oxalis, while rooks, willow tits, and robins soared in and out of the sunlight, their calls in lyrical counterpoint to the woodpeckers' drill.

The peasants plowed the rich dark earth of their lords' fields and the strips they held as their own. Lambs gamboled near ewes, and those serfs lucky enough to have cows led them out to the common pastureland, often with calves frisking at their heels. All were thankful the cold, dark times of winter were over, that the salted meat had held out, and that soon there would be fresh vegetables to eat.

Eleanor, in her formidable fortress on the hillside in Angers, had heard the calling of May, and made no attempt to resist its lush appeal. Though now six months pregnant, she'd insisted on mounting a party to go hawking. Her palfrey was perfectly smooth in her paces and would carry her safely sidesaddle, as always. Her ladies were powerless to refuse her, and truthfully saw no great need to do so, for Eleanor was accustomed to riding, and it should do the babe no harm. Besides, they were as eager for an outing as their duchess. Beyond the cold dark walls of the chateau the verdant Loire valley summoned them also.

The party spread out down the hillside across the Maine, making bright dots of color over the green background of spring foliage. Ysabeau, clad in a riding dress of becoming salmon pink that accentuated the natural color of her cheekbones, was mounted on the same little chestnut mare, Vielle, that had carried her in Poitiers.

The duchess allowed an appreciative sigh to escape her lips as the master falconer, Maître Raymond, prepared to loose her new haggard, a long-winged saker hawk trapped in the wild last fall. This was to be her maiden flight, a test of the falconer's painstaking care over the long winter months when he had gentled the bird by keeping her in the dark, then depriving her of sleep, offering her tidbits, always speaking to her in his soothing Provençal voice, until the hawk calmed merely at its sound. She had been taught to stoop to prey by the aid of wounded pigeons tied to a kite, as well as rabbit fur stuffed with chicken entrails.

The lords and ladies gathered near as the

falconer removed the red velvet hood stitched with gold thread and ornamented with a tiny crown of pearls and feathers. The saker blinked and swiveled its head around, gripping the hawker's glove restlessly with sharp talons, causing the bells on its legs to tinkle merrily.

All held their breath, then cheered as the hawk was launched into the cerulean blue of the Anjou sky. This was the critical moment. All the training and care of the falconer might go for naught now, if the prospect of freedom was more attractive to the saker than the lure.

The falcon soared ecstatically, seizing the updraft, and soon it was a tiny brown speck above them. The party craned their necks, watching, eyes shaded from the sun with their gloved hands.

Far below her the saker spotted a hare, invisible to the riders against a rock of the same color, contentedly munching pink-blossomed clover. The falcon stooped; plunging with astonishing speed, talons first, she seized the hare, and, ignoring its piteous cry, rose again, long wings flapping.

Maître Raymond now swung the lure, a red cloth ball studded with bits of meat, in wide circles, calling to the bird in sibilant Provençal, until at last she deigned to return, bringing the limp carcass to the triumphant falconer.

"Eh, *voilà*!" he called, and again the lords and ladies cheered.

Ysabeau heard a familiar voice join in the cheers behind her, and, turning in the saddle, saw that Philippe de Melle had joined the hawking party. He grinned as he held out a sheer length of white cloth.

"Your veil, *ma jolie damoiselle.*"

"Ah, *grande merci*, my friend," she answered. "I felt it float off back there, but by the time Vielle stopped, I couldn't see it anywhere."

"I found it on a bush, and knew it instantly to be yours," Philippe said with a gallant flourish as he handed it to her.

"A lucky guess," Ysabeau retorted teasingly. "You can have no idea what I was wearing, for you were nowhere to be found when we set out. We even had Rene look for you. Where were you, Philippe?"

Suddenly, it was as if a pair of shutters closed before his eyes; he looked to where the duchess was stroking her bird.

"I had some business to attend to," he muttered, shrugging.

Ysabeau frowned. Here was another instance of Philippe's evasiveness. Now that Ysabeau had grown accustomed to his company at court gatherings, she noted that all too often Philippe was absent, or came in late with no explanation. He had not been overindulging in the local vintage, for his breath seemed free of wine and his eyes clear, though lit by a strange light. Or could he be courting someone, she wondered. Frequently, when walking the battlements on a clement spring evening to escape the attentions of some lovesick *chevalier*, she had noted the troubadour striding out of the castle gates into Angers.

She meant to press him further, but then Eleanor voiced a desire to return to the castle, so the lords and ladies began to rein their palfreys in the direction of home.

"Hold, your grace," called out Philippe suddenly. All eyes turned to him as the duchess eyed the troubadour curiously. "I believe your mount's girth is loose. If you will allow me, I would consider it an honor to tighten it to assure your safety. I assure you, you need not dismount—just shift your leg slightly, so . . ."

The troubadour ran his hand up under the white mare's saddle, seemingly fumbling to reach the fastening of the girth and pull it tigther. His forearm was hidden by the folds of Eleanor's rich blue riding dress. The horse swiveled her long elegant neck around and laid her ears back, while Philippe gave her belly a thump as grooms frequently do to keep the horse from holding its breath, thus allowing the girth to remain loose.

"Why, Philippe, I had no idea you were so versatile," the Duchess praised him in her husky voice. "Thank you for noticing that."

"*Ce n'est rien, ma Duchesse*," Philippe said, humbly bowing.

Eleanor waited until the wiry troubadour remounted, and then touched her heels to the mare's flank in a signal to head for Angers.

Just then a spring demon seemed to possess the white mare. After a few abortive attempts to rear and buck, the palfrey seized the bit of the gaily decorated gold bridle and plunged at a reckless gallop ahead of the group. Cloth of gold trappings and clods of earth flew out behind horse and rider.

The duchess was an excellent horsewoman,

but she was hampered by her fear for the safety of her baby, and had dropped one of the reins. Gamely, Eleanor fought to slow the beast, but was not able to lean over and grab the dangling rein.

"Oh, *Sainte Vierge*," breathed Ysabeau in horror. "She will fall! She will lose the babe . . ."

Many of the lords were already in hot pursuit, but Philippe's long-legged bay was fastest. Within a few heartbeats he had drawn alongside and seized the wayward mare's headstall, bringing her and her rider to a stop. Quickly, he jumped off his mount and ran his hands soothingly over the mare. Again, the folds of Eleanor's riding dress concealed his hand as it reached beneath the saddle blanket to remove the sharp bone needle he had implanted in the mare's hide moments before.

"Oh, well done, Philippe!" cried Eleanor. "You have saved not only my life, but that of Henry's heir. You have but to name your reward, my good man."

Ysabeau's mount had caught up with the rest in time for her to hear the praise and see the triumph glittering on the troubadour's sharp features. As her mare curvetted, impatient at the sudden halt, Philippe turned and eyed Ysabeau for a moment. His eyes were unreadable.

"Well, my good Philippe?"

"Your grace, I would have you know I did what any of your court would have done, strictly for love of you." Ysabeau did not miss the look he shot at Bernard de Ventador. "But there is one boon I would ask, if your grace does not consider it overbold."

"Fear not to ask," Eleanor encouraged.

"I would, your grace, have you ennoble me."

Several of the onlookers gasped at his daring.

Eleanor was silent for but a moment, then chuckled deeply. "Why, Philippe, I had no idea that you aspired so high. I thought that simply making music for your duchess was all you desired in life."

Ysabeau could imagine the painful struggle raging within her friend as he attempted to frame a tactful reply, but his answer astonished even her.

"It was, your grace, until I fell in love. Then I wished for a way to be worthy of my ladylove, whose station seemed as far removed from mine as the sun or the stars. You hold it within your power to make me worthy of her."

"Mere rank does not render a lover pleasing according to the laws of courtly love," Eleanor reproved.

"But I would do more than worship this woman, your grace. I would wed her."

Instantly there were speculative murmurs about the lady's identity. Ysabeau herself was curious, wondering if Philippe's many secretive trips into town had been visits to one of the many houses where members of the court dwelled, for there was not enough room in Angers Castle for all. She smiled, sincerely glad for her friend, thinking that he would now have someone for himself and could put aside his bitterness at Eleanor's fickle patronage.

She entirely missed the look of concern directed at her by Matilde, after she had exchanged a meaningful glance at Rene.

Eleanor's laugh of pleasure rang out in the clear spring air. "*Eh bien.* Granted, although I confess I am consumed with a desire to discover the name of the woman who has stolen your heart from me. But I know that you cannot divulge it until she accepts you.

"Now, as to your ennoblement, a baron must have lands, *bien sûr*. One wonders if you are privy to our correspondence, Philippe, for we were informed only this morning by our seneschal at Poitiers that the Baron de Melle has died, leaving no issue and a wife who wishes only for the peace of Fontevrault."

"Oh, he left issue, your grace, though born on the wrong side of the blanket. I am the natural son of the Baron de Melle and the daughter of one of his tenants." He made his declaration proudly, almost daring any to decry his birth.

"It would not be the first time a bastard achieved high station, Philippe. Only remember my lord's great-grandsire, who first conquered England." Eleanor, too, looked at those who ringed her. With this remark, Eleanor made a slur on Philippe de Melle's parentage equivalent to casting aspersions on Henry's proud ancestry. "Very well, we will grant you the barony of Melle, and a suitable ceremony will be conducted as soon as possible. Meanwhile, it is only fitting that you become a knight, to be worthy of defending your barony and the duchess to whom you owe fealty."

Philippe groaned good-naturedly, for he had been plucking tunes and composing *chansons* while youths of the nobility had been learning swordplay and tilting at the quintain.

"I will do my humble best to be fit to serve you and my lady," he answered, bowing from the waist while still mounted.

Chapter Sixteen

Ysabeau sat on the grass under the concealing branches of a willow in the castle pleasance, enjoying the warmth of a June afternoon. The air was filled with the drone of bees and the scent of lilies growing riotously thick in a bed against the castle wall nearby. Ami, his head in her lap, dozed lightly, a blissful expression on his face as she occasionally scratched behind his ears.

She had escaped the stuffy atmosphere of the duchess' bower, pleading a headache, which had diminished as soon as she had gotten away from the chattering gossip of the ladies-in-waiting. The primary topic was, of course, the identity of the mysterious ladylove of the Baron de Melle.

The ceremony had been this morning. Philippe, clad in a fox-trimmed dalmatic of scarlet silk, had put his hands within those of the heavily pregnant duchess and had sworn himself her vassal with these words:

"Your grace, I swear to keep faith and loyalty to you against all others, and promise to guard your rights with all my strength."

Eleanor, in turn, had replied, "We do promise to you, vassal, Philippe de Melle, that we and our heirs will guarantee to you the lands held of us, to you and your heirs against all others, and we swear to guard your rights with all our strength."

The Duchess had then bent and kissed Philippe on the mouth. The new baron arose, and laying his hand on a gold-encrusted reliquary containing St. Radegonde's finger-bone, swore the oath of fealty: "In the name of the Holy Trinity and in reverence of this sacred relic, I, Philippe de Melle, swear that I will truly keep the promise which I have made, and will always remain faithful to Eleanor, Duchess of Aquitaine and Normandy, and Countess of Anjou."

Then Eleanor's seneschal had stepped forward, giving Philippe a lance, symbolizing transfer of the fief, and the witnesses had cheered. The flushed and happy Philippe had been borne away, the guest of honor at the midday meal, invited to sit at the high table next to Eleanor herself.

It had been a lovely ceremony, though lengthy, and now, alone with her thoughts, Ysabeau again wished her friend good fortune in his quest for love. She hoped he did not equate noble status with happiness, though; in her months with the duchess she had seen that the humblest peasant in his cottage had more potential for peace and contentment than did one of the nobles at court, where romantic intrigue and machinations were rife. She had many admirers now, but certainly she had not found happiness in playing the dazzling breaker of hearts. Only her heart had been truly broken.

It had been half a year since she had seen Simon de Winslade, and in all that time she had heard no word. Almost against her will, she prayed every day for his safety, while damning him for rejecting her.

She would send him no letter—not she! It reminded her too cruelly of the way Jean had ignored her messages. If only she could forget him as easily as she had Jean; getting over her infatuation with her girlhood friend had taken relatively little time, and only a few tears and painful memories. It was nothing, compared to the near-constant ache she carried within her breast now, a reminder of the love that would not fade for the handsome Norman baron.

"I thought I'd find you here," said a friendly voice, interrupting her sad reverie. "I hope you weren't thinking of me, my beautiful friend, with such a *triste* expression."

Ysabeau looked up to see Philippe bent over, parting the hanging fronds of the willow to peer into her hidden retreat. He was dressed in mail, and had pushed back his metal coif, revealing a forehead damp with sweat. The mastiff had come to full alertness and was now on his feet, tail held stiffly out in back of him. He glanced back at Ysabeau as if to see what she wanted him to do, but receiving no order, he dropped back to his haunches and contented himself with watching Philippe.

"I've just come from the tilting field, where Sieur André is doing his best to kill me," he announced ruefully, rubbing his shin. Sieur André was the castle's master-at-arms, and was in charge of squires' training as they strove to become knights. "He was able to splinter my lance and unhorse me, but I managed to drag my broken body over here, knowing you would give me consolation. Just the sight of you eases the agony that racks my body, I swear by the Virgin." He leaned over to pluck an errant lock of hair that had curled around her throat, for Ysabeau had removed her barbette and veil and unbraided her thick brown tresses to feel the play of the gentle summer breeze.

"Why, thank you, Philippe, for the flattery, though perhaps I should say, 'thank you, my lord.' " She smiled up at him, eyes shaded against the intruding rays of sunlight that now stole beneath the overhanging willow branches.

He dropped to his knees so that their eyes were nearly at the same level, letting the curtain of branches fall behind him. The foliage created a private green world that isolated them together. "I wish you *would* call me 'my lord,' Lady Ysabeau—that is, I would wish to be your lord in all truth. I love you."

For a moment she could only gape at him, open-mouthed. Suddenly it was all clear—the gleaming, speculative glances leveled at her by the ladies of the court, and the whispers ever since Philippe had confessed he had a secret love.

"Philippe, you must be joking," she managed to say at last.

His face fell, and he dropped his eyes.

"I knew it. I knew you would not consider me worthy."

"*Non, non, mon ami*, I beg you to believe it is not that!" she cried, immediately crouching at his side and touching his averted chin, so that he turned to face her, his gray eyes clouded with pain. "I have no regard for these things. When I came to court I felt that my heart was irretrievably lost to a peasant boy I had grown up with. It is merely that it would not be fair to you . . . I cannot . . ." She did not want to tell him how much she still cared for Simon, did not want to put a name to the feeling that raged within her and gave her no peace.

"If you hesitate because you're in love with Simon de Winslade, be easy on that score. I have known it for a long time."

She did not know what to say; denial seemed impossible, since the truth was so obvious to him. She nodded mutely.

"I also know you haven't heard from him since he left, and I can see how you grieve. *I* would not make you unhappy, my dear lady. I would only comfort you, love you, treasure you."

How much she wanted to seize that love, and hold it till her pain receded, knowing that as Philippe's wife she could ignore this courtly love nonsense, could become a virtuous matron. Perhaps they would even go to Melle and forget about court life altogether, creating a perfect paradise in his fief. It sounded peaceful, serene . . . She could give Philippe babes and make them her world, and try never to remember the man who had taught her ecstasy—and heartbreak.

But wasn't it wrong to give yourself to a man who adored you, when you could never give him your heart? Never mind that most marriages among the nobility had nothing to do with love, that as her father's heiress she could expect to be given to a noble acceptable to the duke and duchess, someone who had served Henry in battle well, perhaps. She would be the payment, herself and Ré.

But love was a higher law than feudal custom, an inner voice argued.

She was on the point of replying, when she heard Matilde's voice calling, "Ysabeau! Ysabeau! Where are you? There's someone here to talk to you."

Simon. It *had* to be Simon, her heart chorused joyfully as she dashed from under the willow frond, leaving Philippe to follow more slowly, groaning with soreness as he struggled back to his feet. *Mon Dieu*, what if Simon thought that she and Philippe . . .

But it was not Simon de Winslade. A knight in mail stood next to Matilde. His expression was somber. He was not of Eleanor's retinue, and yet his face was vaguely familiar to her. He was from Ré, one of the few knights in her father's service!

"Sieur Reynald!" she said, her heart pounding, her mouth suddenly dry.

"Yes, Lady Ysabeau. It is kind of you to remember me. You were a mere slip of a girl when you left, and now look at you—a fine, beautiful lady of the court. My lord, your father would have been so proud . . ." He choked on his words, his eyes welling up with tears as he looked at her.

"My father . . ."

"My lady, it is my painful duty to inform you that the Count is dead. He died of a fever that consumed him in one day; by nightfall he was dead. There was no time to bring you to his side, though his last thoughts were of you. You are now the Comtesse de Ré, my Lady Ysabeau."

Chapter Seventeen

"Why so melancholy, Simon? I invited you to celebrate, not to show a long face," drawled Henry, lounging comfortably in his tent with his head cushioned in the lap of his whore. "I'd certainly call the relief of Wallingford Castle without the loss of a man cause for cheer, or don't you agree?"

Simon was startled, and ceased his unfocused staring into the firelight to meet his duke's curious gaze.

"I'm sorry, your grace, I didn't mean to dampen the mood. I was just woolgathering, I guess."

"Perhaps you're sorry there wasn't an opportunity to bash heads. A lot of my barons were spoiling for a fight. That's understandable. I was tempted to splash on across the Thames and put an end to a few of Stephen's loud braggarts, myself,'' admitted Henry, speaking to Simon but gazing up appreciatively into the voluptuous, half-exposed breasts of the blowsy young camp follower who'd been his bedmate ever since they first began their campaign in the west. He chuckled as the young woman greedily guzzled the wine in the golden goblet, then tilted the cup so that a few drops went into his mouth, spilling over on his cheek, which he wiped carelessly on the sleeve of his bedgown.

''No, my lord, I wasn't sorry to see the siege of Crowmarsh end peaceably. We've certainly seen plenty of action this summer—taking Tutbury and Warwick, besieging Nottingham—certainly enough for even the bloodthirstiest of Your Grace's followers.'' Simon smiled with the recollection of the successes of the campaign. He leaned back amidst a pile of cushions, propping one long leg against the other knee, and took a deep draught of his wine.

''Then what is it? D'you object to Hikenai?'' Henry pursued, gesturing to the buxom brunette. ''If you want to play at dice, or just talk, I can send her on to bed—which she'll keep warm for me.'' He spoke in Norman French, which the English wench could not follow as yet, though she obviously heard her name being mentioned.

''Ah, perhaps you're in need of a little of the kind of comfort my Hikenai provides,'' Henry said, as if he'd seized on the only logical explanation for his vassal's quietness. ''Why don't I send her to get one of her friends for you?''

Simon had to laugh at Henry's enthusiasm. ''*Non*, my liege, though mayhap I'll seek a wench out later."

"Ah, so you *do* need a woman. That's what's eating you." Henry was triumphantly smug in his diagnosis. "Well, a good roll in the hay will do wonders for that melancholy, I promise you. I doubt you'll find any as delicious as this one, though," he continued, reaching up to pat the young whore's painted cheek. "Did I tell you she's carrying my child already?"

"No, my lord." Simon was not sure what to say, though Henry was patently proud of his virility.

"My Duchess is due to give me an heir within a month and I've already sown at least one bastard in England. Shall I call them by the same name, d'you think?"

"It . . . might lead to confusion, my lord, should you take the child into your household later."

"Yes, I suppose so. Of course I'll take the child—Eleanor will understand. She loves me," he confided with wine-induced candor. "You don't suppose this *fille de joie* could provide the future for my child that I can, do you? I can see the boy now, a prince of the Church someday." He flung his brawny arms wide, causing Hikenai to spill the wine down the deep valley between her plump breasts.

Henry guffawed as the ruby droplets lay there, glistening invitingly, then raised up and licked the wet skin. The girl giggled huskily as he forced her backward and pulled her bodice down farther so as not to miss a drop.

"Your grace, I'll return another time. . . ."

"Nonsense!" roared the Duke, still laughing, struggling upright again. "You'll not weasel out of the question that easily. So—what's her name?"

"What?" Simon stood stock-still at the entrance to the rude dwelling commandeered for the night. It was dark and small, and smelled like the odorous peasant who had been put out of it, but it was a damn sight better than what most of the rest of the nobles in Henry's train had. If Simon was lucky, his dry spot in the byre was still being guarded by Geoffrey, his squire.

"What's her name, I said. The woman who's got you so mesmerized that you sound only lukewarm about a frolic with a winsome camp follower. I've seen that faraway look in your eyes a lot lately. God's eyeteeth, man . . . out with it!"

Simon made a gesture of acquiescence to the ducal will as Henry bade the wench excuse them for awhile, then settled back with a refill of his goblet.

"I met a lady in Poitiers, your grace. She's one of your duchess' maids-of-honor, actually . . ."

"I'll wager it's that petite, luscious little armful they call *La Maraise*," Henry guessed, then gave a crow of laughter when he saw he was correct. "I don't blame you a bit, Simon. If she weren't so close to my wife I'd want her myself. A pretty little wench, to be sure. Those eyes! A man could get lost in them. And that hair . . . does it really reach down to her—but never mind, tell me what happened between you two."

Simon soon gave an edited account, from their first clash in the garden to his failure to receive any answer to his message.

"I don't know if she ever even got my letter," Simon concluded with a preoccupied frown. "Anything could have happened to the boy I paid to take it. Likely he pocketed my coin and went on his merry way."

"He never came back to claim the rest of the fee? He was to be paid whether she replied favorably or not?" Henry was amazingly tenacious about details even when in his cups.

Simon nodded. "Only half-paid. But the priest who was to give him the second installment has not seen him around Barfleur since we left."

"These are troubled times, *mon ami*," Henry said. "A man's throat can be cut if another merely covets his cloak. That's the sort of thing I'll put an end to when I'm king." Then he shook his head and went on. "Well, I can see you'll be no earthly good until you've settled your mind about Ysabeau de Ré," Henry said, clapping Simon on the back. "I can't spare you yet, but as soon as this treaty is settled, I want you to carry a message to my wife. Eleanor and the court are at Angers now, did you know? Perhaps that's how your *billet-doux* went astray. By then you can bring news of my newborn son to me, *hein*?"

As Simon had feared, however, the negotiations which began after the truce at Wallingford soon occupied Henry and his nobles' attention fully, as did the antics of King Stephen's son, Eustace.

Eustace had been enraged by what he saw as

the spineless actions of his father, who seemed to be giving away his heir's future crown before Eustace's very eyes. Eustace had a temper tantrum, pillaging Suffolk during the first part of August.

Not even sacrilege was too heinous a crime for Eustace. He and his retinue had stopped at the abbey of Bury St. Edmunds, and though he was royally treated by the good abbot, he demanded tribute to help pay for his continued rebellion. This was refused him, just as he and his parasitic cronies sat down to feast on stewed eels, Eustace's favorite dish.

Eustace had grown livid, then reddish purple with anger; his eyes bulged and his face became cyanotic as he choked to death in front of all assembled. A dire judgment of God, the monks pronounced piously, on any who dared behave as Eustace had done.

With Eustace died any reason for Stephen's continued resistance. His younger son, William, had no interest in being king; Stephen's wife was dead, and Stephen was too old and tired to think of producing any more heirs.

"Ride for Angers, Simon," Duke Henry told him jubilantly. "Tell my Duchess she'll soon be a queen, and take care of your own business while you're there. But be quick about it! No doubt Eleanor will want you to bring the news of my heir back with you, and there'll be much to do here to get Stephen to stop dithering about, or I miss my guess."

Chapter Eighteen

Simon handed his destrier over to a lackey in the inner bailey. He hurried to the quarters assigned him by the seneschal, calling for a bath as he strode down the corridor. He looked for Ysabeau everywhere, expecting that she might have heard word of his arrival. He was eager to see her, but really hoped to get the stink and grime of travel washed away and be dressed in clean, presentable clothing before he met her.

"What news of Duchess Eleanor?" he asked the serving wench who was scrubbing his back. His thoughts were so focused on Ysabeau that he hadn't even noticed if the girl was comely or ugly. What a change from my arrival at Poitiers last year, he chuckled to himself. Ysabeau, what magic you have wrought! He smiled even before he heard the serving girl's excited answer.

"My lord, she was delivered of a son on the seventeenth day of August."

"God be thanked!" he said sincerely. "I will need to see the duchess today, if at all possible. I carry news from her lord, for her ears alone."

As soon as Simon was bathed and dressed, with his hair still hanging in damp, tawny-gold strands, he was directed to the duchess' bower.

Surely Ysabeau will be with her, he thought, as he was led down the corridor. I will assess her mood when our eyes meet, and though no words may be spoken, we will meet later as if by accident. He grinned as his heartbeat accelerated in anticipation.

Eleanor's chamber was vast and luxurious, laid with thick Oriental carpets rather than the usual malodorous, musty rushes present in most castles, Simon noted as he was ushered into the Duchess' presence. Though Eleanor, comfortably esconced in the middle of the huge bed and wearing a rich bedgown of cloth of gold, was the central figure of the room, Simon's eyes made a quick survey of her attendants as he knelt respectfully by the bedside. Ysabeau was not there.

"Your grace," he murmured. "I congratulate you on the birth of a son."

Eleanor was openly jubilant. "I wish I could see Henry's face when you tell him, my Lord Simon. I'm glad now we hadn't already sent a messenger—we did have some concern, at first, for the babe seemed so frail, so we did not send word at once. But now he seems to be coming along nicely, don't you agree?" At a regal gesture, the nurse handed her a swaddled bundle from a richly carved, padded cradle on the other side of the wide bed. From within the bundle issued a fretful whimper.

"There, there, *mon petit, soyez tranquille*," cooed Eleanor, then held the babe so that Simon could see Henry's heir.

The newborn still seemed rather pale and wan, thought Simon, who, though he was no expert on babies, recalled his own son's ruddy healthiness. But perhaps, he reasoned, Aimery had been pale like this in his first fortnight—Simon had barely seen him in the midst of his wild grief over Rohese's death.

"His Grace will be very happy," Simon said with a smile.

"I have named him William," Eleanor went on proudly, "not only because it is the traditional name of the Dukes of Aquitaine, but for Henry's great-grandfather, who conquered the island my lord is busy with now."

"An auspicious choice."

"And do you bring good tidings from England, Simon? I hear that you do." Eleanor was suddenly a regal duchess again, handing the babe back to his nurse and ignoring the pitiful bleating as he was carried off to be fed.

"Yes, your grace. You may have already received word of our coming to the aid of Wallingford by besieging Stephen's neighboring castle at Crowmarsh, across the Thames, which is very narrow at that point. Your lord and Stephen had a conversation in full view of both armies, but out of our earshot, which resulted in a truce."

Eleanor nodded, to encourage him to go on.

"My news, however, is that on the same day on which your grace was delivered of a son, Stephen's son and heir, Eustace, choked to death over supper at the abbey of Bury St. Edmunds. 'A surfeit of eels,' is reported to be the cause of his demise, though the devout, of course, say it was because of his godless behavior."

If Eleanor was triumphant before, she was exultant now. "Henry *will* be King—it's obvious God wills it!"

"And you will make a lovely queen, Your grace," Simon returned dryly, grinning at her infectious confidence.

"Why, thank you, Simon, you rascal," she said in that attractive, husky voice, and Simon was again shown the powerful sensual appeal that made this woman a magnet for troubadours and princes alike.

"What now? When will my lord at last settle these affairs, so he can come home to see his son?"

"As to that, Your Grace, I cannot say. Stephen's excuse for resistance is over, but he seldom does anything quickly and decisively. He may dawdle for weeks now, listening to everyone's ideas, changing his mind once a day before he formalizes the agreement. For this reason, it is a critical time. Henry dares not leave England now."

"No, of course not." Eleanor's mouth was set in a petulant line and she made a gesture of irritation. "Oh well, we've waited too long to chance losing all now." She stared out the wide oriel window, suddenly very distant. "It was good of you to bring me this news, Simon."

"My pleasure is to serve you, my Duchess, but I asked to come for my own reasons also. Your grace, I have not seen your lady-in-waiting, Ysabeau de Ré, about the chateau since my arrival. Is she still with you?"

Eleanor turned back to him, her attention fully focused on the young baron. "Ysabeau was summoned home suddenly last month with the news that her father, the *Comte*, had died. As his only child, she had a great many matters to settle on the island. I'm not sure when she will rejoin us."

Simon's face drained of color, thinking of Ysabeau suddenly alone in the world. He would have given anything in the world to have been there to comfort her. Poor, lovely girl!

"Is she . . . is she all right? There are many dangers that can beset a young noblewoman alone—" He feared he was making a great fool of himself, in his anxiety.

"Oh, Simon, you great ninny! Of course, I know that. Was I not nearly kidnapped myself, on the way home to Aquitaine? Ysabeau's vassals are there to guard her, and I sent several of my own, as well. No one will seize her and marry her against her will." For a moment, Eleanor's heart twisted in envy; for all his love and passion for her, Henry was still ruled first and foremost by ambition. She doubted he would have joined her so fast after her divorce from Louis if *her* dowry had been only a humble island such as Ré.

"I'm sorry, I should have known you would not let her go without ample protection," Simon apologized humbly. "Perhaps I could speak to Matlide de St. Gilles, who shares a room with Ysabeau? I have a message to leave."

"Simon, she took Matilde with her," Eleanor answered with a gesture of regret.

"I also share the room with Ysabeau and Matilde," a voice purred from the shadows behind Simon. "Surely you could entrust the message to me."

Simon turned to see a statuesque blond standing behind him. He studied the icy beauty for a moment, silent while he attempted to recall her name.

"It's Blanche de Limousin," she said cooly, startling him with her apparent perceptiveness.

"Ah, yes, of course." He stared at her openly. A flush of irritation stained her perfect cheekbones. The woman was much taller than Ysabeau, nearly at eye level with him. She was dressed in a gown of pale aqua that would have been lost against Ysabeau's dark features. But on Blanche, the pastel tone harmonized with her wintry perfection. Not a woman to warm one on a cold winter night.

"Might we be excused, Your Grace?" he asked Eleanor.

"Of course," she replied immediately.

He then stepped into the corridor with Blanche, conscious of a vague sense of uneasiness. Be careful, Simon, he told himself, or your feelings will show and the woman won't do you any favors. Briefly, it occurred to him that tall blonds used to be just his type. But not this one, who seemed somehow arid and charmless next to the memory of the petite Ysabeau!

Blanche inclined her head toward him. "It has been long since you were at court, my Lord Simon. We have missed you." She smiled a dazzling smile and moved a step closer to the tall baron, showing even, pearly teeth between her full lips.

"Yes. Henry has kept me rather busy since I left Poitiers. I wanted to return ere this, but it simply wasn't possible."

"Ah, affairs of state are indeed more pressing than those of court. But court has been so tedious since you left," she sighed, and her breast brushed his arm, which had been outstretched as he leaned against the wall. "Dare I hope you missed us?" Her tongue snaked out to lick her underlip. Her pale blue eyes gleamed.

"*Bien sûr*, my Lady Blanche. Who would not miss the lovely flowers of Aquitaine when one is mired in the muck of battle?" he returned lightly, forcing himself not to jerk back his arm too quickly lest he betray his distaste for her overt maneuvering. "But I missed one lady in particular, as I indicated in there," he said, jerking his head toward the Duchess' bower. "I wonder if you would be kind enough to deliver this small casket to her, together with a letter which I shall go and write now, and have brought to your room?"

"I have said I would," she responded impassively. However, she could not hide her interest as he drew a small silver box from a pouch at his belt.

If he noticed her curiosity, he made no

move to satisfy it. "I sent her a messenger earlier in the year, but I had no answer. Possibly something happened to the youth along the way—I don't know. I'd just like to be sure this reaches her safely."

A smug smile curved the tall woman's lips. "Oh, you may be sure it will get to its rightful destination."

Suddenly the uneasiness Simon had felt earlier returned, stronger now. "Oh, I'm sure I shouldn't trouble you with such a task. If you'll just send for the tiring-woman who assists you, I'll have her take care of this."

But it was too late. "As to that, Ysabeau's taken her along to Ré, too," Blanche replied, unable to conceal the flash of irritation she felt at having to share a tiring-woman with several other ladies, when Blanche had bullied Marie into giving her priority attention. "No, do not fear, I'll take care of this for you"—she was once again all sweetness and light—"and of anything else you might need during your stay here. One hopes you can remain until you are thoroughly rested." Her eyes roamed across the Norman's powerfully built form, giving him her most seductive smile. *Mon Dieu*, she thought, the man was a pleasure to look at, even if he had thrown away his heart on the wrong woman. She'd correct that.

Philippe was surprised to receive a summons that evening from Blanche. The woman had never deigned to notice his existence, except to applaud desultorily at his songs and accord him routine civility when they met in the hall. He would have been amazed, indeed, had he known how she had paced the floor since she first started looking for him this afternoon. She had been unable to find him, for he had been in the city.

It was past supper now as he made his way to the room Blanche occupied alone at present. He wondered briefly if Ysabeau's roommate had decided he was an interesting fellow now that he was of the nobility. Perhaps she'd decided to seduce him . . . not likely, he decided. He sensed the woman was incurably frigid, and the fact that she had never had a serious liaison, that is, one that went beyond the posturing of courtly love, would seem to support his theory.

His knock was answered before he had time to drop his hand to his side.

"Ah, Philippe!" she cooed, ushering him in with a graceful gesture and a swirl of aqua silk. "I thought we should have a talk." She indicated a comfortable, padded chair which he took, but she continued walking restlessly around, reminding him of a caged tigress. She stopped suddenly and faced him.

"You are in love with Ysabeau de Ré, is it not so?"

He was startled that his feelings had grown so apparent, but saw no use in denying it.

"Yes, I am."

"And you would not care to see her wed to another?"

"No, I would not. What are you getting at, Lady Blanche?"

"Simon de Winslade is here, sniffing about for her."

"I see," he said as his heart gave a sickening lurch. De Winslade's absence from court had given him hope that he might coax the lovely Ysabeau into caring for him, once she recovered from her loss. He watched as Blanche pulled a gold chain from beneath the low neckline of her gown and began to play with the large, rectangularly cut emerald dangling there. He had never noticed her wearing the jewel before; the chain's delicate workmanship appeared Saxon to his eye.

"I intercepted this bauble, and a letter he left for her in which he declares his passion for your ladylove. Perhaps you would like to deliver it? Ah, I see you would not. I would advise you to act quickly to secure your little marsh bird if you do not want to see her—and her fief—joined to that Norman."

"My interest in Ysabeau has nothing to do with her lands, only in the lady herself. I love her," he protested with righteous indignation.

"Certainly you do, my dear Lord de Melle—which is good, since I hear Ré is all sand and seagulls."

"What if Simon de Winslade is heading for Ré also?"

She gave a short laugh. "Fortunately for you, Philippe, he can't, for he must return to Duke Henry's side to help him finish snatching the English throne. That gives you precious time to make her your wife before he's free to return for her. Wouldn't you like to see her fat with your babe by the time the two see each other again?"

Her cynical, earthy comment disgusted

him.

"What I want to know is, what are you getting out of all this, Blanche? I know you're not doing it out of friendship for me," he said cooly.

"Why, Philippe, I have always cherished your friendship. I thought you felt the same," she pouted, then laughed, realizing he could see through her. "I? I am getting a clear path to Simon de Winslade, my little lordling. I want him." Her eyes shone greedily.

"Are you sure you'd know what to do with him if you got him?"

For a moment, he thought she would strike him, but then she lowered her head and turned her back to him stiffly. Her voice was hard and icy. "Don't make me sorry that I've helped you, you little upstart minstrel. I'm sure you're not eager for *La Maraise* to catch wind of your clandestine meetings and religious leanings. She seems to attend Mass rather faithfully."

Her words had their intended effect, for Philippe's face drained of color. "Your pardon, Lady Blanche," he said stiffly. "I am most grateful, indeed, for your help."

Philippe lost little time leaving Blanche's room and returning to his own quarters to pack his belongings for the journey to the Île de Ré.

He had offered to accompany Ysabeau to the island, but she had wanted to be alone, to see to her father's obsequies. Though he had promised not to bring up the subject of his marriage proposal, Ysabeau had been politely adamant. "I would feel pressured to decide, don't you see, just by your patient presence," she had said, and of course he could not persist. He had meant to allow her a longer time, but he could not afford to now that he knew the Norman was still interested. She'd been away a month, and by the time he arrived on her little island, she would welcome a face from court . . . as well as someone who was eager to let her cast the responsibilities of governing the island fief on his capable masculine shoulders. He would win her heart before Simon de Winslade ever had a chance to return, though it seemed that the English succession would be settled very soon now.

He was appreciative of the assistance Blanche de Limousin had given, for by not being in the castle today he had nearly missed knowing of Simon de Winslade's presence. But he doubted if making Ysabeau unavailable would automatically render Simon Blanche's plaything. No one who was attracted by Ysabeau's petite loveliness and ingenuousness could be equally charmed by the blond woman's icy artifices. But he thanked her silently for mentioning the jewel she had stolen, the one she now proudly flaunted about her neck. That would provide him with a wedge to drive between Ysabeau and her Norman baron.

Ah, he could just imagine Ysabeau as his wife. And on their wedding night he would explain all about the group to which he belonged, and their unusual beliefs; no doubt, soon she would convert and become one of them, if only for love of him. She would soon forget that Norman scoundrel who had seduced her. The thought made him grind his teeth in helpless jealousy, but he was determined that the loss of her virginity need not affect his love for her. After all, had he not been taught that such things did not matter to those who believed as he did?

Chapter Nineteen

Ysabeau loved to walk along the shore just at dawn, when the mists began to be pierced by the early morning sunlight and the gulls took off to begin their wheeling, day-long quest for food, filling the air with their raucous cries.

She savored her solitude as she padded along the pebbly beach just at the waterline, carrying her shoes, and the cool shock as each wavelet met her bare feet. Only Ami accompanied her on these walks, which was as she preferred. Matilde and Rene were still abed, and she needed to be alone with her thoughts, to consider the changes that had taken place in her life, and to decide what to do with herself.

Her father, Martin, le Comte de Ré, had been laid to rest in the vault of the Romanesque church just outside the crumbling walls of the château. His tomb was next to that of his wife,

Ysabeau's mother, who had died so many years before. Ysabeau was now *la Comtesse*, and these people were her people.

Life would go on much as before for the people of the tiny Île de Ré. Her peasants would tend her olive groves and orchards, and harvest the salt from the marshes, giving her her portion and taking theirs without striving for more. They were a good people; she had seen that from the lack of change evident since the fief had become hers. They cared little for events on the mainland. All they wanted was that life should go on undisturbed as it had for decades.

She wanted peace for them, too, but knew she could not ensure it alone. Ré needed a good *seigneur*. Alone, she was at the mercy of any unscrupulous scoundrel who might force her to marry him, then squander the island's bounty and bring turmoil to its shores. Remaining husbandless was a luxury she, as an heiress, could not afford.

Perhaps she should accept Philippe's proposal, she told herself. But she had been glad when her father's death gave her an excuse to postpone a decision. Wasn't that a sign he was wrong for her?

She had not wept more than once since coming to Ré. It was not that she had not loved her father, but for most of her life he had been a distant figure, away on crusade with King Louis and his then-Queen, Eleanor. They had loved one another, but never quite achieved the closeness Ysabeau longed for.

Suddenly, Ami began to bark, splashing through a little pool left stranded by the tides and disappearing around a tall rock. He's probably found a gull and is fighting him for possession of a dead fish, mused Ysabeau. She was startled when no gull, but Philippe de Melle materialized from around the black boulder.

"Ysabeau, your dog found me before I could find you, but he doesn't seem to remember me," Philippe said, for the huge mastiff was still barking at him.

"Silly Ami, it's Philippe!" she laughed, snapping her fingers so that the big dog trotted back to her side, but continued to watch the young man warily. "Philippe, what are you doing here? I was just thinking about you."

His sharp features broke into a grin. "Now that, my lady, is more than I dared hoped for! You see, I just couldn't stay away any longer. I know you asked me not to come, but it's been awhile, and I missed you . . . please let me stay? I will say nothing you are not ready to hear." He was so endearing, like a little boy who was afraid he'd be denied a sweetmeat, that she didn't have the heart to send him back.

"All right. I'm ready for some company from court. I was wondering what was happening there, though I did have word of Eleanor's son. What else is new?" Tacitly, they agreed to keep strolling at the water's edge, which the rising sun had begun to illuminate in sparkling splendor as the mist disappeared.

"The news from England is good," Philippe ventured, stealing a glance at her beautiful profile, her dark brown hair streaming loose in the breeze, dotted with sea spray. He had to speak louder to be heard over the waves, for the tide was coming in. "King Stephen's son, Eustace, died in a fit of temper, choking to death while trying to defraud some abbot. Without an heir, Stephen's fight is useless. They say there will soon be peace."

"I am glad. The Duchess must miss Henry, and long to show off their son to him."

"Yes . . ." Philippe was silent after that, stopping every now and then to throw a shell out into the blue-green water.

"Who brought this news?" she asked carefully.

"Simon de Winslade—Henry seems to like using him as a messenger boy." He studied her, and did not miss the sudden pallor in her glowing, sun-kissed complexion.

"And how is he?" she forced herself to ask casually, but not daring to meet Philippe's eyes.

Philippe stopped her and turned her to face him. "Ysabeau, I think you should know—after he left, Blanche de Limousin was sporting a rather large emerald on a gold chain of Saxon workmanship. She said de Winslade gave it to her."

Ysabeau's hands tightened convulsively at her sides. She felt as if she had been struck in the stomach, as if she needed to gasp for air, then curl up in the sand and sob. "Indeed. Well, she always did lust after that man. I'm sure she gave him his money's worth."

She made getting a room ready for him an excuse to return to the château as soon as possible, her joy of the morning vanished. She left him in the great hall to break his fast while she climbed the winding tower stairs to ready his chamber.

It was here that Marie found her, shaking out bed linen onto the goosedown mattress and sobbing.

"My lady, why are you doing this? This is servants' work—oh, my dear, what is it?" the plump woman cried, enfolding her in her arms.

The story was out in a few moments, between pauses to blow her nose.

"I *thought* the sparkle had gone from your eyes after we left Poitiers, and my Lord de Winslade the reason. I must say I'm surprised. I thought the English lord had a good heart in him, though he clearly was—how shall I say it—used to getting his way with women. I can't believe he would substitute that cold fish, Blanche, for you, my lady," Marie said loyally.

"Nor I," said a voice from the doorway, and the two looked up to see a sleepy-eyed Matilde, chewing on a crust of bread. "I just came from the hall. What's Philippe doing here? You told him you didn't want him to come, didn't you?"

"Yes," Ysabeau admitted, "but now I'm glad he's here. I haven't told him yet, but I think I will marry him, Matilde."

She'd decided it as she spoke the words. She was tired of pain. She would marry Philippe, and put the bonds of marriage forever between her and the love that had brought her only misery after such short-lived pleasure.

Marie dropped the hour candle she had moved to dust off the nightstand; it fell with a heavy thud in the silence that had suddenly filled the room.

At last Marie found her voice. "You can't be serious! One doesn't marry the first man who asks you, merely because another man disappoints you. And anyway, I don't believe the tale about Blanche and that necklace."

"Don't you? I do," said Ysabeau bitterly, her back to both of them, staring out the unshuttered window which looked over the bay. Her back was very erect, her voice bleak.

"A man like that wouldn't waste his time on her, much less his coin. She has no heart, and she's used to puppet-men, not a real man. She probably bought it for herself, did you ever think of that?"

"You certainly are Simon's defender," observed Ysabeau. "But you always liked him. Face it, my good friend, I trusted him, and he wasn't worth it. Now I want a husband who'll protect my lands and give me babes. Philippe will do those things. Be happy for me," she said and the almost pleading note in her voice wrenched Matilde's heart.

Matilde put her arm around Ysabeau, drawing her close. Her body resisted tensely for a moment, then relaxed. "All right, forget Simon if you will, though I think you're wrong about him and Blanche. But my mind misgives as to this troubadour. Think, just months ago he was nothing more than a freeman who happened to have a talent. Just a music maker. And he's so . . . secretive. No one knows where he's been disappearing to in Angers. And ever since Bernard de Ventador became Eleanor's favorite troubadour, he's been odd, somehow . . ."

"He needs me—he needs someone to love

him," Ysabeau protested. "He'll be fine, once he's sure of me. You'll see."

"But can you love him, Ysa?" asked Matilde doubtfully. "After a man like Simon de Winslade?"

"Yes," she said fiercely, "I must!"

Though Ysabeau had made her decision, there could be no question of an immediate marriage. As Eleanor's lady-in-waiting and ward, she and Philippe had to apply for the Duchess' permission, and wait for the banns to be posted.

Nonetheless, Ysabeau hastened to set her affairs in order on Ré, and turn the administration of the island back over to Sieur Reynald, who had served as her father's seneschal and would now be hers.

It was, thus, mid-September before Ysabeau, Philippe, Matilde and Rene rode back into the bailey of Angers Castle, accompanied by their retainers.

Philippe assisted Ysabeau to dismount, catching her about the waist and holding her there for a moment longer than was necessary, his touch proud and possessive. His eyes left hers to scan the courtyard and see if any noted his new closeness to the most beautiful woman in Eleanor's court.

Ysabeau had been right about Philippe. Once she accepted his suit, he became a new man, no longer the bitter, cynical, moody fellow he had been of late. He was now confident and assertive, his step almost a strut. He was tenderly considerate with her, anticipating her needs, never forcing his affection on her. He had kissed her only twice, and both times his lips were cool and dry, and stirred her not at all. He had attempted no further intimacy.

"You will ask the duchess about our betrothal today?" he said, darting a challenging glance at Matilde.

Matilde, once his friend, had made no secret of the fact that she disapproved of the match. Her opposition was painful for Ysabeau, but she could not be convinced that the decision to wed Philippe was making Ysabeau happy. "Look at you, *chère*. You have deep shadows under your eyes. Marie tells me you toss and turn all night," she had told Ysabeau several days ago.

"I have had a great deal to contend with lately," Ysabeau had reminded her. "I lost my father, became countess of my fief . . ."

"You were coping wonderfully until Philippe came," Matilde had retorted darkly.

Ysabeau now replied to Philippe's anxious reminder. "I will ask her the first time the opportunity presents itself. I have been away a long time, and Eleanor has been without the help of two of her ladies. I mustn't speak of leaving her the very moment I return."

"But you wouldn't be leaving," Philippe countered. 'You could remain in her service."

They had been through this before, in their discussions on the Île de Ré. Philippe was in no hurry to leave court and assume administration of his barony, thinking of the future only vaguely.

"But you are a baron now," she had protested, surprised that he felt no immediate duty to his lands. "Don't you feel a responsibility to your people? And court is no place to raise our babes. . . ." She had blushed at that, and he had looked strange, as if the thought was startling.

"There will be time enough for that later," he had muttered vaguely.

Chapter Twenty

A few days later, Blanche de Limousin was seated in the window embrasure of the Duchess' bower, stitching tiny pearls onto a pair of Her Grace's riding gloves; she allowed herself to smile secretly as she listened to Ysabeau, Countess of Ré, make her request to marry Baron Philippe de Melle.

It had worked. When she had first encountered Ysabeau, Blanche had made sure she was wearing a low cut *bliaut* that displayed the glowing green jewel prominently against the snowy linen of her undergown.

"It is true, then," Ysabeau had murmured tightly, and Blanche had smirked to see those brown eyes grow liquid with pain.

"An old friend sends you greetings, Ysabeau—Simon de Winslade. Do you remember that handsome fellow? He was such a delight to be with when he was here. Too bad you missed his visit. Anyway, he told me during one of our many long *tête-à-têtes* to be sure to say hello to—as he put it—'that little girl from the marshes.' " She laughed her silvery, high laugh then, and Ysabeau's hand itched to slap her haughty face.

Ysabeau figured that last jab was purely fictitious; Simon was probably too busy enjoying Blanche's lush charms to make such a remark.

Just now, Blanche and Ysabeau were the only ladies attending Eleanor, the others having gone hawking in the crisp early fall sunshine.

"I can't believe you're serious, Ysabeau, dear," Eleanor cried when Ysabeau announced her desire to wed Baron Philippe de Melle. Eleanor's green eyes widened doubtfully. "But I thought that you and Simon de Winslade . . . when he was here, he seemed—"

"Excuse me, your grace, but my Lord de Winslade seems a little too . . . shall we say, distractible?" She darted a look at Blanche, which her rival returned, full of gloating triumph. But Ysabeau had not shot her final bolt. "I find I have reached a stage in life where I require a steady, true love, rather than one who is fickle and goes after the first *putain* who throws herself at him."

Eleanor was aware of the tension in the room, but focused on Ysabeau's earnest, pale face, rather than on Blanche's hate-filled one.

Ysabeau had no way of knowing that Blanche was the more angry at the taunt because it was inaccurate. She could hardly be a whore when she was still a virgin. She had merely stolen the jewel, not earned it.

But Ysabeau was wasting no time enjoying her rival's discomfiture. "Please, your grace, give us your consent. We want so much to marry."

"Do you love him?" Eleanor asked suddenly, watching her charge from under lowered lashes. Ysabeau could not meet her gaze.

"I . . . we . . . *bien sûr*, I do, *ma dame*. He is a good man."

"You are surprised that I mention love in connection with marriage."

Ysabeau nodded.

"Well, it's certainly difficult to find in marriages among my nobles, and the higher one's station, the harder it gets, my dear, what with considerations of lands and heirs carrying so much weight. But without love—or at least, passion—the bonds of marriage soon become intolerably heavy chains. Witness my marriage to that monk, Louis," she finished.

"I see, *ma dame*."

"And you still want to wed him?"

"I do, your grace."

Eleanor was silent for a long moment. She had been so pleased to think that the handsome Norman baron was in love with Ysabeau. She had even thought there was more hope their passion would endure, unburdened by the weight of dynastic ambition that drove Henry and herself. Ah well, apparently Ysabeau had caught him fondling some wench. If only she could convince her that even the best men were seldom perfectly faithful. She never expected Henry to live chastely during the time he was away. If one expected little one was not disappointed.

"All right, Ysabeau. If you're sure, the banns may be cried. But I think it prudent that you wait to be wed until the first of December."

"As long as that, your grace?" Ysabeau cried. "Pardon me, but why?"

Eleanor thought: So that Simon de Winslade may yet have time to dissuade you from the folly of marrying that pleasant, but increasingly strange young man I unfortunately ennobled. But she only said distantly, "Because I think it wise, Ysabeau. These things should not be done hastily, you know. Besides, my lord may be home by then, and would it not be wonderful if he could be present for the ceremony? The betrothal, of course, need not wait so long."

She watched as Ysabeau struggled to smother the rebelliousness she must be feeling. No doubt, Ysabeau felt she could very easily dispense with the honor of Duke Henry's attendance if it meant she could wed sooner.

Ysabeau said only, "As your grace wishes. May I be excused for a little while, to tell Philippe?"

On November 6, King Stephen and Duke Henry met at Winchester and agreed on terms of peace, and then went amicably on to London together, where all the chief nobles of the land were summoned to see the treaty drawn up. It was settled: Stephen was to continue as king as long as he lived, with the crown passing to Henry Plantagenet and his heirs upon Stephen's death. As Stephen was obviously a discouraged, sick man, old beyond his years, the prospect of waiting for Stephen's death discomfited Henry's adherents little. The nobles would all meet at Oxford, a fortnight after Christmas, to individually swear fealty to Henry. With the promise of a young, able, judicious king so close, England could begin to enjoy a long-needed respite of peace.

Leaving Westminster Abbey after signing the document, Henry clapped Simon heartily on the back, laughing. "Good heavens, man, why so glum now? Perhaps you want to be my messenger again. Didn't you get that girl out of your system the last time? Though, come to mention it, you looked no better when you returned than before you left. Ha! You thought I hadn't noticed, hey?"

"Indeed, your grace, you *did* have weighty matters to deal with."

Henry taunted, "She wouldn't give in, eh? You're slipping."

"Not exactly, your grace." Quickly he explained why he had been unable to speak with Ysabeau on his last trip.

"Yes, too bad you had to rush right back. It would've been a good time for you to show up in her bailey. A grieving woman will refuse a man nothing . . . that is to say, you could have been a great comfort to her." Henry could not suppress the twinkle in his blue eyes. "Simon, I want you to do one thing for me, besides carrying the news of the treaty to Eleanor."

"Of course, your grace."

"Send that rascal Bernard de Ventador to

me," Henry commanded. "There's entirely too much gossip about him and the Duchess. I'm going to nip their little affair in the bud."

"Your grace, surely you jest! He's but a troubadour. I saw nothing amiss when I was there." Simon was amazed. He was seeing an entirely new side of Henry Plantagenet—an unreasonably jealous side.

Henry stopped to face Simon, entirely serious in his indignation. "Every crowned head in Europe has heard that he calls her *mos aziman*—my magnet, in that oily Provençal dialect of his. I will not, by God's bloody toenails, begin my reign wearing horns! It's not as if she's never been accused of hanging them on a man before."

"Your grace, I will give him your command, but I urge you to believe there is no cause for concern," Simon said reassuringly.

"You had better be right," Henry growled, completely forgetting that less than half an hour before, he had been making plans with Bishop of Winchester to place Hikenai's bastard in the Church, should the child be male.

"Take my advice, Simon," Henry bellowed in farewell, "sling her over your shoulder if you must, but make sure of her now, before she gets distracted by one of those slippery Gascons. I'll see you at the fealty-swearing six days after the New Year. Tell Eleanor I'll be home directly after that."

"I will, your grace."

Thinking over the conversation, as he left London by the Dover Road, mounted on his great war-horse, Noir, Simon smiled ruefully. Henry was and always would be a law unto himself. Bernard de Ventador would take a trip across the Channel he probably had no desire to take. If he refused, Henry would be sure he was guilty of something, and track him down. If he went, Henry would achieve a separation between Eleanor and the troubadour, and even if de Ventador were allowed to rejoin his patroness, there would be a constraint between them, knowing Henry's eagle eye was trained on them. And all for nothing. There may have been some truth to the rumors about Eleanor of Aquitaine in her youth, but Simon was certain there was nothing to them. Eleanor adored being adored, that's all there was to it. For her to allow de Ventador to make love to her would be as laughable a notion to Eleanor as to him.

Simon wasn't laughing at one of Henry's other remarks, however—the one that reminded him that his beloved was hundreds of leagues away. He could not be at peace until he saw Ysabeau again, and found out why she had never responded to his note and the emerald necklace. He guessed grimly that he could probably lay the blame at Blanche de Limousin's door. He cursed inwardly to think of how his need for haste had forced him to trust a woman whom his every instinct cried out against.

Even now, Simon could envision Ysabeau, surely the desired prize of every sensible man who saw her. And she was now an heiress. He had lands of his own and was not greedy about acquiring more, but all men were not like him. He remembered what smooth talkers those southern Frenchmen were.

"*Ďepêches-toi, Noir!*" He set golden spurs to the destrier's flanks, and the big horse responded, hastening him along to the port city and his ship to France.

Chapter Twenty-one

Even the large chapel of Angers Castle was not judged suitably large or grand enough to hold all who would attend the nuptials of the newly knighted Sieur Philippe, Baron de Melle, and Lady Ysabeau, *Comtesse* de Ré. So it was on the first of December that the lords and ladies of the court gathered in front of the abbey church of Ronceray, all craning their necks to see the bride's approach.

They were not kept waiting long. Before it could be seen, the procession announced its coming with music, a delightful cacophony of shawmns, trumpets, harps, psalteries, nakers, and tambours. Then came the attendants of the bride and groom. Since both were orphans, Rene de Limoges rode beside Philippe; Matilde and—honor of honors—Eleanor of Aquitaine, beside Ysabeau.

The bridal pair were mounted on matching chestnut palfreys caparisoned in green samite, with headstalls of gold.

Ysabeau was beautiful, if pale, dressed in a *bliaut* of cream velvet with sleeves that were loose over her upper arms and tightly fitted at the wrists, embroidered all over with golden suns. Her *camise* of pale peach samite showed at the neckline, which was round except for a slit down the front. Her girdle, a present from the duchess, was of woven gold threads and studded with pearls. Her hair, freed for this occasion from its usual coiled plaits, flowed in rippling waves of brown, confined only by a gold fillet holding in place a short veil of the sheerest silk.

Very few eyes lingered long on the groom, with Ysabeau to gaze at; however, Philippe was handsomely dressed also, from the tips of his pointed shoes of gilded leather to the matching circlet that crowned his crisply curling black locks. He wore a fox-trimmed scarlet mantle, as did Ysabeau, and it was carefully arranged to show the magnificence of his saffron-colored dalmatic. The color did not flatter his swarthy features, but such blissful contentment radiated from him, that no one was unkind enough to say so.

It seemed like a dream to Ysabeau, as she was assisted off her mount, her train settled behind her by Matilde. They were met at the church door by the Bishop of Angers, who led them forward. Ysabeau heard Eleanor's seneschal recite the bride's dowry to the assembled crowd. She possessed little besides the Île de Ré: half a dozen horses, a handful of vassals, a few pieces of jewelry which had belonged to her mother. The silver *deniers* scattered to the poor beyond the assembled nobles made a jingling noise that had no relation to her as she and Philippe entered through the massive carved portals of the church.

They were seated in a place of honor at the front of the dark, candlelit church, while the high nuptial Mass was sung. Then the couple shared a Communion cup, with Ysabeau only coming to full awareness as she watched Philippe accept the jeweled golden chalice and sip from it. Or did he? His mouth made the appropriate movements, but she noted no subsequent motion in his throat as he handed it to Ysabeau. It struck her as odd. And the wine tasted sour to her, or was it because of the bad taste already in her mouth, the taste of fear and uncertainty?

"Let this woman," the bishop was saying, "be amiable as Rachel, wise as Rebecca, faithful as Sarah. Let her be sober through truth, venerable through modesty, and wise through the teaching of Heaven."

The Mass ended with the chanting of the *Agnus Dei*, and Philippe climbed the steps to the gilded, scarlet-hung altar, receiving the Kiss of Peace from the bishop.

Ysabeau knew he would now transfer the kiss to her, and she waited expectantly for the feeling of ecstasy, or at least contentment, to rise within her, but all she felt was the trembling of her bridegroom's arms and the cool brush of his lips.

The guests had maintained a respectful

quiet, if not absolute silence, up to this point, but now they could contain themselves no more. Cheers filled the air as the newlywed couple left the church. A feast that might go on for days awaited them back at the palace.

Ysabeau looked forward to putting a little food in her stomach, hoping it would calm the queasy cold feeling within.

Tonight she would be put to bed with Philippe, she thought, as she walked down the narrow main aisle on his arm, mechanically smiling and acknowledging the many familiar smiling faces. How would it be to lie naked with this man beside her? It had been so long since that passion-filled night in which Simon de Winslade had made her his. Would the fondness she felt for Philippe grow into that same consuming fire, that same compulsion to touch him all over, that same ecstatic striving to get even closer? Of course, he would not look like Simon when the men of the court removed his bedrobe and allowed him to climb into the petal-strewn bed with her; he was not only much different in coloring, but he was shorter, slighter, and lacked the broad shoulders of the warrior, Simon. Would he blow out the hour candle, allowing her a maiden's shyness? If he did, would she stare up in the darkness, imagining it was Simon who touched her there . . . and there . . . a Simon who still loved her and had not deserted her?

And what would Philippe do when he found she was no virgin? He had known of her feelings for Simon, but had he really realized that it meant he would not be her first?

* * *

Simon de Winslade reined in Noir in Angers, noting with some impatience that Geoffrey had stopped to observe a wedding party leaving a church. The Norman baron was eager to reach the castle and Ysabeau as soon as possible, but he acknowledged that they had ridden hard since Prime, and deserved a breather. Besides, there was nothing to be done about the delay now. The wedding party was blocking the narrow street that led back to the castle as they remounted.

Probably some count's plump daughter being sold off with a sizeable dowry to an impoverished, pimply *chevalier*, he thought cynically, looking through the milling crowd to see if he was correct. It was difficult to pick out the bride, as all the women were dressed in their finest velvets and silks.

It was not until she was assisted back onto her gold-trimmed saddle that Simon saw her, and in an instant, an icy ball of fear formed in his stomach. No—it could not be Ysabeau! Then he saw Philippe, the troubadour, being assisted onto a matching palfrey, and his worst nightmare was confirmed. He stared as the procession reformed and the noisy musicians recommenced their playing, his blue eyes gone bleak and wintry.

"*Eh bien*, Geoffrey," he said, "it would appear we will be attending a wedding feast."

Ysabeau's feet, clad in the softest of gilded kid leather slippers, trod the newly laid rushes in the hall, releasing the mixed scents of the crushed herbs and dried rose petals that had been interspersed with them. A delicious bouquet rose to their nostrils as she and Philippe entered the great hall, which had been transformed for the occasion. New banners in dazzling colors hung from the massive arched rafters. In tribute to the Nativity season, the long trestle tables were draped with crimson linen cloths and garlanded with pine roping.

She exclaimed aloud with pleasure, then with surprise as she and Philippe were directed to the high-backed carved wooden chairs of the duke and duchess on the dais. Eleanor, speaking at her side, explained, "You and your lord are the cause for this celebration, therefore it would please me to see you in those places of high honor."

Privately Eleanor thought that the squeal of delight Ysabeau had uttered at the decorations was the first happy sound she had heard her make all day. Her favorite lady still looked far too wan. She hoped some of the libations would put a little color into those cheeks. She wished for the dozenth time she had been able to talk Ysabeau de Ré out of this marriage. What had happened to Simon de Winslade? Why hadn't he come back for her? For that matter, where was Henry? She had had no news in so long. . . .

The bishop said grace, and the wedding feast began with the chief cook presenting a roast peacock on a silver platter, to the sound of the trumpet and the applause of all present. He was followed by an endless procession of servants bearing a profusion of dishes: roast beef, pork, chicken, and swan, stewed eels, lampreys in *la sauce d'aile* from Nantes, frogs in green sauce, and an interminable number of side dishes, most of which Ysabeau could not even pretend to taste, though her bridegroom courteously offered her everything. At last came the desserts: baked pears, medlars, walnuts, figs, and peaches, all heavily spiced with ginger to disguise their dried state, followed by sweet wafers washed down with hippocras before the guests arose and heard a final prayer said by the Bishop of Angers.

The wedding guests congregated at one side of the hall, eager to let the servants get in and clear away the benches and trestle tables so there could be dancing. On one side of the gallery the musicians, who had played quiet, pastoral tunes during the feast, picked up the pace with more lively airs.

The dancing began with the *pas de Brabant*, in which each man bent his knee to his lady. Philippe and Ysabeau, as the bridal couple, naturally led the way, followed by the duchess, partnered by a merry Bernard de Ventador.

Ysabeau had only picked at her food. All through the endless meal, it had seemed to her that she was being watched. Several times she had looked up from her meat, certain that someone's eyes were upon her, but though she stared about the vast hall, she could see no one whose look was more than the friendly glance one would naturally cast at a bridal couple. The feeling persisted, however.

The dance was coming to a close when she finally glanced up at that portion of the gallery to which her back had been turned.

There, under one of the arched arcades stood the figure of a man. The high clerestory windows behind him let in the full, blinding late afternoon sunlight, which left the man's face in shadow. But something about his height and shape, those broad shoulders which tapered to a narrow waist, was so familiar that Ysabeau's mouth went dry. She forced herself to look away, hoping Philippe had not seen. But he had noticed something was wrong.

"Ysabeau, are you all right?" he said solicitously. "You finally got the color back into your face, and now you're pale again. What is it, *ma chère*?"

"Ah, Philippe, it's nothing. Just a little too much wine, perhaps. Will you excuse me for a moment? I must . . ." Her voice trailed off.

As the guests began a *danse au virlet*, she climbed the stair to the second level, drawn to that figure as if by a magnet.

When she reached the darkened corridor that led off the gallery, it was empty. She stood there for a moment, blinking in confusion, her pulse pounding in her ears. Could the figure have been an hallucination brought about by her hopeless yearning?

Just then she was seized none too gently from behind—one hand clapped about her mouth and another about her waist—and dragged into a small room behind her.

Still holding onto her with one arm, Simon shot the bolt on the door, then angrily whirled her about.

"Congratulations on your marriage, *ma Dame de Melle*," he growled. "Would you mind telling me why you've done this ridiculous thing, why you could not have waited?"

But his rough handling and unjust anger had lit the torch of Ysabeau's temper, too. "How dare you even touch me, Norman cur? Wait? For what reason? All those months without a word . . . you must think me a desperate creature, indeed," she spat at him, even as his tall figure came menacingly closer.

She was not conscious of retreating in the dark room, but suddenly her back was against the wall, held there by his hard, angry frame, his arms stretched out on either side of her. Their faces were inches apart.

For a moment she could only gaze at him, paralyzed by his nearness. His eyes blazed; his features seemed a hardened mask. She noted a scar on his cheek that hadn't been there before, and wondered absently how he'd gotten it.

"What do you mean, I sent no word? I came, but you had gone to Ré after your father's death. So I left. . . ."

He was going to mention the necklace and the note he left for her, but she didn't let him finish. Lashed to a fury after he mentioned her father without a single softening word of sympathy, she was determined to give him no quarter.

"So you left, after spending your time with Blanche de Limousin instead. How very foolish of me to be absent, mourning my father. I'm so glad your precious time wasn't wasted, though, *mon baron*. And Blanche looks so lovely in emeralds. I applaud your choice." She threw the words up at him through clenched teeth.

He felt the impact of her hurt for a heartbeat before it was drowned by the overwhelming wave of his own pain and fury. "So that's what you choose to believe of me, my lady. Then you fully deserve the likes of Philippe de Melle."

His words were confusing. Did they mean he hadn't given the emerald necklace to Blanche, that he had come to see her . . .

But she was allowed no more time to ponder it. "I had better return you to your bridegroom before he misses you," he ground out mockingly, his lips a breath away. "I wish you joy of your wedding, Ysabeau de Ré."

Then his mouth closed on hers, bruisingly, punishingly, forcing her lips apart and ravishing the soft cavern of her mouth with his tongue. His mustache scraped the soft skin above her lips. She worked a hand free and struck his face, but he only grabbed each wrist in a powerful hand and held them pinioned against the wall, which brought her even closer to him. He thrust against her tauntingly, letting her feel the barely leashed force of his arousal as her breasts were crushed against his rock-hard chest and her thighs melted into his.

Mon Dieu, she wondered as she tried to struggle against the whirlwind of his passion and fury, was he going to take her right here, careless of the wedding celebration below?

"Think of this," he growled against her throat, "when he beds you tonight." Then, after a final crushing kiss, he strode away without a backward glance.

When she returned to the revels below, after nervously trying to straighten her hair and crushed garments, the torch dance was in progress. Each dancer held a lit candle, and capered merrily around to the music, all the while trying to blow out the tapers of others. She was handed a candle and did her best to join in, but her steps were clumsy and her mind preoccupied with wondering if her lips were as swollen and bruised-looking as they felt. The flame of her candle was soon quenched, appropriately enough, by Philippe, and the guests applauded.

"You look tired, my love," he observed. "Perhaps it's time to call your ladies to put you to bed."

Her eyes, which had held the look of a wounded doe, became even larger as she stared back at him. "As you say, my lord," she murmured, backing away and gesturing to Matilde. There was no use in putting it off.

Marie had the chamber ready when the procession trooped in with Eleanor and Matilde taking charge of the giggling, chattering female guests. As if in a dream, Ysabeau was divested of the creamy velvet *bliaut*, the silky underdress, her veil and stockings; her hair was brushed out over her slender shoulders and rose-tipped breasts, its ends touching her gently rounded hips. She was assisted into the petal-strewn bed, and the chattering and lewd jokes rose in volume as they waited for the groom and his men. Ysabeau sat there, responding mechanically to the good wishes of the other ladies-in-waiting and the wives of the knights, barons, and counts who had been invited to the wedding.

She was used to feeling alone, having had

no mother to lean on for so many years, but now even the comforting presence of Matilde and the faithful Marie could not touch her isolation. She had felt she was doing the best thing until she had seen Simon today. But now she knew she was beyond help. There was no one to save her from this. She was doomed, trapped in wedlock and fated to love another—forever.

Suddenly, the crowd of women parted under the tipsy jostling of the men leading in a sheepish Philippe. He was already stripped down to just a linen shirt and a bedgown. But Ysabeau barely saw her beaming bridegroom, so conscious was she of her nakedness in the presence of a dozen leering men of the court. Tradition demanded that she lower the covers at this point, proving that her lord was getting an unblemished bride. She did so, blushing miserably, deliberately avoiding the hot gaze of Joscelin, Eleanor's brother. Instead, her eyes focused on a ruby on the bishop's plump finger as he raised his hand in blessing over the pair in the bridal bed. She thanked the saints that some shred of decency had kept Simon de Winslade from joining the drunken throng that now wished the newlywed pair great fertility.

Then, after a final bawdy jest or two, the bridal couple was left alone.

Chapter Twenty-two

Ysabeau's heart was pounding so loudly that it threatened to leap from her chest. She could not look Philippe in the eye, nor at his pale, wiry body.

"You are even lovelier than I imagined, my Ysabeau," he said, the joy of possession evident in his tone.

At any moment now, his hands would shoot out, he would touch her, make her his . . . and her duty was to submit. He was her lord. He could do anything to her.

"I hope you have had a happy wedding day," Philippe continued diffidently. "I am, myself, the happiest of men, knowing you are my wife. And now I will share with you a part of myself that I have not dared entrust to anyone else at court."

What was he saying, Ysabeau wondered

frantically. Was this some vague euphemism for the conjugal act?

"Ysabeau," he said, touching her chin very gently so that she turned to face him. "I would have you know something. It may help you to relax with me this night, knowing nothing will be demanded of you. But it will also affect the rest of our lives. I am a Catharist."

She blinked at him in confusion, uncertain of what he was saying.

"That is to say, I belong to a small but growing group of men whose beliefs are not those the corrupt Church teaches. . . ."

"You are a heretic?"

"No. Say rather, I am one of the elect few who has seen the error of the Church, who has seen that all contact with the material is defilement."

"*What*? You are a heretic!" she cried, hysteria rising in her voice. This could not be happening. She had wed a heretic. Although for a moment, the term had meant nothing, she was remembering that she had heard of these *Cathari,* a sect that was thriving among the poor and minor gentlefolk. They taught that there was no resurrection, that the Bible wasn't valid, nor was baptism, that the cross was valueless as a symbol; they believed there was no right of individual ownership or purpose in labor, except to merely sustain life. Although their simple, austere lives contrasted favorably with the often corrupt clergy, the Church, Ysabeau knew, had condemned their teachings as heresy.

One tenet especially made icy tendrils of fear and anger coil at her belly. "But the

Catharists believe . . ." she began.

"That all matter is basically evil, especially if it issues from sexual intercourse," he explained patiently, a beatific glow on his face. "We will have a marriage free of the defilement of sex, Ysabeau. I know you don't care for me in that way, *ma chère*, so this is a great burden lifted from those lovely shoulders, *hein*?"

She studied him then, trying to see if he was making sport of her, for truly she felt all the demons of hell must be laughing at her now. She tried desperately to salvage the situation, by reaching out a trembling hand and stroking his arm, willing him to respond to her touch.

"But Philippe, I was prepared to learn to love you, as a good wife should," she pointed out, her voice shaking. "And I know I would love our children."

"Life is purgatory enough without bringing more innocent souls into it," he said rigidly.

"Then why did you marry me?" she cried in exasperation. "You knew I don't believe as you do."

"Why, to bring you to the truth," he said as if it should be obvious. "I loved you enough to want you with me in my beliefs. And if we don't have the concern of heirs, the fiefs we are fortunate enough to possess can be of benefit to the *Cathari*. As of now, I am just a *credente*, a believer. But with you at my side, my believing helpmate, we can become part of the elite, the *perfecti*. . . ."

"But I came to you expecting a real marriage, with babes to bless it!" she said through clenched teeth. "I'll have this bond annulled—''

''When they see this, you won't be able to annull it,'' Philippe interrupted, bringing a small knife up from beneath the rope mattress.

At first she thought he meant to murder her, and she just stared at him, eyes wide with fear. But then she watched as he made a deliberate slit on his left upper thigh, and looked at her with triumphant satisfaction as a slender crimson stream drained down to stain the bed linen.

''There's your virgin's blood, my dear,'' he gloated. ''Try proving now you are no wife to me. I know that thanks to the damned Simon de Winslade, you have no maidenhead to lose. However, as far as the Bishop is concerned, our marriage will seem to have been consummated just as any other.''

''I'll never cooperate with you in this mockery of a marriage!'' she spat, retreating to the far corner of the bed.

''But don't you see, Ysabeau,'' he said, patiently, as if explaining a lesson to an idiot child, ''all know that love cannot flourish in marriage anyway, at least between husband and wife. Now that he cannot wed you, perhaps you and de Winslade can find true happiness in each other, knowing you can never marry and spoil the relationship.'' He laughed bitterly.

It was all too much for Ysabeau. She collapsed back on the feather mattress in a paroxysm of weeping, knowing now that all was lost to her. A loving husband . . . children . . . secure lands and home. She could not take Philippe's words to be permission to sin with

Simon. Just when she believed she had put such a life firmly behind her by marrying, it seemed to be the only option left open that promised any pleasure between now and the grave.

Philippe chuckled again, saying, "It seems you have a predicament, my love," and patted her arm fondly. It came to her suddenly that his laughter had more than a tinge of madness in it, that his deliberate deceit and almost merry acceptance of a cuckold's horns were the actions of an increasingly unstable man teetering on the brink.

He blew out the remaining cresset lamp and turned on his side, away from her; and she was left alone to stare into the darkness, sleepless until the dawn.

Part Three

Chapter Twenty-three

Ysabeau and Philippe returned from their winter honeymoon at Château de Melle in time to join Eleanor's court as it journeyed to Rouen. Henry of Anjou had at last left England and had summoned Eleanor to meet him at Matilda's court.

"I wish my lord would stop in Angers first, and accompany us to Rouen," the duchess grumbled as she directed her ladies, who were once again packing.

"Have you ever met the Empress Matilda?" Ysabeau asked, folding a delicate veil. She called Eleanor's mother-in-law by the title she took on when she married the Emperor of Germany many years before.

"Never, and to tell you the truth she sounds *très formidable*," the elegant duchess admitted with a laugh. "I confess I am a tiny bit nervous at the prospect."

The thought of Eleanor, Duchess of Aquitaine, former Queen of France, herself a very formidable person, being intimidated by any other woman was so startling that Ysabeau was hard pressed not to giggle. But she only said sensibly, "Your grace, you have just given the duke an heir, and by marrying, him doubled his lands. Why should the empress receive you aught but warmly?"

Apparently it was just what Eleanor needed to hear, for she impulsively gave Ysabeau a kiss on the cheek. "Ysabeau, you jewel! You are exactly right! I shall march right up to her, little William in my arms, and say, 'Good day, *belle-mère*, how fortunate you are to meet me at last!' " She chuckled richly, and all the other ladies laughed—except for the sulky Blanche, who merely shot Ysabeau a venomous look. Eleanor left the room then, to consult with William's nurse.

"Ysabeau, dear . . . aren't you a little thicker about the waist since you have returned from Melle?" cooed Blanche in dulcet tones. "Have you an announcement to make, you sly one?"

Ysabeau stopped what she was doing as the blood drained from her face. Her waist was as slender as ever, of course, for nothing had changed between her and Philippe. The marriage had never been consummated, since the troubadour was obstinate in his Catharist belief that physical union between husband and wife was of the devil. Blanche had instinctively sensed the tense, untouched quality that hovered over Ysabeau since her marriage, despite the fact that Ysabeau shared her husband's chamber now when she was not attending Eleanor.

"I'm not *enceinte*, if that's what you mean, Blanche," she replied evenly, "or were you implying I was getting fat? The table at my lord's castle cannot hope to compare with her grace's." She caught the approving look shot at her by Matilde, who then diverted Blanche's attention.

"How are you doing with Joscelin these days, Blanche? I noted you two head to head after supper last eve, and that you were wearing that pretty pale blue *bliaut*. It becomes you well, even if it is a bit tight in the bodice. It looked like your breasts were going to burst out of it," Matilde said, the last remark garnering a snicker from several ladies.

Blanche gave Matilde a look of undisguised fury. "Yes, my Lord Joscelin is, shall we say, completely besotted with me. I wonder how you will like having to honor me as Eleanor's sister by marriage soon?" she asked tightly.

"He's already got a wife, has he not?" Ysabeau riposted.

"Pish-posh, divorces are easily had by the great," Blanche answered airily.

"Anyone who marries Eleanor's bastard brother deserves him," Matilde said finally, getting to her feet. "Ysabeau, come back to our chamber. I need to plan how I will wear my hair tonight at the ceremony."

The two women left with dignity, ignoring the livid Blanche, who would have thrown her eating dagger at them, but for the civilizing presence of the other ladies-in-waiting.

The ceremony to which Matilde referred was, at long last, her wedding to Rene de Limoges, who had finally proposed marriage. The ceremony would be much smaller and quieter than Ysabeau's grand marriage in December, held in the Angers Castle chapel and attended by only those close to the bride and groom. This was how both Matilde and Rene wanted it.

"In truth, everything is already arranged," Matilde admitted as they strolled arm in arm down the corridor. "I just wanted to get away from that poisonous bitch's tongue."

"*Grande merci*," Ysabeau said with a rueful laugh, "for throwing her off the scent."

They had reached the sanctuary of the room they had once shared. Ushering Ysabeau inside, Matilde said frankly, "But I could see her words troubled you. All is not well with you and Philippe, *n'est-ce pas*?"

Ysabeau turned troubled brown eyes to her friend. "Ah, Matilde, I should have known I could hide nothing from you. No, marriage to Philippe has not been what I expected . . ." Her voice caught in a sob, and she could not go on.

"He beats you? He gives you no pleasure in bed? What?" Matilde questioned with gentle relentlessness as she held the weeping girl close.

"He . . . takes no pleasure himself either. We have never made love," admitted Ysabeau, blushing with shame.

"He is not able!" Matilde concluded mistakenly as Ysabeau's tears made it momentarily impossible to explain.

"*Non . . . non . . .*" Ysabeau fought an urge to break into hysterical laughter. "It is merely that he is a Catharist."

Understanding dawned then. "But so are most of the troubadours. So is Bernard, but he didn't get himself booted out of Ventador merely *singing* about the joys of adoring his patron's countess. Most of them espouse all the Catharist tenets except that one." Matilde's tone was cynical.

"Yes, he said that many were content to be merely *auditores*, listeners, but he is striving to be numbered among the sect, the *perfecti*. So, I remain untouched. There will not even be children to help me forget . . ." She broke off, aghast that she had spoken aloud of her deepest secret, even to her closest friend.

"To help you forget Simon de Winslade," Matilde concluded for her. "I was afraid of that. You saw him when he was here at the time of your wedding, didn't you? That *coquin* didn't have the decency to keep away from you, did he?"

Ysabeau shook her dark head. "We met briefly. It was long enough to see he regretted nothing, though," Ysabeau said, recalling their bitter words about Blanche and the necklace.

"I still think you were mistaken about the emerald necklace," Matilde said, uncannily reading her mind. "And besides, you have grounds for annulment, you know. Your marriage is based on fraud. You didn't know you were marrying a heretic."

"No, no," Ysabeau said wearily. "I thought of that, but what would be the point? I will never love again, so at least this keeps me safe from the brutes who would marry me for my land, and abuse me. And Philippe is very kind and gentle. We . . . sing together, in the evenings."

"You don't need a singing partner," Matilde retorted bluntly. "You need someone to make babies with. Why don't you take a lover? He'd have no choice but to accept the babes as his, at least publicly."

"I could never do that. I think if he found I was with child he'd immure me behind the dank walls of Melle." She thought of the high, forbidding towers of dark gray schist that flanked the Château de Melle, the sparse, careless furnishings within, the emaciated, hungry serfs, and shuddered that she had been so eager to see her lord's holdings. Melle was in much worse condition than Ré, and would never improve, for it lacked a trustworthy seneschal and hard-working, well-treated peasants.

"Well," Matilde said with a shrug of her shoulders, "You seem paralyzed to act, and that's not like you. I tell you truly, Ysa, this state is not one you will be content with forever."

Chapter Twenty-four

"Be reasonable, Gervase," Simon said, facing his twin across the heavy oak trestle table in the great hall of Hawkingham Castle. He was distinctly glad he had not removed his coat of mail, and that his sword rode in its scabbard at his waist, as he watched the other man's cold blue eyes.

"Be reasonable while you speak of tearing down one of my castles? How big of a fool do you take me for, younger brother?"

Simon felt the heat start to rise within him, that well of anger that Gervase knew so well how to tap. He had ever been thus, had Gervase: sarcastic, cool, seemingly without brotherly feelings.

"It's an adulterine castle. As such, it has to be torn down, according to the treaty signed by *your* king," Simon reminded him. "You knew when you built Chawton you were just taking advantage of Stephen's weakness. It was completely illegal to build it without royal permission. And it's not as if I'm telling you that your principal seat has to be razed," he went on, gesturing around him, "Hawkingham may stand. It's just Chawton that must be destroyed. You can still use the manor there, and if you behave yourself toward Henry, he's a fair man, he'll give you a license to erect it again one day."

"How very kind of your duke and you," Gervase sneered. "If I'm a good lad, and stand peaceably by while you tear down Chawton, perhaps I can put it back together again. You talk as if we were children, building mock castles of blocks!"

"I seem to remember then you insisted on having all the blocks," Simon said, making an attempt at humor.

"So now you have your revenge," retorted his twin. "How sad the war had to end. How you would have loved seeing me executed as a rebel. Then you'd have had all the lands once possessed by our grandsire, Guy de Bayeux."

"Nay. Not so. You are still my brother. It might just as well have gone the other way. Stephen and Eustace could have won, and you'd have been my overlord then. Would you have been content carrying out gentle Stephen's orders?"

"That fool!" Gervase said with a derisive laugh. "While he lived, I'd have given him lip service. But make no mistake—if Eustace had lived to come to the throne, your kind would have died traitors' deaths, and your lands would have been forfeit, to me, as the loyal brother, of course."

"Of course. But it didn't turn out that way, as you know." Simon stood, his lips compressed to a tight, furious line. "Here's the king's decree," he said, taking a rolled-up sheet of parchment and spreading it out on the table. "See for yourself. It authorizes me to tear down Chawton, save for the manor house, and orders you to do nothing to impede me or my men."

"You just love this duty, don't you, brother?" Gervase snarled, his hand at his dagger. "How much did you have to pay in bribes to get this particular honor?"

"I asked for it, you're right," Simon admitted evenly, his eyes warily watching the face so like his, but transfigured by hate. "Not for the motive you'd assign, though I wanted to make sure only the walls and keep were torn down, that the manor wasn't despoiled, and the village maids raped and the crops trampled, as will be happening elsewhere when Stephen's brigands and Henry's greedy, land-hungry Angevins do the razing."

"I'm indebted to you, *mon frère*," Gervase said sardonically. "All right, do it. You will find no cause to run crying to Henry because of me. Oh, by the way, how is your heir getting along? Does he thrive on that serf bitch's paps?" he inquired with silky menace.

"Aimery is weaned, I believe," Simon replied icily. "Why do you ask?"

"Just interested. After all, he's still my only heir, since my sickly wretch of a wife died without giving me a single living child," he said with callous disdain. "Until I get a legitimate boy on a woman of my class, Aimery stands to inherit all. Why don't you send him to me, when he's of an age to be fostered?"

"Aimery will never spend a moment under your roof," Simon said with cold finality. "I'd not want him to absorb your attitudes, brother. *Au revoir.*"

Simon turned his back and strode from the hall, aware he was taking a tremendous risk in doing so. One should always keep one's eyes on a dangerous snake coiled to strike. He allowed himself a small sigh of relief when he reached the door, aware of Gervase's eyes boring a hole in his back, but he did not really begin breathing easily until he and his men-at-arms had clattered over the drawbridge.

"All right, there's no use wasting the rest of the day," he told his men. "Let's round up the workmen we left in the wood and start for Chawton. The sooner this is done, the sooner my Lord of Hawkington will get over it."

He wondered, despite his calm, reasoned speech to Gervase, if he *had* been foolish to take on this duty, even with the motive of doing as little damage to his brother's fief as possible. They had never been close, but now Gervase would blame the destruction on Simon, as if it had been his idea.

Simon also realized that Gervase's mention of Aimery had not been accidental. Certainly there was enmity between Gervase and himself, but would he harm the boy out of revenge? Surely there were some depths to which the scheming knave would not descend!

He was glad that the end to civil war would also mean he need not be away from Winslade as much as he had been since the boy's birth. He had missed so much of Aimery's infancy, and now Aimery was toddling around, his head covered with a mass of dark curls. He needed a mother. Hulda, his nurse, had married Alf Carpenter soon after gaining his permission, and before long be busy caring for the pack of brats Alf would, no doubt, give her.

He supposed he had better start looking about for some gentle girl of good birth to marry, who'd mother his son and keep his bed warm, who'd help him forget the Poitevin girl.

There was the problem. He could not forget Ysabeau, though God knew he had tried to drown his love in anger when he found her newlywed to that jumped-up minstrel. Damn the foolish wench! How could she believe he'd give that cold supercilious bitch Blanche anything?

Henry had invited him to come along when he left London for Rouen, gaping in surprise when Simon politely declined, citing the need to return to his fief.

"Am I hearing correctly? You, who have practically worn a path across the Channel, don't wish to go? What's the matter, did you and your little French sweetheart have a falling-out?"

"She married another, your grace." He briefly described the day he had arrived in Angers.

"The devil! Well, don't let that stop you. There's lots of luscious womanflesh in Eleanor's retinue. Or you might find someone at Matilda's court in Rouen. Come, Simon, no one keeps me amused as you do," Henry cajoled.

But Simon was adamant. "It's probably best that I stay away, my lord. If I see her with that upstart I just might have to run him through, and that would hardly endear you or me to your lady mother."

Henry sighed. "No, I suppose not. You're too damned honorable for your own good. You ought to just go snatch the wench off to some place for awhile, just to get her out of your system—or make her never want to leave you. Eleanor ennobled a troubadour, you say? I can see she's been left to her own devices long enough. I'd better go get her pregnant again."

"Will you be allowing Bernard de Ventador to return to France, your grace?" Simon inquired, glad to divert Henry's attention from his own problems. A man who was a man, and not merely a capering courtier, did not wear his heart on his sleeve for a foolish woman.

"Not on your life!" snorted Henry. "Though I don't know which is worse, having him making calf-eyes at Eleanor or writing his moonstruck poetry to her from this side of the Channel and complaining of the cold. No, I'll keep him here at my pleasure until he tires of the idea of pursuing Eleanor from afar and goes on to greener pastures. All right, then, if I can't persuade you to come to Easter court with me, I'll see if I can't get that silly marriage annulled. There must be grounds, if one looks hard enough."

"Please, your grace, there's no need. The wench has made her choice," Simon said stiffly and finally.

If he could only forget her and stop daydreaming about what she must be doing with her new husband. The thought of Philippe de Melle—or any man—touching his Ysabeau filled him with a white-hot, murderous rage. God damn the whoreson if he ever caused her to shed a tear, he thought, forgetting his anger at Ysabeau. Or would it be better if the troubadour made her unhappy, so that he, Simon, would have the excuse needed to act on Henry's outrageous suggestion?

Chapter Twenty-five

Marie was drowsily combing out Ysabeau's mane of rippling chestnut hair after having helped her mistress out of her blue sarcenet gown and assisting her into a light woolen bed-robe. They were alone, for Philippe was off at one of his religious meetings, which Ysabeau had politely refused to attend.

"I feel guilty for awakening you, Marie," Ysabeau murmured; nonetheless, she was enjoying the plump tiring-woman's ministrations as she sat on a low-backed chair, growing slumbrous herself. "Surely you have too much to do, what with Matilde, Blanche, and I all in separate chambers these days."

"Now, my lady, I told you I'd be expecting you to call," admonished the woman kindly. "How were you to undo those back laces all by yourself? As for me, Matilde retired early with that handsome husband of hers, and I think my Lord Rene provided all the help she needed to disrobe," chuckled Marie, rolling her eyes. "That other so-called lady has not summoned me yet, but I saw her earlier, strolling in the gardens with that Lord Joscelin. I wonder when she's going to figure out she's in over her head with that one?" Marie asked darkly, not really expecting an answer. "He won't be content to merely play at courtly love, not that one. He'll toy with her and cast her aside, mark my words."

"No doubt, you are right. . . ." Ysabeau murmured, when there came a feeble knocking at the door. Through its massive wooden planks, Ysabeau heard a woman cry, "Open! For the love of God, help me!"

Both women sprang to the doorway, Marie sliding back the bolt and opening the door just in time for a dirty and disheveled Blanche to collapse into Ysabeau's arms.

"Blanche! What means this? What happened?" cried Ysabeau, taking in her split, swollen lower lip, blackened, puffy eye, ripped bodice, the scratches and tearstains on her once perfect cheeks, surrounded by tangled, wild blond hair. They assisted her to the bed, then Marie busied herself with pouring water from the ewer into a basin and sponging the dirt and blood from Blanche's face, as Ysabeau handed the weeping woman one of her own fine lace handkerchiefs.

"Who did this to you?" Ysabeau asked grimly, knowing the answer already.

Blanche regarded her through flooded,

reddened eyes. "Joscelin, of course . . . I allowed him to get me alone in a dark corner of the pleasance. I thought he was going to promise to divorce his wife, and marry me. Instead, he said he was tired of my teasing and . . . forced me . . . Ysabeau, that *salaud* raped me! And because he is the Duchess' bastard brother, no one can help me!" she sobbed hysterically.

"Lie back, my lady," Marie directed gently; she then pulled up the torn, grass-stained skirt of her gown, and sponged away the telltale dried blood on Blanche's slender thighs, though not before discreetly showing it to Ysabeau. Ysabeau's eyes met Marie's above the prostrate woman. Blanche had been a virgin. Ysabeau dared not think of that fact in relation to Simon de Winslade just now—Blanche's need was too great. And she was probably right. She had finally been robbed of the prize she taunted every man with, and Sieur Joscelin would likely go his merry way. How could a married lord be punished, save for banishment from court? That, it was whispered, had happened before, but even if Eleanor banished lord Joscelin from court permanently, the lady in question was still ruined.

"Mother Mary . . . I am so ashamed . . . I feel so soiled . . . I didn't want to come to you, Ysabeau, but I didn't know where else to find help. I didn't want to be seen by any more people than I had to. . . ." She continued to weep.

"I'll never mention it to a soul, Blanche," Ysabeau assured her without a second thought. The once haughty Blanche had fallen so low that

Ysabeau couldn't imagine taking revenge on her former enemy now. "But I think Her Grace should be informed of her brother's heinous behavior, so that she can deal with him."

"What would Eleanor do that would help me? Force him to put away his wife? Not likely!" Blanche laughed bitterly. "What is likely if it is brought to her attention, is that somehow the tale will spread like wildfire around the court, and all will know of my humiliation. No thank you. I will not have them all, from the Duke to the lowliest scullion, laughing at me. No, there is nothing that can restore my lost honor."

"You should have thought of that before you started casting your lures at that married scoundrel," Marie retorted before Ysabeau could silence her, then had the grace to look ashamed. "I cry your pardon, my lady. Indeed I'm sorry for your trouble."

"Never mind, Marie. All would say I asked for it, just as you did—unless I go on as if nothing had happened," Blanche said with determination. But, Ysabeau thought, there was a brittle quality to her that had not been there before.

That night, long after Philippe had come to bed and lay snoring next to her, Ysabeau lay on her back, staring up in the dark and thinking about Blanche.

She had been a virgin before tonight. The emerald necklace must not have been, as she had imagined in her jealous torment, a payment for her favors. Was it the symbol of a promise? Had Simon intended to come back for the tall beauty, perhaps to wed her? Would she be forced to stand helplessly by, and watch as Blanche was given in holy wedlock to the man she loved, would always love? And what would Simon think if he knew his wife-to-be was sullied, another man's leavings? Men like Simon took what they could get, but they expected their wives to be pristine and pure, she thought sourly. And I'd wager Blanche won't tell him, which will serve him right after what he did to me.

The court departed for Rouen the next morning at dawn, having tarried a week while Eleanor's son recovered from a worrisome cold. It was not difficult, in the confusion of moving so many people and household goods, to keep Blanche out of sight. The chill weather of early spring gave the perfect excuse for Blanche to be swathed in concealing cloaks, veils and wimples, while her scratches healed and bruises faded. The black eye, now a greenish-gray, could not be hidden; but Blanche told the few who noticed a convincing account of a horse tossing its head at her as she mounted. However, Ysabeau noted she laughed nervously while telling it and could not quite look the listener in the eye.

The bruise to the woman's soul would take longer to fade. Luckily, Lord Joscelin had not chosen to come along to Rouen, perhaps deeming it a wise time to return to his own château and play the devoted husband; or possibly Eleanor had not thought it polite to take her bastard brother along to meet her intimidating mother-in-law. In any case,

Ysabeau breathed a sigh of relief when she realized he was not among the company, for if he had imposed his leering, obnoxious presence on her, she knew she could not have remained silent about the rape to Eleanor.

Henry had already arrived in Rouen and was impatiently awaiting his Duchess when the party reached the capital city of Normandy.

Ysabeau felt as if she was witnessing a meeting of eagles as she watched the Duke presenting Eleanor, who looked elegant and regal even though she was in a riding dress, to the elderly but still queenly matriarch, the Empress Matilda, Lady of England.

True to her word, Eleanor had walked into the great hall proudly carrying her son, whom she presented to her husband and mother-in-law. She smiled as the infant set up a lusty wail upon being handed to his grandmother.

"Your grace, and my lord, I give you William, your heir, future Duke of Normandy and Count of Anjou. . . ."

"And someday King of England," promised Henry confidently. "I noticed you do not also style him 'future Duke of Aquitaine.' "

"My husband and lord, we have so many possessions between us and are still almost newlyweds—I fancy we may yet make another son to receive my duchy."

Even the old Empress joined in Henry's appreciative chuckle at this bold sally. He raised Eleanor's hand to his lips, and murmured so that only she could hear, "I vow, we will begin that project tonight, my love."

Ysabeau would have been surprised to know that the first topic introduced when Henry and Eleanor were alone together that evening was not *amour*, but Simon and herself.

"Eleanor," Henry said as he poured a goblet of mulled wine, "why on earth did you ennoble that monkey-faced minstrel and then marry him to Ysabeau de Ré?"

Eleanor flinched at his tone. She had expected him to be in an amorous mood, not a critical one, when he had arrived clad only in a bedgown. They had been apart so long, she had been so many months without his touch—the longest time she had ever been celibate. Couldn't he see that? "Could not such petty matters be put off till the morrow?" she asked pettishly.

But Henry was not one to delay discussion of what was on his mind.

"Your thoughtless actions have turned one of my best barons into a lovesick fool," he said sharply, ignoring her caresses as she stood by him, stroking his heavily muscled neck.

Eleanor reacted as if she had been slapped. Her temper ignited. "*My* thoughtless actions? I gave Lord Simon and Ysabeau every opportunity to be together, and like any typical man, he couldn't resist pawing the first available slut when Ysabeau was not around!"

"What do you know of typical men, my dear?" Henry's eyes narrowed dangerously. "You seem to concentrate on pretty troubadours."

"You had no right to take Bernard from me!" shrieked Eleanor. "He did nothing wrong! He was my only comfort during those long months you were away, probably consorting with all manner of low camp followers!" Her bosom heaved with fury.

He licked his lips avidly, distracted from his complaint. Women like the earthy Hikenai were fine when one was on campaign, but there would never be another woman like Eleanor. The well-remembered charms of her voluptuous body beckoned him even as her eyes flashed fire at him. "Come here, Eleanor," he growled. "Come prove you're better than all of them."

"I won't! You make me so angry, Henry, and then you expect me to play the whore for you." Eleanor stamped her foot and her hands clenched into fists at her side.

He shrugged, and made as if to leave. Eleanor lost the battle in that moment. He was eleven years her junior and her lands were now his. He could have any woman, from highborn lady to scullery wench, but she wanted only him.

"I'm sorry, my lord. Don't go. The time I have been without you has given me a shrewish tongue," Eleanor said contritely, barring his way to the door. Then she let the bedgown of crimson sendal slide from her naked form into a pool at her feet.

Chapter Twenty-six

Life quickly slipped into a routine in Rouen, much as it had in Angers.

Eleanor, using all her natural charm and suppressing much of the arrogance of her nature, soon achieved a fairly cordial, if guarded, relationship with the Empress. This was fortunate, for the two women were often left in each other's company while Henry was off on duchy business: quelling a revolt in Aquitaine when certain lords thought to take advantage of their duchess' absence; securing a firm rule in Normandy; even negotiating with Louis, Eleanor's former husband. How the two men could deal amicably with one another was a mystery to Eleanor, and one that made her frankly nervous, she confided in Ysabeau.

Ysabeau gave some innocuous answer, thinking that the Duchess had ample reason for irritableness, with Henry off dealing with Louis, leaving her alone to deal with her mother-in-law. What was more, Henry had lost no time in making good his promise to get another son on Eleanor, and she was already experiencing the queasiness that marked the early months of pregnancy.

She was not the only one pregnant at court, though the other mother had, perforce, to keep her state a secret. Blance de Limousin had conceived as the result of the brutal rape. She had already made plans to retire to a covent in Rouen before her condition became too apparent, but for now, she was a sombre, silent figure, taking only the minimum of care with her appearance; her once glorious blond tresses were now lanky, greasy braids, and her lushly pouting lips were generally pursued in a tightly compressed line. Without understanding why, Eleanor obviously felt uncomfortable around her lady-in-waiting, and rarely called upon Blanche to attend her. The Duchess' avoidance of her caused Blanche to sink further into her sullen despondency. Ysabeau feared for the health of the baby Blanche carried, but her words of encouragement fell on deaf ears.

Philippe seemed well content in Rouen, Ysabeau mused. Perhaps it was that Eleanor, bereft of Bernard de Ventador, required his singing more often. A Poitevin, he saw nothing inconsistent in combining minstrelsy with knighthood, though a *chevalier* of northern France would have; and he was oblivious of the way Duke Henry's lip curled in his presence.

However, it was more likely, Ysabeau

thought cynically, that his contentment grew from finding a cell of Catharist believers in Rouen, though they were rare in the north. When not expected to play for the Duchess, he was often gone from court, and would return to their chamber late, eyes glowing with a fantatical light.

He had not ceased to urge Ysabeau to attend his religious meetings with him; she could see that he felt their marriage incomplete only in the fact that she had thus far refused to take part. She stubbornly continued to see it as heresy, however. How could a religion be true that condemned babies as the physical issue of the devil? More and more, she ached to have a babe suckling at her breast. Perhaps if he had not been so rigid on this point, she would have been more open-minded, for she didn't believe her church possessed the only absolute truth. She could have been a good wife; she could have pushed Simon de Winslade into the past where he belonged; but she had married a man who had deceived her monstrously. She would never forgive him for preventing her from having the children whose warmth would drive that other presence from her heart.

No longer did she try to seduce him, wearing sheer night rails, or none at all, pressing herself close to him, allowing a kiss to deepen whenever he brushed her cooly with his lips. Such tactics had won her nothing but a sense of shame at her lack of pride and wanton behavior. When she behaved so, he would firmly put her from him with a sad smile and a gentle, dismissive caress.

She had made herself vulnerable, and he had taken advantage of her, and after a while she could no longer forgive him for that. The real affection she had once felt for Philippe de Melle died. Ironically, the more detached she became, the more possessive he acted, watching her wanly. His wedding night injunction to her to seek her happiness in Simon de Winslade's, or some other handsome *chevalier's* arms, seemed to have been rescinded.

Your vigilance is quite in vain, *mon èpoux*, she thought, for that part of me is forever dead. Oh, there's many a randy knight to satisfy the ache, but only one man could fill my heart, and he's proven himself to have feet of clay. I want a man capable of being forever faithful, and if there is no such man, my arms will stay as empty as my heart.

She no longer had any urge to take up her duties as châtelaine of Melle. During the winter she had become aware that Philippe was not a good lord, a lord who cared about his people and tended his lands; and Ysabeau could see that he would never bestir himself to learn. He wanted the status of a barony, but assumed his fief would somehow magically run itself and continue to provide him with whatever he needed. She had tried tactfully, but with increasing frustration, to point out that his seneschal was robbing both him and his peasants blind. He had promised to look into it, but never did.

The most she could hope for was that he would not remember the relative prosperity of Ré and cast avid eyes to its profits, on behalf of his church. She was content for now to stay at court, and took care not to remind him of her island fief; she carried on all necessary correspondence with her steward only when Philippe was away.

Blanche retired to a Benedictine convent in the fall, smiling distantly when Ysabeau, accompanying her there, promised to visit her often.

"Come if it pleases you," she said, her eyes seemingly fixed on a point somewhere just above the other girl's forehead. There was a pinched, drawn look to the once lovely woman's face, and dark shadows under her eyes; it was the only part of her that did not seem swollen. She did not glow with radiant health as did Eleanor in her pregnancy; her color was pasty, like the melting tallow of a candle.

"Of course, I will come," Ysabeau said determinedly. "For you must keep up with the gossip, so that you will be *au courant* when you return to court, slender as a reed again."

"Perhaps I'll never leave the convent," Blanche said, staring fixedly at the austere statue of St. Benedict in a corner of the visitor's room. She plucked absently at the rough serge habit that had been given to her.

"*You*, a nun?" Ysabeau attempted to tease her out of her gloom. "Chief flower of loveliness at Eleanor's court? Stay here? Who will be on hand to hold the men's hearts captive, Blanche, if you do not return?"

"You don't truly believe I could go back there, do you?" Blanche said sardonically.

"I don't know why not," Ysabeau protested stoutly. "As far as they know, you have come here to be nursed for an illness. And you have nothing to atone for—you were forced. You are no more guilty of the sin than the child you bear."

She thought Blanche looked at her strangely for a moment before answering. "Eleanor knew, I'm certain of it. There was something in the way she looked at me. Someone must be punished, Ysabeau. Obviously Joscelin never will. . . ."

"Blanche," Ysabeau soothed, putting her arm around the other's shoulders, "an expectant woman has strange fancies, I'm told. Everything will be all right, you'll see." But she was seized with foreboding as she left the sparsely furnished room. The woman's staring eyes had seemed to see into a bleak future.

Her further visits did nothing to reassure her. It was always, "Lady Blanche is at her prayers," or "Lady Blanche is in solitude and wishes not to be disturbed," until one day the message given her by Sister Portress was, "Lady Blanche is ill, and sleeping in the infirmary. She can have no visitors." Attended by Marie, Ysabeau walked, heavy of heart, the short distance back to the red tile-roofed ducal palace with its clear Caen limestone walls.

Late that same night, she was awakened just after midnight by a sleepy Marie, whose plump face looked ghastly in the illumination of the rushlight she carried. Philippe, who had come to bed not long ago, much affected by some potent beverage, mumbled crossly in his sleep and turned away from the light.

"Wake up, my lady, please! The Abbess

has sent a message. Blanche has been in hard labor since sunset . . ."

"But she can't be! It's too early for the baby—it can't live!" Ysabeau breathed as she struggled to full alertness.

"Yes, it seems unlikely that *le pauvre petit* will survive," Marie said. "And there is worse news. Blanche is hemorrhaging. It seems as if she, too, will die. She calls for you. Will you go, *ma dame*? There is a need for extreme haste!"

When Ysabeau and Marie reached the convent, she found that the windows had been draped with heavy sackcloth, even though there was no light on this moonless night to be excluded, only air. The atmosphere was fetid with the odor of sweat, and blood, and death. Two nuns endeavored to add more linen padding beneath Blanche's wasted legs at the lower end of the bed, but even in the dim light of the flickering tallow candles, Ysabeau could see the spreading crimson bloodtide engulfing the bleached linen sheets.

The only color in Blanche's pallid face was the bluish cast that stained her lips. Her cheeks were even whiter than the linen beneath her, and her eyes were dilated.

The babe had already been delivered by the time Ysabeau arrived, taken a shuddering breath, and died; it lay now cleansed of birth-blood, on a clean clout, barely the size of Ysabeau's hand.

"Ysabeau, you came . . . ." Blanche's voice was a hoarse whisper that came with great effort. She struggled as if to rise, then sank back, completely exhausted by the effort.

"No, dear. Lie back, and rest now," soothed Ysabeau, kneeling at the bedside and smoothing back the drenched dull gold strands of hair.

"It . . . is good of you to come . . . I didn't know if there would be time . . ." gasped Blanche.

"Certainly I came! But don't worry. The nuns will make you well—you'll see. You'll just need to rest—"

But Blanche was impatient with these patent lies. "They can't stop the bleeding! You *must* listen now!"

"All right, what is it?"

"I have much to repent for, regarding you, Ysabeau de Ré. I was spiteful and mean when you first came—"

"But I survived. It is all past. . . ." Ysabeau murmured.

But Blanche went on as if she didn't hear. "I wanted Simon de Winslade with all my heart, but he had eyes only for you."

"He's of no importance now, *ma chère*. He decided he wanted you after all, and I wed another."

"Ysabeau, listen for my soul's sake, if you won't listen for yourself!" Blanche cried, and Ysabeau marveled that the dying girl could summon so much vehemence. "He never stopped loving you. He still does. He brought the emerald to *you*, and bade me to give it to you, with a message of his love. I read it—its sincerity twisted my heart with jealousy. I destroyed the note, and kept the necklace, and let you believe a lie. I have done you a great wrong."

Ysabeau could only stare at Blanche, horror-stricken, and repeat her words. "Simon still loved me . . . the emerald necklace was for me . . ."

"It is in a casket of my jewels in the sisters' keeping," Blanche said with difficulty, so softly that Ysabeau had to strain to hear. "It was wrong of me to come between two who were meant for each other. I repent my grievous sin. . . ."

Ysabeau saw the moment in which the light faded from Blanche's eyes. After a silent prayer she straightened and pulled the sheet over the sightless eyes.

"Ah, *Dieu*, poor Blanche. How she suffered . . . the agonies of shame . . . and then for both of them to die like that . . ." Ysabeau said, gulping back a sob as she and Marie trudged back through the dark streets, accompanied by two burly men-at-arms.

"Yes, a very tragic end for a beautiful woman," agreed Marie somberly, though privately she was more touched by the selfless quality of Ysabeau's forgiveness of Blanche de Limousin. "What was that she was whispering to you, just before she died?"

Ysabeau turned a tearstained face to her. "Oh, Marie, he never stopped loving me. The emerald necklace was for me, and she kept it, poor misguided woman. She hoped somehow to turn his eyes back to her."

Aha, I thought so, the plump woman thought. I knew that scheming blonde was up to something, when I saw the jewel around her skinny neck. She watched her mistress, wrenched by her sorrow for all that might have been.

Simon's words came back to haunt Ysabeau, now that it was too late. "So that's what you choose to believe of me, my lady. Then you fully deserve the likes of Philippe de Melle."

He had come to her, not understanding why she had never acknowledged the loving, generous gift, and had found her in the midst of her marriage feast. And she had refused to listen when he would have explained all, though even then it was too late.

Beneath the long sleeve of her outer dress she clutched the emerald in her hand, but it was cold comfort.

Chapter Twenty-seven

Ysabeau had felt compelled to tell Matilde the true story behind the tragic death of Blanche de Limousin. All three women, Ysabeau, Matilde, and Marie, attended the brief, simple funeral service behind the convent walls. Blanche would be buried behind the chapel among the departed *religieuses* and Masses paid for by the Duchess would be said regularly for her soul.

"Poor Blanche," sighed Matilde, still shocked by the revelations about her former roommate. "She was so beautiful, and it brought her only misery. If she had only found a good man like my lord—" She smiled briefly, for happiness to her involved nothing more than the love of a good man. "But she used her loveliness to get what she wanted from men, and gave nothing. To think that all the time that necklace was meant for you. How differently things might have turned out. I could not believe it when I saw her flaunting the jewel." Then she saw how her words had upset Ysabeau. "Oh, my dear, I'm sorry. It must be so painful for you, now that you know the truth. . . ."

"I'm sure we should be praying for Blanche," sighed Ysabeau, wiping away a tear with a lacy *mouchoir*. "There's no use thinking of what might have been. I'm married to Philippe now. Someday, I will look at the emerald and it will bring me comfort to know he did love me, after all."

"Nonsense, my lady," spoke up Marie, with the liberty of a faithful retainer. "You speak as if you were an aged woman. You're too young and beautiful to live on memories." By now they had left the graveside, exiting through the forbidding iron grille that gave way to the street.

"What do you suggest I do?" queried Ysabeau, amused, despite her grief, at her tiring-woman's boldness.

"Go to him, my lady," was the plump servant's unhesitating reply.

"But Marie!" sputtered Ysabeau, laughing now. "Even if I would, he's in England! How am I to get there?" Her heart had begun to beat rapidly, catching fire with hope, despite the cold rational voice in her head that said such talk was crazy, she could never be an adulteress, and Simon didn't want her now, anyway.

"Sell your jewels," came Matilde's practical voice. "The emerald alone will bring you more than enough for passage across the

Channel, and you have a few other pieces, as I recall."

Part with the lovely green stone that burned with a passion of its own, set in the gleaming gold that felt like a cold flame against her neck? She had taken the necklace out while alone last night, and savored its beauty, the feel of it against her skin; she had held it to her lips, thinking of the man who had come for her. . . . But, of course, she would sell it, if that was what it cost her to go to him.

No! This was insane!

"I cannot do this. We must not talk of it." She insisted shakily, her fingers clenched at her mouth, her eyes closed tightly, as if she could shut out the visions that ran riot within, of selling the jewel, embarking for England, and running into Simon's arms.

Matilde put her arm comfortingly around Ysabeau's slender shoulders, and they walked the short distance back to the ducal palace silently.

There was no way she could bring herself to do such a thing. So why, as soon as she had a free moment from her attendance on Duchess Eleanor, were her feet flying for her chamber, carrying her to the little silver casket in which the necklace rested?

I just want to look at it, to hold it, she insisted to herself, to imagine what it would be like to act upon this mad plot my crazy friends propose out of their love and pity for me.

She reached the sanctuary of her chamber, and went immediately to the ironbound chest which held her belongings at the foot of her bed. The room was still, so still she could hear the thudding of her heart and her panting breaths after she had ascended the winding steep stair, practically at a run. Reaching under several folded gowns, her hands found the cool, heavy box where she had left it, and brought it up. Kneeling, she placed it on top of the chest and with a sigh of anticipation, raised the lid.

The necklace was gone. The silver casket was empty.

She rocked back on her legs, gasping, just as the door creaked open behind her and she heard Philippe's voice.

"Oh, I see you have noted that the necklace with the pretty green stone is missing," he said blandly, as if he were discussing the weather. "I knew you would not want to keep a jewel given you by another man, now that you are a married woman. It would be improper, and what's worse, it would grieve me—and I know you don't want to do that. You want to be my loving, faithful wife, don't you?" He knelt by her side and took her chin between two fingers, and smiled.

"Where is the necklace, Philippe?" she asked emotionlessly, hearing her own voice as if in the distance, over the roaring in her head.

"I sold it," he replied airily. "The money has gone to benefit several of the *Cathari* who are impoverished. A gift from my wife, I said, who will not openly join us but who wants to make her lord happy. *Don't* you, my dear?" His eyes glittered in the fading light of afternoon.

She made no reply, and reached, instead,

for the other box that held the few poor items of jewelry that were a legacy of her parents: a gilt chain, a silver paternoster with beads of jet, a garnet brooch.

"I took the liberty of putting your family jewelry away for safekeeping," Philippe said, straightening and going to the narrow window to stare into the inner bailey below. The late sunlight bathed his narrow face in an orange glow. "Don't worry, I didn't sell it. Those pieces wouldn't have brought, all together, what the emerald did. I'm merely guarding them, so that your grief—for Blanche, of course—doesn't tempt you into foolishness."

"Philippe," she began, striving to be calm. "The emerald necklace was a legacy from Blanche. She wanted me to have it. I don't know where you can have gotten this fanciful idea about Simon." She essayed a laugh, as if such an idea was ridiculous. "*Certainement*, he gave the necklace to her, but it's not as if—"

He was at her side in a split second, and hit her so hard that she felt blood running down her chin from her lip. "Don't ever lie to me, or think to play me for a fool, my Ysabeau. I knew the whole story from the beginning. Blanche warned me that Simon had come looking for you—'twas just after you left for the Île de Ré. So I came after you, to save you from your folly," he added righteously.

"You could have told me," she murmured brokenly, her face still stinging from the blow, her mind reeling at the transformation of the gentle troubadour into the sneering brutal man before her.

"I loved your soul more," he retorted. "I thought you would see the truth easily . . . as I do, but you're a stiff-necked, close-minded—" He pounded the nearby chest in frustration, and Ysabeau flinched at the barely leashed violence she had never before seen him exhibit. "I can see I've been too gentle with you, but no more. I must make you obey me."

"I cannot believe your religion teaches you to be this way," she said, and held her breath for fear he would strike her again.

"Oh, it doesn't, Ysabeau. However, as your husband I am free to behave any way I choose, to discipline you if you so much as look at me the wrong way." He grinned fiendishly. "Perhaps I shall begin to behave as your husband in other ways, since I can see that stepping out of character has finally got your attention." He bent to her again, cupping one of her breasts, pinching the nipple cruelly through the soft wool of her *bliaut*. He smiled to see her grimace and attempt to draw back. His hand held her shoulders inexorably close. "Yes, I think this will work. You will finally be subject to my will, as a wife should be." He began fumbling at her *bliaut's* neckline, seeking the lacing at the back.

"Philippe, no. I don't want this—"

"A wife's will is her husband's," he said softly, then grabbed her chin and pressed his lips on hers, punishing the torn flesh of her underlip as his tongue forced its way inside.

It was awful, an embrace full of hate and strife, and it would get worse. She struggled to push him away, to free herself, but he was too strong. Already he was pawing at her skirts, too impatient to remove the gown. She could smell the sour wine on his breath, mixed with the rank, animal smell of lust.

Just then, the horn sounded for dinner, and Philippe pulled away, breathing raggedly. "We shall have to continue this later, wife. I am expected to play for her grace, or we'd stay and finish this first lesson in discipline." He stood up, straightening his chausses, and went to the basin on the bedside stand, splashing some water on his flushed face.

Philippe stared back at Ysabeau, who still lay back, propped on her arms, staring at him in horror. Her hair was a tangled mass, and her veil lay in a rumpled heap at her feet.

"Straighten yourself, woman. You look like a strumpet," he said coldly. "I'll expect you in the hall very soon." Then he turned on his heel and left.

The evening meal was well under way when Ysabeau slipped into the hall and found an inconspicuous place below the salt, hoping that no one of any consequence would notice her reddened eyes and puffy lip. The imprint of his hand across her cheek had vanished, but she could still feel it in her soul.

"I'll keep Ami with me from now on," she vowed, unaware she had spoken aloud.

"Pardon me, my lady?" asked the tiring-woman sitting next to her.

"Nothing. I'm sorry." She had been allowing the mastiff the freedom of the hall during the night, where many of the other dogs roamed. He had originally spent his nights at her bedside, but once she had married, Philippe had complained about him. He disliked the dog's staring eyes and frequent rumbling growls whenever he moved near her. So she had put the dog out, thinking to please Philippe. The mastiff still eyed her reproachfully whenever she banished him for the night, though she was quite certain he was happy to rummage for forgotten bones and tidbits among the rushes and maintain his mastery over the other dogs.

"My lady, pardon me, but look, there's a messenger," the servant woman said, interrupting Ysabeau's reverie.

Indeed she spoke the truth, for striding toward the high table on the dais was a man, dusty and still flecked with mud and horse's sweat.

"He's ridden hard from somewhere," murmured Ysabeau curiously, as the man knelt in front of Duke Henry and awaited permission to speak.

Ysabeau could see the Duke nod, and the man said in tones that carried throughout the entire hall: "Your grace, King Stephen of England did depart this life on the twenty-fifth day of October, after a bloody flux, and was to be buried at Faversham. You are now the rightful King of England. Long live the King!"

The cheer was taken up by those at the high table, rising to salute Henry of Anjou with raised goblets. Soon everyone in the hall was on their feet, chanting, "Long live the King! Long live the King!"

Chapter Twenty-eight

The death of King Stephen provided everything Ysabeau could wish for in the way of diversion. There was no time to worry about being alone with her husband. The entire court was in an uproar. This was the moment for which Henry of Anjou had planned all his life, and his mother, Matilda, before him. Time was of the essence. The crown was his by right and treaty. Archbishop Theobald was protecting it for him, but he was eager to get to England and claim it.

Ysabeau was to attend Eleanor the night the messenger arrived, but long after she was dismissed to sleep on her pallet in the anteroom, she could hear Henry and Eleanor talking, excitedly planning their swift removal to England.

It seemed she had shut her eyes only

moments before when she was aroused to a day of whirlwind preparations. By now, of course, she was used to the process of packing all the Duchess' clothing and overseeing the dismantling of the massive bed, and could participate automatically, while her mind was left free to absorb the meaning of the changes that had happened to her mistress, and how they related to her.

The entire household of Henry and Eleanor would be departing for Barfleur at dawn the next day, if, indeed, Henry could be persuaded to delay even that long. Just when Ysabeau had despaired of ever having the means to get to England, where her love was, history had conspired to give her a way. Granted, Philippe would be with her, but she would be on the same side of the Channel as Simon, who was bound to come to court. Even if he no longer cared, at least she would see him again, and her heart would be eased.

When the ducal household arrived in the Norman port, a storm was raging in the Channel and it was obvious there would be a delay. While Henry was still grinding his teeth and shaking his fist at the lowering November sky, the scramble for lodging began.

Ysabeau found herself quartered in a stuffy airless spare chamber, along with almost all of Eleanor's maids-of-honor, in a small town house belonging to the widow of a local tavern keeper. She was fortunate to get even that, and it would mean sharing a bed with two others. There was no question of being able to have a private chamber with Philippe, and for that she was heartily relieved. It was bad enough just being around him, knowing what had passed between them the last time they were alone, knowing that beneath the gentle demeanor he showed before others, lurked a much darker side.

The weather remained unfavorable for an entire month, with gale winds and sleet, and in that time Henry Plantagenet's temper went from bad to worse. The lords and ladies, crammed into taverns and barns, were no better; the crowded conditions and uncertain departure date provoked tears and petty squabbles among the ladies, fistfights and even swordplay among the courtiers.

At last, on December 7, the wind slackened ever so slightly, but it was enough for Henry. "We go! It's the feast day of St. Nicholas, patron of sailors. I'll wait no longer!" he roared from the dock to the ships' captains, who already had most of the huge party's belongings stored in the holds of their ships.

The captains, as a group, sought to dissuade him, saying the winds were still too strong, the coast too cloaked in fog. One even cited the White Ship Disaster, which had cost Henry I his son and heir, and led to the wretched reign of King Stephen.

Henry turned a distinctly jaundiced eye at this rash individual; quickly, the man blanched and mumbled a temporizing remark.

"I'll have no faint-hearted captains transporting my men," he growled. "The English may say we came on the wings of the storm, but set sail now we will!"

The next 24 hours were filled with tossing, lurching misery for Ysabeau, who was seasick, as she had never been on the little boat that had taken her from Ré to the mainland so many times. She felt fortunate to be on the same boat as Henry and Eleanor, while Philippe was forced to embark on another ship in the fleet. He had coolly taken his leave and said he would see her when they reached the English shore. Once the big square-masted merchant vessel began its storm-tossed passage, however, Ysabeau did not know or care if any shared her damp, chilly berth. She was certain she would die of seasickness.

Fortunately, Eleanor was a splendid sailor and did not require her favorite lady's attendance. But even she spent no time on deck in the tempest, commenting that this passage was worse than any she had encountered on her return from the Holy Land with Louis.

When they made landfall near Southampton the next day, the ducal ship was alone, having lost the others in the storm. Ysabeau was weary beyond words. Briefly she hoped that her lord had perished in the tossing gray-green icy waves, and that she need never see him again, but felt instantly repentant when she recollected seeing Matilde and Rene board the same vessel.

She would have kissed the English ground in gratitude for her safe arrival, had not so many curious English been on hand to witness their landing. Ysabeau felt like a bedraggled waif, in contrast to her mistress, who was dignified and serene, appearing every bit as relaxed as if she had just been rowed across a calm lake.

Ysabeau's assumption that they would wait here for the others to catch up was mistaken. Evidently, Henry felt it was up to the rest of the party to rejoin them, so as soon as they had eaten, on they journeyed toward Winchester, where the English barons were waiting to greet their new king and queen. While she missed Matilde, Ysbeau could not be sorry that they were to go on, for it meant an extension of her temporary freedom from Philippe.

They only stayed overnight at Winchester, the ancient Saxon capital, which still housed the royal treasury. By dawn the next morning Ysabeau was mounted on her chestnut mare, riding directly behind the Duke and Duchess.

Until she left Winchester, she had been too weary to do more than stay in the saddle and remain alert to her mistress' needs. Now, feeling somewhat more fit and rested, she was getting her first real glimpse of England and the English. She felt as if all her senses were alive, drinking in the new sights, sounds, and smells of this strange country that seemed blanketed with mist. The road was frozen in some places; in others, mired in mud. But the chill December sun shone and Ysabeau absorbed the warmth of her horse's flanks, feeling very adventurous to be in a strange land so far from her sunny island in Aquitaine. Ami trotted at her palfrey's legs, his tail carried happily aloft as if he, too, was content to be along on this expedition.

As they neared London, more and more English folk lined the road, eager for a glimpse of the long-awaited young ruler and his notorious duchess. Ysabeau glanced curiously at the ruddy faces along the way, feeling encouraged by their cheers, touched by the sight of them, with their feet wrapped against the snow, huddled in their rough, ragged cloaks.

More nobles and churchmen joined the London-bound procession, making lodging increasingly difficult to find, despite the profusion of abbeys and inns along the way. Inevitably, Henry would decide to stop for the night at some manor house which welcomed its new king and queen in royal fashion, but left the growing party fighting over hovels one courtier pronounced, "not fit for pigs." Ysabeau, however, was privileged to attend her mistress, and had no need to look for more than a corner in which to stretch out her pallet.

One morning they passed a castle being torn down. The workmen enthusiastically tossed their caps and shouted greetings to the swelling cavalcade as they passed. The name of the keep, Chawton, meant nothing to her; had she known it belonged to Simon's brother, the Earl of Hawkingham, and that Simon had been in charge of its razing, she might have viewed it less dispassionately.

"I see the distruction of adulterine castles is going on as agreed, my lord," she heard Eleanor remark to Henry.

"Yes." It was obvious he was pleased. "And I'll not be happy till I get every one of those damned foreigners Stephen let loose, out of England, as well, by the Rood!" He was ebullient, his ruddy complexion glowing with confidence as he neared London. Their attendants relaxed increasingly as they saw how their lord and lady were welcomed.

Philippe, Rene, and Matilde joined them in Guildford with a harrowing story of being blown far down the coast in the storm and having ridden like demons to catch up. Indeed, they looked as if they hadn't stopped to rest; their clothing was mud-spattered, their horses and they themselves obviously weary.

Ysabeau was apprehensive when she was dismissed from Eleanor's side for the night—but she need not have worried. Philippe was snoring lustily on their pallet, his features still pale with fatigue. He looked so boyish and defenseless in sleep that Ysabeau felt guilty for her harsh thoughts. This did not look like the face of a husband who had struck her and informed her he would rape her into submission. She changed into her woolen nightrail, taking care not to waken him, and gingerly settled herself on the pallet, bidding Ami to sleep in the rushes beside her.

Chapter Twenty-nine

No conquering Roman general ever made a more triumphal entry into Rome than did Henry Plantagenet into London, at the head of the swollen procession that had joined him and his Duchess since they had landed on English soil. The cheering was deafening as they rode through the narrow streets. The houses were decked with banners and greenery that proclaimed the Londoners' joy in welcoming the new King whose name had come to symbolize peace and justice after the long chaotic reign of Stephen.

Ysabeau's eyes were wide as she took in the bustling atmosphere of the vast city, with its streets set aside for specific trades, its many large, beautiful churches, its hospitals, and the teeming docks on the Thames, where she could see ships from many lands unloading silks, wines, furs, gold and precious stones. She regretted that all passed so quickly before her, for the Duke was in a hurry to get to Westminster, but she looked forward to exploring later the many points of interest of this fascinating place in which she was to live.

In contrast to their joyous arrival in the city, their reception at Westminster was vastly disappointing. It was obvious from the first moment the ducal party entered the great hall of the palace that no one had restrained Stephen's minions from doing exactly as they pleased.

There were signs of terrible neglect everywhere. The stench of rotting rushes had met their noses even from the outside. Inside, they could see that the floor was littered with bones, dog manure, and decaying food. The tapestries were ripped and singed, hanging crazily askew. Birds flew to and fro and nested in the rafters, let in through broken windows. Weather damage to the wood where rainwater had leaked in unchecked was apparent in many places. There were even obscene words and drawings scrawled on the walls.

"But Henry," expostulated Eleanor, so surprised she forgot to address him formally in front of her attendants. "It's not as if they didn't know we were coming! That they have left the palace this way is an outrage!" Within seconds, she had recovered from her bewilderment and overwhelming disappointment and had worked herself into a truly queenly rage. Her back had resumed its ramrod-stiff posture; every inch of her radiated royal anger.

Henry, too, was looking around in disgust,

his blue eyes flashing ire. But he had a man's ability to live with what he could not immediately change, and merely said evenly to her, "Yes, it will have to be cleaned up before it is fit for royal residence. No doubt, they can find us a few chambers where we can stay while it's being done." He seemed to look on it as one more military campaign, where one was forced to bed down in the midst of disagreeable conditions.

But Eleanor had arrived in the country where she was to be queen and had no intention of settling for less than royal conditions. Her bearing became absolutely rigid and her jaw set, as she said decisively, "This place is not fit for your horses and hounds, let alone the next King and Queen of England and your heir."

The royal household took up temporary residence that night in a borrowed hall in Bermondsey, across the Thames from the Tower of London. Baby William's nurse had her hands full; her charge had not enjoyed the tiring day of bouncing along in the litter, wrapped in fur robes. He was cutting a tooth, and it was clear the damp, cold climate did not agree with his somewhat frail constitution. The ladies took turns rocking and walking with him, but he was inconsolable until at last he slept from pure exhaustion.

It was now late Wednesday night, and before retiring, Eleanor informed her attendants the Coronation would be on Sunday. "So we will have much to do, ladies," Eleanor said, her face reflecting weariness after the trying day. "That gives us just three full days to prepare. On the morrow we will select what I will wear and consult with the seneschal as to the details of the feast."

"Where will the feast be, your grace?" questioned Matilde, obviously thinking of the ruined hall they had just left.

"Westminster, of course. Our displeasure as to its state has been conveyed to the proper men. It will be ready by then. Oh, I know repair of the woodwork will take longer, but the tapestries from Poitiers and Angers that I brought, and fresh rushes and whitewash will hide a multitude of sins."

Three days. Just three days until the ceremony with the feast to follow, when every noble in England would be present. Among them would be Simon de Winslade, of that Ysabeau was certain. She would gaze at him in three days. And if he saw her, and still loved her, she would see the truth of it shining in his azure eyes. She had to tell him what Blanche had done, that she knew about the emerald necklace, that she had never stopped loving him. If she could just do that, she could live the rest of her life at peace, no matter what Philippe chose to do. She told herself those things, repeated them like a novena. The part of her that wanted more, that struggled to break free and throw herself at Simon, damning the consequences, had to be thoroughly suppressed.

She had confessed her guilty longings to the priest, pouring out the sad story to Father André, including her husband's strange beliefs about marital love, confident that the seal of the confessional would prevent him from acting against Philippe's heresy. "And perhaps he will find no one here who believes as he does, Father, and his heresy will wither for lack of nourishment."

Father André groaned inwardly, knowing he must dash her hopes and wishing he could counsel her to leave the wicked man.

"I'm afraid I must tell you I have heard of their presence in England, although they are few. As you have been told by others, evidently, you do have grounds for an annulment, should you seek it before he truly makes you his wife."

There was silence on her side of the grille. Ysabeau sat there with her eyes tightly shut, her fist clenched to her mouth to keep from crying out in her agony of indecision. Her heart raced. Annulment. That was what she wanted to do, but it was too easy . . . surely in a new land Philippe should be given a fresh chance. And Simon very possibly did not love her anymore, having become disgusted with her lack of trust in him. No doubt, he had married by now, and she would see him at the Coronation with some fair English or Norman beauty on his arm. Perhaps he had always been wed, her guilty, tormented mind screamed. Blanche had not said anything about that. Perhaps he wanted her to have the necklace as a token of his love for her, while another lady wore his wedding ring.

"But what of my sin, Father?" she said at last, "what of my adulterous love for another man?"

Completely understandable under the circumstances, he thought, but not excusable under the Church's laws. So he doled out a penance, and she left, feeling she had done the proper thing as an obedient daughter of the Church, but feeling no lighter of heart. Her love for the tawny-haired Norman baron was unabated and could not be banished by a few Aves and Paternosters.

On the day of the Coronation, Ysabeau and Matilde arose while it was yet dark to prepare their mistress for the ceremony. They were the two chosen to assist Eleanor into the cloth of gold Coronation dress of stiff brocade that did much to conceal the fact that the Duchess of Aquitaine was fully seven months pregnant. A wimple of ivory linen covered her glorious golden hair, for on her head would rest the crown of the Queen of England. There was a collar of multicolored gems at the gathered neckline of the gown. Over all she wore a pelisse of purest white miniver.

"I wonder what my lord has chosen to wear," fretted Eleanor aloud. "Surely he knows he can't go to his Coronation dressed as if he's on a campaign. The English nobility will expect him to appear magnificent, or they won't respect him."

"I'm certain his grace will rise to the occasion," soothed Ysabeau as she settled the folds of the pelisse over the Duchess' shoulders. "After all, he has awaited this moment all his life."

"Dear girl, as always, you know how to calm me," sighed Eleanor, smiling gratefully at Ysabeau. "It's just that we've had so little time together to talk since arriving in London.

Henry's always off consulting with Archbishop Theobold, or his assistant, young Becket. You're quite a lovely sight today yourself, Ysabeau."

"Thank you, your grace. It's kind of you to notice on such a momentous day." Her flush of pleasure at the compliment heightened her already radiant glow of excitement.

Ysabeau was dressed in a mulberry velvet gown made up for her by the seamstress, Yvette, who had followed the court to Rouen but had chosen to go back to Poitiers rather than make the trip across the Channel.

"My joints swell enough in the winter, when it's damp," she had said, showing the gnarled joints of her callused work-worn hands to Ysabeau. "I imagine they would be one constant ache in England—they do say it's always damp there. I'll be here when you and your mistress return, I warrant. Eleanor will never stay away from Aquitaine for long, nor will she find a seamstress to make clothes for her as I do," she had cackled confidently.

When Ysabeau would have paid her for her painstaking work, the thin woman would take nothing, saying, "It's a leftover length, too short for anyone else but one of your height, and too vivid a color for any of these blonds. No, take it, my dear, with my blessing. It will look wonderful on you."

Ysabeau had never worn the gown in Rouen, and she had been thankful as she had drawn up the side lacings that molded the fabric to her lithe curves. A woman should always wear something new on the day when she hopes to see the man she loves.

Philippe, dressed for the ceremony in a fur-trimmed short dalmatic that unfortunately clashed with Ysabeau's gown, had awkwardly volunteered her jewelry the night before, fumbling as he handed back the items he had previously confiscated. "You can wear them at the Coronation, my dear."

"Don't worry, I'll give them back to you when the day is over," she had said coolly.

His mouth had tightened at her remark, but he added, "Here's an additional gift to go about your slender waist, darling," and handed her a gold link girdle with black velvet ribbon threaded through it that would indeed set off her tiny waistline to perfection. "There's no need to return these things."

"No, for we're in England anyway, aren't we, my lord?" she had retorted before she could stop herself. He went white, but made no move toward her, though his gray eyes narrowed and grew slate-hard.

She wished she had not said it, though it was true. There was no more need for Philippe to worry about her selling her jewelry to flee across the sea from him.

Now she only wanted a glimpse of Simon. Philippe couldn't stop her from that. And nothing he could do would make up for what had gone before.

Chapter Thirty

"I am granting and giving by this charter, confirmed to God and the Holy Church and to all my counts, barons, and subjects, all the concessions and grants, liberties and free customs which King Henry, my grandfather, gave and granted them. Likewise I outlaw and abolish for myself and my heirs all of the evil customs which he abolished and outlawed."

In those few words following his anointing, Henry erased Stepehn's reign, as if he had never existed, as if no ruler between himself and Henry I had intervened. The choir of monks sang vigorously as he stepped down, echoing the enthusiasm of the pages, knights, barons, bishops, priests, and abbotts who had filed into the abbey to witness their new ruler's consecration. The bells above tolled with a ponderous joyousness, as if threatening to break loose from their bonds, and soar.

They could soar no higher than Ysabeau's heart, for she had seen Simon de Winslade.

He had been in the procession of barons, as had Philippe, though fortunately the two men were not near one another, and now the Norman lord sat just three rows up, across the aisle from Ysabeau. He could easily see her if he but glanced over his shoulder, for she was near the aisle. She prayed he would do so, but as the Coronation ceremony began she was content just to simply drink in the sight of him.

Surely it was not fair for a man to look so devastatingly handsome. He was wearing black, and the contrast between it and the gold of his hair gave the latter an extra sheen. She longed to bury her fingers in that thick mane that curled slightly over the back edge of his black velvet mantle. As he turned his face slightly, she could see that he looked thinner, that his cheekbones stood out more above the lean planes of his face, his finely chiseled nose, and sensual lips. The sight of his golden mustache sent tremors through her as she remembered how the tender flesh above her lip had tingled when he had kissed her, and the slightly different sensation when his mouth had sought her breast, and then ventured lower.

As if conscious of her scrutiny, he glanced backward, looking from face to face as though he heard someone calling his name. Then he saw her, and those blue eyes locked on hers. His gaze was unreadable. She wondered what he was thinking. He glanced to her side for a moment, as if to break the contact, while her heart screamed, *No, don't look away yet!* And then his eyes came back to hers, more searching now, as if he would know her thoughts.

Hear this, then, Simon: *I love you. I have never stopped loving you. I want you. I* need *you. Please come to me.* Her eyes shone with a liquid luminescence, her pink lips quivered, and her delicate nostrils flared.

And suddenly his eyes took on the jewel-bright hue of the stained-glass sky behind him as his tightly held mouth relaxed into a smile that was meant for her alone.

The organ swelled just then in the glorious opening notes of a joyous anthem and the high pure voices of the choir leaped to meet it.

Philippe de Melle, sitting far down the row in back of Simon, chanced to look back at his wife just in time to see her face become transfigured with radiance. He thought that the December sun must have broken through the clouds and was shining through the window, catching her in its bath of light. But then he realized that the Abbey was no brighter than before; the only light was from the hundreds of candles that glowed from the altar, the side chapels and at points along the aisles. It was only her face which had taken on such incandescence. With a darkening suspicion snuffing out his appreciation of her heightened beauty, he followed the path of her gaze until his eyes rested on its source.

He had known before he looked it would be Simon de Winslade. His hand went unconsciously to his sword hilt, but, of course, it was not there; in such an hallowed place and at such an event, arms were not worn. So, his fist could only clench upon itself as his jaws tightened and his gray eyes turned cold and thoughtful.

The ceremony was over at last, and Westminister Hall began filling with the hundreds of nobles, prelates, knights and servants.

The army of workmen that had descended on the hall in the early hours of Friday morning had, indeed, worked miracles. Though much remained to be done to make it livable, the banquet hall itself was once again a monument to the ambitious building program ordered by the flamboyant, scandalous William II, Henry's great-uncle.

Fresh rushes from upriver, mixed with sweet herbs, lay underfoot, almost entirely banishing the foul odors that had nearly overpowered the royal party just three days before.

At the center of the high table sat the newly crowned King Henry and Queen Eleanor. Henry had risen to the occasion, and was a truly royal figure in a scarlet velvet dalmatic embroidered all over with snarling, gold, rampant lions. In contrast to the voluminous cloaks worn by the English, his ermine mantle came only to his waist. Ysabeau had seen them point to its length and refer to the new King as "Curtmantle," a sobriquet that seemed destined to stick. On his right sat the aged Theobold, Archbishop of Canterbury, who had set the crown upon his head. On Eleanor's other side sat Henry, Bishop of Winchester, who was the late King Stephen's brother; he had played both sides of the fence for so long that his face was permanently molded into lines of easy amiability. Even now, he was laughing, vastly amused at something Eleanor had just leaned over to say.

The spaces at the side tables were still filling as the hundreds of banqueters sought their places. Ysabeau, sitting next to a silent Philippe and sharing his trencher, let her eyes watch the pantler as he approached the high table. He had a towel draped around his neck, so long that he held an end in each hand. His outstretched left arm balanced King Henry's napkin, seven loaves of white bread, and four trencher loaves; in his left hand he carried the salt cellar for the high table. Assisted by the ewerer and the butler, he placed the salt on Henry's right and the trenchers to his left. He gave two knives to the carver and one to his Sovereign, then cut the trencher loaves into bread plates with his own special knives.

Next, the ewerer approached the dais, laden with two basins, and after straining the water through cloth, a specially honored knight tasted it. Only then was the water deemed fit to wash the King's and Queen's hands.

Ysabeau could see all this clearly, for no one had taken the place opposite hers, obstructing her view. However, as the basins were presented all over the hall and all the guests washed their hands, she saw out of the corner of her eye a broad, black-clad pair of shoulders fill the vacant spot. Handing the damp linen towel back to the page who served their table, she looked up, prepared to give a civil greeting to their tablemate, but the words died in her throat.

It was Simon de Winslade who was settling in there, smiling affably at her. Her face paled and she could feel her heart accelerate into a runaway rhythm.

Simon, you must not sit here . . . I can't dissemble with you sitting so close, she thought.

But there was no need for pretense, for she saw Philippe scowling at her as if all her thoughts were naked to him.

"Find another place, de Winslade. Surely you know you're not welcome here," Philippe growled menacingly as the two men's eyes dueled above her. Philippe's voice was hoarse with suppressed rage.

Simon's lips moved, snarling beneath his golden mustache before he answered with a deceptively amiable drawl, "I fear I cannot, my lord. The latecomers must take what is left, and I can see nothing else available. Surely you do not expect me to sit below the salt?" Something about his derisive glance to the lower area implied that Philippe must know how awful that would be; he had all too recently left that status. Only his ennoblement and marriage to Ysabeau entitled him to sit where he was now, and Simon's manner suggested that he was still not quite worthy.

The air was thick with tension, and Ysabeau feared that they might come to blows. She was thankful that neither wore a sword, but they each carried eating daggers, and even a fistfight would be sufficient to land them in the Tower with charges of treason for brawling at such an event. Her eyes begged Simon to go elsewhere, anywhere, but he would not look at her. He knew what she was thinking, anyway, but he had waited too long for this opportunity, and now neither heven nor earth would move him.

Mercifully, the Archbishop of Canterbury arose at that moment and in stentorian tones led the assembled guests in saying a Latin grace. Then a profusion of dishes were brought in for the first course, and Ysabeau busied herself with choosing an appropriate sampling, despite the fact that her appetite had quite deserted her. She was entirely too aware of Simon's presence across the table, though she tried to make bright chatter to her sullen spouse to preserve appearances for the benefit of those sitting near them.

Simon now had a trenchermate, a golden-haired countess; whether this was by design or she had sat there due to the crowded conditions, Ysabeau could not tell. But after Ysabeau avoided Simon's first few glances, he began to flirt outrageously with the blond woman, who was evidently of the Anglo-Norman nobility. Ysabeau wondered sourly why her husband was not partnering her at table, until the woman happened to ostentatiously mention her "dear, departed lord," all the while smiling archly at Simon.

Ysabeau felt a sickening lurch of jealousy. She stabbed viciously at a slice of roast swan, an action which did not go unnoticed by Simon.

Philippe had seen the byplay between de Winslade and the Countess and had relaxed slightly. He even unbent enough to lavish some of his rarely displayed charm on the delighted woman, and she began to play the coquette in earnest, thrilled to have two such handsome gentlemen paying her compliments.

Has Simon known her long, or have they just met? Does she warm his bed already, or will he bed her for the first time tonight? Perhaps she has a rich demesne, and he will wed her. . . . Ysabeau could not stop torturing herself with these thoughts.

The Coronation banquet went on for hours, but Ysabeau heard little of the pretty speeches, and did not really taste any of the food. She only knew she longed for it to be over, so she could escape to her chamber, though it meant being alone with Philippe, who was in a very dangerous mood. Even if he chose tonight to avail himself of his husbandly privileges, she vowed her cup of misery could be no fuller.

At last the sweetened wafers and wine that signaled the end of the feast were served, and all arose, so that the trestle tables could be dismantled and the hall cleared for dancing. The beggars at the gate would eat well tonight, for there seemed to be as much food left as had been consumed. Even now the head almoner was gathering bits of meat and leftover heels of bread from the tables.

It was easier for Ysabeau to dissemble once the dancing began, to pretend that her heart did not ache as a succession of flushed, merry, and usually tipsy lords partnered her. Accompanied by the *hautbois* and tambourine, they did the *galliarde*, in which she and her partner, standing opposite one another, advanced, bowed, and retired again and again to the sprightly music. And after awhile, her mood lifted with the music.

Following the first dance, it seemed that

everyone wished to dance with the lovely *Maraise*. Around her the gossips were telling the lords and ladies of the English court, who admired her dark loveliness, all about Ysabeau de Ré: Such a provincial girl she was when she first came to Poitiers! One would hardly guess it to see her now, *hein*?

Frequently, when she caught sight of Philippe, it was to find him watching her, though at other times he appeared to enjoy himself enormously while dancing and chatting with many partners. The English and Norman women found him as engaging as Ysabeau had, she could tell. Philippe had never had any difficulty being charming when he wished. It was only she who knew his darker side.

After the first couple of dances, she lost sight of Simon. Probably bedding the Countess already, she thought viciously, but a few minutes later, during the rapid-paced *tourdion*, she saw the woman dancing, apparently content, with a Gascon knight. *Eh bien*, perhaps the Baron de Winslade was favoring someone else. What did it matter, though, the miserable voice inside her insisted, for he could have almost any woman in this hall. She had seen the women's eyes following him just as they had in Poitiers.

King Henry led the applause as Queen Eleanor began the *branles*, a Poitevin dance, with her brother, William. Eleanor was clearly at the height of her glory tonight, for she was again a queen. She had proven she had known what she was doing to divorce the King of France to marry a mere Duke many years her junior, for now Henry and she were master and mistress of a vast empire. Ysabeau smiled as Eleanor graciously acknowledged the cheers, looking many years younger. She knew of no other woman who could appear so agile, though heavily pregnant.

Then suddenly, as the dance ended, she found Simon standing in front of her.

"The next dance is mine," he said.

On hearing his demand, she stiffened and pulled away, but his strong hand had already reached to claim hers. "Are you sure the Countess can spare you, my lord?" she hissed acidly.

He looked amused. "Lady Edyth? She's danced with every man in the room tonight. Paying her court at table was just an act, and you know it."

"I know no such thing," she insisted, her body still rigidly resisting his pull toward the dancing.

"What would you have me do, make eyes at you through the whole meal, as I wanted to do?" he shot back. "Your darling Philippe looked as if he would put a dagger in my back. . . . Come on, Ysa." It was particularly difficult to resist him when he called her by her nickname and used that sweet coaxing tone.

"Which is precisely why I can't dance with you. You'll undo all the good you did by your acting. I'll warrant you suffered mightily throughout it, my lord, though none could tell from your fatuous look."

He looked so absurdly pleased at her furious compliment that she wanted to strike him. "I was convincing, wasn't I? Come on,

Ysabeau. I particularly want to dance this one with you."

"I cannot!" she insisted, for she could tell from the opening strains it was a *danse au chapelet*. She dared not. Her feelings would be too transparent. "Philippe—"

"—would not object in this crowd. Besides, no one does this dance with their spouse—it's quite frowned upon." He looked down his nose, as if he was a troubadour making a judgment at a court of love, until Ysabeau giggled in spite of herself, and let him lead her into the throng.

Conflicting emotions churned within her as their bodies swayed in the intricate movements. His eyes remained on hers until she felt hypnotized, robbed of her will. She longed for the end of the dance as much as she dreaded it.

The *danse au chapelet* finished with a kiss on the lips. There had been much ceremonial kissing that day, and much of what Matilde referred to as "drunken trenchermate kissing," in which one endured the attentions of an intoxicated dinner partner, perhaps pleasurably if one was a little tipsy too. But the kiss between Simon and Ysabeau as the sweet strains of the music came to a close was neither of these. Though they touched with no part of themselves but their lips, there was a depth of feeling to the kiss which seemed to isolate them from the rest of the crowd, much as two expert dancers will find themselves dancing alone while the rest of the crowd draws back to admire.

At the first touch, it was as if a bolt of lightning hit Ysabeau; then her lips clung to his, seeking and demanding. His lips felt so good, the sensation of warmth washing over her as familiarly as if he had kissed her only yesterday. Eyes closed, she drank in the sweet honey of him, swaying toward that hard body, but not allowing herself to bend against it, for she knew if she allowed herself that contact, she would never let him go. She would play the wanton for all the court to see.

As it was, all the other dancers had long finished their brief kisses and many were staring at the pair who obviously did not want the moment to end. And she knew Philippe had seen them—she knew it without even being sure of where he stood. There was malevolence in the air.

Ysabeau fancied every murmur was about them as she turned nonchalantly away from Simon, then looked desperately back at him after they had walked a few paces through the crowd. As the musicians struck up still another dance, she turned to him again.

"Simon, I am afraid. Philippe—"

"You fear what he will say. Ah, my love, I'm sorry . . ." He, too, was shaken by the intensity of the emotion he'd just felt. All he had wanted was this dance, and a brief kiss at the end. But he knew it had seemed a lover's kiss to anyone watching.

"It is not his words, Simon, that frighten me." Her fear showed in her eyes, those lovely, expressive liquid eyes with their slight upward tilt that so enchanted him. He cursed himself that they were now full of panic. She was like a doe that has ventured into a snare, and now the snare was jerking tight. "He will beat me,

Simon, and worse . . ." She wanted him to understand without her saying the words. "There is much you do not know. I must talk to you. . . ."

He thought she meant she was afraid for her life, she could see. He did not know that she and Philippe had never truly been man and wife, that there were worse things than death, now that she knew Simon still loved her. He had not said it, in so many words, but she could tell from the moment they touched.

He had been thinking for desperate moments while she stared anxiously at his face, then blankly at the careening dancers, as if still enjoying the festivities. "Go back and join the dance, Ysabeau," he said in low tones, staring out, as if also watching the dancers. "He is still here, dancing. Keep him here, at all cost. Within the hour, your tiring-woman will deliver a flagon of wine to your chamber. It will put him to sleep very quickly, and better yet, he will have little remembrance of this evening's events. It will seem like a dream. Make sure he drinks it, *ma chère*. It will not matter if you drink too, if you cannot avoid it—you will only sleep rather soundly."

Oh, it would matter, her heart cried at once. *I would hate to lose the memory of that kiss!* "How do you come by such a potion?" she said. "Are you a sorcerer? Or is it that you are experienced in deceiving husbands?"

He smiled. "Neither, I'm glad to say. Just a trick an old crusader taught me to get away from an enemy."

She smiled tremulously. "Thank you,

Simon."

"Try to get him to drink it as soon as he comes in. I'm sorry, my darling, to have endangered you. . . ."

He dared not touch her in this throng, where so many eyes were upon them.

"It's all right. I would have dared it all over again to see you, to touch you again. I did not dream of a kiss."

He smiled, and her fears burst like a bubble within.

"We will talk soon. Tomorrow, if possible. Do not miss any opportunity to leave the hall. Never fear, I shall know your movements, and find a way to be with you. Now I must go."

Chapter Thirty-one

She managed to dance a half dozen more dances, and then passed from one chattering group to another, before Philippe appeared at her side like a sullen thundercloud, grabbing her elbow and propelling her toward the door of the banquet hall. She forced a rueful smile to her face as they passed several groups of lords and ladies, a smile which said, "My lord is surly with drink. Please pardon his rudeness," though inside her heart quaked with fear. Would the wine be there? Had she given Simon enough time to get it to Marie? How would he know where to find their chamber? Would Philippe drink it, or refuse, having already drunk enough to ensure a splitting head at dawn?

All the way to their chamber he mumbled threats. "Wait till I get you alone, *ma dame* . . . cuckold me in front of all eyes, will you, slut . . . I've waited too long as it is . . ."

She need not have worried. Marie was there as they entered the small chamber, yawning sleepily and rubbing her eyes as she rose to greet them.

"Good eventide, my lord, my lady. I've heard it was a magnificent Coronation and banquet. I've taken the liberty of bringing you some mulled wine. It will help you rest and awake refreshed on the morrow. You must be tired, after such a long day. I'll just assist my lady from her *bliaut*, my lord, while you have some of the wine." Her back to Philippe momentarily, the tiring-woman's eyes met Ysabeau's meaningfully.

Ysabeau breathed a brief prayer soundlessly as Philippe settled himself on a bench by the brazier after pouring a cup of the warmed beverage. She watched him sip it broodingly as Marie unlaced the gown with deliberate slowness, first undoing the tight-fitting mulberry sleeves, then the back.

He watched her insolently, knowing she was humiliated by his leering face and lewd remarks in front of her servant.

"Ah, yes, let's see your bare shoulders. That's it, lovely . . . now turn around, show me your back . . . the gown does lace clear down to that tight little ass, doesn't it? That's it, lift it off, woman . . . ah , delicious nipples. I can see them through your chemise . . . growing hard, are they? You must be thinking of the feel of my hand on them. . . ."

Marie raised anguished eyes to Ysabeau's bloodless face, silently assuring her that she'd be nearby should her mistress cry out. But Ysabeau shook her head, almost imperceptibly. It would be all right. It had to be. Simon said it would be.

"You're too laggard, bitch," Philippe said at last, draining the rest of the cup, then tossing it away with a flourish. Ysabeau stood in her chemise, trying not to tremble. "I'll take it from here," he said. He gave the plump woman a shove, and she retreated from the room, giving Ysabeau a last worried glance before Philippe bolted the door behind her.

"*Maintenant, ma chère*. Uncover yourself. I will do what I should've done long ago."

With fingers that shook as if she had an ague, she pushed the sheer silk garment that was the last barrier between herself and Philippe down to the rushes at her feet and waited for his onslaught.

He stalked her as a wolf does a deer. As he came closer, he murmured, "Thought you could betray me before my very eyes, did you? And with de Winslade, that Norman scum. . . ."

But she was determined not to give in to fear, for in a moment she would be screaming if she did, and like a wolf, he would launch himself at her. She wondered how she had ever considered him gentle. He was deadly at this moment. She must stall him, win time for the drug to work.

"My lord, I thirst. Surely you would give me leave to drink some wine first. I vow, my throat is parched." She strolled casually toward the little table, aware of his hot eyes on her nakedness. At least, if the drug didn't work quickly enough to save her, it would dull her remembrance of what would follow.

His arm shot out as she passed by him. It felt a trifle unsteady, but it caught her waist in a bruising hold. Then he shoved her roughly against the stone wall and chuckled as she winced in pain. "No, my lovely, all the wine is for me." With one hand he waved an admonishing finger at her as he used the other to pour the remaining contents into his cup, which he then grabbed—unsteadily. Yes! His speech was thicker, too.

"Jusshhh like . . . all of you ishh for me," he finished as he again poured the potent beverage down his throat in a couple of gulps.

He slammed himself against her, his mouth cruelly biting her lips as she sought to deny his tongue entrance. His hand pinched her tender nipples as he forced her to feel his insistent manhood pushing against her through his velvet tunic.

"Now, you undresshh me, wife, and we'll see how a husband treatshh a wife who is shhtraying. . . ."

Silently she did his bidding, wondering when the wine would take effect, her mind screaming, *Now—please now!* She removed the tunic and light woolen undergown, and he was left in shirt and chausses, grinning blearily at her. The fine linen shirt came next, smelling of stale sweat and spilled wine.

"My *chausses*, my wife . . ." He shoved her to her knees, where she could reach the woolen hose that were tied to his belt at several points. She tried to ignore his manhood jutting obscenely at her. With shaking fingers she undid them, rolling each one down as slowly as she dared.

"Ysabeau, I—" But he could not even finish his sentence. Suddenly the drug reached his brain, and he fell across her like a log. He began to snore as soon as his head settled on the rushes.

"Thank God," she whispered. He was surprisingly heavy for such a slightly built man, but he had only pinned one of her legs in his fall, so she was able to struggle free without much difficulty. She covered him up gingerly with a blanket from their bed, and then settled herself to sleep.

Chapter Thirty-two

The next morning, Ysabeau was up at prime, planning to avoid her husband as long as she could. She knew Queen Eleanor would desire to return to the hall at Bermondsey, for the state apartments at Westminster, where they'd spent the night, were still not fit for royal residence.

The drug had apparently worked as Simon had promised, for when Ysabeau finally encountered Philippe at the midday meal in the hall at Bermondsey, he smiled at her as if nothing untoward had happened, and said, "Thanks for covering me up, my love. I guess I celebrated a bit too heartily, eh?"

"You're quite welcome, my lord. I only wish I could've gotten you into bed, but you were dead weight. I hope you are not too stiff?" She gave him her sweetest smile, but felt guilty inside at her duplicity. By the rood! It was incredible that he had the power to make her feel that way, especially after the events of last night!

Ysabeau knew she was still in jeopardy. If some wagging tongue or virtuous wife present last night should consider it his or her duty to mention his wife's scandalous conduct, Philippe might remember everything. It was unlikely to come from anyone from Aquitaine, however. Flirtations outside marriage were such an accepted element of courtly love that it was really more unusual to be in love with one's spouse. The Anglo-Norman court was more unpredictable, for they had never held as closely to the tenets of *le gai savoir*.

Ysabeau was to be frustrated in her desire to see Simon for five long days, for the Queen kept her ladies hard at work in Bermondsey, organizing the household and preparing for Christmas, stitching tiny articles of clothing for Prince William and the coming baby, and magnificent festival vestments for the Archbishop of Canterbury. Eleanor herself sewed the matched pearls in place on the splendid cloth of gold chasuble. The elderly Theobald would be mightily pleased with his gift.

She knew Simon was being kept busy also, for Henry was determined to totally reorganize the government and the English legal system, and was conferring for hours every day with his nobles. She had seen him once or twice at mealtimes, but always from a distance. He was careful not to put her in peril again. But when it was safe for a few fleeting seconds, their eyes met, and what a wealth of emotions were conveyed in those glances! It was those looks which kept her believing that the dance and the kiss had not been a dream.

Then on the Thursday before Christmas, King Henry's favorite destrier, who had not been thriving since the Channel crossing, was found dead in his stall. Queen Eleanor felt she had finally been given a solution to her dilemma of what to give her lord for a New Year's gift.

"How providential," she said to her ladies as they assembled early the next morning, "that a horse fair is held at Smoothfield every Friday. That is where we shall go today. Matilde, summon my seneschal to order an escort for us, and bid your lord to accompany us—oh, and that rascal, de Winslade, as well. I value their judgment in horseflesh, and Simon, especially, will know my dear lord's taste in mounts."

It was all Ysabeau could do to restrain herself and not clap and laugh with glee. Her eyes met Matilde's joyously and her mouth broke into a triumphant grin. In such a party, surely there would be a chance for private conversation—if only it was possible to avoid having Philippe go along.

Fortunately, because it was Christmas Eve, Philippe was in the midst of preparing some verses for the banquet on the morrow.

After changing into her royal blue riding dress and squirrel-lined, hooded cloak, she went to the outer courtyard, where everyone was to assemble. Ami trotted excitedly at her heels, sensing an adventure in the offing. Ysabeau had not the heart to deny him permission to come along, for he had been cooped up much of late, due to the damp, foul weather of an English

December, and the huge dog needed exercise. He was always well-behaved, staying right with Ysabeau and her mount and generally ignoring the temptation to stray.

In the courtyard the horses stamped, impatient to be off, their breath forming clouds of stream in front of their tossing heads. There was an enclosed cart for Eleanor, whose physician had pronounced her too pregnant to ride any longer. The Queen chafed at the restriction, grumbling, "This thing shakes me worse than a bucking horse," but complied, perhaps remembering the incident in Anjou when Philippe had caught her runaway mount.

It was the first clear, crisp day since the Coronation, and everyone was eager for fresh air and diversion. But Ysabeau was experiencing much more than just pleasant anticipation as she prepared to mount her chestnut mare; she was in transports of joy, for Simon would be with her. They would not be alone; there were two other of Eleanor's ladies, and six men-at-arms, but it was enough.

Rene and Simon joined them just as Ysabeau was settling her long skirts in the saddle. Though the Norman gave the Queen a warm greeting which brought a flush of pleasure to her cheeks, his gaze went immediately thereafter to Ysabeau.

His eyes told her that she looked exceptionally beautiful today as she sat her palfrey. The mare had caught her tension, and was curvetting around the courtyard, but Ysabeau controlled her with easy skill. The amused tilt to Simon's mouth told her he knew exactly why the mare was behaving so.

The party clattered across London Bridge, up Lombard Street until it turned into Newgate Street. The famous horse fair lay in the shadow of the Priory of St. Bartholomew, just outside Newgate.

The field was filled with horses of every description: warhorses for knights, palfreys for everyday riding, pack and cart horses, plough horses, and unbroken colts. Ysabeau was surprised to also see cattle, pigs, and sheep in another corner of the field being inspected by sturdy yeomen. The air was full of stallions' whinnied challenges and barnyard smells.

Simon was at Eleanor's side, pointing out this horse's strong haunches, that one's intelligent eyes, another one's sloping shoulders. Still, he contrived to keep Ysabeau near him, occasionally giving her a look of such blazing intensity that she could have sworn it was not cold enough to snow after all.

He steered Eleanor clear of a destrier she admired, fearlessly grasping the massive stallion's head and revealing the short teeth, thereby exposing the would-be seller as a cheat and a liar, for he had sworn the horse to be only four summers old.

"Ah, Simon, you have saved me again," said Eleanor. "I would have purchased that handsome beast in a trice. Should we buy the chestnut Flemish stallion, then?"

"Yes, I think His Grace would be very pleased with him," Simon answered. "But what about the black mare over there for yourself, my Queen? She has Moorish breeding—see her fine head, those alert eyes? She would carry you well, and is surely fit only for royalty."

"Yes, I remember that breed well from the Crusade. Of course, I must have her!"

Ysabeau could see the Queen was flattered by Simon's words, though she felt no jealousy. His charm and loyalty had made him valuable to both Henry and Eleanor, and that had brought him into her life.

The party began to remount once two horses were paid for and delivery arrangements made. Eleanor rubbed the small of her back before climbing wearily into the cart. She tired much more easily than was her wont, now that she was at the latter stages of pregnancy.

Ysabeau, however, was regretful that the expedition was nearing its end, and wondered what Simon was feeling; but then he edged his mount closer and said softly, "If you were mine I'd have bought you the black mare. Someday, when you *are* mine, we'll return here."

She closed her eyes as the wave of longing swept over her. "Simon, you must not say such things."

He was silent, which did not constitute an apology for his words. She looked away from his compelling eyes, and saw Ami looking up at her sympathetically.

Sometimes the dog looked so thoughtful, she was sure he would begin to speak to her. He always seemed to mirror her moods—quiet when she was pensive, merry and playful when she was happy. Now he was studying her face, and looking at the Norman baron, cocking his head as if to try and understand the tension that ran between them.

They reentered the City through Newgate and Simon maneuvered his destrier so that he was next to her.

The party stopped outside a vintner's establishment because Eleanor had heard he stocked a particularly good wine from Bordeaux. While the lords and ladies waited outside with the Queen, talking and laughing, a squire was dispatched to order several tuns.

Simon edged his mount over close to the eaves, where a rakish gray tomcat was grooming himself atop a barrel. "Hello, what's this? What a handsome beast you are," he crooned soothingly as he leaned over and plucked the cat from his perch.

Ysabeau eyed the Norman baron in surprise as the beast settled itself amiably in Simon's arms. "Why, Simon, I didn't know you liked cats! Are you troubled with mice in your chamber?"

"No," he said softly, for her ears alone, and his blue eyes danced with mischief. "Actually I cannot stand the creatures—they make me sneeze." As if to prove it, he did so, noisily, but continued to hold onto the tabby. At her puzzled look he whispered, "Watch and wait. I cannot let our time together end so soon."

He whistled for Ami, who had been nosing around the periphery of the group, and surreptitiously showed him what he held in his arms. "Look, old fellow, isn't this a nice kitty? You *like* kitties quite as well as I do, *n'est-ce pas*?"

The gray cat bristled and hissed, trying to retreat up Simon's shoulder. Ami danced excitedly around the horse, barking and jumping at the feline.

Suddenly the cat had had enough of this silly game, and with a throaty yowl, clawed his way out of Simon's grasp and dashed between the other horses' hoofs to escape. Ami was in immediate pursuit.

Simon's muttered imprecations were lost in the neighing and plunging of his stallion as he struggled to control the horse, for the cat had scratched the destrier's withers as he launched himself groundward.

"Ami!" called Ysabeau after her pet, who was flying down the narrow sidestreet after the fleeing gray blur. She was sure that he would stop in his tracks, obedient as always. But he did not.

"Simon, he'll get lost!" cried Ysabeau in distress, and spurred her palfrey after the dog.

After calling an apology to Eleanor, who had peeked out her curtains at the commotion, Simon joined Ysabeau in the chase, grinning at the success of his ploy.

Up and down the winding streets they galloped, Ami a black and tan flash ahead of them. Ysabeau could no longer see the cat, and wondered as she held on for dear life why her pet was being so willful. It was not at all like him. Often, they narrowly avoided hitting pedestrians or upsetting carts of fruits and vegetables. Curses followed them when Simon's mount overturned a stand bearing pots and pans, scattering them over the street with a tremendous clamor.

The cold wind stung as Ysabeau struggled to stay in the side saddle. They were near the river now—Ysabeau could smell it—but she had no clearer idea of their location than that, nor had she any idea how to get back to Bermondsey.

Suddenly she could not see Ami at all, and she reined in her horse, disgusted at her pet, but worried for him, too. Simon pulled up also.

"I suppose we had better go back. I don't see him anywhere," she said reluctantly, breathing hard.

"Yes. By the saints, Ysabeau, I'm sorry. I feel awful about this. I merely meant to stage an excuse for us to go off by ourselves for awhile. I never meant for you to lose your pet." A glance at his troubled face showed the sincerity of his words. "I promise, I will post notices about the City. I will offer a reward for him."

"Please don't blame yourself, Simon, I'm not angry at you. I can't believe he would be so heedless of my call. Were you hurt when the cat fought his way off your horse?"

"No, my gauntlets protected my wrists," he assured her, but she insisted he remove them so she could see for herself. As her slender fingers touched his strong hands, he suddenly noticed how cold they were. On an impulse he carried a hand to his mouth and kissed her fingers, the gesture bringing a small smile to her face though her eyes were welling with tears.

Chapter Thirty-three

And around the next corner sat Ami, tongue lolling out, as if he had merely been waiting for them to catch up. He did have the grace to look remorseful, however, after noting his mistress' stormy expression.

Ysabeau was off her mount in a flash. "Ami, shame on you! You have never been so bad! I was so worried." But her remonstrance turned into a hug as the dog sought to kiss her face in greeting.

She looked ruefully at Simon, but he was grinning.

"I never thought he would cooperate so enthusiastically with my little ruse. Look at him—he was never lost! I suspect he knew exactly how far behind we were, didn't you, scoundrel?"

Ami wagged his tail in agreement.

"*Eh bien*! We are all together again. Now why don't we take advantage of this time together? What shall we do? Obviously I cannot keep you out till dawn on the excuse of hunting your dog, though I would like to. . . ."

Suddenly he noticed her cheeks were white and pinched and her nose very red. "Ah, my dear, you're frozen. We must get you inside and warm you up, or you'll get lung fever again, and then I shall murder your dog just before your loyal Marie murders me. I have it—we are just across from Southwark now. We'll go into the cookshop and get some food and drink to warm us. I'm sure you are hungry, *n'est-ce pas*?"

It had been hours since she had last broken her fast, so Ysabeau agreed.

She had heard of the famous cookshop on the southern bank of the Thames that was open at all hours of the day and night, and served all manner of food. She could smell the delicious aromas drifting in the clear, cold air from several yards away.

Inside, the smell of roasting meat was almost unbearably enticing. In less time than Ysabeau would have imagined, she and Simon were comfortably seated at a trestle table in the corner, feasting on succulently roasted capon and washing it down with a delicious Rhenish wine, while at their feet Ami contently gnawed a meat-encrusted bone. Though there were many in the establishment, from nobles to merchants and their plump, rosy-faced wives, they were quite alone at their table.

The crackling glow from the nearby fireplace lit their faces.

"I wanted—" she began.

"You said—" he started to say at the precise same moment.

She laughed, then her breath caught as his strong hand captured hers on the roughhewn wood table.

"I have wanted to be alone with you for so many days. . . ." he murmured caressingly, and she felt the glow quicken in the center of her being. "You said you had things to tell me, my Ysabeau, but first I must know this—do you love me?"

It surprised her that he should even have to ask. "You know I do. I have never stopped loving you, though I tried, when I thought you did not care." She gazed at him shyly, hardly daring to breathe as wonder took hold of him and with a victorious cry he pulled her close and kissed her, right over the remains of their dinner.

He was grinning when he released her. "You know, I thought *you* didn't care for *me*. I could not undertand why I couldn't forget that haughty court damsel, especially after she married another." His last words sobered them, made them remember why this day was so bittersweet. "Why *did* you marry him, Ysabeau? And what's wrong with it now? Something is, or you would have forgotten this foolish Norman long ago."

She then explained how jealousy and despair had led her to accept the solace Philippe had seemed to offer, and how she had sought to comfort Philippe, too, when Bernard de Ventador had so threatened his feeling of worth.

"But—" he probed.

"He is a Catharist, and would not be a true husband to me. It means I will never even have his children to love." What an agony of humiliation this was, to speak of these things to him! Her husband would not even make love to her. How undesirable it must make her appear. Even men who despised their wives could bring themselves to sire heirs on them. She closed her eyes as if in pain, and a tear escaped from under the sooty lashes.

He had been sitting across from her; he came now to sit by her side, an arm about her shoulders.

"He has never made love to you?"

She shook her head, still fighting a flood of anguish.

His hand stole gently to her cheek, brushing away the drop of moisture, then he gently forced her chin back toward him. "Ysabeau, look at me." His gravelly voice was honeyed velvet to her ears. "Listen to me. I am glad he has never touched you. You are mine, and would have been with me for months had we both not been so foolish."

She smiled tremulously, but continued, "Now he threatens to . . . have me. He's known that I love you ever since Blanche died and I . . . found out about the necklace." His shocked looked necessitated a brief recounting of Blanche's tragic story. "I would have come to you then, but he sold the emerald necklace and I couldn't. I had no way. And then King Stephen died. Now he knows I want to be free and he's going to . . ."

"Force himself on you," he supplied, the look in his eyes boding murder.

"Simon, he's changed. I think he is a little . . . mad. I'm afraid of him now. He's nothing like the charming gentle man he pretends to be in front of others."

"Ysabeau, you are not staying with him," he pronounced decisively. "It's too dangerous. I'll speak to Henry. He'll intercede with the Church."

"Simon, an annulment takes time," she said, fear seizing her in its icy grip.

"Indeed, but I'll not have you in his clutches in the meanwhile. You'll go away with me. He need not know where you are."

If she went away with Simon, she could be branded an adulteress and then Philippe might divorce her. But perhaps that would make it difficult for Simon; he had not said anything about their marriage. Perhaps he was not free to marry, or perhaps he was not willing to give his name to a divorced woman, though he would give her his protection. For the moment, though, none of that mattered. Her mind was whirling with apprehension, knowing she had to take some dangerous step. She could not endure things as they were, nor would Simon permit her to. There was, at least, a wonderful sense of haven in that. She could see from the faraway look in his eye that he was plotting a way for her to come to him.

"I don't like to think of you being with him another night," he said, after taking a long draft from his goblet. "Yet it's already late, and I'm sure you'll need to make some preparations. . . ."

"You needn't fear for me, Simon," she interrupted, "for I attend her grace tonight."

He was visibly relieved. "And tomorrow is Christmas. The banquet will take up most of the day. *Bon*! It will be a good time to slip away."

"Yes, especially with Philippe performing for the King and Queen. But Simon, I haven't said I will go. . . ."

A winter chill cooled his eyes. They became wary, guarded. "What game is this, lady? Do you play me for a fool?"

She sensed his hurt and was sorry for it, but his summary manner had both amused and frightened her. She had only been seeking to lighten the atmosphere with a little playfulness, but she could see he thought she was still playing the capricious court lady.

Ysabeau looked at him from under her lashes, mockingly pretending to be as wounded as he. "I would never," she pouted, "go away with a man who doesn't love me." Yet it was not all teasing; she had to be sure.

"Love you? *Love you*? By the eyes of God, woman, I *adore* you!" Holding her face between his two large hands he lowered his mouth to hers, seizing her in a kiss that set off explosions within her. It went on for endless moments, until they were both gasping.

"Now, my darling Ysabeau, will you go away with me, tomorrow night? I'll find you someplace safe to bide until you are free of that bastard. Henry and Eleanor will help us."

She did not doubt it was possible. "With all my heart, my love. But forgive me. I am afraid.

Will we be shunned, banned from court? I do not care for myself—I only want to be with you. But it would trouble me greatly if your love for me cost you your chance of advancement."

"Silly girl, do not fear. We will free you of your mistaken marriage, and we will plight our troth in a real, flesh and blood marriage. You will be the Countess de Winslade, and I promise I will give you babes until you cry, 'Hold, enough!' " He had seized both her hands in his; his eyes mirrored the shining joy in hers.

The moment was interrupted by the proprietor of the cookshop, who had approached their table diffidently. "My lord, please pardon me, but it's Christmas Eve, and I planned to close down—in honor of the birthday of Our Lord, you understand."

The place was empty. They had been so intent on one another that they had been oblivious of the passage of time. It was now late in the afternoon. They could see through the oiled parchment windows that the winter sunlight was fast fading.

"*Mais oui*, my good man. We were having such an enjoyable talk that we forgot the time. Pardon us." The gold coin Simon handed him made the taverner's forgiveness a certainty.

Chapter Thirty-four

Fortunately Southwark was near Bermondsey, but it was fully dark by the time Simon and Ysabeau, with Ami trotting faithfully behind, rode into the courtyard.

"And just where have you had my wife, Baron de Winslade?" came a voice from the shadows as they handed their horses to a waiting page and were entering the hall.

Philippe de Melle lounged lazily against the wall, obviously watching for Ysabeau.

"We have been chasing Lady Ysabeau's foolish dog, my Lord de Melle," answered Simon, his voice short.

"Till dark? God's bones, a merry chase it must have been!" retorted Philippe stiffly.

"Saints, man! Lady Ysabeau was chilled to the bone. We stopped to warm ourselves and have something to eat at the cookshop in Southwark. I suggest you spare me the outraged husband act." Then, as Simon began to stride on into the hall, Philippe made a move as if to stop him.

The Norman baron turned on his heel. "I'm very tired and cold, my lord," Simon said, his voice menacing. "Drop your silly suspicions or you'll feel my steel. And you have a voice to preserve for tomorrow's festivities. I wouldn't want to hear you've made yourself hoarse haranguing your wife, who is equally fatigued. Good eventide, my Lady Ysabeau . . . my Lord de Melle."

Philippe stood there, glaring impotently at Ysabeau as Simon disappeared down the passageway. "Don't imagine you have heard the end of this, Ysabeau," he growled, but Ysabeau noted he kept his voice low. "Just because yon strutting stallion whinnies, don't think I cower, you slut. . . ." He waved a thin finger menacingly in her face.

Ysabeau opened her mouth to deny his unspoken accusation, but no words came. She shrank back, truly afraid of the viciousness she saw in his eyes.

A throat was cleared behind him. Ysabeau whirled, wondering what had brought Simon back so quickly, but it was only the Queen's seneschal.

"Excuse me, Lady de Melle, but her grace bade me send you to her as soon as you returned."

She murmured her acquiescence, thanking the saints for their heaven-sent interruption of Philippe's tirade.

Eleanor was already preparing for bed when Ysabeau arrived in her apartment. "We thought to make an early evening of it, Ysabeau. I'm more tired than I care to admit from our excursion today. I'm too old to be jaunting about, great with child, I suppose. And Bishop Henry will be saying a special Christmas Mass in the chapel at midnight. Did you find your dog? Ah, I see you did," she finished, for Ami had padded along behind Ysabeau, certain of his welcome in Queen Eleanor's apartments.

"Bad doggie. You gave your mistress a scare," cooed Eleanor, scratching the big dog's ears fondly. "Such irresponsible behavior from one about to be a father, too."

Ysabeau grinned. The Queen's prized mastiff bitch, Circe, was expecting to whelp a litter fathered by Ami any day now. "He did lead us on quite a chase before he decided to give himself up. I hope you didn't mind, your grace, but we were so hungry by the time he allowed us to catch up, that we stopped for a bite to eat in Southwark, and lost track of time." She colored, realizing she might have said too much.

Eleanor's clear gray-green eyes missed nothing. "Your meal certainly seems to have agreed with you," she said, noting the girl's blush, which was due to more than the winter wind. "Of course it did not matter. You'd have missed supper entirely, had you not stopped."

"Yes, your grace." Ysabeau began to comb out Eleanor's lustrous, wavy blond hair. The Queen, already clad in her bedrobe, relaxed as Ysabeau bent to her ministrations, wielding the silver-backed brush and comb with soothing skill. There was silence for long moments, punctuated by the occasional hissing sounds of coals in the brazier and the whistling wind beyond the shutters.

"Ysabeau," said Eleanor suddenly in the stillness, turning to her and looking penetratingly into her eyes, "I have lived with two very different men, and have known several others. . . . I know what is said of me. Part of it is true. But I will tell you that love, true love, for all the pain it must sometimes involve, is worth daring everything you have and are." Eleanor's eyes were no longer focused on her; they seemed to be looking inward, remembering her own tumultuous youth: her marriage to Prince Louis of France in her teens, her boredom with his monkish ways, her glamorous, dangerous participation in the crusade, her suspected love affairs with Raymond of Antioch and Geoffrey Le Bel, Henry's own father.

Why had Eleanor said that to her, Ysabeau wondered. The last thing they had discussed was her supper with Simon. Could Eleanor read minds? Could she know what had been discussed, that even now Ysabeau was planning to flee her cruel husband and her marriage vows? Could Eleanor be drawing a parallel between her own passionate struggles to find the right mate and Ysabeau's quest for love? Was she giving Ysabeau her tacit blessing to do whatever was necessary to be in Simon's arms? Her questions were not answered, for Eleanor lapsed into a thoughtful silence once again.

As soon as the tall woman was comfortably ensconced in the great bed, Ysabeau curtseyed to take her leave, but at the door, she blurted out impulsively, "Your Grace, I just wish you to know I have b—I *am* happy in your service. I have learned much from you." She blinked to hold back the tears. This would be the last time she would ever perform this bedtime service for the Queen.

"Dear Ysabeau," said Eleanor, touching her cheek with her slim, elegant fingers. "I have grown so fond of you. You have met and surpassed all the expectations that I had of you when you came to me. Such a waif you were then! Merry Christmas, my dear. And be happy."

She knew, then. She had to know.

Marie found a moment early Christmas Day to speak with Ysabeau alone.

"It's all arranged, my lady. Lord Simon bade me tell you. His squire will have your mounts outside the gates at the appointed hour, and will follow afterward. You'll have a few things in a pack on your saddle, of course."

Ysabeau was startled. She hadn't known Simon would involve her tiring-woman and hoped it would place her in no danger when her mistress was discovered gone. Before she could voice that apprehension, however, Marie added, "I'll follow in a few days with the baggage wain, once we get word where you are."

"But Marie, how can I expect you to leave court? What about Matilde?" She was dumbfounded that Marie would be willing to give up her position at court.

"As to Matilde, she's already given me

leave, and her blessing. I'm sure she'll find a way to speak of it to you later. *Moi*, I tire of the constant hustle and bustle of court life. It's even worse here in England. I desire to go with you, my lady, and serve you, and care for your babes someday."

She was touched, and spontaneously embraced the fat Marie, though it was no easy task to reach her arms around her broad shoulders. "Oh, Marie, I'm so grateful to you! When you talk I can almost believe Simon will be my husband and there will be children. . . ." Her voice was choked with emotion.

"Never you doubt it, *ma dame*. And today it begins. Do not fear, we'll get you away. And Ami will stay with me, until I come."

Ysabeau nodded. "Doubtless that is best, since I don't know where I'll be."

Later, Ysabeau found Matilde and Rene readying themselves for the feast in their chamber, and slipped inside, after seeing that the corridor was empty. She wanted to avoid Philippe as long as possible.

"Matilde, I thank you for your generosity regarding Marie . . . and for your friendship. And yours, my Lord Rene."

The couple gathered her into an embrace, until all three were laughing, though with misty eyes.

"*Eh bien*! I am just glad you are finally doing the right thing!" Matilde said at last. "I have watched Philippe carefully of late, my dear, and the look in his eyes frightens me to my very soul."

"He is a mad dog," agreed Rene soberly.

"Be careful, *ma petite* Ysabeau. I care for you as for a sister."

"Simon will take good care of her," Matilde told her husband, then turned back to her friend. "Where are you going?"

"I don't even know myself," Ysabeau confessed with a nervous shiver. "I suppose that is for my safety, so that Philippe can in no way learn how to find me before our marriage vows are sundered."

Matilde nodded. "That's very wise. You will be in good hands with Simon de Winslade. He is a good man." Then, with the tears rolling from her eyes, she said, "When all is settled, my lord and I will come and visit."

Ysabeau was too overcome to speak. She just nodded, and fled the room. It was all beginning to seem real. If they succeeded in their plan, for better or worse, nothing would ever be the same again.

Chapter Thirty-five

The hours before the Christmas feast were endless to Ysabeau. She had not slept much the previous night. Knowing she was expected to attend the midnight Mass with the Queen, she had lain wakeful through the early hours of the night, wondering what the morrow would bring; after the service in the chapel she had achieved, at best, only a fitful doze, tormented by fantastic nightmares in which a monstrously transformed Philippe kept snatching her from Simon's arms. Now the fatigue added to her high-strung state of anticipation made a very volatile mixture within her, indeed.

At last Queen Eleanor was clothed for the feast to her satisfaction, and her ladies attended her as she took Henry out to the stables to receive his gift. It was a week till New Year's Day, but the King was becoming suspicious as to why he was forbidden to enter the stable.

He was delighted with the horse, gleefully inspecting the handsome Flemish destrier from all angles before vaulting into the saddle, still as agile as a new-made knight. There was much of the boyish show-off still in Henry Plantagenet.

"You did very well, my dear. He's magnificent," he boomed to his wife. Eleanor smiled serenely, well pleased herself with the gold collar Henry had given her; on it, a leopard rampant grasped a large blood-red ruby in its forepaws.

"We must give Simon the credit for selecting the horse," Eleanor said. "You must remember to mention it when he arrives for the Christmas court. He insisted he would have to be a bit late for some reason." Ysabeau, her nerves already stretched to breaking point, could have sworn Eleanor gave her an odd look, but just then her attention was distracted as Ami ran to her side.

"Oh, no! Ami, how could you?" she exclaimed, annoyed to see him, for she had left the mastiff in the keeping of one of the pages. The dog had seemed to catch her mood, for he had whined inconsolably as she had left and strained against the boy's hold on his collar. If she had to take him back in now, she would be unable to attend her mistress in the formal procession into the hall.

Young Raymond, his dark curls flying as he caught up with his charge, panted, "I'm sorry, Lady Ysabeau. I went to take him to the kitchens, thinking a bone would settle his fidgets, but he charged out the side door after you."

"It's of no moment, boy. Just let him come along, Ysabeau," Eleanor commanded in her decisive fashion. "No doubt, half the men will have their prized hawks screeching on their arms as they arrive, including your crony, Thomas Becket," she said, looking at Henry. He and Theobald's archdeacon had become fast friends, inseparable, in fact. "Ami's always well-behaved, and waits patiently for his tidbits from the table."

"Thank you, your grace," Ysabeau said gratefully, though she heard Philippe beside her mumble, "Damned animal." He carried his *viole* with him, and was in a high state of exultation about his upcoming performance. He had boasted to Ysabeau that, in addition to a carol in tribute to the Infant Jesus and the Virgin Mary, he had composed a couple of *pastourelles* and an excellent *sirvente* that would have everyone roaring with laughter.

Good, she thought, then you and the rest won't see me escape. She was glad that his buoyant mood apparently blinded him to her nervousness.

The King's cook had outdone himself in the multitude and sumptuousness of the many dishes set before them.

Ysabeau was half-crazed with tension, but forced herself to eat, not knowing when she would next have the chance, and washed it down with a potent wine that calmed her to some extent.

A page slipped a message to her while

Philippe was making conversation with an ascetic-looking abbot on his right; the crumpled scrap of vellum bore the words, "When Philippe sings, slip out as if to the garderobe," scrawled in Simon's bold hand.

She looked over to the other table, where he was sitting, and found his eyes upon her. He winked, then went back to the hunk of beef he was devouring with his customary good appetite.

Would that I could appear so carefree, thought Ysabeau as she crumpled the missive unobtrusively and threw it under the trestle table, among the rushes.

She casually excused herself as the sweet wafers were being passed, pleading a need to answer nature's call now so as not to miss his singing.

"Good idea. There is plenty of time before I will be called. I think I'll go and do likewise," he said affably. She screamed inwardly in vexation, for she had seen Simon stroll casually out, as if bent on the same errand, sometime during the last course, and she knew he would be waiting for her. The men's and women's chambers were on opposite sides of the same passageway, so she was forced to hide her irritability as he escorted her there and back, for all the world like her jailer.

"Mary, His Mother, in robes of blue,
Echoing Heaven's celestial hue,
In the manger, of comfort bare
Laid the Babe all pink and fair . . ."

Ysabeau stifled the impulse to edge toward

the door as Philippe sang the first lines of his carol, for his eyes were on her. To the others, he must have appeared the doting husband, singing his heart out to his wife. She, however, knew she must wait until he shifted his attention to his royal patroness, which he did after he began the second song.

"When I around Poitiers did roam,
I spied a milkmaid, all buxom and gay . . ."

She gave him a last, long look, and despite everything, tears began welling in her eyes for all that might have been, had Philippe been the man he pretended to be to the rest of the world.

"Stay, Ami," she bid the mastiff, who had been dozing at her feet. He looked up alertly as she eased herself from her seat. "I'll be right back," she added, more for those nearby than for the dog.

A pair of torches flared in the inner courtyard, casting unreal shadows as Ysabeau stole out the side entrance, walking carefully on the icy cobbles and shivering as she peered through the moonless dark. There was no one out there—where could he be? Perhaps he had abandoned the idea, having had time to think of the dangers. . . .

"Here I am, love," a voice said, nearly in her ear. Startled, she threw her arms up as if to ward off a blow, only to be caught around the waist and whirled in the strong arms of Simon de Winslade.

"Oh, I thought you had grown bored waiting for me!"

"I've grown frozen," he laughed, stamping

his feet. She could see his breath steaming out before him as he talked. "Don't worry, I knew you would be out as soon as you could. I just feared he would find a way to keep you there."

She grinned up at him, savoring the way his white teeth gleamed in the flickering torchlight. "The horses—"

"They await us by the outer gate, all loaded and ready to go. I couldn't take the chance that someone might see your mare and wonder why it stood tethered with mine out here, so I have bought you a black mare, not an Arab as I promised, but a pretty thing all the same."

"You're so clever . . . you think of everything," she praised, then seized his face between her two small hands and kissed his sensual mouth.

Her spontaneousness took him by surprise, but he didn't let it slow him down, returning her kiss thoroughly, pulling her against his hard body, melding her to its contours as he plundered the sweetness of her mouth.

"I will be taking you to my sister, who is a nun in a convent at Chertsey," he said between kisses, his mouth against her neck. "You can wait there while the Church processes your annulment. But it will take us a day's hard ride to get there, and when we stop for the night at an inn, I mean for us to get thoroughly reacquainted—if you're agreeable?" He grinned teasingly down at her, his merry eyes already certain of her answer.

"You rogue! I should refuse, and make you woo me as is proper."

"I courted you once, *ma dame*," he said

with a mock groan, his lips a teasing inch above her moist, eager mouth. "And an endless month it was, too. Not again, I beg you." His free hand cupped her breast, stroking the nipple through the velvet of her gown. His other hand, fanned over her buttock, held her firmly against his long torso.

"I think you should," she purred, her own breathing coming raggedly in response to the fire his hands were spreading.

"Should what? Court you again?" he groaned again, in earnest now as her hands began their own exploring.

"Nay—beg," she laughed just before his mouth came down hard on hers, punishing her for his aching state of arousal, which he could not satisfy until they were safely away. The cold of the December night forgotten, they kissed and embraced for long minutes.

"*Oui*, I'll beg," he promised her. "I'll beg to touch you—here, and stroke you—here, and kiss you—there . . ." His bold fingers left no doubt as to his meaning, lingering suggestively in the last location, until, moaning, she arched toward him, wishing her heavy skirts gone, wishing they were lying right now on a bed before a crackling fire, naked and intimate.

"*Mon amour*," he said at last after touching her sensitive ear with his playful tongue, "perhaps we should go, or I will take you right here in the bailey."

"Simon!" she screamed.

If he had been kissing her at that moment he would have died, for she would not have seen the dark figure launching itself at him. But she was merely standing in his embrace staring dreamily over his shoulder, and so had a precious second of warning as the knife-wielding attacker plunged at her lover's back.

Simon was unarmed, and cursed himself as he dodged away for carelessly leaving his eating knife in the hall. It would not have been much, but it was more than he had now against Philippe de Melle.

Simon knew it was the troubadour even before the torchlight revealed his livid, crazed face. Philippe fought with the superhuman strength the devil gives the mad as he threw himself at Simon again, his short, wicked blade gleaming evilly in the dancing light. Simon would have to depend on speed alone.

"I'll kill you, you Norman cur!" he grunted as he stalked the warily circling taller man. "No one can have my Ysabeau. I'll send you to hell!"

"I thought you Catharists didn't believe in such a place," taunted Simon, seeking to enrage his attacker.

"I believe in it now," retorted the smaller man bitterly, still watching for his moment. "Hell is where I've been, while watching *my wife* lust for another man, wanting to possess her, but knowing that even if I did, it would be useless sin. She'll never be pure enough; I've seen how she pants like a bitch in heat. . . ."

Unfortunately, Philippe had succeeded in maddening Simon with his blistering disparagement of Ysabeau, who shrank against the stone wall, terrified of the menace Philippe posed with his knife, knowing there was not time to summon the steward, knowing that her cries might distract and endanger Simon. With a roar of pure rage, Simon charged the wiry fanatic. As he moved, though, he slipped on the icy cobbles, falling heavily at Philippe's feet, rolling away from him, but not before Philippe had leaped on him, the deadly blade held high before it descended.

Ysabeau's scream filled Simon's ears as he struggled to hold off the weapon and the thin man's scratching, clawing hand that sought to close around his throat.

She threw her own eating dagger then, but it lodged only in his upper thigh. Philippe heeded it no more than an angry bull would a fly.

Then, there was a low-throated growl and a sudden blur of black and brown as Ami came bounding, seemingly from nowhere, and leaped into the writhing mass of the two men locked in mortal combat.

The grunting and gasps for breath turned to cries of terror as the big canine efficiently separated his mistress' hated oppressor from the man she loved, pinning the luckless troubadour on his back. Ami's slashing fangs were to work; he snarled and snapped as Philippe screamed.

He might have settled for thoroughly mauling the troubadour, but Philippe's hand still held the dagger, and after he managed to work it free, he plunged it into the dog's massive chest just as the strong jaws seized upon his neck. Crazy with pain, the dog ripped open Philippe's throat, collapsing on top of him with a whimper as Philippe's last bubbling protest ceased.

For a moment there was silence as Ysabeau stared, horrified, at the bloody scene. It had all happened so quickly. "I'm all right, Ysabeau," Simon called, though his breath was still labored. She would have gone to him, but he gestured her toward the prostrate furry heap as he struggled to his feet on the cobbles that were now slippery with congealing blood.

The dog opened fast-glazing eyes as his beloved mistress bent, sobbing, over him. He licked her fingers with his great pink tongue, then was gone.

"Philippe is dead, Ysabeau," Simon told her soberly.

Chapter Thirty-six

At first she didn't hear him. Once she had seen that Simon was all right, his voice became faraway to her, as if he was speaking to her through a layer of carded wool.

"Ami," she cried brokenly. She cradled his limp head tenderly, stroking his brindle muzzle and thickly muscled neck, now streaked with crimson. Her hand came away blood-stained and absently she wiped it on her wine-colored velvet skirts. "He died for you, Simon,' she cried. "He gave his life to save yours."

"Yes," he agreed, kneeling beside her, trying not to hurry her, and fully aware of what he owed the dead mastiff. "I will always be grateful to his memory. He probably saved *both* our lives, if truth be told. Philippe was mad, you know. He was not responsible for his actions."

Only then did she really see the horribly

mangled, limp form that had been Philippe de Melle. "Oh, my God . . . he's dead," she screamed. "He's dead, and I murdered him."

He thought she believed her knife, still lodged like a thorn in his thigh, had somehow ended his life.

"Nay, beloved, never think so," he soothed, fighting to hold her close while she flailed at him, struggling to break free. "Hush, hush . . . the dog killed him, but he did it to save us. Philippe was deranged, and he had a knife. He might well have killed both of us." At all costs he had to get her calmed down before the guards found them like this. She was too hysterical to know what she was saying, and though he knew that Henry would not hold them responsible for the troubadour's death, he didn't want to subject Ysabeau to any ugly scenes right now. She had been through too much already. How much, he hadn't fully suspected, even after Ysabeau had told him of Philippe's strange religious beliefs. But then he heard the madman's raving. Ysabeau had been living in hell, and all the time he had been sulking in England about her.

Her sobs quieted slightly, enough for her to pronounce the words, "I am a sinful woman . . . a slut . . . Philippe was right. I deserve to die for my sins."

A cold ball of ice formed in the pit of his stomach. Damn de Melle, most of all for doing this to her, he thought miserably.

"Come on, Ysabeau. We're going now," he said, his tone harsher than he realized.

"No, I can't. Can't you see? I must stay

and pay the price for my wickedness." In her voice was a rising note of panic that he might try to stop her.

"*You did no sin. You didn't kill him*! I will get word to their graces about what really happened here, but I'm damned if I'm going to see you wear a hair shirt over this. I've known some Catharists, Ysabeau. They were gentle people who believed in less contact with the things of the world, much as our monks and nuns do. And most of them don't deny themselves lovemaking and children—they put off becoming *Perfecti* until they're old enough to do without it," he said cynically, then added, "Not that I could ever imagine being too old to want to make love to you."

He couldn't reach her, he could see that. She just continued to try to struggle free of him; her lips were blue with cold, but she was not conscious of that, either.

"I must go in and confess the murder," she cried loudly, with stubborn determination. She began to fight like a wild thing, sobbing, small fists flailing indiscriminately at his shoulders, chest, and face.

"Ysa, you didn't—God's wounds, be quiet!" She was hysterical, so he did the only thing he could think of: He aimed a stinging blow at her right cheek. There was no other way.

He succeeded too well. Used to the force necessary to swing his broadsword, the blow fell lower on her jaw than he intended and with much more force. She fell at his feet like a crumpled flower, unconscious.

Perhaps it was just as well, he thought. He

would not have been able to get her out of there, kicking and screaming; he had not brought any rope, of course, and while he had bribed the gate guards to ask no questions, even they could hardly ignore a noblewoman being taken away against her will.

He carried the inert body easily over his shoulder until he reached the horses. After wrapping her limp form in her own fur cloak and hood, he laid her across his saddle bow for a moment while he tied the reins of her black palfrey to the crupper of his destrier. Then he mounted, holding her against him on the saddle. For a moment he bent low, his lips touching her forehead, breathing in the floral scent of her hair, which reached him even through the fetid smell of the blood that stained them both.

Giving a low word to the black destrier, he gathered up his reins and rode through the gate.

"He must like them drunk before he works his will," muttered one guard cynically, taking a swig of ale from the common jar.

"A noble as well-favored as the baron? Go on, Raoul. Sounds more like your style to me. It's likely the only way you can get 'em to put up with you," one of the others guffawed, his raucous laughter reaching Simon's ears even if his words did not.

She first felt the sensation of an icy rivulet running down her neck, though the rest of her was blessedly warm.

Ysabeau opened her eyes tentatively in the dim light and found Simon bent over her, holding a ball of snow in a cloth to her jaw. She looked at him confusedly for a moment, her mouth opening to ask why he was doing such a silly thing, and then the pain lanced across her cheek.

"Easy, love. I regret to say you have an enormously black and blue jaw, thanks to me. I'm very sorry. I never meant to hit you so hard. But the bone seems sound enough, though I'm afraid you'll have to eat soup for a few days." He strove for a light tone, but his blue eyes could not hide their concern, and his face looked utterly weary.

"You hit me?" she repeated after him.

"You were hysterical."

"I . . . was only trying to do the right thing," she said, speaking with difficulty.

"You're to say no more about being guilty, do you hear? You've had a nasty shock tonight, seeing me almost carved up by that madman—and never doubt he would have turned on you next—and seeing Ami sacrifice himself for us. But you are not responsible. If anyone is guilty, it's I, for having been blind to the danger Philippe posed to you and letting you nearly waste your life with him. Now," he said, arising from the bed and dropping the shrinking ice ball into the basin with a sigh, "the innkeeper has a letter to be delivered to the King and Queen in the morning, explaining what happened. I'm not the least worried that anyone will try to blame either of us. It's obvious that Philippe died from the dog's attack, not the minor flesh wound from your eating knife. And Matilde knew what Philippe was like. She'll tell Eleanor. And Henry knows me well enough to realize that I'm not the sort to stoop to murdering a husband—even the husband of the woman I've loved to distraction these two years."

She began to relax under the influence of the determined love in his voice, but seized on something he said earlier.

"The innkeeper? What is this place?" She looked around the low-ceilinged room, with its dark rafters and plain, serviceable appointments.

"We're still in London, at The Boar and Bear. You couldn't go any further tonight, in your condition. We'll set out for Winslade in the morning."

"But your sister at Chertsey . . ."

"She need not keep you for me now. There's no longer any need. Philippe is dead. He can't hurt you any more, and you're free. You're a widow, Ysabeau. I'm taking you to Winslade keep, where we'll be married, once preparations can be made."

She could feel the paralyzing sense of guilt dying within her, but then it reared its head one last time. "I'm not sure I shouldn't go to the convent, if only for a few days, to arrange for Masses to be said, to pray for his soul, to contemplate my role in what has happened. . . . Don't you think that would look more seemly to the court?" The prospect sounded unappealing, even as she said it.

She could see he was having trouble reining in his impatience as he turned back to her, his blue eyes blazing. "I'm not going to stand patiently by while you force yourself to mourn for a crazed bastard who would have eventually slain you in a religious frenzy. If you want to have Masses said, by all means, Father Richard can do it at Winslade. And as for those at court, I don't give a damn if anyone is harsh enough to judge us, but I think you'll find the people who matter—Eleanor, Henry, and our friends—will understand completely."

It was true. And at the moment there was nothing she wanted more than to ride out of London at this man's side, away from the curious, probing eyes of the court, to a much deserved solitude together at Winslade. She felt her guilt slip from her soul like a loathsome burden, and the first tentative beginnings of joy begin to well up within her. She opened her arms to him, sitting upright in the featherbed.

The sudden motion made her sorry, indeed. Pain exploded in her jaw and forehead, and caused sweat to bead up along her brow. She realized also that she was naked beneath the sheet. Cheeks flaming, she sank back against the bolster.

He noticed her discomfort immediately. "I'm sorry, love, I felt it best that you didn't wake with that bloodstained gown still on. Here, drink this." He poured a cup full of an amber liquid from a jar on the nightstand. "This is from the innkeeper's wife. It'll lessen the pain, and you'll sleep well."

It was on the tip of her tongue to reject the potion, but she didn't have the energy to frame the lie. Her jaw ached abominably. She was so weary . . . it felt soothing and safe to merely drink down the vile-tasting concoction and let the drowiness steal over her.

She meant to watch as he stripped naked, to indulge herself with the sight of his powerfully muscled shoulders flexing as he washed from the basin of melted snow. But her eyelids were too heavy, the call of slumber too seductive. By the time he was toweling himself dry, her breathing had grown regular, and he smiled. She roused briefly when she felt him pull her close into his arms, and thought that the embrace felt very good, indeed. Then she slept, dreamlessly.

Chapter Thirty-seven

When they left the inn at prime the next day, the city of London was waking as usual: Vendors were beginning to set up their booths; housewives were calling out shrill warnings as they emptied chamber pots from overhead windows; shopkeepers were throwing back shutters to let in what little light could be gleaned from the cloudy day. It seemed incredible to Ysabeau that life could go on as it always did in these streets, after the events of the night before. It could matter little to these Londoners that a minor courtier died in such unusual circumstances, she told herself; it was said they didn't even care who sat on the throne at Westminster, as long as their businesses and rights were undisturbed.

By the time they left London a mizzling rain was falling, which shrouded the city walls as

Ysabeau glanced backward.

They stopped for the night at an abbey where they were given a single room after Simon announced them to the porter as, "the Baron de Winslade and his lady." While the austere-looking monk padded away to arrange the lodgings, she giggled at him, "His lady indeed! For shame, lying to a monk!"

"He doesn't care as long as my coin is good," Simon retorted. "An I did not tell that little falsehood, they would have given us separate beds in separate rooms. You'd probably have ended up sharing a pallet with some fat merchant's daughter who snored, my love, while I would have had the joy of trying to sleep with her father! No, *ma chère*, I had something else in mind for us tonight. We have been apart long enough, don't you think?" His eyes caressed her warmly, bright with intent.

For a moment she could not get her breath. "You mean . . . that we will sleep together here? In an abbey?" Somehow she had not pictured their physical reunion happening in such a setting.

He grinned. "We will share a bed, *mon amour*. I shall not promise how much *sleep* we will get."

Just then the monk returned. Worried that the Benedictine had heard Simon's words, Ysabeau blushed to the roots of her hair. But her eyes were shining.

They dined at the abbot's table, gratefully consuming the simple fare, feeling the weariness recede from their saddlesore bones. Silence reigned at the table according to the rule, with requests to pass more of this or that dish being accomplished by gestures, while one of the community read aloud from the stories of the martyrs. Simon and Ysabeau, however, heard but little of these spiritually uplifting tales, for they were totally intent on one another.

How soon could they courteously take their leave of these kind, but otherworldly men, Ysabeau wondered as she saw Simon gazing at her over the rim of his plain wooden mazer, undressing her with his eyes. She didn't know how much longer she could take this . . . she was on fire for him, and he wasn't even touching her, except when his fingers surreptitiously caressed hers as he handed her a bite of roasted chicken or passed her the wine. Glancing across the room, she saw a young monk staring at them with open interest. She looked back sternly at Simon, shaking her head, silently begging him to stop. He smiled in an amused fashion, then arranged his features into the proper degree of solemnity and pretended great interest in the reading. Beneath the tablecloth, however, the long hard length of his thigh continued to press against hers so that she had the greatest difficulty maintaining her decorum.

After the meal, the abbot, a tall spare man whose build reminded her achingly of her father, bade them goodnight, saying his abbey was honored to lodge the Lord and Lady de Winslade, and thanking Simon for his generous donation.

Later, for an extra silver penny, a pair of monks brought a sturdy tub and several steaming buckets of water into their sparsely furnished chamber.

"I thought you'd like a bath," invited Simon.

She looked at the steaming water longingly, already knowing how it would soothe the ache from her weary thighs, how good it would feel to wash off the grime of travel. Still, she wanted to place his needs first, because she loved him. "Nay, get in, Simon, and I will scrub your back."

"There is room for both of us," he pointed out, "if we are willing to be at least friendly. And I intend to be a great deal more than your friend this night, Ysbeau de Ré." He rejoiced to see that her eyes glowed with the same passion as he felt threatening to explode within himself. She nodded her assent.

He gathered her into his arms then, smoothing back the tendrils of brown hair that had strayed from her braid during the day of traveling. He kissed her for a long moment, his tongue touching hers in sweet greeting as their lips melded together.

They undressed each other; Ysabeau, quite adept now as a substitute for his squire, Simon, fumbling as he struggled to unlace her gown with fingers suddenly clumsy with passion. His progress was infinitely slow, for he insisted on kissing every silken inch of her as it was bared; first the lovely, creamy shoulders, then the graceful curve of her back as he removed her linen undergown; next, he lingered over removing her slippers and unrolling her silk hose, sucking at her toes until she pounded at his shoulders in torment, as his tongue caressed the sensitive area at her knee and made a path of fire up to her thigh. His nearness was unbearably taunting, for he was already naked, the evidence of his need touching her thigh as he leaned toward her to remove her chemise. She moaned in an ecstasy of anticipation, pulling him close, thinking a bath might be equally delightful—after.

But he evidently meant to prolong her torment, perhaps as sweet revenge for the many times she had taunted and refused him, until he had wanted to rip the clothes from her sweet body and bury himself in her. Lifting her in his arms, maintaining contact with her moist, honeyed lips, he stepped into the tub, lowering her into the heated water slowly, letting her lush, satiny body slide down teasingly against the full length of him until she sat in his lap in the water.

Then he seized a cloth, making a pretense of washing her very thoroughly, lingering with studied casualness at her rose-tipped breasts, gazing at her with heavy-lidded intensity as he submerged the cloth beneath the water. She had never been so thoroughly clean, nor so ambivalent about lingering in the pleasurable warmth of the water. Half of her wanted to stay in the oaken tub forever, feeling his hands upon her and knowing what was still to come—either in or out of the water. The other half wanted him now, wanted to lie with him on the plain abbey bed. That part won out as she took her turn, washing him with equal completeness, but in a less leisurely fashion. She had partly arisen in the water, and was about to reach for a towel when he pulled her into his lap, so that her back lay against his lightly furred chest.

"*Non, mon amour,* not so quickly. We have all night."

She found it very pleasurable, indeed, to lean her head against his shoulder, her neck thrown back in abandon as his hands fondled her breasts and his lips alternately licked and murmured sweet nothings into her ear.

They briskly toweled one another dry, not wanting to linger in the chill air when the bed, with its freshly aired linen and unbleached wool blankets beckoned.

Once there, he made as if to resume passion's play, but she whispered urgently to him, "Simon, take me now! You have made me so hot I cannot wait any longer!"

He was happy to comply with her request, bringing her quickly to a shuddering, whimpering climax with his consummate skill before he spent himself within her.

Chapter Thirty-eight

They reached Winslade Keep late in the afternoon of the next day, just as the sun was disappearing behind the wood to the west.

Ysabeau stared curiously at the gray stone castle which belonged to the man mounted next to her. It was of a squat, oblong shape, with a storeroom on the ground floor. A wooden, removable staircase gave access to the great hall on the second floor; above this, she knew, would be the great chamber which was occupied by the keep's lord and lady.

"There was once a wooden keep here, in the Conqueror's time," he told her, watching her take in the sight of his home. He had yearned to have her here for so long. "It was not until late in the first Henry's reign that permission was granted to rebuild it in stone, and to crenellate the walls."

At intervals along the parapet there were timber huts that jutted over the edge, for the purpose of defense. From there, Simon's men could step out, protected, and drop heavy objects or boiling oil on attackers.

He followed her gaze. "Perhaps I will be able to take that timber hoarding down, if Henry can build a lasting peace. Come, let's go inside."

The man in the barbican tower had spotted them, and recognizing his lord, was even now lowering the drawbridge. The windlass creaked as the heavy wooden drawbridge landed on the bank with a thud. The portcullis slid up more smoothly, and Simon urged his destrier forward.

When she followed him Ysabeau felt as if there were dozens of eyes trained upon her from the gate towers and the outbuildings, but actually only three men-at-arms were on guard duty; the rest were consuming their supper in the hall.

They passed through another gatehouse and were in the inner bailey, and she glimpsed a pair of scullery boys heading inside from the kitchen through a pentice, laden with steaming platters of meat.

The hall lay before them, high clerestory windows outlined by the final rays of the setting sun.

"You are welcome, Lord Simon," said an older man of average height, who took the reins of their horses. "Supper is just laid." He looked discreetly at Ysabeau, smiling slightly, but waiting to be introduced.

"I have the honor to present Lady Ysabeau de Ré, from Aquitaine and Queen Eleanor's court. When all is arranged, she will become my wife. Lady Ysabeau, this is Thomas, my seneschal."

She inclined her head graciously, and hoped she had not blushed when he announced his intent to wed her. Thomas, however, broke into a grin.

"My lord, that is, indeed, good news! Welcome, my lady Ysabeau!" His beaming smile was reassuring to Ysabeau. He seemed genuinely to care for his lord. Then he said, "If I may say so, my lord, Aimery will rejoice that you have brought him a new mother."

Simon looked uncomfortable, and cleared his throat. "Thomas, give the horses to the stableboy, and we'll go in. We'll not stop to change, since the supper is ready now." He paused to unlace his coif and pull it off, then, after handing it to Thomas, he placed Ysabeau's small hand on his arm, as if they were at court. He avoided her gaze, which was turned to him in curiosity as they entered the hall.

Who was Aimery, she wondered. She was to be his new mother? Evidently Simon had a son, perhaps a love child born of some village wench. It was not unknown for a lord to take in his bastard, particularly if it was a boy who showed promise. Henry had already done so; the boy was named Geoffrey, his mother rumored to be an English camp follower, one Hikenai. While Eleanor didn't like it, she had apparently decided to turn a blind eye to it.

Her mind awhirl with questions, she nevertheless took a few moments to notice her surroundings as the seneschal directed the laying of fresh linens before the central places at the high table.

The hall was moderately large, aisled, with larger carved timber posts supporting the timber-beamed ceiling. Against one side wall was a massive stone fireplace in which several burning logs crackled merrily. The high clerestory windows which Ysabeau had seen from the outside were on that wall; the opposite wall featured blind arcades.

The dais itself was of stone, with two tables intersecting at right angles; at these, the castle folk dined, or rather, pretended with varying degrees of success to do so, while they gaped at Ysabeau.

The inhabitants of the castle had been nearly finished with their dinners and soon began to'disperse, leaving Simon and Ysabeau to their privacy. Seeing that Simon was not forthcoming about Aimery, Yasbeau applied herself to a slice of venison cooked in a pepper sauce. She realized she was as fatigued and famished as Simon appeared to be. Perhaps after he had eaten and bathed there would be time for questions.

The necessity of questioning him never arose, however, for as Simon was wiping his mouth with a linen napkin, a female approached, carrying a wriggling, dark-haired toddler who clearly wanted to be set on his feet. The blond woman, whose plain woolen kirtle proclaimed her peasant status, gave in to the child's excited cries and let him loose as they reached the dais, saying something to Simon in the gutteral language that Ysabeau knew to be English. Liberated, the boy jumped straight into Simon's lap, crying, "*Mon père! Mon père*!"

Simon dismissed the woman, then turned his attention back to the boy, who was chattering away to Simon in a mixture of English and Norman French.

She noticed the woman giving her a long, measuring glance before leaving, which Ysabeau returned frankly. This must be the child's mother, yet Ysabeau saw nothing of her broad, peasant features or straw-colored hair about the boy; he had an unruly thatch of coal-black hair and his father's penetrating blue eyes and slender build. The woman was stocky and full-hipped, and had breasts that strained the bodice of her russet dress.

Then the woman gave her a shy, but genuine smile, which Ysabeau found astonishing, since she was sure the entire castle already knew that she was to wed their lord. Did she not resent Ysabeau for intruding into her relationship with Simon? Had he forced her against her will, with this dark, handsome child as the result? Or was it merely that she considered the noble lady no competition for a man of Simon's lusty appetite? The woman looked from her to Simon and the boy as her smile broadened to a grin, and calling something that sounded like a farewell, strode from the hall, her full hips swaying gracefully. There was an earthy beauty to the woman, and suddenly Ysabeau saw the basis for Simon's attraction to her.

"Ysabeau, I would like you to meet my son, Aimery," said Simon with a proud smile, turning the boy in his lap to face her. "I am sorry you had to hear of him in such an offhand fashion from Thomas. I fully intended for you to meet him tonight, if he was not abed by the time we arrived. I hope that it is not too much of a shock to you. Aimery, this is Lady Ysabeau, whom I want to marry me. Do you not think she should?"

The child seemed not the least whit shy of the strange woman seated in the great carved chair next to his father, and said unhesitatingly, "Pretty lady. Yes, I like her."

"Oh, unfair, my lord, to have two such handsome men pleading the same cause." In truth, she had already quite lost her heart to the charming little boy who was a black-haired copy of his father.

"He seems quite taken by you, too," Simon said in amusement as the little boy held out his arms to Ysabeau. His voice became thick with emotion as he drank in the affecting sight of his son clinging affectionately to Ysabeau's arms, as if he had known her all his life—indeed, as if she were really his mother. An unbidden bit of moisture stung his eyes, but vanished as he heard Ysabeau's questions, uttered over Aimery's head:

"Simon, the woman who just left the hall—is she his mother? Please understand, I do not judge you; many nobles have relationships with peasant women, and children as a result. . . ." Her voice trailed off as he looked at her in consternation. For a terrified second she thought she had made him angry, then he roared with laughter.

"Hulda? God's blood, Ysabeau, you certainly have a Provençal's frankness!"

"My lord, I have never seen any profit by pretense. Perhaps that's why I was no success at *l'amour courtois*. I should prefer you to be direct, also."

"No, Hulda is not Aimery's mother," he answered, looking her in the eye, "though she served as his wet-nurse when his mother died."

Now she was even more startled, as he had known she would be. "In certain areas, Simon, I fear I do not know you at all."

"I realize that. It's a lack I intend to remedy immediately. Aimery's mother was my wife, Lady Rohese of Basingstoke. She died a few days after his birth, of childbed fever."

"And you loved her very much."

"Yes, I did. That was a couple of months before I came back to Poitiers and met you the second time.

"Then you were married when I first met you in the garden. I sensed a . . . distance in you."

His blue eyes swept over her, heating her blood. "Yes, one I knew I could not maintain if I had further contact with you—so I didn't. I had taken vows I meant to keep. And then, when I returned, I was quite angry still that Rohese had left me. I viewed her death as a desertion, and I fear that was the cause of my cynicism toward women. I half expected any woman I cared for to leave me, as Rohese had—and my mother, before her."

Her dark eyes were huge and liquid as she listened to his words, leaning forward with the child cuddling happily in her arms; unconsciously, she pressed her lips to the boy's head every now and then.

"Your mother, my lord?"

"She ran off with a minstrel who visited the castle when my brother and I were very young," he said bitterly. "We never heard from her again, though several years later the abbess of a convent in London wrote to say that she had died there of the French pox, quite insane before she expired."

Holy Mother of God, no wonder he was so disdainful of the troubadours who prattled about the joys of courtly love! She saw clearly now why he had at first sought merely to bed her. He had wanted her, but did not want to make himself vulnerable to hurt. He had felt enough pain already.

"You have a brother, too? You spoke of your sister, the nun," she encouraged him to continue.

"Yes, Gervase was the oldest, and as such, holds Hawkingham, the principal castle of the original holdings of Guy de Bayeux, the Norman baron who came over with William the Conqueror. I believe Aimery gets his coloring from old Guy, for Rohese was even blonder than I. Gervase also holds title to Lingfield and Chawton, though the latter was razed recently since it was adulterine. Gervase, you see, was a supporter of Stephen—at least until he began to lose."

"Yet you are not his vassal?" Again she

was surprised, for it was an unusal arrangement.

"No, my father wisely saw how things would go in England, and was an adherent of Matilda. He arranged for me to do homage directly to her for my fief. Now, Gervase had better watch his step, for Henry means to restore things to the way they were in the first Henry's day, and he won't be patient with disloyalty." He meant to mention that he and Gervase were twins, but her next question distracted him.

"You do not like your brother, do you? Is it because he was for Stephen?"

He sighed heavily before answering, and when he did, his eyes were troubled. "No, it's more than that. I guess it's because, more than anything, Gervase is only for himself. Stephen just gave him the chance to satisfy his selfish greed more than Matilda would have. I razed Chawton at the King's command, but he hated me before that. If it weren't for me, he'd have it all—Winslade in addition to Hawkingham, Lingfield, and Chawton. He hates the fact that I chose the right side, though I did it because I felt the Empress had the greater right, not because I thought she—or her son—would win."

"And what of your sister?" she asked him, knowing instinctively that this was a happier line of questioning.

"Adèle—or Sister Mary Agathe now. We've always been close. I visit her whenever I pass near Chertsey. She's fully five years younger than I, but I could always talk about anything with her. She used to follow me around the castle like a puppy, from the time she could first toddle. I used to dread the day she would go away to be wed to some young lord, even though I left to be fostered, in my future father-in-law's household. I was troth-plighted to Rohese when Adèle told me she wanted to be a Bride of Christ rather than marry. But fortunately, her order is not so cloistered that she cannot visit occasionally—and she is often granted permission to do so since my father and I have been generous to the abbey," he finished with a grin. "I haven't talked so long in a twelvemonth!"

The boy had been watching his father's face, and then gazing back delightedly at Ysabeau's, but now as Simon noticed him again, his dark head drooped on Ysabeau's breast and his regular, even breathing told them he was asleep.

Their eyes met over the sleeping child, hers shining with her enchantment at the boy, and he gave her a smile of such singular sweetness that for a moment she forgot all the pain and tragedy that had preceded their journey here and longed to surround herself in the love of this man and child forever.

The tallow candles had burned low, and the servants lingered around the edge of the hall, obviously waiting to spread out their pallets and seek their rest.

"Come, we will take the boy back to Hulda. He sleeps in her chamber."

They climbed the steps past the third floor to the floor above the lord's chamber, where Simon paused at the door and knocked softly.

There was a rustling in the rushes and Hulda, with a blanket covering most of her thin night rail, opened the door. Beyond her in the small room Ysabeau could see that a man lay sprawled in slumber on the bed which the woman had obviously just left. A tiny baby slept in a cradle at one side of the bed, while Aimery's trundle bed lay waiting for him nearby.

"Thank you, Hulda," Simon said as the serf woman yawned and smiled sleepily at the somnolent child whom she accepted into her arms.

She murmured something in English, obviously a question which concerned Ysabeau, for her pale eyes darted uncertainly to her and back to Simon.

He answered with an affirmative nod, smiling, reaching out to touch his son's head before Hulda carried him off to bed.

Then they headed back to the stair, now arm in arm, going to the great chamber, which they would share for the rest of their lives.

Chapter Thirty-nine

She could not control the yawn that escaped her as they stood before the carved oak door that led to the great chamber. Fatigue was so mingled with anticipation that she could not separate them.

"I can see I've worn you out with my family saga," he teased. "Never mind, it has been a long day. And after a fortnight at court, I shall be very glad to sleep in my own bed—especially with you in it," he said with a familiar gleam in his blue eyes as he pushed the door open.

It was a room much like any noble's sleeping chamber, with a fireplace whose smoke exited through the same chimney as the great hall's. Narrow windows were shuttered now against the winter night air. A massive bed with hangings of forest green velvet stood in one corner, and next to it, a tall wardrobe, a couple of backless chairs, and a low table.

Ysabeau had been silent for a few moments as she took in her new surroundings. Now she moved toward him as if to help him undress, but he stayed her hand.

"A moment, first, if you please. You claimed that night in Southwark that you had never heard me say I loved you, and I promised you vows of love. I wanted to make those vows here, in my keep, in our chamber. But you felt my love for you last night, did you not?"

She nodded, eyes luminous as she thought of the night of passion spent in the abbey, where their lovemaking was punctuated by the sound of the abbey's bells.

His armor had been put away by a servant while they dined, but he'd retained his sword. Now as he drew it from the jeweled scabbard, it made a sibilant hiss. "Kneel with me, Ysabeau," he invited, his blue eyes livid in the dim light of the room. Propping it against the low table so that it stood on its point and the hilt formed a gleaming silver cross, he folded his hands together and said solemnly, "I, Simon, Baron de Winslade, swear by the cross formed by this sword hilt, to you, Ysabeau, Comtesse de Ré, my eternal love and faithfulness, to be shown by the devotion of my heart, soul, and spirit to your good and the worship of your body by mine. I will wed you as soon as the Holy Church gives her blessing, and will be your husband until death parts us."

She was so moved by his earnestness that tears welled up in her great brown eyes, gleaming in the firelight, and unbidden, she made her own vows: "I, Ysabeau de Ré, swear by this cross to love you truly, Simon de Winslade, and you alone, all the days of my life, holding back nothing, to be a good mother to Aimery and such babes as God will give us, to be submissive to your will"—here, her eyes danced with merriment and he could not resist making a skeptical face—"and to be thankful for your love for eternity."

They sealed their vows with a kiss, and felt themselves as committed to each other forever, as if the priest had already celebrated the Sacrament of Marriage before them.

In the morning when Ysabeau awoke, Simon was gone, and for a moment she felt a pricking of uncertainty. Her body was still rosy with the aftereffects of a night spent in his passionate embrace, for he had brought her to fulfillment twice in the deep of the night before she slept, drugged with happy exhaustion. Now, she wrapped the blanket around her slim form and stepped over to the shuttered window. When she opened it she could see the sun just edging over the village's thatched roofs.

Mother Mary, she had slept half the morning away! He must think her a lazy, useless court parasite! Suddenly his good opinion of her mattered terribly much as she struggled into her clothing, found scattered about the room. She blushed, thinking about the night before as she pulled on the rumpled silk chemise and retrieved her linen undergown from on top of the iron-bound chest. She hoped Marie and her baggage would arrive soon, so she wouldn't have to keep putting on the same travel-stained *bliaut*. Certainly she could not wear the wine-colored velvet gown ever again, for it was encrusted with Philippe's and Ami's blood. But how, she wondered, was she to get the back laces fastened?

Just then, there was a soft scratching at the door; when she opened it, Hulda stood there with Aimery balanced on her hip. The child laughed at the sleepy-looking lady still in her undergown, for the rest of the castle had been astir for three hours.

"My lord bade me come and see if you needed help," Hulda said in hesitant, but passable French. "He said you were to feel free to use my lady Rohese's gowns, at least until your clothing arrives." She spoke shyly, but under her lashes assessed the impact of her words.

Ysabeau found that a practical solution, though she wondered how Simon would feel, seeing her in his dead wife's clothing. As she stepped to the tall wooden wardrobe, she caught Hulda eyeing the rumpled bedclothes, and wondered what the woman thought of her, a lady, sharing the lord's bed without a priest's blessing. Suddenly she sensed that Hulda and Simon *had* at one time been intimate, and unconsciously she froze, staring at the peasant woman, her mouth half open in shock.

"Do not worry, my lady," Hulda said, reading her thoughts with startling precision. "You have nothing to fear from me. Aye, my lord and I were together once, but once only. My Alf is more than enough for me now," she added with earthy frankness. "I am glad he has finally found one of his class whom he can love as he did my Lady Rohese—she was a dear sweet thing and loved him truly, but you are better for him, I think. I sense he has braved much to bring you here."

"Yes," Ysabeau said, amazed at the woman's wisdom and intuition. She selected a pale blue kirtle from the closet, smiling tremulously at Hulda, who relaxed visibly after that. The confession had been risky for her, Ysabeau realized. It was not unknown for a serf woman in such a position to be put out on the road to fend for herself when the lord took a wife. But she sensed she had nothing to fear from Aimery's nurse, and that the woman could do much to aid her.

"Thank you, Hulda. I believe I'll try this one," she said, indicating the blue garment in her hand. If you'll just help with the lacing—"

Hulda did so. Ysabeau soon realized that Blanche's taunts about her flatness two years ago no longer applied; at least, she certainly had more curves than the unfortunate Rohese had had, for her breasts strained against the fabric of the bodice, emphasizing her tiny waistline and gently rounded hips. She eyed herself with some satisfaction in the polished silver mirror as the woman plaited her hair into a serviceable braid down her back, then held out her hands to Aimery.

"Perhaps he and I could get better acquainted this morning. I see you have your own babe to care for."

Hulda was grateful. "Yes, my lady, and

she'll no doubt be clamoring for her second feeding by the time I get back to her. Thank you."

Ysabeau was gratified to see Aimery come to her arms without hesitation. He certainly was a sunny, fearless child, she mused. Evidently his rough-and-tumble life, spent mostly with the wet-nurse while his father was away, accounted for that; but it was also evident that Simon had spent time getting reacquainted with his son since his return to England, for the boy obviously loved his sire. Her heart warmed the more to Simon as the two-year-old gave her an engaging grin so much like his father's, and she went to seek him in the great hall below.

Chapter Forty

But she was not to see Simon until midday, for he had broken his fast early and ridden out about his demesne. Of course, he would have much to do, reasoned Ysabeau with a pang of disappointment, as she coaxed Aimery to eat some more of the gruel she was spooning toward his pursed lips. Simon was a responsible lord and had neglected his barony for over a fortnight while he attended the Coronation and then lingered in order to rescue her.

Determined to prove herself worthy as his châtelaine, she soon scooped up Aimery and began exploring the keep, meeting the folk who lived within its walls, the priest, Father Richard, Edwisa the cook, Helwyn, the laundress, and so many scullions, men-at-arms, stableboys and serving women that she soon forgot their names. All seemed friendly and respectful, further supporting her opinion that Simon had always been a good lord to them. After Philippe's lack of interest, this was refreshing, indeed.

She made herself familiar with the inner and outer baileys, peering into the many outbuildings, such as the smithy and armory, that made Winslade a self-sufficient castle. Although she was aware that Simon had been away a great deal during the last two years, nowhere did she see evidence of neglect.

Marie arrived with Geoffrey and the sumpter mules late the next day. Ysabeau was glad to see her for her own sake, of course, for a winter journey was not without perils. Her arrival also meant she would not have to wear the late Rohese's clothes, which made her uneasy no matter how practical it was. What she most wanted to hear from Marie, however, was what was being said about the unusual circumstances of the death of Philippe.

"I left before very much was said, so all I can tell you is what happened the next morning. Of course those foolish hens are clucking," Marie said with characteristic frankness, speaking of the ladies at court. "It's winter, and they're bored silly, that's all. Never you mind, though, by this time se'enight, they'll be pecking at someone else. Of course, around their graces strictly the truth is allowed to prevail—that Philippe was the victim of an unfortunate accident and that you have retired from court in shock."

"That's scarcely the whole truth," Ysabeau retorted.

"Those who care for you know the whole story, and why you acted the way you did, and as for the rest, they aren't entitled to know more,'' Marie said firmly, and put and end to the discussion.

Ysabeau had had some concerns that life in a baron's country castle would seem dull to Marie, after the glamour and intrigue of court, but she need not have worried. Marie took to Winslade keep and its folk like a duck to water, becoming almost instantly accepted, because she did not put on airs as she might have felt entitled to, having been a servant among the great. With her fund of anecdotes about the new King and Queen, she was easily the center of attention among those who kept the household of Winslade.

Ysabeau's days at Winslade were full and busy, and she fell into the great bed at night fatigued but happy, having watched the castle run in its well-oiled style; but she knew she made a valuable contribution to it in some way every day, too, whether she spent the day sewing clothing for the servingmen or supervising the cleaning of the tower guest rooms. And she knew deep within that her most meaningful contributions were to the happiness of Winslade's lord and the emotional well-being of his son, who throve under her attention as a flower with a regular supply of sun and water.

One night, after they had curled up under the blankets together and were enjoying the brick-heated warmth of the bed linens and each other, Ysabeau asked, ''Simon, what ails you? Is it the King? Is he wroth with you for taking me off without his consent?'' She probed teasingly, for she realized that Ré was not such a rich prize that Henry would be upset at Simon for taking her with him. It was an expected courtesy to await the King's formal permission before they married, however, so she was just as eager to receive word as Simon was.

With one hand behind his head and the other smoothing his mustache—which he did when pensive—he studied the beamed ceiling, avoiding the merry eyes and delectable form hovering over him. He gave into the impulse at last and pulled her onto his chest, so that her sweet breath warmed his skin and her lush dark tresses, freed from their proper daytime plait, tickled his nose. He smoothed her hair with one strong hand while the other held her close, murmuring, "Yes, I suppose you could say it is the lack of a message from their graces that troubles me. But also, Gervase was here today, and I didn't give him what he wanted."

"Your brother was here? Why didn't you call me to greet him? Is it because—" She stopped suddenly, shrinking away from him, shame dulling her shining brown eyes. Living with him as she was, outside the bonds of the Sacrament of Marriage, she must appear to his brother as no better than his mistress. She could not as yet greet him as the rightful châtelaine of Winslade.

"No, silly one. It's Gervase who's not worthy to greet you," he soothed, holding her chin so that his blue eyes gazed into her brown ones. "You were with Aimery in the outer ward, and you two appeared to be having such a pleasant time that I didn't have the heart to interrupt. Especially since Gervase was being his usual charming self." He made a wry face, mostly to hide the apprehension he'd felt as he and Gervase had walked along the parapet and talked, and the elder twin had spied her and his son as they frolicked in the newly fallen snow.

"Lovely . . ." he had sighed. "Is that one from the village, or did you bring her from a London stew, brother? I'll vow she's as luscious between the legs as her face is," he added. "Care to share her?"

"No more than you ever did, brother," Simon said, fighting the urge to throw his twin off the parapet. "And guard your tongue. That's my intended wife, the Lady Ysabeau, Comtesse de Ré."

"Ah, a thousand pardons, Simon. Please don't take offense. I'm so glad you've found someone to replace the late lamented Rohese at last. No doubt, you'll soon have a handful of sons to pass your little keep to—should aught happen to Aimery, of course," he added with unctuous concern. "It's good that he should not be your only heir. And have you told her we are twins? Perhaps she should have the opportunity to meet the one with the larger possessions, since we are equally well-favored of face."

"Perhaps you should get to the real purpose of your visit, Gervase," snarled Simon, jaws clenched and hand resting on his sword hilt. "You didn't know of Ysabeau, so you didn't come to look her over. . . ."

"I wish you would believe it was just a brotherly desire for closer ties between our keeps, Simon, but you always had such a suspicious nature. Welladay, I suppose I must go ahead and ask you: I need your intercession with Henry to rebuild Chawton. It's an insult to our family name, lying there in its tumbledown state, a constant mockery to me, and I curse Stephen every time I look at it. If you'd talk to Henry, I'm sure he'd give consent." Gervase stopped and leaned against a merlon, fingers hooked casually in his swordbelt. "And," he added, "I need money to rebuild it."

Simon stopped pacing and stared at Gervase, giving his twin a short bark of mirthless laughter. "You overestimate my influence, *mon frère*, and certainly my funds."

"Why, brother, you always had led me to believe you and the Angevin were like this," he said, holding his index and second finger together under Simon's nose insolently.

The truth was that Simon probably could have asked that favor of Henry Plantagenet with a good chance of success, but presently he was awaiting the King's permission to wed Ysabeau, and had no intention of asking too much just as Henry was taking up the reins of government. With feigned control, he ignored the fingers so near his face and said, "I have no intention of going to London anytime soon, Gervase. I've just returned from there, and I fully intend not to stir from this keep without a good reason now that there's a fair monarch on England's throne. If it can wait awhile, I'm expecting his grace's messenger soon and will convey your request through him. As for money, surely you remember I'm the younger son, and have only the one keep. I can't help you there."

"What would you have me do, go to the

Jews?" hissed Gervase, his handsome face darkening in anger. "Marry your fair Poitevin, then, and get ahold of some of her coin. I do believe you said she was a countess—"

"I'll not spend a *sou* of her money replenishing the castle you lost through your own folly," Simon said with quiet firmness, though his eyes blazed blue fire.

"I see your little bedmate leads you around by the nose," taunted Gervase. He saw that Simon was too secure in his love to be vulnerable to his jibe, and tried another tack. "Perhaps you've forgotten Aimery is my heir. Surely you would like to safeguard his future?" His eyes, a cloudier blue than Simon's, looked sly.

"Gervase, you have time between now and your demise to raise up a quiverful of sons, if you'd spend more time doing it and less time backing the wrong cause," answered Simon with more lightness than he felt. "Aimery will always have Winslade, whether he has Hawkingham, Chawton, and Lingfield, or not."

"Don't be too sure," Simon thought he heard his twin mumble. "I must be going."

"You're leaving already? What about supper? Your men must be tired—you're welcome to stay the night." He hoped he did not sound as insincere as he felt about the offer of hospitality. The sooner he saw Gervase ride out over his drawbridge, the better, though it was a shame his brother's retainers would probably have to set up a cold camp out there somewhere. If Gervase left, he could avoid presenting Ysabeau to him; he did not wish his twin to rest those lascivious eyes on his beloved, or for

Ysabeau to try to extend a welcome to Gervase. One did not put one's beloved within striking distance of a poisonous snake.

In bed, Ysabeau was still looking at Simon with eyes shadowed by doubt. "Are you certain it was Gervase who was being difficult, or was it that you just did not want to explain to him why we have not wed as yet?"

"I'll be thankful when we get word from court, so you'll stop talking like that," he sighed, and realized he had sounded too harsh. "It's just that a scoundrel like my brother would try to use your husband's death somehow to his advantage; he'd twist the story until you sounded like a veritable Jezebel. It seems clear he has not heard any gossip of it yet. Keeping him clear of you just increases the chance he won't catch wind of it."

She seemed reassured, for he felt her body relax against him. "Did I tell you what Aimery called me today, Simon?" she said, changing the subject, much to his relief. He would have to see that she never left the castle unprotected, for he did not trust his treacherous brother any farther than he could throw him. Yet he did not want her living in fear. . . .

"What's that, my love?" he answered, again forcing his troubled mind away from the subject of his brother. He delighted to see how well his beloved and his only son were getting along. Aimery had never known his real mother, and he had instantly adored the beautiful Ysabeau. Like father, like son, he thought with satisfaction.

"He said, 'May I call you *mère*, my Lady

Ysabeau? I want to call you *mère*.' " Her eyes shone with delight as she watched his smile. "Of course, I said yes. You don't object, do you, Simon? Perhaps I should have made him wait until the wedding."

"You are so silly—of course, don't make Aimery wait!" he chuckled. "I can see he loves you as much as I do. Thank you, love," he said, stroking her hair, "for loving my son. I had hardly dared hope for that. I want you to feel free to give Aimery anything he asks for." His eyes danced with a gleaming mischief which he allowed her to see.

"Simon—" She looked at him, trying to see where his joke was leading.

"Tonight as I put him in his little bed he asked me to give him a little brother. My love, you wouldn't deny my son anything he wanted, would you?" He held her with one arm while his other began to arouse her in that way he knew so well.

"I suppose not," she sighed, her breathing already quickening. "It seems I cannot deny his father anything he wants, either."

Chapter Forty-one

They had barely attended Mass and broken their fast the next morning when the steward announced that a party had just been admitted into the outer ward and was making its way to the great hall.

Simon's eyes lit up. "The King's messenger, at last!"

"I'm sorry, but no, my lord. It is two religious women, mounted on mules."

"Ah, my sister!" he groaned to Ysabeau through fingers splayed over his face. "I knew I should have sent her a message, telling her why I didn't show up at Chertsey with you. Now I'm in for it! Adèle can be the wrath of God personified." He didn't look seriously alarmed, however.

Adèle—Sister Mary Agathe—entered the hall only moments later, trailed by another nun who had accompanied her on her journey. The tall Benedictine gave a very un-nunlike whoop of joy and was seized in her brother's embrace and whirled around, her black woolen skirts flying.

"Oh, Simon, put me down. This is most unseemly. You'll shock Sister Marguerite," she commanded with mock severity. As he did so, she turned to include the amused Ysabeau in her greeting.

"You must be Lady Ysabeau, my dear," said Adèle in a musical voice, deep for a woman's. Ysabeau could see her resemblance to Simon: she was tall and fair-complected, with sparkling azure eyes very like Simon's, and if any hair had shown under the severe starched wimple she was sure it would have been yellow. "Now, brother, tell me why you failed to bring this lovely lady to me as you promised. You're a naughty boy to worry me so. I could not imagine what had happened, after you told me why she was coming."

"I'm truly sorry," Simon said, "but circumstances forced us alter our plans. Perhaps you should come to the solar with us and we'll tell you what happened," he continued, glancing meaningfully at the many servants in the hall, breaking their fasts and beginning the task of clearing. "Thomas, bring the sisters some bread and wine, and have their things stowed in the guest chamber."

". . . and since Philippe de Melle was dead there was no need to bring Ysabeau to sanctuary at Chertsey. I'm sorry, I meant to send you a message. . . ." Simon concluded apologetically.

His sister was sitting on a backless bench near the brazier, facing Simon and Ysabeau, who sat together.

If Ysabeau had had any doubts that his sister would find her innocent of wrongdoing, they were banished now as the Benedictine turned to her sympathetically. "Ah, you poor lamb! You have, indeed, been through a terrible experience. It's truly a miracle that the awful heretic did not slay you! I thank God and all the saints for your deliverance!" Her graceful hands fluttered as she talked.

Ysabeau relaxed as the nun's sympathy washed over her. Here was the first outsider's reaction to the events that had culminated in the dreadful incident outside the banquet hall.

"I can see you could do naught else," Adèle said warmly. "Of course, you would want to bring Ysabeau out of that atmosphere of intrigue and gossip after such a nasty shock. And when will you be married?"

Simon explained about the necessity of awaiting the King's permission, and that he expected word any day. "But you know how unpredictable royalty can be, Adèle. Henry may have weighty matters of state that are absorbing his attention at the moment."

"Quite so. But Simon, would it be all right if I stayed to witness the wedding? I have the abbess' permission to be absent awhile, and it would mean so much to me." She sounded wistful.

"Of course, you must stay," Simon said firmly, beaming. "I wouldn't have it any other way. Besides, there's the fact that you're my favorite, if only, sister; you'll be the only family member present."

The nun sighed and fingered her crucifix. "I can see Gervase and you are not getting along any better than usual. Never mind, *mon frère*, I know it's not of your doing."

The two nuns were then shown to their chamber, and Simon and Ysabeau were still chatting in the solar when the seneschal brought word that the guard at the gate tower had at last spotted the long-awaited envoy from the King, accompanied by a half-dozen knights.

"At last! Direct him up to the solar, Thomas," Simon ordered.

A few minutes later the seneschal announced, "Thomas of London, my lord."

A glance at Simon's startled face as she rose to greet the visitor revealed that he had not been expecting Henry to send the Archbishop himself. Then she turned to study the tall, lean man known as Thomas à Becket.

Becket was dark, and possessed a Norman beak of a nose, piercing gray eyes, and black hair. He was ascetically thin, and towered over Simon and everyone else. She knew by reputation that although Thomas was not a priest, he remained as chaste as any cloistered monk. She wondered what such a man must think of the actions of Simon and herself.

If he had any views opposite those of his good friend, Henry Plantagenet, however, he gave no evidence of it.

"Greetings, my Lord de Winslade, and my Lady Ysabeau de Ré, from Their Graces, King Henry and Queen Eleanor. I had business near here, so I agreed to bring word of their graces' permission and fondest wish that you marry." He smiled to see the radiant joy that lit Ysabeau's face, but added warningly, "However, my Lord, His Grace the King begs your presence immediately in London for a consultation of his barons, to make new laws and renew old ones from the first Henry's reign. He does not anticipate needing you above a fortnight, my lord, but he begs you will return with me tomorrow."

Simon groaned aloud. The request was a royal command which could not be ignored.

"Of course I will attend, as his grace wishes," he sighed. There could be no other response. Damn his eyes, Henry snatched away with one hand what he had just given with the other!

"Never fear, Simon. I will be waiting for you when you return," Ysabeau said calmly later in their chamber after arranging for a formal midday meal to be served in the hall to Thomas and his retinue. "I wish we could marry sooner too, but I have much to do to ready the chapel and hall for a fitting wedding and feast. And your sister has agreed to help me make a new dress, so that your bride will dazzle you."

He appreciated her consideration, her willingness to put the needs of the realm first, though he noticed the liquidness of her fine dark eyes. The unshed tears added brilliance to her gaze as she tried to mask frustration with serenity. What a lucky man he was that such a beauty as this loved him and his son!

"Are you sure?" he queried, blue eyes probing her face. "You could go to London with me. Perhaps we could be wed there. . . ."

"And have you leave our bridal bed in some crowded inn or borrowed chamber at the crack of dawn and disappear all day on court business? No thank you, my lord. I have waited long enough for this that I do not want it done by half measures. And Aimery fully trusts me—if I were to disappear now he wouldn't understand. No, I am well able to wait two weeks or so until you return to us, and we can be wed in Winslade's own chapel. All the same," she whispered into his ear, pulling his tawny head down to hers, "come back to me just as soon as you can, my love!"

She could feel his fervent agreement in his kiss.

Chapter Forty-two

The two weeks Henry had promised turned into more than two months, as Simon had privately feared.

The barons had not got down to business at all the first three days they were assembled at Bermondsey, but had had to humor Henry in his twin passions for hunting and hawking. A seemingly tireless individual, Henry could chase the red deer all day and expect his favorite nobles to keep him company drinking and wenching all night. More than one yawning, weary noble darkly mumbled that the rumor of the Angevin's demon blood was more than fable.

When the barons and the King finally sat down in council together, Henry first announced his new appointments, a masterful combination of Stephen's old supporters and men who had changed their allegiance to Henry during the war. Perhaps the most surprising choice of all, however, was Thomas Becket, as chancellor.

They had been working only a few days on the revision of the laws, when Henry received word of the defiance of a few remaining barons. Henry decided to use the rest of the winter to sweep the country clean of rebellious barons, remaining unlicensed castles, and Flemish mercenaries who had stayed on as robbing brigands.

Ysabeau received a letter in March, saying that they were besieging a castle in Suffolk and were going on to do the same in York. It was a loving message, full of anguish that the King's business was keeping them apart for so much longer than planned. He said that he had hoped that Henry would wind up his campaign soon, for he had received word of the birth of his new son on February 28, in London. The child had been christened Henry, and already promised to be more sturdy than the sickly Prince William. He went on to mention that the barons and bishops were to meet in Wallingford later in the spring to swear fealty to William, and then to young Henry, in case the first son failed to survive.

"Ah, saints, I could weep in vexation," cried Ysabeau to Adèle. She had read the missive aloud to Simon's sister and her companion, Sister Marguerite, as they sat by the fire, working on Ysabeau's wedding dress. "Henry will probably want to keep Simon with him till after the fealty-swearing, which means we can't be married for weeks. Hasn't Henry Plantagenet had enough of war? Why can't he leave the fighting to some of his other vassals—most of them act as if they can't stand the poor women they're married to anyway," she finished fretfully. She wished now she had gone to London with Simon. They could have been wed by Eleanor's own chaplain and she could have been with Eleanor when the new baby was born. Possibly Eleanor would have even reminded her royal husband he was keeping his favorite baron from his promised honeymoon.

"Patience, my dear, all will come to pass in God's good time," counseled Adèle, laying down the decorative border she was embroidering for the hem of Ysabeau's wedding dress. Sister Marguerite did not even look up from the matching silk underdress she worked on. Adèle had explained one day that Marguerite was nearly totally deaf, as the result of her father having boxed her ears rather too soundly when she was a child. Ysabeau understood then why Sister Marguerite's voice was hesitant and strange on the rare occasions she did speak, and why she always studied those talking so carefully.

Ysabeau looked fondly at Adèle, though she was not at all sure she could be patient much longer. She could not imagine how she would have got along with Simon gone all these weeks without the nun's presence. She had made herself handy in dozens of ways. She told stories to a rapt Aimery; she assisted with the many tasks of running the castle; she entertained Ysabeau with tales of Simon as a boy, which delighted listener and teller alike.

Her reverie was interrupted just then by the

entrance of the captain of the guard, who came to tell her that Simon's brother, the Earl of Hawkingham, was outside the walls and desired speech with her.

"Hmm, that is a problem, isn't it?" she replied, her brow wrinkling in concern. She knew Simon did not want his brother admitted into the keep in his absence, for he did not trust him; Gervase had already come once, a month ago, and been politely refused entrance, then told Simon was expected home at any time. They could not lie to Gervase about Simon's absence and say that Simon did not wish to see him; the lord of a castle never hid behind his seneschal or a woman's skirts. Still, she could not feel carefree about admitting to Simon's distrusted sibling that she had no idea when her lord would be back.

"I suppose I could speak to him from the parapet," she answerd the seneschal, rising from the settle by the fire and reaching for her furlined mantle. She was loath to leave the fire's warmth for the windswept walkway behind the crenellated walls, but the sooner it was done, the sooner she could return.

The sky was leaden as she climbed the stairway to the parapet; tonight there would, doubtless, be snow. The wind whipped about her legs, stealing under her skirts to chill her limbs even with their woolen stockings.

From her vantage point, she could see Gervase of Hawkingham, mounted on a gray destrier at the head of six armored men, but she could discern little of his features. Like his men, he wore full mail, including a coif and helm with a nasal piece. She could see that his eyes were pale and that he possessed his brother's high cheekbones; he wore a pointed blond beard instead of just a mustache, like Simon, but more than that she could not discern. She had been curious to see the degree of similarity between the brothers.

"Greetings, Lady Ysabeau," he called up to her. "Obviously, my dear brother has not returned, or you would not be up there, exposing your fair cheeks to winter wind. Will you give my men hospitality, so that I may hear the news Simon has doubtless sent you, and offer my services for anything you may need in his absence?" His voice was confident, courteous; he had said nothing she could find offensive, yet there was a smooth quality to it she could not trust.

"I regret to say, my lord, that I am under previous instructions by my Lord Simon not to admit you in his absence."

"But surely he did not mean for you to refuse shelter to myself and my few men, who will otherwise be exposed to the winter storm! That is hardly hospitable. . . ."

"My impulse to hospitality must be overcome, I regret to say, my lord, by my obedience to Lord Simon's wishes. I will be glad to make your acquaintance when my lord returns."

"Which will be when?" he countered.

"I expect him daily," she insisted stubbornly, "though I cannot say exactly when, for Simon is in his Sovereign's service, and those serving the King cannot just leave on a whim."

"And did he wed you, before he left to

follow the Angevin? If congratulations are in order, I would not leave them unsaid."

"No, my lord," she answered stiffly. "We will wed as soon as he returns."

"Certainly," he called back, but that simple word managed to somehow convey doubt. "You will be good enough, I'm sure, Lady Ysabeau, to have Simon notify me upon his arrival home. I would dearly love to attend your nuptials."

She thought it extremely unlikely that Gervase of Hawkingham would be invited, but good manners and prudence prevented her from saying so.

With that, he rode away, and Ysabeau returned to the keep, filled with anxiety.

"You did just right," Adèle assured her when Ysabeau told her of the meeting. "I don't know what makes two brothers different on the inside, though so alike on the outside. But as a girl I could always count on Simon to soothe my hurts and dry my tears, while Gervase usually caused them."

Meanwhile, Gervase, who had loudly demanded shelter at the Augustinian abbey at Greywell, was smacking his lips gleefully as he thought of the encounter. Simon was still away, and the delectable Poitevin wench obviously had not a clue as to when he'd return. She must be getting rather lonely, cooped up in his brother's keep in the midst of winter, with opportunities for diversion few and food supplies diminishing. And Simon hadn't married her yet . . . she was an heiress, and if he could wed her first, then her revenues would come to him. His eyes gleamed as he imagined his brother's anguish, knowing he had snatched his delightful morsel away from him, and put her forever beyond his reach. And he'd never let her go. . . . He'd have her in his bed nightly until her belly was full with his seed, and he could disinherit that bright-eyed brat of Simon's.

Chapter Forty-three

It seemed like an answer to Ysabeau's prayer when on the very next day, she received the letter from Simon de Winslade.

"Please read it now, my lady. Your response is needed quickly," the messenger urged, when she would have put it in her sleeve to savor later, for she was right in the middle of candle-making with the rest of the castle women. Her hair was tied back, the sleeves of her serviceable woolen kirtle were rolled up past her elbows, and she knew flecks of the smelly melted tallow marked her skirts.

The messenger was unfamiliar to her, but he might be one of Henry's men, she surmised. The handwriting, too, was not in Simon's familiar bold scrawl, though this was explained in the opening paragraph: "To Ysabeau, Comtesse de Ré, from Simon, Baron de

Winslade, greetings." Here, Ysabeau frowned, for he normally included some endearment in the salutation, and without it the letter seemed austere and cold. Nonetheless, she read on. "Forgive me for this strange hand, but I am unable to write, and must rely on the assistance of a monk. I have missed you, and as the time dragged on I found myself unable to wait to make you mine. Perhaps it was because of you that my concentration lapsed, causing me to be grievously wounded in the shoulder with a cross-bow bolt in York. It was removed without incident, and I obtained leave from Henry to return to Winslade and recuperate under the tender touch of your hand, my own dearest angel. However, en route, the wound festered, and I sought refuge in the abbey at Greywell. Here I lie, sick, perhaps unto death. Mayhap, the sight of you and my son can give me the will to live, I don't know. It's in God's hands now. By your haste you may make up for my fatal carelessness, which was always keen before I fell in love with you. . . . Given at Greywell Abbey, March 17, 1155."

She gasped aloud, her face as pallid as the vellum sheet she clutched. Simon, dreadfully sick . . . he might even die! "I must pack!" she cried, virtually throwing the missive into Adèle's hands as she flew from the room toward the stair. The mental picture she had of Simon, a nasty, gangrenous wound sapping his strength, his body feverish, thinking only of seeing her and his son again, gave wings to her feet as she climbed the steep staircase toward her room.

She was soon joined there by Simon's sister.

"Ysabeau, are you sure Simon wrote the letter? There's no seal impressed in the wax," began the nun hesitantly.

Her worry fraying her temper, Ysabeau snapped, "Of course he did not! He says a monk wrote it! And he may have left his seal behind in the camp . . . blood of God, Adèle! You don't suppose his arm was amputated, and he fears to tell me?" She was frantic, and in her frenzy rushed from one corner of the room to another, succeeding merely in transferring piles of clothing from place to place.

"But, to tell you to bring little Aimery out in this weather . . . would Simon do such a thing?"

"Adèle, he may be dying—and it's my fault! We will do exactly as he says!" she cried. Visions of Simon standing before the besieged castle, daydreaming of her as she so often did about him, filled her mind with horror. It was her fault. . . .

Sister Mary Agathe's voice came again, more sure of herself now. "Ysabeau, I know my brother. Does it seem like him to imply you are at fault for his wounding? He's a warrior, Ysabeau. He knows he takes a risk every time he dons mail and belts on his sword. He wouldn't blame the woman he loves for that."

That was the piece of the puzzle that didn't fit, Ysabeau realized, but her sense of guilt shoved it aside. "Perhaps his wound makes him fretful," she said. "We can't all be sweet martyrs—" She saw the nun flinch and grow pale. "I'm sorry, Adèle," she said in a moment, clasping Simon's sister to her in tears. "I'm just so frightened. I must go to him! I cannot rest until I see him! If you're coming along, fine. If not, please understand. I can't take the chance of ignoring this message."

"I'll go pack a few things for Aimery," Adèle said quietly, and left the chamber.

Ysabeau packed a change of clothing for herself and gathered up a few packets of medicinal herbs she thought Simon might need, though usually the care in an abbey infirmary was the best that existed anywhere. Expecting to be met in the bailey only by three men-at-arms and Adèle, she was dismayed to see Sister Marguerite mounted on her sturdy mule.

"Sister Mary Agathe, I have to get there quickly. Every person added to this procession slows me from reaching Simon's side," she cried.

"The rules of my order forbid me to travel without one of my fellow sisters, but never fear, Sister Marguerite will keep up," the nun promised firmly. "If Simon is gravely ill, we may all have to nurse him in shifts."

As it turned out, the nuns were as good as their word, but the fetlock-deep snow retarded their progress, and they all were chilled to the bone by the time they arrived at the abbey gates at nightfall. Aimery had fallen into a doze for the last few furlongs, and awoke as Ysabeau pulled her mount to a halt. He was fretful and confused, whimpering for his supper and his father. He did not understand why Ysabeau had ordered the cold ride across the downs, with snow swirling about his cold cheeks.

"I'll hold him, Ysabeau," Adèle offered.

She had already dismounted and handed the reins to one of the retainers. "I'll follow you in, as soon as I've given instructions to Sister Marguerite."

She watched Ysabeau approach the grille at the entrance, where a monk stood waiting to greet her, his head swathed in the black cowl of the Augustinians. Then, speaking softly so that her voice would not carry beyond the men and the nun, Adèle said, "Something about this doesn't sit right. Perhaps I'm getting fanciful, but I can't shake the feeling. Therefore, do not come in, Sister Marguerite, till you see me beckon. And began now to tell your beads. If I've not come out before you've said ten Aves and ten Paternosters, mount and ride to Lord Simon at York, or, failing that, King Henry himself."

Sister Marguerite had watched her intently, lip-reading, for she couldn't hear the soft-spoken words as the man could. Her eyes widened with alarm as the implication that this was a trap, and that Lady Ysabeau and Sister Mary Agathe, whom she idolized, might be walking into danger. Her florid cheeks paled at the idea of riding so far with these rough men to bring aid. But if Sister Mary Agathe had asked it, she would have ridden to the mouth of Hell.

From her vantage point at the gate, Ysabeau could not see the hooded figure stride down the cloister walk with un-monkish haste toward the infirmary. Once there, he threw back the cowl, revealing an untonsured head of coarse black hair.

"She's here," he announced with smirking triumph to the elegant figure lounging on the comfortable but narrow bed in the infirmary. "I told you she'd take the bait. Went white as a sheet, she did, when I gave her the message, and even insisted I ride on ahead to encourage you with the news that she and the brat were on their way."

"Yes, yes, Osbert," replied Gervase, a little distractedly, as he hurriedly climbed under the covers, expecting his brother's luscious mistress to come dashing through the doorway at any moment. "Now, get you gone, but hold my men in readiness to subdue her, lest she give the alarm too soon, before they've seen to her escort." He chuckled, rubbing his newly shaven chin, and then heard her rapid footsteps down the hallway, guided there by one of his henchmen, disguised as an abbot. How Sir Ralph had protested the shaving of his pate!

"It was thinning up there anyway, old boy," Gervase had said, enjoying his vassal's discomfiture. "You're the only one fat enough to wear the abbot's robes—I could hardly depend on that pious goat to lead the lamb to the slaughter!"

Father Anselm was, at this very moment, soundly gagged and trussed in the chapel, as were the rest of the small community. That Father Anselm had promised to see Gervase excommunicated troubled the earl little; he figured the matter would be dropped when the monks came to no harm. All he wanted was a means to lure Ysabeau de Ré and Simon's brat out from behind the walls of Winslade keep, and then he would leave the abbey in peace forever. Anselim would rest quietly enough after a fat donation, he assumed.

The door opened and he quickly shut his

eyes, feigning sleep. He heard the sound of several pairs of feet and Ralph's voice saying soothingly, "He fell asleep after supper, for the effort of taking his broth exhausts him. He is in some danger yet. I will wear out my knees in prayer until he passes the crisis, never fear."

God's little toe, Gervase thought, struggling not to laugh. He never knew Sir Ralph was such a good actor. He was really embellishing the role. He shifted slightly then and groaned, as if in his sleep, wondering if Ysabeau had spotted the blood-stained bandage over his collarbone yet. The dried blood on it looked so very realistic, though it was only that of a chicken, filched from the monks' barnyard.

Then came a voice familiar to him, and he groaned inwardly.

"Father," his sister, Adèle, was saying, "has he any fever? Have you tried a tisane of boiled willow bark? I've found it to be an excellent febrifuge."

He hadn't counted on his sister coming, in fact, had not even known her to be at Winslade. She'd see through his disguise as soon as he opened his eyes, perhaps sooner. Even though he'd shaved his beard, so that he now wore only a golden mustache like Simon, he knew he could never fool Adèle. He had hoped for at least a kiss before Ysabeau realized she'd been trapped.

"Ysabeau . . ." he moaned, allowing his eyelids to flutter open.

"Simon, you're awake!" cried Ysabeau gladly, and dropped a kiss on his brow. "How are you? I've been so worried," she murmured, studying him. In the background she could hear

Adèle carrying on a spirited discussion with the abbot over the best medicaments to use, while Aimery began crying.

"I'm fine, Ysabeau, now that you're here."

It was like looking at Simon's reflection in a murky stream. His image was blurred, somehow, the eyes a cloudier blue. She knew that wounds and fever cause a loss of weight, but Simon's cheeks seemed fuller than before. He looked so . . . dissipated, somehow, as if he'd been long at the wineskin lately. In fact, a faint scent of stale wine on his breath reached her even now. "Simon?" she questioned, as the man in bed returned her gaze unblinkingly.

Aimery had succeeded in struggling loose to go to his father, whom he'd heard was very ill and who would not be able to play with him. He clambered up onto the bed, only to scoot, whimpering, back toward Ysabeau. "Not Papa," he said decidedly, then looked to see what Ysabeau would make of Uncle Gervase masquerading as his father.

As if in a dream, Ysabeau recoiled. This man had Simon's face, spoke with Simon's voice, but everything about him was wrong.

"Gervase . . ." she heard Adèle murmur in horror, and the man in bed openly grinned.

"Shame, Sister, coming along and spoiling my fun. I wanted to enjoy the pretty Ysabeau's company a trifle longer as Simon. Welcome to Greywell Abbey, Lady Ysabeau, and I'm charmed to make your acquaintance at last. Gervase, Earl of Hawkingham, Chawton, and Lingfield, at your service. I'm sorry for my little trick, but it seems you were too shy to meet me any other way."

"My lord, if this is your idea of a joke, I beg you to spare me any further exposure to it. Suggesting that the man I love is grievously ill can hardly be funny. Am I to understand that Simon is not injured?"

"Not so far as I know," he answered breezily, in the voice so like Simon's.

"Then you will excuse us if we continue this introduction at a more appropriate time," Ysabeau said stiffly, rising from the bed and going to Adèle's side, with Aimery in her arms. "We have just galloped across the Downs in the snow for no good cause, my lord, with a young child—"

"I'm sure you'll find my hospitality agreeable," responded Gervase smoothly. "You can't leave now, especially with Simon's beloved son and heir." Something in his tone and his eyes as they rested on Aimery made icy shivers steal down Ysabeau's spine. No one should look at a child that way. "In the morning, we'll all leave, of course, and you'll be my guests at Hawkingham."

He laughed evilly as both women backed toward the door, only to be halted as Sir Ralph drew his sword from the scabbard under his robes and barred their way with its length, guffawing at their distress. Aimery, sensing disaster, set up a wail.

". . . now, and in the hour of our death. Amen." Sister Marguerite finished her last prayer, and stared anxiously at the gate. No one had appeared, though she had prayed very slowly. Something was very wrong.

"Let us go," she said in her strange voice, and one of the men held her stirrup while she mounted the patient mule.

They were swallowed in the darkness moments before Gervase's mailed knights came out looking for them. It was snowing so hard that their tracks were already half-obliterated, leading north over the Downs. Gervase's men were on foot.

One of the knights gave a snort of disgust. "By the time we are mounted they'll be leagues away, and in what direction will they head? My lord needn't worry. We'll be safely behind the walls of Hawkingham before his brother even hears of this. Once in there, Winslade can whistle for his leman, for all the good it'll do him."

"Perhaps when he tires of her, he'll share her," speculated another. "What a lovely creature to look on, with those dark eyes! I wonder if what they say about Provençal women is true?"

Chapter Forty-four

"You'll never get away with this, you know," Ysabeau said tightly as her palfrey, held by a leading rein, headed southward to Hawkingham. "Simon will rescue us." She and Adèle, who carried Aimery on her mount, were surrounded by Gervase and his men-at-arms. Escape was impossible, unless they met a stronger party en route that she could persuade to aid them.

"My dear Lady Ysabeau, soon to be my lady, in truth," came his carefree reply, "Simon will have no idea that you're gone until it's too late. He's busy fighting with Henry, as you were so kind to inform me. By the time he returns, you will have seen the splendor of my much superior castle and decided that it's better to be wed to an earl than a mere baron."

"Never!" she said, jaw clenched as her

dark eyes flashed at him. "Even if you doubt Simon's love for me and mine for him, he'll never let you hold his son."

"Oh, I'll have no reluctance to free the boy."

"You won't?" she turned to him, hope flaring for Aimery's safety.

"Nay, what do I want with Simon's brat, once you've given me a son of my own?" he said, reaching out a mail-gloved hand to turn her averted chin to him. "I said a boy, mind you. None of your puling girls, like my dead first wife gave me." Something glittered within the depths of those cloudy blue eyes that frighened her to her very soul.

"I'll never marry you," she repeated.

"Oh, we'll see about that," came his reply. "Remember what happened to the other nun and Simon's retainers."

He had told her he had murdered Sister Marguerite and the three men-at-arms who had escorted them to Greywell, and Ysabeau had been nearly demented with horror, grief, and anger, until the whispered conversation she had had with Adèle in the middle of the night.

Adèle had told her of her suspicions before the trap was sprung, how Marguerite had been instructed to leave after a certain interval if she did not reappear. Adèle had every reason to think that the four had gotten safely away and were even now riding to summon help from Simon at York. After all, they had seen no bodies, and Gervase would not have scrupled to display them like grisly trophies, the nun insisted. The snow was melting, which should cover their tracks if Gervase sent any men to pursue them, though that also meant the roads could turn miry and slow them down. But Ysabeau must pray and continue to assume that Simon would soon rescue all of them.

Ysabeau cursed her own foolishness. How gullible she had been! An unmarried heiress must always guard against abduction and forced marriage, not go jaunting about the countryside on fool's errands. The words of the message hadn't sounded like Simon's, but she had let her guilt spur her on when prudence would have dictated otherwise.

How was she to avoid wedding the unscrupulous Earl of Hawkingham? Would he rape her and get her with child, making marriage a necessity? Would he threaten the safety of Simon's son and Adèle? She knew she could avail herself of a dagger and plunge it into Gervase's treacherous heart, even though it meant exposing herself immediately to the rapacious wolves who were his retainers. Death would be welcome, once they made her their plaything, as their leering looks promised. And she had no right to endanger Simon's sister and his innocent son. Oh wretched day when Simon had ever entangled himself with her! If not for her, he might have married some knight's daughter long ago and be living in peace.

These thoughts and others tormented her as they rode southward, and she was mostly silent until they crossed the drawbridge to the tower keep of Hawkingham.

While Ysabeau imagined her love to be hard

at work besieging the Count of Aumale's fortress at York, Simon lounged at relative ease with his liege in Scarborough Castle. The reputedly impregnable fortress on its rugged peninsula had been surrendered along with his other royal properties when William le Gros realized that Henry II meant business, unlike his feckless predecessor.

They had been there several days, enjoying a much-deserved rest after the hard march northward. It was a rainy, drafty night, and the chimney wasn't drawing well; Simon's eyes smarted from the smoke that couldn't escape. He was staring into the fire in the great hall, his eyes gazing unfocusedly at the dancing flames, while he wondered how Ysabeau was coping with the diminished stores and the restlessness of being cooped up against the chill winds. He wondered also how soon he was going to be able to take his leave of Henry. He knew the King fully intended to deal with Peverel of Nottingham and the Bishop of Winchester on his way south; whether he would be willing to do so without Simon was open to question.

Three years ago Simon would have gloried in the successful campaign, even in the midst of winter. They had scored victory after victory, taking castles without crossing swords with any of the rebels or destroying a single stone. He could practically see justice and order spreading over the land, as recalcitrant barons learned that Henry Plantagenet always followed up a threat with swift action if obedience was not forthcoming. He would have enjoyed, also, the increasing favor bestowed on him by Henry, who seemed to thrive on his company nearly as much as that of his Chancellor, Thomas à Becket, though Henry did not understand his reluctance to join him as he dallied with the Yorkshire wenches.

"You're as bad as my Becket. You've been as chaste as a clerk ever since you met Lady Ysabeau. Did you ever wed the girl?" Henry queried, lolling on some cushions with a cup of malmsey.

"No, my liege. We did not have the chance, and I'd like to speak to you about that. . . ."

But they were not to complete the conversation. The steward ushered a man-at-arms into the room, still in his boiled-leather hauberk and dripping a trail of water across the rushes as he came. Another dispatch from London, Simon assumed; there was a constant stream of them coming and going, as Henry governed his realm from wherever he happened to be.

With a start, he suddenly realized, however, that the man was one of his own sargeants, Harold le Rouge, named for his flaming red mop of hair. He arose, which helped Harold to spot his lord in the smoky great hall.

"Harold? Is aught amiss at Winslade? Ysabeau? Aimery?" The man's drawn, sober face did nothing to reassure him as he waited for his answer.

"We've ridden as fast as we could, my lord, from Greywell Abbey. Lady Ysabeau, your son, and the holy nun, your sister, are taken—"

"Taken? How? What were they doing at Greywell Abbey?" None of this made any sense. Henry was listening now, too.

"I know not, my lord! We never saw the villain lying in wait, but your sister suspected treachery, that the letter was not from you."

"Letter? I sent no letter!" Simon's face was a thundercloud, and Harold's face reflected fear of his lord's wrath.

"My lady received a note saying you were sorely wounded, and might not live, and lay at Greywell. You summoned her there . . ."

"I did no such thing!" roared Simon, and Harold took a step backward.

"No, my lord, of course not, I meant the letter said it was from you—"

"Hold!" interrupted Simon, realization dawning. "Has my brother, Earl Gervase, been nosing around the castle? Did anyone tell him I was gone?"

Harold le Rouge cleared his throat uncomfortably. "Yes, my lord, the very day before. Your lady had to tell him when he demanded entrance at the gates."

"God damn his black heart, it's Gervase who has taken them! I should have known he'd stop at nothing to do me ill."

"But to take two women and an innocent child!" exclaimed Henry.

"We went to the Abbey as the letter requested," the man went on, watching as the baron paled and then flushed with anger, hand tightening convulsively on his sword hilt. He'd not care to be the Earl when Lord Simon caught up with him. He went on to explain how the nun had not reappeared immediately as planned, and they had ridden off at a gallop, fearing the worst; he had spotted Gervase's armed retainers come dashing out of the abbey just as they topped the hill and disappeared from view into the falling snow. They'd left the nun at a convent they passed on the way northward, knowing they'd be able to make better time without Sister Marguerite on her mule. The nun would be able to make her way back to her own convent at Chertsey without much difficulty, Harold was confident. "But I know not where he's taken them, my lord, or even if they've left the abbey—"

"Of course they've gone—he can't defend such a position," Simon interrupted grimly, his well-chiseled lips tightened into a thin line. "They'll make for Hawkingham. It's better fortified that Lingfield, and Chawton's little more than a manor house now." Then, turning to his Sovereign, who was by now standing at his side, he said, "By your leave, your grace, as you can see I must go, and my men with me. My lady and my son are in great danger, for there's little that blackguard wouldn't do to avenge himself on me." His eyes, which held a murderous gleam in them, stared down at the shorter man, awaiting his certain permission.

"No."

"*No*?" He couldn't believe his ears. Could Henry of Anjou be serious? Was he so selfish that he could see no other cause but his own? He wouldn't stay, even if it meant breaking his fealty. His love and his only son—and yes, even his sister—were in deadly jeopardy and that transcended even what he owed his King.

"Calm down, Winslade." Henry laid a restraining hand on his subject's shoulder. "I merely mean that you will not go alone. I'll go with you. I've no more liking for rebellious nobles in the south than in the north, and I've been watching your brother for some time now. I'm aware he was never one of my supporters or my mother's, and when I ordered you to raze Chawton, he had less cause than ever to love either of us. By striking at you, he's struck at me, Simon, and I won't tolerate that."

"But . . . Your Grace, what of Nottingham? The Bishop's lands?" How could he refuse Henry's help? How could he explain that waiting on the entire army would slow him down too much, and in that time Ysabeau might be forced into marriage with Gervase? The thought of his brother touching his beloved in any way caused a red mist to swim before his eyes.

"I don't propose to bring my entire force," Henry assured him, reading his subject's mind. "We can take a couple hundred men, and surround the castle. When they see me, his knights will surrender the castle whether your fool of a brother agrees or not," Henry promised, his successes of the last month buoying his confidence.

"You don't know Gervase as I do," Simon countered grimly. "He's never scrupled to hire the meanest scum that came his way. Hawkingham is manned by a motley collection of Flemish mercenaries, Enlgish brigands, and any cutthroat who comes to the gates. None of them owe you any allegiance, for they know you'd give them short shrift. No, if we're to get in, it will have to be by deception." Then he was silent, pacing the floor.

"I have it!" Henry announced. "Eleanor and Thomas have complained often enough that I look like anything but a king." He gestured toward his rude, stained russet jerkin and held up his callused hands with their ragged, dirty fingernails. "We can take advantage of it, for once. Now stop wearing out the floor, Simon, and listen to the plan. . . ."

Chapter Forty-five

They had coverd the eight-league distance between Greywell and Hawkingham in one grueling day precisely because, Ysabeau thought, Gervase did not wish to hazard meeting any stronger party of riders, or Simon himself. Fortunately, it had been warmer than the previous day, and the snow was receding into scattered patches in shaded spots. Still, Ysabeau was exhausted when they reached Gervase's castle, and a glance at Adèle holding the sleepy Aimery, confirmed that the past two days' exposure and hard riding had taken their toll on the nun also.

Ysabeau's fatigue prevented her from properly appreciating the aged beauty of the tower keep of Hawkingham as it rose above the sparkling River Meon, though she knew it was one of the very first stone keeps built in

England. While others of the new Norman conquerors were erecting hastily built wooden palisades and keeps, Guy de Bayeux had built in stone, symbolic of his enduring commitment to his new land.

As they crossed the moat and entered the outer ward, Ysabeau could view the splendor of the limestone castle that had been enlarged and improved by succeeding generations since Guy de Bayeux. Gervase leaned down from his destier and said softly, "Gaze upon all that will be yours as my countess."

She returned his look with one of intense loathing and uttered one word contemptuously: "*Jamais.*" Never would she consent to live life as the plaything of this cruel scoundrel who was but a distorted copy of his brother; never as long as she had breath in her body would she endure him touching her at will, forcing himself on her in bed, requiring her to bear his children. What a mockery of love it would be to see that face so like Simon's beside her. Yet how unfair it was, that Aimery's safety depended on her acquiescence!

Ysabeau had noted when she was first shown to her room in Hawkington's tower that the only bolt on the door fastened on the outside. She made no comment about it, but resolved to make sure the eating knife she carried with her was always secreted on her person. She would be no easy victim for any attempt at force by Gervase, though she knew she could only use the little knife to try to hold him off. The fact that he held Aimery and Adèle, housed elsewhere in the keep, limited the amount of resistance she could afford to put up.

Gervase had indicated that he would not further impose his presence on her that night, merely showed her to her room and promised that hot water and towels would be brought up as well as a late supper.

"But may I not see Aimery, my lord? He's had a very difficult two days . . . he's grown used to having me there. Please. I want to assure myself he's not sickening from the cold." She hated asking him for anything, and now she was begging, and he obviously delighted in it. Damn him, I'd like to stick my dagger into his ribs, she thought. Then who would beg! That would wipe the smirking smile off his evil face!

"Certainly, my dear." His agreement surprised her, and she took a step forward, until he added, "the moment you agree to become my countess, you'll have the run of the castle." He chuckled at her crestfallen face. "How I will delight in giving you sons of our own, so that you needn't grieve when we give Simon back his little runt. It delights me to see what a devoted mother you have become—though you won't be nursing our babes. No," he said, grinning, reaching out a hand to grab her breast, "our babes shall have wet nurses, and I will be the only one to suck from these lovely breasts." His face loomed so close that she could smell his wine-laden breath.

She struck him then, her blow landing with stinging force on his right cheek. As he backed away, still laughing infuriatingly, she screamed every foul Provençal epithet she had ever heard.

Then he had stepped forward, pushing her

with such force that she landed on her backside in the rushes. Still chuckling, he had slammed the door shut and thrown the bolt, leaving her alone and afraid.

At a midday meal worthy of a royal banquet, she was reunited with Aimery and Adèle. The little boy ran to her with a glad cry as she entered the hall, then drew back as he saw the man who looked so much like Papa at her side.

"It's all right, Aimery," she said encouragingly, stooping to his level, her mulberry-velvet skirts spread all about her. "Your Uncle Gervase won't hurt you." She looked warningly at the Earl over the boy's dark head as he hugged her tightly, babbling in a mixture of French and English.

Gervase directed her to be seated at the high table at his right, sharing his trencher, Adèle and Aimery on her right. On Gervase's other side was a man he introduced as Father Édouard, Hawkingham's priest.

The man was so grossly fat that for a moment Ysabeau could only stare. He had at least three chins, and his small eyes were set so far into fleshy rolls that they looked like raisins set in a suet pie. There was surely enough fabric in his robe to make a tent.

"Charmed, my lady Ysabeau," the priest answered unctuously. "I will look forward to conducting your nuptials." When he smiled, his eyes disappeared altogether and he bared a mouth with several blackened teeth.

"There will not be any wedding, Father. Surely you are misinformed. I am already contracted to my lord's brother, Baron Simon de Winslade."

Father Édouard looked startled for a moment, for he knew a betrothal was a formal contract which would not be broken lightly. Ysabeau prayed that he had no way to find out that she and Simon had had no time to draw up such a contract. After a glance at Earl Gervase, however, he cleared his throat mightily and said in fulsome tones, "I'm sure any such difficulties can be easily overcome."

So the priest was Gervase's creature, Ysabeau could see. She could look for no help from that quarter, not that she had really expected any.

"Which union do you think would be recognized by the Church—betrothal, or a marriage in every sense of the word, as a result of which you were swollen with my seed?" sneered Gervase.

She was humiliated that this speech had been heard by Adèle, who bristled and glared at both men, and by several of the retainers who sat at the lower table, who looked at her with open lasciviousness. Simon never would have tolerated their attitudes. At Winslade, she had been treated with honor and respect.

During the meal Gervase turned to the fat priest at one point, giving her a chance to speak privately with Adèle.

"Are you well-treated? Are your quarters comfortable?" she queried.

"Yes, you are not to concern yourself. We

have all we need. Aimery is with me, and though he asked about you when we woke, he is well, as you can see." Aimery was sitting in Ysabeau's lap, teething on a crust of bread. "And you? Did Gervase—"

"No, not last night, and he'd better not try!" Ysabeau answered heatedly.

"Well, don't worry about us. I don't believe my wicked brother will harm Aimery and me, but be careful what you do, my dear. Stall him, Ysabeau—give Simon the time to come to your rescue."

"But how will he ever get in?" Ysabeau whispered despairingly. "Hawkingham's walls are even more formidable than Winslade's."

"I don't know what he'll do, but remember to pray for him," reminded the nun with a smile and a twinkle of her blue eyes.

Ysabeau gave a wan smile in return, but privately she was less convinced than Adèle that Gervase would hesitate to harm his sister or nephew to achieve his ends.

After the meal he took her on a walking tour of Hawkingham, for the day was again mild. At every turn he attempted to impress her with splendor of the older, larger keep.

She saw the orchards, whose trees would be laden with cherries and apples in summer, the tiltyard, the armory, the quietly beautiful chapel which had stood in the village since Saxon times, the kitchen gardens, the kitchens themselves, and finally, the stables.

He had been content to play the gracious host, showing her his possessions proudly, her arm tucked firmly through his. However, in the depths of the stable he had seen no grooms about, and quite suddenly pushed her into an empty box stall and attacked her.

He roughly pushed her to the haystrewn floor, his mouth coming down with brutal force on hers as his hand pushed its way into her bodice.

She struck her head against the manger on the way down, and for a moment stars and pinwheels danced before her eyes, but then she began to fight him with every ounce of strength at her command. She scratched and bit and kicked, finally landing a telling blow with her knee to his groin. As he clutched at himself, bent over in the corner, she scrambled up from the straw, finally able to reach her eating knife which she had concealed in her chemise.

"Touch me again, *canaille*, and I'll carve out your heart," she spat at him. She crouched, blade at the ready, her breasts heaving with her ragged breathing, her hair pulling loose from its ladylike plait under her veil. She didn't know it, but she presented a very enticing picture to any man, with that wild, free, disdainful expression on her face.

"I don't think I'll give you the chance," grunted Gervase heavily as he struggled to his feet, making as if to edge past her in defeat.

Then, suddenly he was behind her, pinioning her arms painfully within his steel grasp, all traces of hesitation gone.

"Now, bitch," he hissed into her ear. "The final part of the tour, and one I hoped to omit.

It's a good thing you ate heartily at midday, for by the rood, it may be a long time before you eat such fare again!"

Chapter Forty-six

And now she was alone in a small subterranean chamber, with only a small candle and a ragged blanket. The straw was rotten and damp, giving off an odor of mold, and slime grew on the walls. Apparently the dungeon was near the river. Half buried in the straw, she found a rude wooden bowl. The ceiling was so low that a tall man would have to stoop to enter the cell.

The damp, cold air soon penetrated her very bones. She wrapped the filthy blanket around her and held her hands near the stub of a candle, knowing it would soon gutter out. She forced herself to pray rather than give into the panic that threatened to envelop her as she saw the tiny red eyes that waited just outside the circle of light, squeaking and rustling the straw when she threw the bowl at them. Rats. They would crawl over her if she slept, their scaly tails dripping. She was determined not to sleep, and prayed that she would stay awake until Gervase decided he had punished her enough.

Hysteria was but a breath away as the candle flickered out. Total blackness descended, filled with the scurrying movements of the rodents. Ysabeau kicked at them, standing in the corner of her cell. As one bold rat brushed up against her leg, she lost control and screamed, "Simon! Simon, for the love of God, help me!" She went on until she was hoarse and all she could do was cry soundlessly, her throat burning, until no more tears would come.

She slept at last, or perhaps it would be more accurate to say she lost consciousness, for when she awakened she saw that a new candle had been left, with a hunk of black bread, some thin gruel and a spoon. The candle looked as if it would last the day, at least—would she be down here that long? She wondered briefly if Gervase had brought the items, or whether he had entrusted the task to one of his lackeys. Had he looked on her sleeping form and lusted after her? Could such a man feel any pity for the terror-filled night she had spent? A twinge at her lower leg as she moved led her to hold the candle to examine her skin. There was a pair of puncture wounds surrounded by a small circle of redness, just above the bone of her left ankle, clearly made by rodent teeth. She shivered, remembering the ugly gray rat she had seen inches from her oustretched hand when she awakened. She hoped it would not fester, for she had nothing to wash it with here.

She called out, but no one answered.

She could hear no sound outside her cell to indicate there were any other prisoners in the dungeon; and it seemed the jailer did not spend any time here except to bring her food. She forced herself to sing songs to fill the silence; she sang every song she had ever heard, including all of Philippe's compositions. She conducted imaginary conversations with Simon, with Queen Eleanor, with King Henry himself. She composed a letter to her seneschal on Ré; she imagined showing her island home to Simon and his son.

Ysabeau wondered what hour it was; she had absolutely no outside light. She could only guess at the passing of time. She sneezed as she sipped the last of the cold, greasy gruel, and wrapped herself up in the blanket. Her leg still hurt. When she examined it by candlelight again, the circle of redness seemed larger than it had when she awoke, and there was a thin line of redness streaking up to her calf. The pain throbbed with every heartbeat now.

She awoke with a shaking chill, with bones that ached. The lung fever again, she thought, until she realized that the most pronounced area of pain radiated up from the bitten ankle. It was swollen and hot, and the streaking had reached her thigh. The wound was infected, and the infection was spreading into her bloodstream.

Will I die of blood poisoning, she wondered as panic threatened to take hold. A poultice would draw the poison out, but she had nothing with which to make one. She thought of the wounds she had seen cauterized by her father's steward, and of the one knight who had perished, screaming in pain until he lapsed into a coma, because he feared the red-hot iron's burning more than he feared the risk of infection. His arm, wounded in swordplay, had become reddened and enormously swollen, and the same streaking she was seeing on her leg had spread into his armpit. The smell of his rotting, gangrenous flesh had become so awful, that when he finally breathed his last he had to be buried in the same hour, for fear of contagion.

I will probably die in much the same way, she thought desolately, with no one to even find me before it is too late. No, she thought with fierce determination, eyeing the low-burning flame of the candle, which was again close to guttering out. Not while there is anything I can do that will give me a chance—I will be brave enough to try! Before she could lose her nerve, she grabbed the candle, grinding the flame against the festering area until she screamed, dropped it, and passed out of consciousness.

Later, she awoke, burning as though this cell was the antechamber of hell. Have I died, she wondered dazedly, and was I such a wicked woman to have merited eternal punishment for my unsanctified love for Simon de Winslade? Will I meet Philippe de Melle within these unholy, burning walls—is that my fate, to spend eternity by his side in hell?

At one point her father appeared before her, his old worn robes bathed in a benign light that transformed them into cloth finer than any emperor could hope to wear. She smiled to see that face so dear to her, and he smiled back.

She sensed he knew all that had befallen her since his death; had he come to lead her out of Hell? She arose, and would have gone to him, but as she reached his tall, spare form, he faded and she felt the wet, cold wall of her cell.

She didn't realize that at the height of her fever she removed her clothing in a futile effort to cool her overheated body. She was quite naked when the serf assigned to feed her brought her bread and soup. Alarmed, the peasant immediately sought the seneschal, who informed Gervase.

In a fury, Gervase struck the serf who stood worriedly beside the dungeon's entrance, though the poor man had only been following orders. The impact of his fist threw him against the wall.

Ysabeau's limp form was brought up from the underground chamber swathed in a blanket, and then placed in her chamber. Gervase lost no time in summoning Adèle.

"They teach you nursing of the sick at the Abbey, don't they?" he inquired sourly. At her distracted nod, for she had already felt Ysabeau's baking skin and found the charred center of the infected ratbite, he added, "Then heal her. She's of no use to me as a corpse."

She stared at him, amazed by his cold dismissal of Ysabeau's condition. "God help you if I can't save her. When Simon catches up to you there won't be enough of your corpse left to bury."

He recognized the truth of that, but he was not about to say so. Turning on his heel, he directed his seneschal to make sure his sister had everything she required.

She never knew how close Adèle had come to despair, thinking that the only treatment that would cure her at that stage was amputation of the leg, and knowing that she had neither the skill nor the proper tools to perfom the surgery. It was just as well, the nun had thought, for her spirit quailed at the thought of amputation. But after a day and a half, the medicine she had ordered prepared in the kitchen was pronounced ready, and Adèle began to note some gradual improvement in the appearance of the wound.

Ysabeau recovered rapidly after Adèle applied poultices of bread covered with blue mold to the bite and alternated them with hot compresses. Once she was awake enough to swallow, she was given her tisanes of boiled willow bark every few hours. When she began to be awake for longer periods of time, the nun spooned meat broth mixed with wine past her reluctant lips. Her appetite was slow to recover. She lost flesh and her skin became nearly translucent; the fine dark eyes regained some of their luster, but she had lost the radiant glow of her cheeks. The skin seemed stretched tightly over her finely sculpted cheekbones.

She saw very little of Gervase, thankfully, during her recovery; he would arrive suddenly, stare silently at her for a moment, and leave. Adèle saw to it she was never alone with him. She offered him no speech either; she was aware that if she opened her mouth, she would be unable to stop, and what little strength she had regained would be lost in a futile tirade. She was regathering her strength. She was not sure when it would next be tested, only that it would be.

Once she was up and around and eating normally, she quickly found out. Gervase entered the room one morning, just after Adèle had left to see to Aimery.

"You needn't shrink from me, my dear," he cooed reassuringly as he sat down in a chair by the brazier.

"What are you talking about?" she asked suspiciously, a growing dread cold within her.

"Your future, and that of my sister and little Aimery," he answered easily, smiling. "When shall our wedding day be?" he asked her cheerfully, as if he expected a glad, agreeable answer.

"My brush with death has not endeared you to me," she replied acidly, sensing that he was playing a game of cat and mouse with her. "I will never marry you. I am betrothed to Simon, and I hate you."

"Hate me you may, but no contract ever existed, my dear liar. I've had time during your illness to have the parish records of Winslade investigated. You and my twin were never betrothed, so you are quite free to marry, being the widow of Baron Philippe de Melle. I look forward, my dear Comtesse de Ré, to seeing the fief I will gain through you." His eyes gleamed evilly.

"If you hope to regain your squandered wealth through me, my lord, then I can save you the trouble. Ré's keep is in little better shape than Chawton," she said wryly. "It's not a rich fief, just a few olive groves and salt marshes."

"Peasants can always be . . . encouraged

to produce more," he said coldly. "And the island is far enough away, I should think, in case Henry won't forgive me for marrying an heiress without his permission."

"It's part of Eleanor's duchy, and she's his wife."

He laughed cynically. "And you believe those two will live happily ever after, the aging Queen and the younger King already famous for his womanizing? Not a chance. Pretty soon it'll be what was hers, is hers alone, though Henry will seek to control it and her with an iron hand, mark my words."

It made her sad to think his words might be true, but she couldn't let herself be distracted at this point. "Time will tell. However, that's all beside the point. I won't marry you."

"Then I'll have to put your other choice into effect."

"Which is . . ."

"Aimery shall have to suffer for your foolishness. If you haven't regained your senses by dusk, I'll put the little boy into the cell you recently vacated."

She gaped at him in disbelief. "You wouldn't dare!"

"Wouldn't I?" He chuckled unpleasantly. "If I put you back down there, you'd just sicken and die, in your weakened state. Adèle is the stuff of which martyrs are made. She'd will herself to die before she'd let her sufferings change your mind, so I can't use her. Who is left, but the boy?"

His face was twisted in a sneer. She longed to claw it off with her fingernails. She could feel her fingers clenching into talons.

"I hate you," she said again.

"I know you do. So did my late first wife, by the time she died. Fortunately, it won't stop me from getting sons of you. A woman's willingness—or lack of it—has never affected my potency."

She tried another argument. "Does it never occur to you what Simon will do, my lord? His service with Henry will not last forever. He will be home any day now, and it will be a simple matter to trace me to Greywell and then here."

"I sent a man north who reports that the King is in Nottingham, and then bound for the Bishop of Hereford's holdings. No, by the time Simon is free to aid you, as I've said, it'll be too late. How long will his love last, think you, if he sees your belly distended with another man's child? Till dusk, my dear." He arose, turned on his heel, and left, carefully barring her door on the outside.

His words sounded like a death sentence. Simon was still in the north, fighting for his king. He would be too late to save her.

The image of herself that Gervase had painted rose to mock her—her abdomen hideously swollen—only to be replaced by another horrible nightmare picture: Aimery, that tousle-haired, affectionate, trusting child, being thrust into that damp darkness, to be gnawed by rats, to freeze to death, wondering why Uncle Gervase hated him enough to do such a thing, and why Lady Ysabeau allowed it to happen.

She screamed, and screamed again, and

kept on screaming until at last one of the guards came and unlocked her door, looked in to see what was amiss. "My lady? My lady, please! What ails you?"

"Send your lord to me," she told him dully.

He kept her waiting for hours, wondering frantically if he'd done the heinous deed out of spite. When at last he reappeared, her nerves were at the breaking point. She practically fell at his feet, so relieved she was to finally see him.

"All right, my lord. You have won. I will wed you." At his triumphant smirk, however, she held up a hand. "But I will not be yanked down to the chapel in what I have on, like some peasant wench, to have your fat priest run through a mumbled Mass. I demand that this thing be done properly, as is due to my rank. I want a few days to arrange proper raiment, and for a suitable wedding feast to be prepared." She threw the demands arrogantly in his face, her heart quaking within. She was just playing for time—anything to give Simon a chance to get here.

"You cool French bitch! To stand there and make demands when I could snap your slender neck like a reed."

"I wish you would, my lord," she retorted. "I only wish I could will myself to die, but I can not, more's the pity."

"All right," he said surprisingly. "There's a chestful of my wife's clothing still around. You can make something over from there. But I'll only give you a se'enight's grace."

"Every day you give me is one day less I'll be married to you," she snapped, turning her back rigidly to him.

"Ah, my Poitevin turtledove, what tender sweet nothings you murmur," he answered sardonically. "I'll see the priest now, and give him the happy tidings."

"Send Adèle to me, if you would be so kind, my lord," Ysabeau requested with mocking courtesy. "We have much to plan."

When the nun arrived, Ysabeau explained what had been going on. "Don't you see, Adèle, there is no other way?" Ysabeau sighed in despair. "We have no way of knowing where Simon is, and how could he help us? Gervase has the advantage, since he holds Aimery—and I'll endure anything before I allow him to harm one hair on the child's head. I couldn't allow him to put Aimery in that cell. It was awful beyond imagining, I tell you. Aimery would not survive it—"

"Surely you have lessened your time in Purgatory," Adèle agreed sadly. "I have seen the dungeon—you may recall I grew up here—but it was never used in my father's time." The nun sounded as defeated as Ysabeau felt. "But you must not stop praying, my dear sister. A week is a long time. Our Lord created the heavens and the earth in less. Anything can happen in a week."

Chapter Forty-seven

I will never live with him as his wife, thought Ysabeau grimly as she endured the evening meal, trying hard not to let her feelings show when Gervase made the announcement of the wedding to the household. Later in the meal, and after considerable overindulging in wine, he pawed at her until she pulled her high-backed chair as far away as she could. Making a loud, lewd remark about her coldness and what he planned to do about it, he nevertheless allowed her to keep her distance. She glared at him, her face burning with shame.

I could not stand a lifetime of this, she thought, being humiliated in front of his coarse knights. If Simon does not come in time, I'll see Adèle and Aimery released, and then I'll plunge a dagger into his black heart before ending my own life.

Whether she had the courage to carry out her plan, she didn't know; but surely it would be better to end her life quickly than to face the slow death of being his lady.

Much as a condemned prisoner watches his scaffold being built, she watched the busy preparations for the wedding during the next week. The kitchens were beehives as huge haunches of roast venison and beef, and a whole fowl were roasted on spits, while the cooks argued over their style of preparation. Apparently, Gervase's kitchens were not suffering from the usual depleted supplies as winter drew to a close; but after seeing the lean, gaunt-faced peasants, Ysabeau assumed Gervase was not usually so free-handed with his stores.

She and Adèle had found the musty trunkful of the late Lady Yvonne's clothing, but its contents had been too moth-eaten, stained, and threadbare to consider using, even had the dead woman been Ysabeau's size. Gervase's first wife had been reed-thin, Adèle informed her, and grew progressively more emaciated as life with her evil husband sapped her vitality. Eventually she had died of a wasting disease, cursed by Gervase, whom she had failed to provide with an heir.

"She expired with a smile on her face," Adèle said forthrightly, "which I am convinced was as much due to her release from Gervase, as to her first sight of Heaven. Oh, I pray you never have to wed my brother!"

They were fortunate enough to find a bolt of gold velvet, deep in one of the chests, that had mostly escaped the ravages of time. Yellow tones did not complement Ysabeau's rosy skin tone, but she said it did not matter; she did not care about being attractive to her bridegroom anyway. With Adèle's help, the cloth was cut and sewn into an respectable looking bridal dress within the allotted time.

Aimery watched all the proceedings with keen interest. He seemed to think that for some inexplicable reason, the promised wedding between his adored father and the lovely kind lady he had brought home to Winslade had merely been moved to his uncle's castle. Surely his papa would appear soon. While he still hadn't warmed to the cold-eyed man who otherwise resembled Papa, he was again free to be with Lady Ysabeau, and that made his two-year-old heart happy.

As he chattered on in his artless fashion, Ysabeau realized his mistaken idea and her heart ached, but she dared not shatter his peace of mind just yet. Perhaps Aimery's father would still arrive in time.

To that end, she made frequent trips to the old Saxon chapel, both with Adèle and alone, to light candles and pray. The village folk were impressed with the seeming piety of the new Lady of Hawkingham, but Father Édouard was not fooled.

Ysabeau slept late on the day before the wedding, taking refuge in sleep to avoid Gervase's smirking presence as long as possible, but at last she realized she must come down to the hall. There was still much to do. She had missed Mass, but that was no loss; she found no peace in the fat priest's mumbled delivery and no sense of God's presence. Perhaps breaking her fast would help dissolve the lump in her throat.

Upon entering the hall she found the chief cook and the butler airing a noisy dispute before Gervase, who watched them lazily from his chair.

"She's using your best Bordeaux to baste the venison, my lord!" complained the florid-faced butler in injured tones. It was his responsibility to keep track of the wine in the Earl's cellar. "But there won't be enough to drink at the weddin' feast an she does that, for your knights have, ah . . . been hard at it this winter," he said, eyeing Ysabeau's approach warily. If he made the Earl look foolish in front of his bride, he'd be cuffed for it later, he knew.

"But I know just how me lord likes his venison, I do!" screeched the plump cook stridently.

It was clear that Gervase was annoyed at being bothered with such petty problems. Fortunately, the seneschal stepped up to Gervase's side. "If I might interrupt, my lord, a fellow waits without the walls who might be able to solve the problem. I know you said we were to admit no one unfamiliar this week, but the fellow happens to be a wine merchant, and there are several barrels in the back of his cart. He says he has a very good tun of Bordeaux, by coincidence."

Gervase raised his eyes heavenward. "Thank God for small favors. An end to this cacaphony!" Then, remembering caution, he added, "The fellow couldn't be a knight in disguise, could he? Is he tall and well-built?"

"Oh, no, my lord," assured the seneschal. "Not a knightly sort of person at all. Very rough, in fact, and stocky, with torn clothing, a patch over one eye . . . But his wine is good," he hastened to add after Gervase turned his suspicions glare toward him. "I demanded a taste of one of the barrels at random, and a very good sort of vintage it was." As if to underline the truth of his words, a rather loud belch escaped that self-important offcial's lips, and even Ysabeau had to smile.

"I think I will go down to the bailey to look this fellow over, and bid him welcome to Hawkingham. Perhaps he carries news," Gervase said. "Care to join me, my lady?"

"No, thank you," was her quick reply.

Ysabeau might have gone about her tasks with a lighter heart if she had greeted the bearded fellow below, but as it was, she was merely relieved that there would be wine to drink after the ceremony on the morrow. She would need it to get through the following night. And perhaps she could encourage Gervase to drink very deeply. If he was too fuddled with wine to molest her, so much the better.

"God's blood, Sire, d'you mean this is the very first opportunity you had to let me out of this cage? I thought I'd suffocate in there," muttered Simon as Henry at last pried the top off the huge barrel in which he had been concealed. Stiffly he climbed out, rubbing wrists and ankles numbed from the cold, cramped position he'd held for several hours.

He'd exulted as the portcullis had been raised and the cart driven by Henry, King of England, had clattered across the drawbridge, only to be stopped by the officious seneschal who'd demanded to test their wine. Simon had hardly dared breathe as he heard the King say, "Ah, they are all the same, yer worship, I promise ye! Let's try that barrel at the back there, it's the easiest to get at." Henry's English-accented French was as flawless as his rough appearance. No one would have thought this one-eyed, humbly clothed fellow could be a knight, let alone the King.

But the seneschal was not about to be cozened so easily. "Of course you'd be sure to have a good wine within easy reach," he said with pompous suspiciousness. "No, let me pick one at random. My Lord the Earl would not be pleased to serve inferior stuff to his bride."

Bride! Did that mean that his thrice-damned brother had already wed her? It was all Simon could do to restrain himself at this point and not start shouting within his barrel to be freed.

"Oh ho! Do I come in time to celebrate a wedding?" Henry boomed, apparently a happy merchant who scents the possibility of a good meal as well as a good profit.

"Indeed, my good man. On the morrow the Earl of Hawkingham is to wed Countess Ysabeau de Ré of Poitou, a lovely lady, formerly of the royal court."

I'll see him in Hell first, Simon had sworn within his barrel, as his heart resumed a more regular rhythm, now that he knew he was not too late.

The seneschal had picked a tun in the middle of the wagon, and after he had sampled and pronounced the wine fit, he had added grandly, "I believe I may welcome you to stay for the wedding feast."

"So after that condescending bastard was finished, your damned brother strolls up, as you heard, to bid me welcome, and invites me into the hall, for all the world the most gracious of hosts. But he really wanted to sniff out the news as to what Henry Plantagenet was doing. I told him I'd been in Cornwall of late, and really was not well-informed, but a peddler of pots and pans I'd passed said the king was still in the north. I kept telling him I had to go out and see to the unloading, Simon—I was afraid he'd have some of his lackeys do it, and your barrel certainly doesn't *slosh* like the others. But he kept plying me with questions and the worst Rhenish I've ever tasted!" He grinned at Simon in the dim light of the stable, where he'd taken the horses and the barrel which had concealed him.

"Now you'd better hide yourself, and I'd best round up some of his lazy louts to take the rest of the wine to his storeroom, before I'm missed. I'll meet with you here, after everyone in the hall's asleep. You're sure you can get to the postern to open it for the men tonight?"

"Certainly, especially if you can get the guards on watch to start their celebration this evening," Simon promised confidently. "Did you see aught of my lady, or my son, or my sister, your grace?"

"*Oui*, that I did. Lady Ysabeau was sitting sewing by the light of the fire when I was in the hall. She looked very strained and melancholy. Your little boy was playing at her feet with a ball, and for all I could see, looked content. He's a sturdy lad, such as I wish my William was. Mayhap I'll have better luck with young Henry."

"Did she see you, Sire?" Simon inquired worriedly, a look of apprehension lighting his azure eyes. If Ysabeau recognized Henry, and was too surprised to conceal it, all might be lost, and his sovereign in real danger.

"Looked right through me, Simon. She seemed preoccupied. Never fear, my friend, we'll soon have her and the rest of your family safe and free."

Chapter Forty-eight

The day dawned mild and clear, surely a mockery of the desolation Ysabeau felt when she awoke and realized that the siege, with the walls of Hawkingham breached and the garrison surrendering, and Simon proudly riding up to the hall to claim her, had been but a delicious, futile dream. It was not to be. This was the day.

She arose and put on a furred bedgown against the chill air, and summoned the servants, who brought in an oak tub and buckets of steaming hot water. She bathed efficiently, joylessly, not lingering in the soothing warmth. Adèle entered just as she finished drying off, and wrapped up in her robe once more, was combing out her luxurious dark, curling tresses in front of the brazier's heat.

It was obvious that the nun had been

crying; her puffy reddened eyes took in Ysabeau, and the tears welled up again.

"I don't understand it, Ysabeau. I have prayed all night to Our Lady," she sobbed. "How can she allow this to happen?"

Ysabeau had no answers. It seemed incredible that after her hellish marriage to Philippe de Melle, she could be entering a union which promised to be infinitely worse. "Please," she pleaded, "you must stop crying, or I will start again. I don't want to give your brother the satisfaction." She squared her lovely shoulders, and forced herself to think strictly of the tasks at hand.

Once her hair was dry, Adèle assisted her into the gold velvet *bliaut*, which had turned out very well in spite of the lack of enthusiasm both women had had for the project. It had a brocade trim, which they had removed from another dress, at the round neckline and hem, and sleeves that were loose at the shoulders but close-fitting at the wrist. When Ysabeau had informed Adèle that this was the very latest fashion at court, that Queen Eleanor's gowns were styled so, the nun responded with shy interest, remarking that it had been years since she had concerned herself with such worldly matters as the cut of a gown.

"I don't envy you your life," Adèle murmured now, helping to fasten the barbette and veil that framed Ysabeau's lovely, if melancholy, features. "It was pleasant, getting out in the world to visit Simon, but I had forgotten how full of strife the world is. I'll be relieved to have the walls of the convent around me, to have nothing more weighty to worry about than whether to tell Sister Marguerite her wimple has a spot on it."

In spite of herself, Ysabeau giggled, then straightened, kissing Adèle gently on the brow. "Dear Adèle, you have been so good to me, and here I have embroiled you in such a disaster. The abbess will be sure you have eloped with a sailor! *Maintenant*, you have reminded me of something I have to do. Please send Gervase to me."

"Before the wedding? But he shouldn't see you—" the nun began, before Ysabeau held out a hand to interrupt.

"This is no joyous occasion," she insisted, "and all the bad luck that will ensue is that I am marrying the wrong brother. So I think we need not stand on tradition . . ."

Several minutes later, Gervase barged into the room, saying, "My dear Ysabeau, you wished to see me? I hope it is a brief matter. Father Édouard is ready to start whenever we appear, and as we can't break our fast before the Sacrament, I'd just as lief get on with it. By the way, you look lovely, my lady, if not precisely radiant."

"You are quite handsomely appareled yourself, my lord," she replied formally. Almost as handsome as Simon would be to me now, if he appeared in sackcloth, she added to herself. "You do me too much honor." Gervase was wearing a dark blue dalmatic with a gold geometric pattern and a matching cape lined with gold silk.

"When the Earl of Hawkingham marries, he does so with fitting style. Now, as to why you summoned me?" he asked again, a trifle impatiently.

She took a deep breath. "I wished to discuss with you the fulfilling of your promise—"

He cocked an eyebrow at her.

"—that following our wedding, Sister Mary Agathe and Aimery are to go free. You will have them escorted back to Winslade?"

"But of course," he said, coming closer to where she stood, staring down into the morning light which illumined the inner bailey now. "I trust you will agree that tomorrow is soon enough? They need not miss the festivities, nor the sight of the happy, blushing bride." She really is a lovely thing, he thought hotly, even with the violet shadows under her eyes that bespoke a restless night. Tonight I'll be between those sweet thighs, and we'll see if all they say about Poitevin women is true. "I think I deserve a kiss from my soon-to-be wife to seal the bargain," he said, striding inexorably closer.

"Touch her and you're a dead man, Gervase," said a familiar voice.

Both of them whirled, and the emotions within each could not have been more opposite. Ysabeau felt transfigured by joy, unable to believe the beloved tall figure before her was not some image conjured up by her brain. She kept glancing from brother to brother, noting differences in their clothing and demeanor, assuring herself she was not merely seeing double.

Gervase's face was full of consternation and chagrin, for as a nobleman dressed for his wedding, he was not armed. Simon, in contrast, held his unsheathed sword. "How did you get in?" he snarled. "The gates have been guarded, the portcullis down ever since we returned. I've let no one in but a wine merchant—"

"It would have served you better to be more familiar with your King, *mon frère*," Simon grinned. "That was Henry Plantagenet driving that cart, and I was in a barrel."

Ysabeau had gone gladly to his side, to be seized into a tight, one-armed embrace while he kept the blade trained on his brother.

"The King is within these walls?" Gervase gaped open-mouthed. Then a look of cunning stole over his handsome features. "But what are two men, against a garrison? You've brought this King into a deadly trap, Simon. Careless of you not to remember the loyalty of my men. They'll not scruple to spit that rude fellow, who claims to be a king, like a pig—after they've stopped laughing," taunted Gervase with a cruel smile.

"Careless of *you* to leave the sally port guarded by only a pair of drunken men-at-arms," countered Simon easily, and watched his brother blanch. "The hall is even now surrounded by a superior force that won't hesitate to slaughter your band of paid cut-throats."

Gervase sputtered desperately, "It's hardly very chivalrous of you to surprise me like this, an unarmed man, unable to fight you. Give me a sword and we'll duel for the wench!"

His words were deliberately inflammatory, impugning Simon's honor, and Ysabeau was dismayed to see the man she loved wavering. "Simon," she pleaded desperately. "It was hardly very chivalrous when he put me into the dungeon until I sickened, and he would have put Aimery there, too, had I not at last agreed to marry him. Let the King punish him, not you!"

Actually her words made him more, not less inclined to plunge his sword through his twin's treacherous heart.

"Would you have me hide behind the King's robes, Ysabeau?" Simon asked, not taking his eyes off his brother. His voice was cool. He gestured with the blade. "Down to the hall, Gervase. I'll see that you get a sword."

Grimly he kept the point of the sword at Gervase's back, and with Ysabeau following, they descended the winding stairway. Once, Ysabeau cried in desperation, "Please, Simon, don't do this! Hasn't there been enough death?"

"Silence!" he thundered. "This is between us, Gervase and me!" And she obeyed, for she had one higher to appeal to: the King himself. Damn men for their constant need to fight!

In the hall an amazing sight met Ysabeau's eyes: the men-at-arms of the Hawkingham garrison were all herded together at one end of the hall, being guarded by knights wearing the King's leopard badge on their surcoats. Henry himself lounged at ease at the high table, enjoying a cup of ale.

"Ah, there you are, Simon. We were wondering when you'd reappear. I see you have all well in hand. Good day to you, my Lady Ysabeau," he greeted her warmly, and watched appreciatively as Ysabeau sank into a deep, graceful curtsey. Simon de Winslade was a lucky fellow, no doubt about that. Too bad he'd seen her first, the king mused, remembering her awkward, ill-clothed appearance when she'd first come to court. "As for you, Gervase of Hawkingham, I've ignored your former support of Stephen and your lack of warmth toward me long enough. You've finally pushed me too far, stealing a royal ward intended for one of my trustworthy barons."

"Your grace," answered Gervase sullenly, "I demand the right of trial by combat. If I win, my earldom is secure, as well as my right to the lady."

"One of the many barbaric customs my new laws will abolish. You shall be tried by your peers, not by combat. Law shall rule, not swords," Henry pronounced loftily.

"Your grace, I beg you to grant us leave to fight," growled Simon. "He'll not touch my Ysabeau while I live."

"Please, Sire, don't allow it, I beg of you!" cried Ysabeau, seizing Henry's rough, reddened hand. "I can't bear to take a chance of losing him forever!"

Henry was undecided, she could see, desperate to resolve the dilemma by law, yet not at the cost of his baron's honor.

"She was delicious, *mon frère*," Gervase murmured silkily into the thick silence. "I certainly understand why you would want to fight for her. Why, she knows tricks not even an infidel whore knows. And she's shameless. She would love me for hours in my chamber in the middle of the day."

"He lies! He never bedded me!" Ysabeau cried indignantly, knowing her cause was lost. They would fight now. But Simon must not go into mortal combat thinking that Gervase had possessed her.

"Is it a lie? How unkind of you, lady, to deny the pleasure we shared." The Earl eyed her coolly.

"Then say, if you can, base scum, on which inner thigh I have a birthmark. If you had carnal knowledge of me by the light of day, as you claim, then you will know."

Gervase paused for a second, staring at her, then answered, "The left, my lady. She loved me to kiss her there, Simon. How she would moan. . . ."

With a roar, Simon launched himself at his brother, dropping the sword, eyes blazing, teeth bared, intent on strangling his twin brother. But he was held back by three of the King's knights.

"My lady had no mark at all," growled Simon through clenched teeth. "You're proved a liar. No more will you foul my lady's name! Give him a sword, Sire."

All the saints could not have stopped the duel at this moment. Recognizing that fact, Henry avoided Ysabeau's pleading eyes and handed Gervase his own sword. Ysabeau must be championed, or Simon had no honor at all. It could be no other way.

There was a rustling and creaking as tables and benches were pushed aside and men moved to make room for the duel. Gervase removed his splendid dalmatic to fight unencumbered in shirt and chausses.

Ysabeau, her lips moving in prayer, watched as the men saluted each other with the gleaming, jewel-hilted broadswords, then circled warily, seeking an opening. Neither man, of course, wore mail or carried a shield. Any attack by one would have to be fended off by the skill of the other with his sword alone.

"May God give victory to the just," Henry said quietly.

Still they had not engaged, and there was a low swell of murmuring as the hall full of knights and men-at-arms watched the two men, mirror images of one another, continue to circle like two wolves.

Suddenly Gervase opened the attack, lunging at Simon, thrusting as if the heavy sword were a mere toy made of ashwood. Simon parried easily, then riposted, his blade catching the sleeve of his brother's luxurious silk shirt and rending it from wrist to elbow. The sound of ripping cloth was lost in the cheers of Simon's men. Then all settled down to silence again as Simon took over the attack, his lithe form driving Gervase relentlessly to the wall.

Attack, thrust, parry. The hall rang with the clash of steel as the two men, so evenly matched in form and skill, feinted and dodged, engaged and disengaged over the rush-strewn hall, the dry reeds crackling in protest as the warriors' booted feet trampled them still further. Once, Gervase had Simon in retreat as far as the high table, and Henry had pulled Ysabeau out of harm's way, but he tripped over a beef bone some hound had left buried in the rushes. He went down on one knee, but recovered quickly as Simon moved with catlike grace to press his advantage.

Both men were a marvel of agility. Their adroitness would have been beautiful to watch had it not been for their deadly intent. Blood lust shone from each pair of blue eyes.

Simon fought in silence, forcing himself not to waste energy replying to his brother's taunts. "Perhaps I was mistaken about the details, brother. We always closed the hangings around the bed, for we wished to be completely alone. So how was I to see a birthmark? But I could feel . . . and taste . . ."

"Liar!" he breathed, knowing that Gervase wanted him to abandon his cool, measured attack and defense, and let rage lead him down the reckless path to a fatal mistake.

Both men were breathing heavily now; both men had scored touches, as was evident by ripped clothing and splashes of crimson on their shirts. So far, though, neither had suffered a serious wound.

Simon refused to think of the larger issues at stake, but only the threat Gervase had posed to the woman he loved, and to his only son. The thought of his darling lying terrified, ill, and alone in that subterranean cell lent fury to his every thrust and counterthrust. He slashed with the blade, a blow that could have severed Gervase's head from his shoulders. But Gervase ducked. Then both men lunged simultaneously, their blades locking, their faces inches away, both pairs of eyes blazing hatred as they separated, for neither could thrust when they were so close together.

Ysabeau's heart was in her throat, and it threatened to burst with fear as she saw Gervase's blade dodge under Simon's guard and open a deep slash in his thigh, which immediately welled up with blood. If Simon was losing, would Henry let Gervase kill him? Would there be time for Henry to call a halt to the fight? Ysabeau glanced at Henry's face, but it gave her no clue, though he acknowledged her look with an encouraging squeeze of her shoulders.

Simon was not about to retreat, however. He redoubled his attack, his blade whistling through the air as he began to drive Gervase through the hall, though he left a trail of blood in the rushes as he went. Implanted deeply in his brain was the idea that this battle mattered more than any he had ever engaged in at Henry's side. The fate of the beautiful Frenchwoman who loved him rode on his naked blade as he drove Gervase relentlessly toward the stair.

Gervase was forced to climb, or die immediately—he had nowhere else to go. And so he retreated slowly up the stairs, making Simon pay a price in agony for every inch he gained, gaining some advantage himself with the greater height he achieved.

Gervase had reached the first angled turn in the stairs, where Simon hoped he would lose his balance. He could not keep his eye on Simon's flashing sword and watch his feet at the same time. He fell backward heavily, the sword clattering uselessly down several steps, out of reach.

Instantly Simon was upon him, his sword pressing with deadly intimacy at Gervase's bare throat.

"Well, whoreson, I think you have an apology to make ere you die."

"I don't know what you mean." Gervase's blue eyes blazed sullen defiance.

"I think you do. The lady is waiting for you to cleanse the stain upon her honor."

"What matters it, if you kill me anyway?"

"Why, brother, do you want to die with a lie upon your lips?" Simon inquired with mocking solicitousness.

Everyone in the hall held their breaths. Simon de Winslade was like some avenging angel, standing there, bloodstained and drenched with sweat, but magnificent in his fury. Would he slay his twin, if he refused to speak? The moment stretched on forever.

Simon pressed the blade forward until the tip pierced, ever so slightly, the skin of Gervase's neck. "Talk, brother, or I promise your death will be neither clean nor easy," he hissed.

Gervase held up a hand, and Simon withdrew his sword an inch. He cleared his throat, now that he had room to swallow what little saliva he had.

"The Lady Ysabeau never lay with me. . . ." he mumbled.

"Louder!"

"I said the Lady Ysabeau is innocent!"

"Louder!"

"She never lay with me, willingly or otherwise! Now end it, damn you!"

Ysabeau was sure her heart stopped beating as she waited for the deadly blade to descend again, but then Simon stepped back.

"I believe I will leave you to the King's justice, *mon frère*. I have what I want," he said, looking to where Ysabeau stood, limp with relief.

"I applaud your decision," Henry said, descending from the dais to where Simon stood guard over his fallen twin. At a gesture from Henry, several men-at-arms came over and hauled Gervase to his feet; they forced him back down the steps and made him kneel at the King's feet.

"Gervase, formerly Earl of Hawkingham, I declare you traitor and strip you of all your lands and possessions and sentence you to exile. You are to be escorted tomorrow—after a night spent in the dungeon, as is fitting—to the coast, where you may take ship to wherever it pleases you, as long as it is beyond my realm. Go see if Louis will have you. Those English knights that have sworn fealty to you may go with you or transfer their fealty to your brother, as they choose. The damned foreigners among them are to leave English soil forever. You and they must not return, on pain of death. Your lands and titles are forfeit; I give them to Simon de Winslade. Come forth and do homage for them, Simon, Earl of Hawkingham, Winslade, Lingfield, and Chawton."

He did so as Gervase was led away, stumbling and shamed. Then he called to Ysabeau, "Where is my son? Bring him out . . . and Adèle!"

But before she could summon them, Simon's face had lost color, and he had fainted against her, the loss of blood taking its toll.

Carefully she eased him to the floor, snatching her veil and barbette off her head without a second thought and pressing them against the wound at his thigh to stanch the flow of blood. Already it was little more than a trickle; she was not seriously worried. He merely needed to rest and have his wound sewn up. The latter could be accomplished much easier with him unconscious, anyway.

Efficiently, she directed a trio of knights to carry him gently up to the great chamber, and then turned to King Henry, who stood ready to assist her. "Your Grace, I have not thanked you and your men yet for your daring rescue. Surely the troubadours will sing of it for centuries to come! Now come, a feast was prepared to celebrate a marriage which, thankfully, will not take place. I know you and your men will not let it go to waste."

At that, there was a cheer for Simon's gallant lady and the hospitality she bade them enjoy, for they had been tantalized by the smell of roasting meats as they'd crept into the castle walls to surround the hall and disarm the guards in their towers.

"I thank you, beautiful Countess," Henry called as she started to follow the men carrying Simon's limp form up the stairway. "But will you not grace the banquet with your presence?"

"Perhaps later, after I've played nurse to my beloved lord," she replied with a smile. "After all we've been through while apart, I'm loath to let him out of my sight!"

There was not a man present, including Henry, who did not wish he could be in Simon's place.

Chapter Forty-nine

Simon began to stir restlessly and groan by the time she'd finished her sewing, but with the aid of a big goblet of potent mead, she soon had him asleep again. He was snoring lustily when Adèle tiptoed in with Aimery in tow, admonishing him with a finger held to her lips, that he must not wake Papa.

Ysabeau put in a brief appearance at the feast, finding everyone, especially Henry, in an advanced state of merry drunkenness. She smiled shyly at their frank toasts and laughed with becomingly blushing cheeks at their bawdy jokes, but was soon content to slip back up to the Earl's chamber. There she could watch him sleep, wonderfully happy just observing the regular rise and fall of his powerfully muscled chest. Soon she lay down next to him, drowsy with the effect of the food and wine. How glorious to feel him beside her again, his strong limbs so warm next to her thighs. She raised herself up on one elbow to kiss his forehead as he slept, and then closed her own eyes and slept till dawn the next day.

They decided to wait until they reached Winslade to be married. Neither of them wanted the ceremony to be performed by Father Édouard, though the fat priest had fawningly offered to do so. "And the dress Adèle and I worked so hard on is back at Winslade, Simon, whereas I wouldn't mind if I never see that gold creation again," she laughed ruefully.

Henry bade them a fond farewell that morning, announcing he was off to London to see his new son at long last, admonishing Simon with mock sterness that he didn't want to see him again until he had wed the Lady Ysabeau. After that he had looked to Ysabeau for approval, and was rewarded with a dazzling smile. "I give you your prisoner of love, Lady Ysabeau."

"I thank you, your grace," she said sweetly. "I vow he will not be paroled until he has carried out your wishes."

"And a few of my own," Simon said with a bold look, causing her to blush hotly.

Despite her "fussing," as he termed it, Simon insisted on mounting his charger for the trip back to Winslade the next day, instead of riding in the cart with Adèle and Aimery. He declared he was not an old man yet, as he'd prove to her very soon. And so he rode back to his barony, though from the firm set of his jaw during the last league or two, she was sure the effort cost him dreadfully.

Men, she thought ruefully as they dismounted at last in Winslade's own bailey; she saw that he had indeed pulled a couple of the stitches loose and that the wound bled anew.

He swore colorfully in his chamber as she had repaired the damage with her bone needle and horsehair thread. She continued imperturbably until the job was done, remarking calmly that his irascibility was a sure sign he was getting well.

"Getting well? Certainly I'm getting well, you impudent French wench!" he pronounced, and proceeded to grab her to him and show her just how well he was already.

"Simon, no! Lie quietly, or you'll pull the stitches loose again." He kept kissing her, stifling her objections, covering her mouth with his so that she could protest no more. Then he whispered in that husky voice that set her blood aflame, "Now, my little nursemaid, I will take you in ways that could not possibly strain your handiwork, never fear. Undress, my love. Make it easy for me."

With the late afternoon sun that stole into the narrow window bathing her in radiance, she arose from the bed, unlacing her *bliaut* deftly, letting it fall to the floor in a blue velvet heap, pulling off the snowy woolen underdress after that. She knew he loved to watch her undress, so she did it with deliberate, studied slowness, watching with a secret smile as his face flushed, his eyes grew a darker blue, and his manhood swelled with his desire. Clad in only her sheer chemise now, she lingered at its fastenings, kneeling at the bedside and giving him glimpses of the bounty it contained. She was careful to hover just out of reach, however, and gave a chuckle as he groaned and reached for her, his fingers closing on empty air. Once the chemise was unlaced at the bodice, she stopped to unbraid her hair, looking sidelong at him as the glorious fall of it spread over her slim shoulders, partially concealing the rosy nipples that peeked out over the pale cloth. She was as seductive as Eve, as elusive as a fairy sprite. At last she reached up and slowly pushed the straps of the thin garment from her shoulders, her eyes never leaving his as the garment fell ever so slowly past her breasts, gliding caressingly over her hips, baring the triangle of dark hair between her legs and the softly rounded buttocks, and coming to rest on the floor. With a teasing motion of her slim ankle, she kicked it away and came toward the bed.

Ysabeau thought he had meant for her to lie atop him, to accomplish their mating with the least amount of exertion for him. She extended a long, slender calf over his thighs, but he stopped her there, saying, "Lie back, my love, let me pleasure you."

She sank back into the goosedown mattress as he turned on his side, his hand reaching between her legs into the dark curls as his mouth closed on a rosy, erect nipple and sucked it tantalizingly. She was very conscious of his manhood lying tense and throbbing against her leg; and as his fingers stroked her, opening her, he thrust slightly at her, teasing while his fingers went deeper within. It felt as wonderful as if he were inside her. She writhed, moaning in joy.

She reached a little peak, sighed, and began the climb, for she knew there were still heights to reach. All the time, he murmured to her, "Yes, Ysa, that's it. Ah, God, you're so much a woman . . . you're mine, always and forever! I love you . . . ah, love, you're so wet for me . . ."

She whimpered in protest as his fingers left her, for she had not yet scaled the mountain, and knew that she was but steps away from the summit that beckoned. Why? And then she felt him rearranging himself as his head left her breasts, and his tongue took up where his fingers had left off, stroking her with knowing, deft thrusts of his tongue until her fingers burrowed convulsively in the burnished tawny gold of his hair. The tiny prickles created by his mustache on her tender skin made the sensation he was creating madly, impossibly wonderful. Yet now she drew back from the height, fearing it. She was too high, too out of control; she would reach the top and fall. . . .

But he urged her on, encouraging by the loving caresses of his hands and the groans he could not hold back. And suddenly she was falling into the abyss, aflame, falling in the midst of a shower of golden sparks.

She must have lost consciousness for a moment, but when she came to herself again she was whole and entire as never before, though utterly drained. She stirred, wanting to give him his climax, though she wasn't sure how she would accomplish it. She was sure her bones had been dissolved, for she felt absolutely without strength. But she wanted him to feel the way he had just made her feel; he deserved this wonderful sense of completion, also.

But he must have known how she felt, for he whispered, "Lie still now, rest awhile." She did, gratefully, feeling her breathing slow, her pulse return to its regular rhythm, and the blood flow into her arms and legs again.

It seemed to her that they both dozed for a brief time. Then she awoke, smiling at his boyish sleeping face. Stealthily, she eased herself out of his arms and knelt on the bed by him, so that the first thing he felt as he returned to awareness was her velvety soft lips closing around the head of his shaft, her tongue encircling it, driving him to paroxysms of madness as it rose.

"Ysa, Ysa, you witch!" he groaned in delight. "I said rest!" But it was clear he welcomed her bold assault from the way his hips arched rigidly and his breathing grew ragged. She was just warming to the task when he sighed, "Oh, no, *ma chèrie*, you'll not get by so easily!" He grasped her firmly and pulled her onto him, watching her as he sank his shaft deeply, but achingly slowly, into her moist velvet sheath. He groaned again as she began to move on him, glorying in the way the soft waves of her hair fell around their faces, curtaining their eyes from all else.

She rode him expertly, and when he would have lingered, leisurely tonguing her ripe nipples, she picked up the pace, determined that he should lose control. But it was she who did so, finding that summit again just as he reached it also, collapsing against him just as he thrust convulsively into her. She loved to watch his face as he climaxed, his lids close over those glittering pale eyes as he cried out as if in pain and rammed into her harder and harder until he lay spent beneath her. Their limbs entwined, his arms imprisoned in the tangled masses of her hair, they slept.

They were married the next morning in Winslade's little chapel, the bride resplendent in the dress Adèle had labored into the night to finish, for it had not been completed when they had left for Greywell. It was of a royal blue silk, bordered in silver, with deep, dangling sleeves lined in a gleaming ivory; an ivory underdress showed at the round neckline and in slashes in the sleeves. The bridegroom had chosen to wear blue also, though of a lighter hue that matched his eyes.

Adèle, holding Simon's son so that he could see as the priest blessed the union of his father and Ysabeau, felt her eyes grow hot with happy tears as she watched the handsome couple take their vows. She would return to the convent tomorrow, her heart at peace, knowing that her dear brother was happier than she had ever seen him.

Just as they were all sitting down to the wedding feast, visitors were announced. Simon rose warily, wondering who came now to disturb their joy. Ysabeau also rose, her heart in her throat, afraid that affairs of the realm had necessitated Henry's breaking his promise to leave Simon at home for awhile. But then she saw who stood just behind Thomas the seneschal, and she ran forward with a glad cry.

"Lord Rene de Limoges and Lady Matilde, my lord," Thomas announced formally. "They said they came from the King and Queen, so I felt you would want me to let them in without further ado."

"You thought right!" Simon went forward and embraced Rene and kissed Matilde on both cheeks.

"We are sorry to hear we missed the wedding, but I see we are in time for the feast," said Rene with a grin, eyeing the magnificently spread tables.

"Rene!" Matilde reproved, laughing. "Where are you manners? Bring in the wedding present from Eleanor that we brought."

"Ah, yes, how careless of me to forget." He and Matilde exchanged a conspiratorial grin. Ysabeau could tell at a glance that all was well between the pair, and that their love had only deepened with wedlock. Let ours do so as well, she prayed fiercely. Rene did not leave them long to wonder, re-entering the hall with his mantle thrown over the right side of his chest to conceal the bundle he carried.

The bundle moved under the heavy, fur-lined robe . . . and whimpered.

"What—" murmured Ysabeau curiously as she walked closer. Matilde stepped forward to pull back the folds of the cape, watching her friends' faces as she revealed a squirming, bright-eyed, brown and black puppy. It was a mastiff, the very image of Ami when he had been but a few weeks old.

Matilde handed it to Ysabeau, smiling as the wriggling puppy struggled to lap her face with its pink tongue. Aimery had rushed forward when he saw the gift unveiled, and Ysabeau set the pup down beside the surprised toddler. Soon both were rolling about in the rushes, getting acquainted, the pup enthusiastically bathing any portion of the boy's face it could reach. Aimery's giggles mingled with the dog's excited, shrill barks, bringing pleasure to all who watched.

For Ysabeau, it was like seeing Ami born again, and her heart, which had felt full to overflowing with joy, swelled anew. She turned to see Simon's eyes tenderly gazing at her.

"I think our gift just became your son's, but I don't mind. The beast will guard him well, and be a good companion as Aimery grows."

"I trust he will be so to all our sons and daughters," Simon said boldly, watching her blush prettily in front of Rene and Matilde. But he saw she returned his look just as frankly, her deep brown eyes sultry in their depths.

"Her grace sent a letter, Ysabeau," murmured Matilde, drawing a parchment sheet from a pouch at her girdle. "Perhaps you should read it."

They sat down together on the dais, and food and drink were brought to Rene and Matilde while Ysabeau read aloud:

"To my very dear Lady Ysabeau, Comtesse de Ré, Hawkingham, Winslade, Lingfield, and Chawton, from Eleanor Queen of England, Lady of Ireland, Duchess of Aquitaine,

Normandy, and Gascoigne, Countess of Anjou, Poitou, Saintonge, Limousin, Auvergne, Bordeaux, Agen, Maine, and Touraine, greetings.

"Bless you, my dear, on your wedding day. I rejoice to hear that you and my very dear friend, Simon, have become man and wife at last. Both of you are precious to me and I am very pleased that you are together at last. May your peace and happiness only grow.

"I have sent you the best of Circe's litter, sired by your wonderful Ami, and I know that you will not mind that she is female, since she looks so much like her sire. I know Archdeacon Thomas has long ago conveyed our understanding about the tragic incident in which your dog died, but I know you will have missed your pet.

"And as for you, my Lord Simon, Henry bids me tell you that your wedding gift from him, in appreciation for your loyal service and friendship, will be a further increase in your lands, as befits a newly created Earl of our realm. When you come to Wallingford in a se'enight"—here Simon groaned aloud—"for the swearing of allegiance to our son William, he will discuss with you what fiefs would best suit you.

"But do not fail, Ysabeau, to have your lord bring you with him, for we love you well and would have your company. I promise you will not have to scramble for a decent chamber together, as you are newlyweds.

"Again, I rejoice to see that you have heeded my words, dear Ysabeau, and dared all for love. I know your way has not been an easy one of late, but I thank the saints that they have brought you both unscathed through your trial, to be together. I feel you have truly discerned the difference between the game of courtly love and love that endures forever.

"Eleanor, by the Grace of God Queen of England, etc."

"Henry promised me he would leave me alone for awhile," Simon groaned. "Will you mind journeying to Wallingford with me, my love?"

"How can you ask? Of course, I don't mind, if I can go with you. At least Eleanor understands that I could not bear to let you out of my sight, in the midst of all those lovely ladies." She laughed lightly, but he drew her near, so that his next words were for her alone.

"How can you think I would even look upon those females with their airs and pretenses? I need no courtly love games, my Ysa, for I have a love that is real and always, whatever may befall us."

"Well said, my forever love," Ysabeau replied with a radiant smile, as her lips met his.

The hall cheered as everyone at the tables raised their cups to Earl Simon and his lady.

Afterword

I would like to extend my thanks to the Hampshire, England, County Library for its invaluable assistance in gathering information about the medieval area of Winslade. Their sources indicate that the modern-day name of the village, Winslade, evolved from the Saxon *Winesflot* of the eleventh century; I have chosen to use the more pleasant-sounding modern name.

Once again, as in *Defiant Heart*, I have used the occasional word or phrase in modern French, with one or two exceptions, as when Bernard de Ventador refers to Eleanor as *mos aziman*. I feel this gives the speech a French medieval flavor without obscuring the meaning, for I would venture to guess few of my readers are familiar with eleventh-century Norman or Provençal French. The latter, indeed, resembled

Catalan Spanish more nearly than French.

Eleanor of Aquitaine has long been a figure of fascination to me, but much more has been written of her later years, her quarrels with Henry, her long captivity, her release and subsequent achievements at an age when most of her contemporaries were long dead. I wanted to portray her at an earlier age, for I believe there was a time in Henry and Eleanor's early married life when they were passionately in love, Eleanor probably to a greater extent than the younger, always-on-the-move Henry. I have attempted to foreshadow the beginnings of trouble between them, however, as in the way Henry handled her probably innocent affection for Bernard de Ventador.

The Catharists were largely tolerated, especially in southern France during the twelfth century, and many of the troubadors and lower nobility did espouse the Catherist faith but lived in peace with their Catholic neighbors. It was not until 1209 that a crusade was ordered which resulted in the massacre of Toulouse, in which Cathars and Catholics alike were mercilessly slaughtered. After the great Cathar fortress of Montségur was destroyed in 1244, the sect was forced underground.

Most of the nobility in the medieval period did wed strictly for lands and heirs, and love was not expected to have any part. Indeed, the outgrowth of the courtly love rituals was an attempt, I believe, to satisfy the real need of men and women for a deeper, more permanent love than was available in the majority of noble marriages. I believe there are always, in any age, however cynical, men and women who find that real and lasting *forever love* such as Ysabeau de Ré and Simon de Winslade forged.

Laurie Grant